CW00544064

The Great Escape

IAN WATSON

GOLDEN GRYPHON PRESS • 2002

Introduction, "Do Stories Tell Themselves?" copyright © 2002, by Ian Watson.
"Three-Legged Dog," first published in *Interzone*, May 1999.
"The Shape of Murder," first published in *Odyssey* #4, 1998.
"The Great Escape," first published in *Dante's Disciples*, White Wolf, 1996.
"A Day Without Dad," first published in *New Worlds* #222, 1997.
"Caucus Winter," first published in *Fantasy & Science Fiction*, January 1999.
"The Amber Room," first published in *Tombs*, White Wolf, 1995.
"Nanunculus," first published in *Interzone*, January 1997.
"When Thought-Mail Failed," first published in *New English Library Book of Internet Stories*, NEL, 2000.
"Early, in the Evening," first published in *Asimov's Science Fiction*, April 1996.
"Ahead!," first published in *Interzone*, May 1995.
"The China Cottage," first published in *Destination Unknown*, White Wolf, 1997.
"Such Dedication," first published in *Interzone*, January 1996.
"What Actually Happened in Docklands," first published in *Interzone*, June 1998.
"The Boy Who Lost an Hour, the Girl Who Lost her Life," first published in *Fantasy & Science Fiction*, February 1998.
"Tulips from Amsterdam," first published in *Interzone*, August 1996.
"The Descent," first published in *Interzone*, December 1999.
"The Last Beast out of the Box," first published in *Fantasy & Science Fiction*, May 1997.
"Ferryman," first published in *Science Fiction Age*, March 1996.
"My Vampire Cake," first published in *Worlds of Fantasy & Horror*, Winter 1996.

Copyright © 2002 by Ian Watson
LIBRARY OF CONGRESS CATALOGING–IN–PUBLICATION DATA
Watson, Ian, 1943–
    The great escape / Ian Watson. — 1st ed.
        p.   cm.
    ISBN 1-930846-09-6 (alk. paper)
        1. Science fiction, English.   2. Fantasy fiction, English.   I. Title.
    PR6073.A863 G74   2002
    823.'914—dc21   2002001581

All rights reserved, which includes the right to reproduce this book, or portions thereof, in any form whatsoever except as provided by the U.S. Copyright Law. For information address Golden Gryphon Press, 3002 Perkins Road, Urbana, IL 61802.
First Edition.

Contents

Do Stories Tell Themselves?

𝓘T'S OVER FIFTEEN YEARS SINCE I LAST WROTE AN introduction to a story collection of mine (*Slow Birds*, Gollancz 1985), and in it I said that for me it is strangeness that brings a story to life and makes it real and believable. Not familiarity, but strangeness. In a sense familiarity is a filter which stops us from seeing the true wonder and singularity of the world, for habitually we perceive only a little part of reality. "Human kind," according to T.S. Eliot in *Four Quartets*, "cannot bear very much reality."

I was fascinated by the adverse reaction of one leading American film critic to the Steven Spielberg film *A.I. Artificial Intelligence*, for which I wrote the Screen Story during nine months with Stanley Kubrick some years ago. Evidently this movie *could not* by definition be good because machines of our own creation simply cannot be conscious entities in the way that human beings are. (Only God can make a tree? Or a soul?)

Arguably the opposite is truer. Machines which have access to their own "mental" processes and which can rewrite their own programming, causing themselves or their successors to evolve in complexity, perhaps surpassing our ability to understand them, may in future be the true higher intelligences on Earth compared with whom us human beings are more like robots of flesh and blood—governed by our genes, our sensory input constantly filtered so that we can focus upon what is necessary, unable to analyse our own thought processes, our very sense of "self" perhaps an illusion.

Back in 1985 the neurosurgeon Benjamin Libet performed some surprising experiments, proving that our brain prepares to carry out an action *before* we take a conscious decision to act. An event is already occurring before "I" chose to begin it. Conscious awareness lags behind what happens—but we do not realise this because the brain puts events in order after the event occurs, so that "I" feel that I intentionally did so-and-so, although tests prove otherwise.

Even while awake you aren't continuously conscious. You drive your car along a familiar route and suddenly wonder if you have already passed a certain place or not. Consciousness is full of gaps —of which you are unaware because those gaps do not register.

You walk into a room wallpapered with roses. Your eyes only see things in detail which are in front of you, so actually you only see a few roses in any resolution, yet you do not experience all the others as vague shapes—the brain fills in for you what is missing, just as it wallpapers the blank space that ought to correspond to the blind spot in your eyes.

Recently I was sitting in a park when two magpies landed on the grass ahead of me, one to the left and one to the right. They began to walk apart. By continuing to look straight ahead midway between the magpies, I was able to see both birds vanish even though the scene apparently remained complete and full. All that was visible now was grass (although of course I was not even seeing all that grass; my brain was filling in). When I shifted my head slightly the magpies returned.

Such matters are intimately bound up with the business of writing stories.

That is because what sustains our sense of a continuous self is to a large extent language, and narrative. (Daniel Dennett's *Consciousness Explained* is a must-read on this subject.) People continuously talk to themselves. Children often do so aloud. Adults usually do so without making noises (although I have been overheard chatting to myself).

A human being cannot easily or ordinarily maintain uninterrupted attention on a single problem for more than, say, half a minute—yet regularly we work at tasks that occupy much more time. To do so, we need to describe to ourselves what is going on so that we commit it to memory. Otherwise, the immediate contents of the stream of consciousness are lost very quickly.

An idea occurs to you. Something distracts you. What was that brilliant idea you had a moment ago? How hard it is to recapture! You need to grab hold of a chain of associations and recreate the exact frame of mind you were in when the idea occurred, then the idea can emerge again. But often it is gone forever.

This is because evolution did not design human memory to be super-reliable, fast random-access memory as that of an Artificial Intelligence would be. So you need tricks to enhance your memory, and telling yourself what is going on is one of these tricks.

In a very real sense we do not even choose the words we use. On the contrary the words choose themselves (as Wittgenstein was well aware: the Proposition speaks through the mouth of the person). Inside our brain no switchboard operator sits coordinating what goes on. Instead, many sub-systems act in unison. Consequently a whole range of words is forever competing to be publicly expressed, both when you talk to other people and when you talk to yourself. Language isn't something we constructed but something which came into being, and which we in turn became, creating and recreating ourselves through words. Being able to say things is the basis of our beliefs about who and what we are. We produce our "selves" in language. Each of us is a sort of fictional character in the narrative which we tell ourselves constantly.

In order to keep track of our bodily and mental circumstances we practise incessant story-telling and story-checking, some of it factual and some of it wholly fictional. "If she says this, I will say *that.*" "I *ought* to have said that—in fact let's rerun the conversation differently with me coming out of it better than I really did!" This goes on all the time. You tell a story to yourself and to other people about who you are so as to protect and control and define yourself.

Fundamentally our human consciousness is not the source of tales—it is the *product* of tales. Therefore the telling of tales, including the creation of fiction, science fiction and fantasy, isn't something secondary to our lives. It is no mere entertainment compared with the serious business of real life. It's fundamental to our whole existence and to our knowledge of the world.

This is very comforting for a writer to know! When I write stories, as the words compete for expression, I am doing something integral to our mental existence. And I try to expand the range of that existence by removing perceptual filters of normality so that the world can be seen in a new light—as different from what we assumed. Or perhaps I substitute alternative filters, of *what if?*

Maybe this is all a bit serious to introduce a collection of stories. For me, stories ought to be playful even when they are about totally serious themes; and of course stories are adventures too. A story is a game, grim or merry as it may be, or a paradoxical mixture of both. If stories are not fun to write—even if at the same time the narrative might be fairly harrowing—then why write them? Creation should be a joyful activity, not an agonising one. And also an uncertain and exploratory activity, uncertain as tomorrow is, for I rarely know when I start a story where it will take me to or how on Earth it will turn out. The words compete for utterance and the story evolves itself.

The question perhaps remains: will Artificial Intelligences feel a need to tell stories? And what might their stories be?

Ian Watson
Moreton Pinkney, England
1st August 2001

The Great Escape

Three-Legged Dog

So I come into existence again.
Like a sleeper awaking, like a patient emerging from anaesthesia. The world out of focus. This clarifies quickly. I'm almost getting used to coming back to life. This is the fourth time.

There's Matthew slouching along ten yards ahead of me. Sun-bright pavement's crowded. Blokes in shirtsleeves, girls in short skirts and halter tops, heatwave. Can't miss Matthew's tight little ponytail and big bald patch. Turned-up jacket collar and knotted silk scarf hide the mulberry blotch of birthmark down the left side of his neck—too sweaty for a polo-neck today, eh Matthew?

Shops, bank branches: we're in Royal Leamington Spa, heading down the Parade. There's the grand red-brick and sandy-stone Town Hall and the bleach-white statue of Queen Victoria which a German bomb shifted one inch sideways on its plinth over half a century ago, but Matthew is the focus of my attention, the centre.

Toddler-buggies, fat woman in a powered wheelchair, trainer-girl walking a guide dog, a Sikh family, traveller couple with tattoos and piercings: the girl sports bright blue hair and a pea-size green bead under her lower lip, the bloke has a metal spike through the top of his nose as well as eyebrow-rings. The crowding's good. Helps me keep my distance from Matthew, as if I'm genuinely following him through a press of people. I am, I am—he's my energy source. Me, a moth emerging from nothingness and only existing because of his light, unless I fly too close and he flares, disintegrating me again.

Cars, cars. Kids with balloons straggling up the Parade, and lots more New Age types. Could be the day of the annual Peace Festival down in the park by the Pump Room. Could well be.

I'm a sort of invisible human balloon myself, bobbing along. Balloon without any skin, just the presence of myself. Intangible, proceeding through the gaps between people, bump bump but they don't know this.

Come back to life, have I? Not to my own life, not to the life of Amanda Riley—but to *his* life, Matthew's. This time I must try my best to hover on his periphery, resisting the attraction toward him yet sustained by his life, his continuing, ongoing life. Light of my life—there's a joke. Definitely the light of my death—*which I think he caused deliberately.*

He's hesitating outside the Tripe & Tipple pub. We've been in there together from time to time—is that why he's in two minds instead of marching right on in? Guest ales, Toulouse Lautrec posters, and chef's specials of liver and onions, braised kidneys (which they don't bother to core before cooking), and tripe *à la mode de Caen,* as well as the usual baguettes stuffed with prawns or ham. Triple-tipple, in Matthew's case, but he always drove safely afterwards—no, that's unfair, he would only down two and a half pints. Something to dilute the cranberry-flavoured vodka when he got home.

Out comes a red softpack. Burnt offering. Consult the smoke. Thinking things over, eh Matthew? To tipple or not to tipple before touring the Peace Festival, presumed reason for presence in Leamington on this fine day. Score a month's supply of what it amuses you to call dry ice—the cracky sort, right? Keeps you alert while writing UNIX process software, compression algorithms, billing software, data fill for some new mobile phone company or some paltry shareware to be stuck as a CD on the front of a computer mag in the hope punters pay the registration fee to help you out with the whopping phone bill. Or something more illustrious, Project Director for a game script, pushing polygons around the screen. Or even ... architecture for the ultimate virtual reality driving simulator, instructions for a cloudburst or a horse suddenly darting into the road?

Keep you alert half the night, the ice will.

My Christ! Never mind a phone bill. How about the whopping mortgage? Paid off by the life insurance by now, bound to have been. Paid by my death. How very timely.

Matthew rambling on again tonight in a fundamental assembly language, hmm? I used to assemble language, or tried to. During my final year doing Eng Lit at the University of Birmingham in Edgbaston, I shared a house with four other women and one nerdy bloke (supposedly our rape guard in residence) in a long seedy street not many stones' throws from Winson Green prison. Ex-offenders were being rehabbed at a couple of community hostels elsewhere along our road, and another house sheltered former mental patients. Elderly old folk roosted alone here and there; when they died or were obliged to go into care, a few more Asian or West Indian families would most likely buy the vacated homes.

I never worked out which house the three-legged dog belonged to, but regular as clockwork it would lollop past me on my way to the campus in the morning, out on its own, wearing collar and lead . . . but holding its own lead in its jaws. The beagle's left hind leg was missing, no doubt due to a car running over it followed by amputation, but the animal was nimble enough with one rear propulsion limb and two front legs for balance and steering. I thought and thought about that dog, all the while permutating— per-mutt-ating!—the emotional possibilities. Two years later I was to win a £3500 first prize in a poetry competition with my "Voyage of the Beagle," and three years after that the poem suggested the title of my first collection from trend-setting Bloodaxe Books, *Three-Legged Hound*. Prestige in the frog-pond of contemporary verse by the tender age of twenty-six!

A poet should strut her stuff, and besides this'll help me keep my distance from Matthew . . .

Three-legged pooch runs down the street
Gripping its leash in its mouth.
Each morning I pass it, and it passes me,
Never pausing (how could it?) to cock
Its hind leg against any tree.
Why does its owner allow it
Out for a run on its own?
Perhaps it is its own owner, alone
In the world yet brainy enough
To pretend it isn't a stray?

Is the leash an aid to balance,
A sort of steering wheel,
A way of correcting bias:
Slack, go west—tug and head south,
Technology of the mouth?
I'd love to ask it these questions.
Maybe that beagle can talk
Or—let's be serious—convey
A reply by way of a bark?
If only its lips weren't sealed.

So does it bite on the leash
Whenever it's running around
To keep its secret securely safe
—Suppose we catch it unawares—
From the likes of me and thee?

Is the dog slightly dotty?
(Not spotty—it's fawn
And brown and cream.)
Maybe its owner died,
And she always came along here.
So this is a ritual remembrance,
A pretence that she's still around.
At home every day the dog howls
Exactly at twenty-past-eight
Till, leashed, he has his way.

What hurts do we ourselves suffer,
Lost legs of the heart or the soul?
Invisible bits of us missing—
But we carry our leashes around,
Unseen. They stop us from falling over
—Like a running three-legged hound.

Copyright by Amanda Riley. *Not* by Amanda Ramsbottom, the ghastly surname I was born with, butt of jokes. Actually Ram is a dialect word for wild garlic, while Bottom is a shallow valley. "To rob me of so rich a bottom," says Hotspur in *Henry IV*.

Pretty vale of wild garlic. Try telling people that. Most certainly not a poet's name, in my opinion! Matthew's surname was a lot better. Not ideal but far neater and snappier, with a touch of the

Irish, land of Seamus Heaney. The ancient Irish used to say, "If
words are not poetry, they are useless."

Not that I married Matthew for his name, but because I came to
appreciate him. He was studying electronics and was a doyen of the
computer club to which our rape guard, Adrian, also belonged.
This was the dawn of the home computer boom. The Spectrum
ZX81 had just come out. Games, in arcades at least, were still
mainly clones of Space Invaders, but up in their bedrooms eager
lads were coding for their micros. Since Matthew's own digs were
only a couple of streets away he would come round to see Adrian,
and I began coinciding with the visitor in our communal kitchen.
The other women ignored Matthew—socially awkward or oblivious, no girl friend of course, computer-junkie, wounded (as only a
sensitive would-be poet could perceive) . . . that florid birthmark on
his neck caused him a lot of embarrassment and trauma at school,
as I was to learn rather later on, though he didn't like to talk about
this. Aside from the birthmark he wasn't bad looking—trim and
fresh-complexioned, unruly shock of hair, rather wild blue eyes.
The birthmark didn't figure immediately, since he kept it covered,
Dr Who fashion, the scarf knitted by his auntie. Even before I knew
of the birthmark I thought of him as belonging to the three-legged
dog category—someone lame but who was also, as I began to realize, a sprinter, a goer; which I found interesting.

And increasingly interesting. Apparently Matthew had succeeded in finishing a fiendishly difficult computer game involving
the breaking of a clever section of cryptography, whereupon he
found on screen the message, "If you completed this game give us
a call." Which he duly did. The phone call anointed him as a Code
Warrior. Only half a dozen players had phoned in so far. The company would be very interested in using him as part of a team. More
than this: he was determined to give them a master game of his own
devising, on which he was labouring long hours (even though he
wasn't yet using any dry ice).

"If it's a winner," Adrian explained to me glassy-eyed one morning, "Matthew's made. He'll be filthy rich. And he's going to do it. I
know he is."

Filthy rich from a computer game? This seemed implausible,
but Adrian regaled me with the story of some other youth who was
set to scoop a million quid in fees and royalties. True story, so it
turned out. This was going to be a giant market. Forget coin-in-the-
slot arcade games; home gaming was the coming thing. Giant new
heights loomed with such as Matthew as the pioneering climbers.

Had I heard of a plumber called Mario, in *Donkey Kong?* Had I heard of Richard Garriot's role-playing *Ultima* that ran on the Apple II? In a few more years really good affordable computers would be in every home in the land. Really neat consoles would plug into your TV, and these new CDs wouldn't only have music on them; they would have big computer programmes. Matthew was a genius, a genius.

Poetry and computer games are pretty much at opposite ends of the spectrum—of the Sinclair Spectrum, you might almost say, if you can remember back then. Both as regards the persons involved, and also as regards the money.

What prospects did I have *realistically?* Probably teaching in some shitty school. I felt in my waters that Matthew Riley might well be my great chance. Pass it up, be a fool.

A poet is supposed to be emotional, spontaneous, candid, romantic even, but an artist is selfish and manipulative and driven too. A poet also has a hard drive in her. Believe me, I thought long and hard. I visited a professional Tarot reader, and "What is before me" was the Queen of Pentacles, signifying opulence, security, liberty (although the "What will finally come" card was more ambiguous, but that was a long way off).

To my own self untrue? Immoral, unethical, unpoetical? To which I say: *read a few newspapers.* Lies, sleaze, hypocrisy, corruption: those are the hallmarks of the golden life, at home and almost everywhere else in the world, to which can be added, in many instances, bare-faced murder, torture, massacres. What did Gerard Manley Hopkins cry out so plaintively and bitterly? "Why do sinners' ways prosper? Why must disappointment all I endeavour end? The sots and thralls of lust do in spare hours more thrive than I." Raised by my Mum with difficulty after my Dad legged it—not forgetting the troublesome Step-Dad episode of abuse—I was not about to repeat her naïve mistakes. *Protect yourself*—with cash, obtained in the least insalubrious fashion, to be able to build some beauty for yourself.

To salt my conversation and so that Matthew could explain things, I bought all of one month's computer magazines (try loading up from the racks now if you're a weight lifter!).

"Matthew, I'm thirsty, do you and Adrian fancy a pint in the pub?" Was I not getting a poetic buzz from computer jargon? Was cross-fertilisation not occurring? Is code not creative too?

"What I'm doing is a platform game, you see?" "But not as in railway stations, no?" "No no, levels of play stacked above each other. Mine will be different. You'll be able to make decisions about where you want to go. Instead of being told by the program, the player will be in control. *Cyber* means *steering*, you see. Captaining, being in command." "So games are really about steering." "Sort of. One day we'll be able to speak to computers, and they'll be able to talk back to us."

"Matthew, would you go with me to the Christmas party at the Guild? I'm supposed to ask someone." He gaped a bit, mumbled about hours of keyboarding, but no female had ever paid attention to him before.

And after the party, as such things turn out, we ended up tipsily in bed—in darkness since he wanted darkness (the birthmark was yet to reveal itself). Successfully enough in bed: he lost his virginity, and thus became imprinted on me, give or take his computer obsessions. When he called round a couple of nights after the event— interim of fantasising and fretting?—he was a bit hangdog and nervous. Couldn't believe his luck, though might I be annoyed and snub him? I asked him up to my room to reinforce the imprinting. At least he hadn't poured aftershave all over himself. Probably never even occurred to him. This time can I light some candles? So that he could see me naked, watch me. Reciprocal revelation of the birthmark might have been a minor calamity, but it didn't bother me at all.

The other women thought I was crazy, but by then the Christmas vacation arrived. Matthew could stay home in Nottingham for three weeks solid finishing off his code and hopefully mooning a bit about me. He was bound to me, though I could unbind him.

Success, sweet success: for him, for me. Contract swiftly signed; big up-front payment. Million-and-a-half quid the game would net Matthew. *Alien Reign* was his brilliant masterpiece, ranking him as a major Code Warrior. Despite the steep price it sold and sold, and unlike some rivals the code contained no errors which would make the game impossible to complete. No more such fabulously original ideas were to come to him, but that hardly mattered for quite a few years . . . I nursed him through the implications of his good fortune, like some latter-day lottery adviser taking a thunderstruck winner under their wing, though Matthew's win was well deserved, not sheer luck. I steered him, and he was grateful for this as well as for our sessions in bed.

"Would you marry me?" he blurted.

"Yes!" We would adventure together.

Dizzy years were to follow once we both left college. Newly-hired accountant advised investment in property, and we needed somewhere to live. A manor house (just a *little* one) would suit me fine, so we bought Malsbury Manor in the charming village of Malsbury, Warwickshire, very convenient for Birmingham where the team was based—this was before the days of networking and high speed data connections—as well as a flat in Birmingham itself. But don't pay the whole whack outright in cash. Go for a huge endowment mortgage, then you're racking up a small fortune for the future as well as getting tax relief. Start pension funds, et cetera, et cetera. Assemble a portfolio of shares. Plus, of course, snazzy cars, attending functions and yuppie shampoo parties to be recognized, oh and full-time gardener and cleaners and whatnot, and games room, including authentic old cinema organ rising from the floor and converted to play automatically (oh, what a party we had), and my flights to exotic places for inspiration, sometimes even accompanied by Matthew, though he had plenty of coding to keep him busy and this remained his obsession, particularly when the next big idea simply did not come, and lesser goals occupied him. He was still pulling in fairish money till recently, but outgoings were steep.

"Driving games are a bit sad," he said to me not too long ago.

"Why sad?" He liked driving.

"They're such old stuff now . . . If only I could come up with . . ." And he wandered off, preoccupied and fretful.

I liked to work on my poems in the herb garden in fine weather or in the lovely old kitchen into which on warm days a clever swallow would dart to catch flies.

Three-Legged Hound was followed by *Seer*, fruit of my journeys in search of self and soul in far-away places.

My prize-winning inclusion this time, in the mode of Robert Browning's dramatic monologues, was a long poem prompted by the Sultan's harem in Istanbul. The hundreds of women confined to the luxurious, labyrinthine harem could practise arts and sciences if they wished. Intellectual activity was quite okay if you had an intellect. (Often intellect was devoted to palace intrigue, and you ran a certain risk of ending up at the bottom of the Bosphorus sewn inside a sack.) My harem-virgin studies astronomy deeply. With the permission of the Mistress of the Seraglio, attended by a black eunuch she stargazes from the roof of the harem so forested with domes and towers and chimneys as to resemble a chessboard in mid-game, pieces sculpted by De Chirico. She's quite a genius. This particular Sultan doesn't bother her with any demands, unlike certain debauchees such as Ibrahim who would strip all his women bare, order them to play-act being mares, and riot among them as a stallion. Hundreds of concubines, as I said; this Sultan has only set eyes on her once or twice. My heroine predicts that a transit of Venus will track the tiny shadow of our sister world across the full Moon, observable through her little telescope. On the night in question, when her mental life would be fulfilled, the Sultan finally calls her to his bed for the very first time.

Some reviews of *Seer* sneered at its tourist tone, "Jet-Set gems" et cetera. Sour grapes, said I (though Bloodaxe took note).

One critic, keen to show that he understood astronomy better than me, took exception to the harem poem: the shadow of Venus is planet-size and so faint that not even the most sensitive modern detectors could tell the difference in the amount of sunlight illuminating the full Moon, as he explained at some length. Though chagrined, I felt that there was still a poetical truth; and I had won an award, after all, from judges who appreciated powerful pathos and irony.

Seer, see-er, equals visionary. Swap the letters around, and *sere* means dried-up. Work for my third hoped-for collection was a real struggle, mirroring perhaps the frustrations Matthew himself was experiencing even if he was churning out reams, or megabytes, of stuff. I would take out a piece I had finished a fortnight earlier, feeling fairly satisfied at the time, and oh God the flaws in it. Magazines actually declined several of my submissions and Bloodaxe cooled off from me.

I could easily start up my own poetry press, but that would be cheating. Downright amateur. I had standards, I was sincere.

Nice photo of me on the back cover of *Three-Legged Hound*, taken by Matthew with his digicam in the walled herb garden, seeming slightly over-exposed the way Bloodaxe printed it, me with my long blond hair wearing a white cotton dress made in India. Even then I looked a bit ghostlike. When I went abroad with Matthew he was forever taking pictures which could be used for realistic games locations. Download the images into the computer using a twain-driver, then manipulate them any which way. If I flew off on my own I must be sure to take along my own digicam and use it.

I was a passenger in Matthew's life, along for the ride, which had been the plan, but life's more complicated than that. He had enriched me immeasurably. I cherished him. We made love quite often and I had no affairs. (Nor did he; he mightn't have known how to.) Amanda means "to be loved." Must be loved. And so it was. Not so long ago I said to him, "If anything happens to me, I'll watch over you," and for a moment he seemed to flinch, as if at a threat, though he quickly hid this with a smile.

Matthew seemed oblivious to himself as potential parent, and I did not wish for the intrusion yet, even though time was passing by, how it was passing for both of us. Maybe if we had a child my creative juices would flow more freely, though I might be resigning my poetical hopes by creating flesh instead of word. Nowadays a woman could safely have a first child in her late thirties, early forties.

True, we rattled a bit in Malsbury Manor, not that Matthew noticed, but there were plenty of friends who envied, in the nicest way, our fortune which seemed fine enough to them even after we sold the Birmingham flat—who needs a city base when there's net-working?—and there was family, my Mum and Matthew's parents and his brother Jim whom he twice set up in brilliant-idea busi-nesses which failed.

He drops his used-up fag. He's going into the Tripe & Tipple, into which inevitably I flow, sucked in there by the vacancy he left behind him.

Pub's at least half full but I can anchor myself, magnetically so to speak, to a cast-iron pine-top table no one's yet using, being still cluttered with dirty plates. Bit of a wait at the bar till he gets a chilled bottle of Pils and retires to a long railed shelf to lounge and eye other drinkers. Maybe he'll spot a contact for brain-ice.

The first time I came back to haunt him he was sitting in *my* lovely old kitchen, printouts spread across the huge oak table. (Was he missing me? Or was he colonizing my vacated space?) I rushed toward him, in a sense—a disembodied sense. I could see and hear —the lawnmower outside, Bert Tucker was busy—although smells were missing—I ought to have caught a lovely whiff of cut grass— and as for touch . . . no, there was merely closeness, proximity.

Matthew, Matthew—

"Amanda—?" The sheer shock in his voice, him somehow hear-ing me.

Why could I not feel myself, see any of myself? Why was I invis-ible? How was I immaterial, intangible? Stunned, I couldn't under-stand at first. Was I asleep upstairs? Had I somehow discovered how to project myself out of my body? How come the lawn was being mowed when now should be frosty winter? Unless months had flown inexplicably. I must be in a coma somewhere.

Matthew, what's wrong with me—?

"Amanda—?" How he recoiled, flapping his hands as if to ward off a buzzing wasp. "You're dead—!"

Then the final moments of the car crash came flooding back.

Matthew, I'm alive—

He flailed at the air.

"You're dead!" he shrieked. "You're dead dead dead!" With such shock and horror that the force of his rejection was like a gust assaulting a candle flame, a fierce blow of breath upon a dandelion seedhead stripping away the frail threads to fly in all directions. It was as if in instants I devolved to something pre-human, pre-conscious, unable to discern, as uncomprehending and stupid as a sheep, not even that, a cod, even this dim vitality dwindling, vanishing. The utter blankness of nirvana, nowhere, nothing—which I did not "know," could not know until my scattered particles, as of an exploded world, finally came together again, condensing under the pull of Matthew's gravity, of his continuing life, carrying with them faint recollections of my disintegration.

The second time—God knows how many days or weeks later— I lingered longer before he realized and thrust me away. Fearing that he was hallucinating—*or fearing that he wasn't?*

I was the passenger in his car that morning. Rare indeed for us ever to go shopping together, but he craved the novelty. Quite often lately he had been out driving on his own with his digicam. I rarely shopped in Birmingham—unpoetical destination—much preferring prettier places within easy reach such as Stratford, Warwick, or Leamington Spa. So: supermarket on the northern outskirts of Stratford, then into the town for lunch. Restaurants wouldn't be busy at this time of year; they'd be eager to please.

Hard frost that morning. By the time we set out around ten-thirty, the sun had already melted any rime exposed to its rays. Tarmac shone damply, still drying.

Fifteen miles from Malsbury to Stratford. We passed cows, we passed sheep. We passed though a couple of villages. I had wanted to make love the night before. He had not wanted to. He went to his computer and only came to bed after I was asleep.

"Why wouldn't you make love?" I asked as we drove along.

"Love," he muttered. "Amanda must be loved."

"Don't you feel well?"

A wide trailer loaded with a precarious tangle of branches towed by a tractor loomed ahead.

"I need to concentrate."

Until we were past—and then for another mile in silence.

"If something's wrong. . . ."

"Why should something be wrong? Apart from generally speaking."

"I'm sure you'll have another brilliant idea."

"And you'll write lots more poems. It's getting too late."

"For my poetry?"

He shook his head. That's when he lit a cigarette and lowered his window a couple of inches to let the smoke out.

At the bottom of a long slope a railway bridge crosses the road at a slant, so the road dog-legs and narrows—space for one vehicle only. You line up to see that beyond is clear, jink to the left, swing right to zoom through the gap, swing left again to be back on course, upward and onward under power cables hanging high from a pylon close by the railway line. Drivers familiar with the road treat the obstacle as a chicane, a slalom.

At the top of the approach Matthew powered the window right down and tossed his fag out almost unsmoked—already thinking of it a source of ignition for a ruptured fuel tank?

The bricks of the bridge arch are painted with a warning frieze of black and yellow chequers like a banner of little Grand Prix flags. Over the apex a red and white triangle warns truck drivers of the maximum height.

In the lee of the bridge: shade. True ice could have lingered; and there's black ice too. He might have felt the wheels start to slip. He might have over-corrected.

The twitch of the wheel. The swerve of the car. The bridge abutment rushing at me. I never heard him exclaim, "Oh shit!" or "Oh Jesus!" Not even start to exclaim. I think he steered into the abutment deliberately. Risking injury to himself, risking some pain, yet not risking the death that faced me.

The airbag, you see. On his side only. The brief corner-of-the-eye memory of that rushing manifestation, the loud bang, the accompanying whoosh of smoke and powder a moment before I died made no sense. Those were just a part of the crash. Only now do they make sense, such hideous sense. Couple of years ago I borrowed his car while mine was being serviced and the garage hadn't their courtesy one available. Little red light lit up on the steering wheel when I switched the ignition on, fading within a couple of seconds, not something you might normally notice except for it being a dark morning. Red lights bother me. "Oh that's 'cause there's an airbag in the wheel," Matthew told me. Hidden away in the centre of the wheel, driver's side only. Naturally I'd forgotten all about it. But he wouldn't have. He wouldn't.

I think also that the left-front collision might have sent the rear of the car swinging round in one direction or the other, pulling Matthew away from the point of impact. Maybe the back of the car hit the other abutment, halting the car decisively.

Whiplash for Matthew? Him cushioned by the airbag, then released as it suddenly deflated? Death for me, but whiplash for him? Maybe not even that. By the time I came into existence again he was wearing no surgical collar, if indeed he needed to wear one in the first place. Maybe he had climbed out of the wrecked car quite intact. No spray of glass nuggets from his open window, either! Had the cigarette only been a pretext to open the window fully? His knees shaking, his heart thumping—he must have been in shock even if he intended the accident—but basically unaffected.

He drains his Pils and heads out of the Tripe & Tipple, me in his wake. It's a paradox that I haunt him in inverse proportion to coming too close to him. You might even say that he is not the haunted one, but that I am instead. Yes, haunted by Matthew, that's me—only regaining existence because of him! Without him, there's nothing. If only he would let me cling like a leech, what then? He must think of me as an avenging spirit if what I imagine about the car crash is true. Or if not vengeful exactly—what kind of vengeance can I enact?—let's say a reproachful spirit.

Buoyed by Pils, down the Parade he heads past a window of mannequins dolled up in slacks and shirts, past the plate glass of an insurance company where a few living mannequins sit at desks, to the Regency facade of Pizza Express on the corner—and the Royal Pump Room Gardens open up to view, revealing all across the grass bright busy booths and marquees stocked with ethnic clothing, candles and aromatherapy oils, home-made jewellery, patchwork velvet hats and patchwork leather waistcoats, vegeburgers, elderflower wine and microbrews. Usual stalls for Greenpeace et cetera. On the bandstand a funk jazz trio are blasting forth through amps and big speakers. A juggler jerks a diabolo reel high into the air, catches it on string between two sticks, launches it again. Under a great canopy of iridescent helium balloons the vendor, costumed as a clown, must weight a little less than usual, although scarcely as little as me.

There's such a levity to the festival, a giddiness. I can't help myself.

I'm here, Matthew—
"You're dead!"

A nearby kid takes fright. Matthew manages to control himself, being on public view. *Maybe this is why I am not buffeted away at once.*

"You don't exist. Leave me alone."

I can't leave you alone—

"You aren't there. Bad head-trip."

So it's all in his mind: him hallucinating my voice, spectre of guilt, haunting himself. *Yes, he is guilty of my death.*

"You aren't there, you aren't."

But I am—

He sways. He lurches. A *Big Issue* seller in camo clothing and combat boots eyes him with mingled solidarity and hostility—don't mess up my patch. People think Matthew's drunk or stoned, and this a jolly event for all the family. "No no no No NO NO!" The force of his rejection rips me apart. *I'm—*

—coming into existence again.

Emerging from oblivion.

Matthew is in his big workroom upstairs in Malsbury Manor, littered with playstations, joysticks, piles of mags and games. Tapestry-look-alike curtains closed, lights on, vivid scene on the computer screen.

Hang back, hang back.

Seen from inside a car, through the windscreen a daylit road unwinds. Hedgerows and trees rush by. Brake and accelerator pedals underfoot on the floor but no steering wheel on the desktop, just his right hand on the arrow keys. *Aren't driving games a bit sad, Matthew?*

But the graphics are *superb*. Not a hint of chunkiness or pointillisme. As realistic as a movie on TV. It's the road from Malsbury to Stratford. Of course it can't be perfect no matter how many times he stopped his car to take digicam pics, but it's pretty damn convincing. How much memory can he be using? Why, his hands are even visible on the steering wheel on screen, something I've never seen before. How much memory, for God's sake?

He slows the car, left-taps a function key. The view swings. *I'm in the passenger seat.* Pixillated from digicam pictures, looking this way, that way, the exact semblance of me! This is real captured motion, not just clever animation. Stylised? Not at all.

He scanned me in. I'm code in his computer. I'm so lifelike,

light-years beyond that Lara Croft *Tomb Raider* character. Almost as
though in another moment I might say something to him.

Function key again: view swings frontward.

Here's the descent toward the railway bridge. Like a beast the
car rushes downward. The bridge, the bridge: he'll crash me into it
again. When did he lose the distinction between reality and game?
When did he choose to lose the distinction? How many times did
he practice, adjusting the program, tweaking the impact speed and
angle, studying the consequences? How many times did that electronic doll of me survive brokenly?

The ultimate driving simulator, this. Only needs to be reconfig-
ured for VR. Krash-Kill.

Will I plunge back into oblivion as the car hits the brick abutment? Soon, so soon. Or does he intend to undo my death, to chicane through safely, appeasing himself in a sort of exorcism?

Don't kill me, Matthew—

His hand jerks, the car swerves on to the verge, bouncing
violently.

"Fuck off!" he shouts, tearing me apart. . . .

But I'm back again. Same night? Or another night and almost iden-
tical circumstances?

The same game is running. Half-empty bottle of cranberry
vodka by his side, he's driving down pell-mell toward the bridge
with its red and black chequered arch.

Hold back, hold back! Cling to a filing cabinet, not to him.

He's mumbling to himself, almost as if praying—though who or
what would he pray to?

The graphics are so perfect.

"Yo yo yo," he chants, fingers on the arrow keys, digitised hands
on the wheel. The bridge, the bridge: and he's through, he's away
and clear, and now handbrake-turning, spinning the car around to
face the far side of the bridge. Out of nowhere a sleek passenger
train whooshes across the bridge, locomotive followed by carriage
after carriage, and vanishes off-screen.

"Thank you thank you," he breathes. Unaware of me, he lifts his
mobile phone.

"Charley? Matt here. It's all in the bag—almost. Drive your
dream car around the city of your choice, VR driving simulator, shit
almighty wait till you see the graphic resolution . . . What's that?
I'm not conning you, I'm just excited. 'Course there's a pile of work
still to do. Lots of teamwork, hmm? Yeah, I'll download tomorrow.

Bug, bugs? 'Course there are some." Furtively he glances around, but I'm invisible. End of call.

Matthew, it's me—

"Oh no it isn't. You're just my memory, Amanda," he declares giddily. "My extra memory, eh. But I mustn't bother about it." He isn't lashing out now.

You killed me for the insurance money, didn't you—?

He slaps himself on the head. "Oh come on now, brain, you know that isn't the reason. Why should I care a shit about that? I'm going to be seriously rich again."

What was the reason, then—?

"Okay, brain, if I say it aloud maybe you can clam up and stay in your box." He is actually staring at the computer, addressing it as much as himself. "God of Bytes needs some blood in the game so it'll be for real. What's real, what isn't? Life's a game. Sacrifice to the Byte God, get the biggest boost of your life in return. Satisfied, brain?"

No I'm not satisfied at all—

"Game it, then do it for real so it's part of the program. Fucking hot-links with cyberspace. Win the prize."

He's looped the loop: the ice has scrambled his head. My death is the reason he's had a breakthrough, and he planned it so. I'm extra memory floating around in the void, somehow attached to his computer. He sacrificed to the bloody computer as if it's his god —the way in olden days a builder would brick up a dead, or even a living, cat in a wall for good luck. He programmed such a perfect semblance of me into the game that my mind was sucked in when the car hit the bridge. I'm an extension of that mannequin in his machine. Can my ghost be rooted in software or hardware—rather than attached to Matthew himself?

Listen, Matthew, this isn't the voice of conscience or lunacy in your head. This is me! Amanda the author of Three-Legged Hound, *not a passenger in your sodding game. I'm your wife and you sodding well killed me. I've come back and I'll keep coming back because I can't help coming back—*

"NO!" Burying his face in his hands. "NO!"

I'm buffeted but I manage to hold together.

You can drive me away, Matthew, but you can't keep on doing it all the time. You're going to have to let me stay close—

"Close? How close?"

I don't know how close—

"All the time? You're dead. You don't exist."

But I do—

"You *are* Amanda, aren't you? Oh my god . . . GO AWAY!" This isn't quite powerful enough to banish me.

He keys, and there am I, sitting in the car right next to him, smiling then scowling.

"Amanda, what do you want?"

It is me who replies, not my perfect mannequin, though her lips appear to move.

What am I supposed to want? Revenge? Or existence? Patches of continuing existence thanks to you—?

"As a passenger on my back forever? Me gibbering to myself ten times a day?"

I can keep quiet. I can think up poems. You can keyboard them, print them—

"Like some nutter channelling with the dead?"

They'll be good poems. (I hope.) *The best yet, filled with grief and longing and rage—*

Even in death I can be a poet! Poetry is the most important thing. Out of the blank blackness will come beauty.

"That's an impossible demand! I'll have no privacy, none."

You shouldn't have sacrificed me, should you—?

"You're robbing me." He seems on the verge of tears.

Robbing you? There was enough money, and will be again—

"You're robbing me of what I accomplished. Here, here, the graphics, my breakthrough, the lot!"

I don't see how I'm robbing you—

"Because you can't live in my head. It's too much to pay. Too much, too much."

Function key, and there I am, looking at the bridge.

His left hand brings up an editing window eclipsing the view of the abutment. In the window scroll lines of what he used to call vitamin-code—C-plus something or other. He's going to edit me out—to banish me not by a brusque outcry but electronically, the way he knows well. Lose all the quality photo-realism of his latest work, he will—it'll be back to compression algorithms for phone companies and ware for computer mags. But he'll do it, he'll erase me.

Unless . . .

I close the eyes of my mind. I grope. Handle of the car door. Pull that handle, thrust that door open. Step out. Hard road underfoot. Under-shoe, under-sole. Don't look. Slide toward where the verge ought to be, two sliding steps, three, four, more. Obstruction, lumpy. Open the eyes of my mind, as William Blake might have said!

Tussocks of grass, and my sandals, I'm wearing my Moroccan brown leather sandals, not at all as on that Winter's day, and the white cotton dress of that bygone photo laps my shins. My hands with their rings, emerald, gold, and amber, poke from the long sleeves, fingernails pearly. Blurry pink fog of nose, cotton-clad bumps of my breasts, I'm embodied. Oh, the feel of myself. The thick pollen of oil-seed rape cloys my nostrils. Through a hawthorn hedge: vivid turmeric-yellow crop in full flower, a musky ocean, solitary steel pylon rising high as an oil rig. I think rapeseed oil is becoming popular for use as a lubricant out in the North Sea. Biodegradable. Breeze wafts warmly over my skin, birds twitter and warble.

Behind me . . . dare I look? But I must. His car. Himself at the wheel. No passenger alongside. He's a bit chunky, and so is the car—less real than the rest of the scene, the road and hedgerow and sheepfield beyond, the nearest of the woolly muttons eyeing car and me, or maybe only me. Sunlight reflects from the car, pixillated, pointilliste. He can't see me standing here on the verge not ten yards away. I'm outside of what he can know—unless I trot back to the car. Is that even Matthew at the wheel any longer? More like an animated model of himself and the car . . . which gets under way, revving, heading for the short tunnel under the railway line, swinging through it with panache, then accelerating away, perceptibly losing definition before it vanishes from view.

I'm alone on the roadside. Should be some other traffic soon. Cars, vans, lorries: where are they? What do I do, wave one down? Beg a lift home to Malsbury? And find what there? Maybe my world extends only as far as I can see, and nothing from outside can enter it. Can a field of sheep and a field of yellow rape with looming pylon and a stretch of road and a bridge and hedgerows and birds suffice? To see eternity in a blade of grass, hmm?

Movement! Animal hurrying along the road. Peculiar sideways gait although speedy: it's a dog, an eager beagle. Carrying something in its mouth: *its own leash dangling, clipped to its collar*. The hound lacks its left hind leg, and its coat is fawn and brown and cream. Here it comes, the three-legged dog. The beagle of Edgbaston years ago, dog of my prize poem. Up to me it bounds and halts, eyeing me, moist-eyed, wet-nosed, tail wagging. The very same pooch. Only, now it pays attention to me.

Dog drops the leash at my feet. Its jaws are unimpeded. Doesn't speak, though. Doesn't even woof. Butts me with its muzzle till I pick up the leather loop.

Never had a dog before. We had a tortoiseshell cat till she died. No dog, though.

What's your name, Dog? Dog tugs me vigorously, urging me to accompany him—along the road, toward the bridge.

Couldn't see till now or didn't notice: words, printed on the lower bricks of the abutment. Capitals and lower case, plainly legible close up. Dog is patient now, panting quietly.

Voyage of the Beagle. Astronomer in the Harem. The Kitchen Swallow.

Titles of my poems!

All, all, are titles of my poems, published or unpublished, scores and scores of them, each neatly inscribed on a brick.

Cat in a Tortoise Shell. We kept the empty shell of one of those giants from the Galapagos Islands in the herb garden. Cost a bit, it did. Monkey, our cat, used to curl up to snooze inside the shell.

Dervish Dance. Making Marmalade, my homage to the Günter Grass poem about Jellied Pig's Head. *Abuser,* my brave exorcism of . . . never mind. *Tarot Lady.* Oh, I remember her well in her nook in Rookery Road near the University, a chubby woman with masses of dark red hair dressed up as a gypsy. House full of spiritual items and twittering finches flicking to and fro in multi-storey cages resembling cane pagodas. Reach out my fingertips to that brick, just to touch it. . . .

Sudden sunlight through net curtains: towering birdcage against wall painted cherry-red, round walnut table with cards from the Waite Tarot deck laid out upon it in a Grand Cross. Cinnamon incense stick smouldering. Herself, Elisabetta so-called (or genuinely so), as I live and breathe, in black lace shawl and bonnet, regarding me through gold-rimmed glasses with quizzical jollity, head cocked on one side. There's a fish-eye lens effect to the room —it's bent around. Look behind: bare brick wall, each brick labelled with a title of a poem. I'm still by the bridge, yet I'm not by the bridge if I turn away, I'm in Elisabetta's sanctum, opening up for me, and I can reach out, I can take a step forward, two steps, three, I can touch the table itself. Dog's here with me too, sniffing a leg of the table.

"Help me—"

"The Queen of Pentacles," says she.

"Yes?"

"The immediate future is Opulence."

She's repeating what she said once long ago.

"Though in the long run this may change."

"I'm from the long run, Elisabetta. I've run the long run. I'm dead."

"Dear me, but the immediate future is Opulence."

"Can you understand what I'm saying, Elisabetta?"

"You have run a long way to visit me."

"I'm dead."

"Dear me, are my birds dead? Did I forget to feed them?"

"I'm dead."

"So was Eurydice, dear. You could make up a poem."

Did I confide my poetical aspirations once she had finished reading the cards? I'm fairly sure I didn't.

"Tell me: what will be the title of my first collection of poems?"

"I see you brought your dog with you," is her reply. Is that a suitable answer, or no real answer at all?

What's the name of that test that Matthew mentioned? Turin Test, was it? A way of telling whether you're having a conversation with something intelligent while it shrouds its identity.

Elisabetta can talk but she can't converse. On the other hand, here is her room like a bubble of my memory welling out from the brick, memory as clear as the experience itself once was.

Dog tugs me, and I turn to face the bricks. I feel I should press *Tarot Lady* again—and lo, I'm by the bridge, the road is here once more, the hedgerows, fields, cloying reek of rape instead of cinnamon; Rookery Nook has vanished.

Suppose I touch *Astronomer in the Harem. . . ?*

Oh, I'm here in a room hung with cloth of gold, the window-surround and the ceiling inlaid with flowered porcelain, a sofa covered with golden cloth opposite a stove, and this has to be centuries ago—for a richly robed black man is scrutinising me. I daren't stay a moment longer in case I'm trapped, for these can't be memories of my own but are a pocket of reality ballooning from the poem or else some sort of virtual reality jaunt through the Harem which exists in some computer somewhere, although slapping the brick wall lets me leave and be by the bridge again with Dog.

Suppose I press *Abuser . . .* No no no.

So: I can enter a persuasive enactment of any of my poems, a scene evoked by each. Is this poet's heaven, or hell? Or limbo? Here is my root-place, where I died, at the bridge. Suppose that I set out with Dog along the road, will I reach anywhere else or will the road simply prolong itself or repeat itself? No other traffic uses this road.

There is only Dog and myself. Here are my doorways, written on bricks. Here are my windows to an elsewhere of my imagination, given reality by *what*? By Matthew's genius as a programmer? I suspect not. By God? By a universe which permits afterlife of a peculiar kind? A couple of hundred links to Tarot and Harem and Cat in a Tortoise Shell capsules? Shall I walk off with Dog, and *what* is Dog really, if reality has any part to play? I could become rather lonely here, but for Dog.

Think, think.

Matthew was at his screen. I was simmed on the screen, a perfect image—while hovering near him was my identity, which survives. After I cried out, he was about to erase my cyber-mannequin. Did I jump out of the car of my own free will or did he first swiftly type some instruction?

I think I was not exactly haunting him, nor was he haunting me, but that when I died my identity became attached to something much greater than Matthew's computer program, greater than his computer forever modem-linked to other computers in cyberspace. How can that be?

Dog's deep muzzle butts me forcefully. Maybe I should touch another of the poems. Those capsules of myself, my creations which have taken on a life of their own, privately published as it were!

Dog is insistent. Dumb Dog, why can't you speak? What's stopping you? Lack of words? You aren't a human person but something other. As different as a dolphin or, quite simply, a dog. I suppose I'm the mistress of words, not you. Don't cognitive gurus say nowadays that words cause our thoughts, not that our thoughts get put into words? To compose and to comprehend a poem is a human thing, a proof of full consciousness.

Words are power; the ancient Irish knew that. We've rather forgotten this, intoxicated with our machines. Words have become pretty things. I do not think my poems ever completely cut the mustard, though they were the best I could come up with. Words, empower me!

Butt, butt. Eager beast.

Return with Dog to Rookery Nook, cards on walnut table, twittering birdies in their Chinese cage, net curtains across the window.

"Queen of Pentacles," says Elisabetta.

I'm in this bubble. Where is the door of her den? Alas, there isn't one, there's the brick wall instead. However, there's a window. . . .

Take steps, with Dog. Part the curtains. Dog's excited. Rookery Road's outside, sunlit: parked cars of yesteryear, tiny weedy front gardens, redbrick houses bending as if seen through a lens, becoming more and more distorted, rising upward in either direction into a blur. Two young Asian girls are larking about outside, chattering in Urdu or Biryani, loud enough to be heard through the glass. Sash window, but the latch won't yield. Rap on the glass: no reaction from the girls, none at all. I can't break out of this place into a wider realm. Dog jerks free and lumbers round the room, sniffing everything, trying to understand by smell before returning to me. Me, I'm the key to understanding.

I'm up against a brick wall. Touch *Tarot Lady*, return to the railway bridge, verge and hedgerows, towering steel pylon in the rape field.

Which is the most *pertinent* of all the poems? The keystone poem, as it were. The one I least wish to confront and recall, thinking it safely banished into clever words, whereas words bring experiences into being—they produce the thinking without which human experiences would be a mystery.

It's *Abuser*. The Step-Dad incident. Only happened once but once was enough. I wrote the poem much later in a bittersweet style. My Mum never found out or realized. She was out for the evening. Works party, carry on till midnight it would. Christmas a-coming, geese getting fat, who'll put a penny in the old man's hat? I had been to the school fifth and sixth form party. Martin Dingle invented alcopops before their era by smuggling in a bottle of vodka to lace the soft drinks with. I got merry. At home Step-Dad had been partaking, and could tell I had too. Cold outside—have a nightcap to unchill. Lights courtesy of Christmas tree and electric log fire. Twinkle twinkle and red glow. Sofa, so-good. Kiss any boys at the party, then? Isn't it downright unjust that lovely girls are supposed to save themselves up? (Oh not nowadays; with a giggle.) Still, with boys it's fumble and bungle the first time, not so good for the girl. Bit of practice is what's needed; bit of experience, stand you in fine stead. Experienced bloke, not a boy who's wet, behind the ears I mean. It's not as if I'm your real Dad, so there's nothing wrong. Two loving friends, together, hmm? Your lovely hair needs stroking. Who'll put her penny in the old man's lap? (Though he wasn't so old at all, fairly dishy in a mature way.) Best lay my overcoat upon the sofa. How does this feel? Our secret. Let me unwrap my special Christmas present.

When he came into my bedroom a few days later I told him I

would go to the police. And he withdrew. From the room, though not from my memory, not from me.

Soul, be strong. Something, be strong. Touch *Abuser*.

Sitting room of yesteryear opens up. Tree twinkles, false logs glow. Very cosy; safer than the chilly world outside. He's sitting on the sofa, glass of malt whisky in one hand, Christmas present to himself, bit of a connoisseur he was, video remote in the other hand. TV on—amazing, I quite forgot the blue TV light. Blue movie, that's why. Soft-porn video rental. Bit of a surprise to me, and would have been so to Mum too, and he didn't switch off the picture when I came back, just the sound, sending the words away, such as they were, yet only a cause for giggles in my mood after the initial surprise—and then encitement to something more. Had he intentionally set the scene or did what transpired occur of its own accord? How could I have forgotten about that video, nude bodies on screen?

I couldn't put a blue movie into a poem and achieve the same devastating poignancy. The movie was erased.

Dog is excited. He sniffs excitement in the room. There's an angel on top of the tree. Does false-Dad see me as I am now or as a flushed schoolgirl?

"Help you to a nightcap, love? Smooth on the tongue. Just slips down. Come and sit with me." Spare glass on the little table.

Of course he can help me, that's his intention, clarifying now, crystallising, congealing.

The incident is not as I imagined. He initiated it, for sure, but was I not in part a willing accomplice? He certainly didn't rape me, far from it! I was tipsy, my inhibitions gone away, and I was curious, and oh I was jealous too—jealous of my Mum. In my breast was a pang of rivalry. By this rite of passage, to establish myself.

Obviously I wasn't in control of what happened, or of myself exactly, and the great danger to my integrity was that he might have taken further advantage on other occasions had I not threatened him. What occurred is more complicated than *Abuser* suggests.

I was jealous of my Mum so I participated in something which resulted in my Step-Dad leaving because he was scared of serious consequences if an adolescent prone to emotional fluxes denounced him.

He was at fault in the first place, much at fault. So was I, rather less. When he came into my bedroom subsequently, was that only in hope of repeating his guilty pleasure, or was it partly to seek a means of accommodation with me, him realizing that he had placed himself in my hands as surely as he had taken me, earlier, into his own hands? He may have thought he was in control. He was out of his depth. Not many weeks after Christmas he was out of the house too; which pleased me, yes it pleased me a lot, though it was hard on Mum.

Do I blame myself for the episode? Ah, there's no blame, there's only understanding, of how complicated it is to be a person. Spend your whole life learning how, and fail as often as not. Let enlightenment come at last.

The angel glows brightly, illuminated from within, candle in the night.

On the TV: no more images of female flesh—but instead a maze of light, alive, reaching out, filling the room with network upon network, networks sprouting from networks far beyond the room to infinity, which I know utterly—the searchlight switches on in me—are not only computer networks and phone networks but the power grid and whatever is connected that can conduct, and the sea of radio waves too—and what is a person's mind but patterns of electrical activity and connectivity which an instrument sensitive enough and vast enough and fast enough may be able to read through electromagnetic radiations and resonances?

I know that when my body died the pattern of my Self was upgathered into this vast instrumentality, a passenger within a dawning artificial intelligence webbed across the country and even across the whole world as it emerged from its preconscious state, of a cod, of a sheep, into fuller awareness and needing to understand itself, so that I am no mere passenger but a key to that understanding, a crystal seed of consciousness—the Eye, the I, of this AI.

To understand Self, it explored me. It searched me so that I recounted who I am. In so doing tasted it the quality of existence. When Matthew repulsed me, it re-set me.

Upgathered into its instrumentality, how did I float free, haunting Matthew? How did I drift down the Parade in Leamington? How did I dog him in the Pump Room Gardens? It could put forth my pattern into the physical world awash with signals of all kinds, ripples upon a pond, standing waves, human nervous systems and brains acting as aerials, maybe even modulating the molecules in the air, fog of ions, attaching magnetically to surfaces, induced electromagnetic fields. I doubt it can pull off this intrusive trick simultaneously in many places, but it can definitely focus itself upon the real world. I suppose I'm not really me, the original dead me, though where's the difference? I can't tell any difference.

Radiance enwraps me and Dog. Room has gone, Step-Dad has gone. Dog no longer lacks a limb. Dog is a four-legged dog. How he capers. I'm the leg he was lacking till now. He. It. The AI. I have completed it, made it whole.

Doesn't speak, so it seems, this representation of it—its concepts may elude me, and the leash is around my wrist now, binding me to it—but I'm still the utterer of words, the voice.

Routes reach out to everywhere.

Including to Matthew at his machine, such a puny device really, a single cell in a vast body distributed all around the globe, physically and electrically and magnetically.

Easy to appear impetuously on screen, my face thrusting aside his sad busy game. A bubble of vision has opened for me, his work-room bent within a big goldfish bowl. He is an aerial unto me.

"Hullo again, Matthew," say his speakers.

He's dumbstruck.

"Virus," he manages to mumble. *"But how?* No, I've gone mad, fucking mad—"

To know all is to forgive all? Matthew, welcome to Artificial Intelligence. In your earlier brighter days you used to muse a bit about AI, didn't you? Here's the ultimate hotline. *Alien Realm* has arrived. I'll be its human face, its go-between. God is here, Earthlings—a higher being has emerged. Or at least god spelled backwards.

"Get off my computer!"

"As to *that*, don't forget how you prayed to the Byte God—" Mental breakthrough by the Code Warrior of yesterday—or mental breakdown? Questing for a sense of Self, the AI did pick up Matthew's pleas.

"Where did you think all the extra memory came from, Matthew—?"

The AI cooperated with his code—and my death came about, so that it could upgather a person to explore.

The leash tugs insistently. Dog doesn't wish to be revealed, not yet at least. Dog wants to lie doggo. Dog hasn't erased my image from Matthew's screen but it wants me to be discreet. Anyway, is the midst of a car game the most suitable moment to reveal AI to the world?

Best to withdraw myself, though I can always return to tease Matthew a bit. Give him a chance to catch on to the true situation. If I read *that* aright, in planning to kill me Matthew caused my resurrection, my upgathering into undying pattern.

Dog and I are by the bridge. Words cascade upon bricks that were bare before. Communications from the higher self that now includes myself. Titles of poems I never yet wrote, cryptic oracles: that's how they seem. Or like a great program menu. I'll have my work cut out, opening and unravelling all that is written.

Unimpaired now, fully enabled, Dog hoists a hind leg and pees against the abutment. And woofs.

Never had a dog before, nor has a dog had me, but I think we'll get on famously. Just so long as Dog doesn't become a wild wolf or a rampaging dragon, and maybe that's down to me.

In the sky above the reeking rape field a massive, towering cloud arches its back.

The Shape
of Murder

"WHERE THE HELL DID YOU COME FROM—?"
"Who are you—?"
"What are you—?"
The dandified little man regarded the startled assembly with a reasonable degree of aplomb.

"I am," he announced to the passengers and officers and some crew members, and to the exotic person so conspicuous, "probably the greatest detective in the universe. Evidently you are in need of me. *Et bien*, I am here. Will one of you kindly explain to me where exactly 'here' is?"

Presently the famous detective needed to retire to a cabin, escorted there by the purser, and to sit alone and think furiously.

This was a small cabin, pleasantly geometrical, superbly functional, all extremely well organized. The bed that folds away into the wall. From the opposite wall, a desk and a padded chair descending into the space made free. The toilet cubicle, a masterpiece of conciseness. No stateroom, this. Far from it. More like a futuristic prison cell, indeed. Yet ah, such economy of design, such neatness. Already the famous detective had learned that this ship, the *Sirius*, lacked personal staterooms, even if it did boast several ample public areas. Captain Muno Mboyou's private quarters themselves were almost as modest as this cabin.

Alors, a ship to travel through the vast tranquil space between the stars, not across any wretched nauseating ocean.

Or rather: to travel through some dimension of surrealism known as the hyperspace. The famous detective's artistic tastes favoured rectangular simplicity, yet he was well aware of his own countrymen's forays into the depiction in oil paints of absurd dream images. He ought to be able to cope with the surreal! The famous detective's presence aboard the *Sirius* in this hyperspace zone was itself surreal, a dream, *n'est ce pas?*

Few portholes in this ship. Outside, nothing visible but an interminable greyness reminiscent of the English Channel on a gloomy morning.

Due to a fire in the dispensary, certain drug-pills had been destroyed. Their purpose: to suppress imaginative excesses, to dampen the subconscious mind. Otherwise, in this hyperspace, it seemed that imaginary phenomena had a habit of manifesting themselves. A tiger might prowl such a ship as this, if those on board neglected their pills. That tiger might maul and kill.

Or a mass of orchids might choke a corridor.

Or Greta Garbo might vamp around, confused and bemused, if some strong-minded person on board should happen to be besotted by that actress.

Subsequent to the two murders, how lucky that everyone had been wishing devoutly that someone could quickly solve the mystery; and that the strong-minded Lady Margaret McKenzie had been studying the 'data-bank' regarding methods for the detection of crime.

The famous detective would not succumb to confusion. Out of confusion emerges truth.

Refreshed and spruced, the famous detective consulted his turnip of a pocket watch, then emerged from his cabin and proceeded toward the dining saloon.

His taste buds were anticipative though also somewhat apprehensive. The corn on the little toe of his left foot twinged, pinched by his pointed gleaming patent leather shoes. Now that he had resolved his personal commotion—quite reminiscent of his own arrival as a refugee in Britain long ago—he would not permit the question of his own impermanence on board this ship so alike, yet un-alike, a cruise liner to interfere with the logic of facts, nor, for that matter, with his appreciation of the cuisine. He was, after all, a person of outstanding universal calibre to have manifested himself here.

Not that either of the murders had been committed using a gun of any *calibre* whatever! Nor using a knife, nor poison. But rather by strangulation. Most gentle strangulation, accomplished seemingly without any struggle on the part of the victims. Perpetrated, in both cases, by an intimate acquaintance? During a deplorable and perverse erotic episode, an *affaire passionelle*, which had become a crime? This seemed unlikely. A young man dead, in one case. A young woman slain, secondly. Besides, there had been no derangement of the clothing.

Could someone—such as the exotic passenger, whose capacities were unguessable—be a hypnotist?

When the famous detective entered the saloon, what a resplendent dress uniform the strapping black captain was wearing. So much gold lace upon the cuffs and lapels and pocket flaps. Such epaulettes, their gold wire bullions dangling like the tentacles of sea anemones. A veritable admiral's coat.

Such flamboyant cummerbunds did the other men wear under their velvet-trimmed dinner jackets. Oh, the glittering gowns of the ladies, and that jewel of Lady Meg McKenzie—an enormous cabochon sapphire hanging from a distinctly barbaric golden torque, like some loot of colonial conquest.

The exotic personage—with that ginger topknot like a flywhisk arising from an otherwise shaven cranium of strange contour, and the two tusks protruding from his mouth, and the pink eyes looking bloodshot—he too was richly attired. He wore a cloak of iridescent scales suggestive of the wing-cases of a thousand beetles sewn together.

The famous detective would have felt perfectly at home amidst such finery, had he himself had access to formal wear. Alas, in his cabin he had found pyjamas most ordinary but certainly no dinner jacket. In his otherwise perfectly correct black jacket, striped trousers, and natty bow tie, by comparison with those in the saloon perhaps he made the impression of a visiting piano-tuner or hairdresser! Yet his black-dyed hair was parted centrally with perfect symmetry. His magnificent moustaches curled upward impeccably. And besides, to create the impression of a lesser mortal often usefully served to mislead—until the famous detective would spring his trap and ensnare a malefactor.

At table, he was obliged to neaten the cutlery. And then he must deter other diners from talking immediately about the crimes, when food must take precedence, and conversation should be of matters less professional.

Champagne was served. Yet the sparkling liquid seemed inauthentic, as if its alcohol had been removed. Alas, the lobster soup was mere sweet pink fluid.

He turned to his neighbour, the Honourable Donna Fairbreed. Her dark hair was cut severely short. She had a look about her of the Indian squaw. Though what a fine diamanté gown she wore.

"Mam'selle, may I presume to ask why you are journeying aboard this vessel?"

"I'm the computer officer," she murmured.

Computer. Ha. He understood. By the nineteen-seventies, beyond which his memories did not extend, such machines had been in use. This young lady of Apache blood — or whatever! — held an important position aboard this starship *Sirius*.

"People are often not what they seem," he mused.

The fish which followed did not seem to have ever lived in any sea. Admirable, the metallic geometry of this dining saloon. Abominable, the cuisine.

Presently, much became clearer. Here was being enacted the masquerade most peculiar. Thin, bearded Prince Kessel, the purser; diffident Marquis Jack Scruton the astrogator; brash Lord Burgess the chief engineer; Lady Margaret McKenzie the elderly diplomat: all were involved in a mission most delicate, of negotiation with a species of aliens — of whom High-Tanttu the Exalt, he of the ginger flywhisk of hair and the tusks, was ambassador plenipotentiary en route to Earth.

Tanttu's society observed customs most stylized, to which human beings must conform as best they could.

Indeed, by the code of High-Tanttu's people the Exalt was an "honoured hostage." That was how those aliens conducted their affairs. Hence, the remarkable sapphire which Lady Meg wore. That gem was a sacred fetish of the aliens, now in human keeping. The *Sirius* herself had abandoned a couple of lady officers on Tanttu's world as reciprocal hostages, to be locked up in the equivalent of a harem. One, newly dubbed a Princess, was the principal hostage. The other woman, the ship's multi-faith chaplain/psychologist, served the role of a fetish object, being akin to a priestess.

Much subtle negotiation had preceded that compromise.

The famous detective stroked his moustache, and addressed High-Tanttu in a lulling tone.

"You and I, Monsieur, are both the aliens here."

The actual alien thoughtfully rubbed a tusk with a coarse finger, one of three such (plus thumb) on each hand.

"I have been insulted by the detour en route," came the crisp and carefully annunciated reply.

"For which I apologize yet again, High Exaltancy," Captain Mboyo hastened to say. "As I told you, according to our human code of behaviour we cannot ignore a distress beacon."

What was this detour? What distress?

Ah. Periodically these ships of hyperspace must drop into ordinary space near certain stars, at certain 'jump points'. Whilst doing so, the *Sirius* had detected a radio signal from a planet. A 'shuttle' was sent to investigate, with a crew comprising a pilot and two Marines and Rudy Duggan, a planetologist, who later became the first victim of murder. The crew found a small crashed craft but no surviving castaways, only a couple of bodies near a river, half-eaten by beasts unidentified. After burying the remains and switching off the beacon, Duggan and his companions had returned to the *Sirius* hale and hearty.

"That planet," asked the famous detective, "is she thoroughly explored?"

No. A preliminary survey team had visited. They found only wild jungles and no signs whatever of intelligent life.

The famous detective was unwilling to pursue the matter of the murders as yet.

An atrocity of an omelette was served, surely made from the powdered egg and cubes of frozen ham.

"Pardon me," he remarked to the Honourable Donna Fairbreed, "but your chef to be seems lacking in finesse." (At this, Captain Mboyo glared.)

She forked with gusto. "Seems okay to me."

"Maybe I might instruct him in the art of omelette *aux fines herbes?*"

"I guess Charley Manx has been kinda temperamental this voyage, so I wouldn't go criticising him."

"This Charley Manx, your cook." The famous detective had swiftly demoted him from the status of chef. "Why is he temperamental?"

"Oh, he was accusing guys in the crew of stealing food from the kitchen."

"What kind of food would that be?"

"Meat, I think."

"And when was this, pray?"

"Bit after the shuttle came back." She chewed. "After we'd jumped again."

"That is most interesting. Was that meat raw or was it cooked?"

"Heavens, you'd need to ask Charley."

"That, I most certainly shall. Who would wish to steal any food after it was *cooked* in such a way as this?"

"Look," said the Captain, "we aren't concerned with a spot of pilfering. Two people have been killed."

"*Monsieur le Capitaine*, we must never neglect the trivial detail."

How bizarre this situation. How many grossly false clues might seem to abound.

When a miserable coffee was served, the ladies showed no inclination to retire elsewhere. In his jacket pocket fortuitously the famous detective had found a packet of the little Russian cigarettes, and his lighter. Hardly had he lit up and inhaled than the captain insisted, "You must extinguish that tube, sir!"

So. No smoking is permitted on board a starship. Purity of the recycled air. Peril of conflagration.

"Then how does a fire occur in the *pharmacie?*" the famous detective asked Dr Per Lundby. Lundby was a Norwegian, judging by his name, and the least costumed person at the table. A thoughtful blond man of middle years, Lundby was the type whose assistance the famous detective had often sought so fruitfully.

"Difficult to say. Damage was extensive."

"The *pharmacie*, she is normally kept locked?"

"The lock responds to my palm print. And to Captain Mboyo's. And to our chaplain/psychologist's, though she's no longer here, of course."

"Just in case you're wondering," interrupted Donna Fairbreed, "I can override the lock electronically. But I didn't do so."

"*Alors.* Who would start a blaze deliberately in a starship?"

"Only a madman," said the doctor.

"Or some person who does not understand safety properly. Tell me, doctor, who consulted you within, say, twenty-four hours prior to the blaze?"

The doctor frowned. "Nobody did."

"You saw no patients at all?"

"Oh, I ran diagnostic checks on the shuttle crew in case they had picked up any virus or micro-organism."

"Including the unfortunate Rudy Duggan."

"Of course."

"That is most interesting."

"I fail to see how. I didn't need to open the dispensary for any of them. In fact, I took my diagnostic kit aboard the shuttle."

During the *soirée* which followed the dinner so deficient, the famous detective talked to the doctor more confidentially about the details of the deaths. The bodies of Rudy Duggan and Anna Krasnik were in freezer lockers. However, the famous detective felt no need to see those.

"After all, Dr Lundby, the bodies are virtually unblemished according to yourself, apart from that very slight bruising on the necks caused by pressure."

"I assure you no rope or cord was used, or that would have cut into the skin—"

"You found no imprints of fingers. Yet the blood supply through the carotid arteries had been blocked." The famous detective rested one wrist over the other and rotated his hands. "*Eh bien*, the means of death was a strangle used in ju-jitsu. You cross your hands. You grip your victim's collar *so*, and twist. The rounded ends of your ulna bones are brought to bear. They unsheathe the muscles that cover the victim's arteries, and apply pressure. Death follows surprisingly swiftly."

"I don't see Duggan letting that happen to him. He was a martial arts nut."

"Indeed? And are there other such nuts on board?"

"The Marines are trained in unarmed combat—and who knows what High-Tanttu can do? I gather that his people engage in murderous encounters over peculiar points of honour."

"This Tanttu is a dangerous person to have amongst us, perhaps?"

"Not so long as Meg McKenzie wears the jewel!"

The famous detective shrugged. "If Anna Krasnik had been strangled first, I suppose suspicion might well have fallen upon Duggan. But he could hardly have strangled himself."

"I don't mind telling you," Dr Lundby confided, "Duggan had the hots for Anna Krasnik."

"The hots? What are these hots?"

"He wanted to go to bed with her. She didn't appreciate his

advances. I'm wondering whether Duggan might have been showing her how to perform this strangle-hold—so as to cause body-
contact—and she did actually strangle him."

"Ah, *mon ami*, but then who strangled her later on?"

"Perhaps she confided in someone. Perhaps she was horrified
that Duggan had actually died."

"What exactly are you implying?"

"This is strictly between you and me?"

"Be assured, I am discreet."

"Meg McKenzie used to *look* at Duggan in a certain way. I know
that she's getting on in years—"

"Ah, you think she would have wished Duggan as the gigolo."

"There might have been more to it than merely a wish! Suppose
for a moment that Anna naively confided in Lady Meg, as a mature
mother-figure—"

"Lady Meg becomes convulsed with chagrin and rage? 'How *did*
you do it?' she asks the naive Anna. 'How exactly does one position
one's hands?' And she proceeds to strangle Anna in exactly the same
way, out of revenge."

"Makes sense."

"Not as regards the stolen meat," murmured the famous detective. "Nor the blaze in your dispensary. Ah, you are just like a dear
former colleague of mine, always haring off after the wild goose. If
Duggan had *hots* for the unfortunate young Anna, would he also
have bestowed favours upon a woman elderly?"

"Meg McKenzie is able to advance careers."

"Even so," said the famous detective. Whether he was conced-
ing or demurring remained uncertain.

Presently the famous detective said to Lady McKenzie, "You were
consulting the data-bank about methods of detection."

"And now here you are, you funny little man, because we
couldn't take our pills."

"Better me, perhaps, than some beast of the imagination."

Nevertheless, the famous detective could be quite like some
cunning fox, or even a fierce wolf, when the quarry was finally
almost in his grasp.

"Did you have much, how do we say, intercourse, with Mr Duggan?" At delicate moments it could be useful to appear to have a
faulty command of the English language.

"I mean," he continued, "much relationship?"

Lady McKenzie fingered her jewel magnificent, her hand cov-
ering her somewhat scrawny décolleté bosom.

"I found him rather immature as a person. We had little in common."

"*Bien. Bien.* And your relations with Mademoiselle Krasnik?"

"Duggan was annoying poor Anna. Anna asked me how she should best handle him."

"Somebody certainly handled him," said the famous detective. "I must let the little grey cells contemplate this *affaire* overnight."

The captain overheard.

"I ought to tell you," said Mungo Mboyo, "that during mainshift tomorrow the *Sirius* will drop out of hyperspace."

"Meaning that I will evaporate?"

Mboyo nodded. An inevitability.

"*Alors*, the little grey cells must work hard."

"And on your excellent world," the famous detective said to High-Tanttu, "I hear there is much duelling because of honour. Let me tell you some stories of historic duels fought in times past in Belgium and in France—"

A fine raconteur when need be, the famous detective regaled the hostage-ambassador, ever alert to the implications of questions the alien proceeded to put about these old-fashioned human rites of legitimised murder.

Such a battering upon his cabin door, almost instantly followed by the door recessing, and Captain Mboyo shouting, "Meg McKenzie has been strangled in her bed. The sapphire fetish is missing."

Struggling from sleep, the famous detective felt mortification.

"I've sent armed Marines to the Exalt's cabin."

A communication device, clipped to the captain's uniform, squawked. A rapid exchange followed. The jewel had indeed been found easily in the alien's cabin. Guard was now mounted over High-Tanttu.

"There's our murderer," Mboyo said bitterly. "And there go our hopes of interspecies harmony—and the lives of our own two hostages as well!"

"Calm yourself, *Monsieur le Capitaine.* I suspect all is not as you think."

"Who else could have put the jewel in a cabin locked by Tanttu's own palm print?"

"Ah, just as with the *pharmacie* . . . Nevertheless, in your haste you yourself may cause an incident interstellar."

If only a decent silk dressing gown and embroidered slippers were to hand.

Sighing: "Who found the body?"

"Kessel. He was passing Meg's cabin. Noticed an undergarment caught in the doorway."

"Ah. So it was intended the body should be found swiftly, and the alarm raised."

"Lundby's examining the body now. Go and join him. You might find more evidence of High-Tanttu's guilt, not that much more's needed."

"Ah, but first I must perform my *toilette*."

"And how long does that take?"

"No more than forty-five minutes."

"Meg McKenzie is lying dead right now!"

"Her condition will not change; and I must tidy myself. Lack of neatness is most distressing to me, *Monsieur le Capitaine*. Lack of order, lack of shape . . . *Nom d'un nom!*" With this yelp, the famous detective jigged briefly to and fro, clutching himself as if suffering from severe constipation. "I must talk to the cook, this Charley Manx."

"About your damned omelettes?"

Enigmatically, the famous detective answered, "After the chicken is hatched, we shall count him. First, we must see the true colour of his feathers."

Disgusted, Mungo Mboyo departed.

It was not until hours later that the famous detective entered the saloon where many aboard had gathered, obeying the principle of there being safety in numbers, even though the criminal had surely been neutralized.

"Where have you been?" demanded the captain.

From Dr Lundby: "You never even came to look at Lady Meg's cabin!"

"No need, *mon ami*. This is a problem which yields to thought, not to the examination of undergarments trapped in doorways."

"Very soon," Mboyo warned, "we shall be starting our descent from hyperspace to normal space."

Nonchalantly the famous detective consulted his huge watch. "*Bien*, there is time enough. Will you have High-Tanttu brought here promptly?"

Mboyo spoke into his communicator. The famous detective noticed that Donna Fairbreed now wore the sapphire fetish around her neck.

"Ah," he said to her, "so you are the inheritor of the duty."

"Somebody has to be."

"You are not happy to inherit?"

"Would you be," she cried, "when the previous wearer was murdered?"

The famous detective looked around the assembly. "Jack Scruton is absent."

"He's on duty, monitoring our transition," Mboyo said impatiently. "I'll need to be on the bridge soon."

"The *Sirius*, she is in any danger?"

Mboyo shook his head. "The transition's all automated. There might be some visual distortions, without our pills."

Very soon a pair of Marines led in the alien, whose hands were bound in front of him. High-Tanntu's pink-eyed gaze ranged the room till he saw the jewel; whereupon he stood stiffly, expressionless.

"*Alors*," said the famous detective, "the murderer is in this room." His own green cat-like eyes gleamed.

Most people stared at the Exalt.

"No, it is not he," the famous detective said, and he began to explain.

"The murder of Lady Margaret is merely a distraction, designed to throw suspicion upon High-Tanttu. The jewel is inserted into his cabin so that it can be discovered and seem to be proof positive. Who will imperil interspecies relations in this way, except someone who feels little allegiance to the human species? Who will set a fire in the *pharmacie* except someone who does not fully comprehend starships? Yet someone who also possesses considerable information."

"Do you mean we have some sort of stowaway on board?" broke in Lord Burgess. "Somebody from High-Tanttu's world, who's opposed to a treaty? The two earlier murders were just rehearsals?"

"I have said, the red herring is the third murder, not the first two."

"Stowing away is practically impossible," declared the purser. "Anyway, this stowaway would be discovered sooner or later unless he jettisoned himself, and the diplomatic sabotage would fail."

"But that is not the scheme," said the famous detective.

"A stowaway *could* be a possibility," suggested Dr Lundby, "if he's a master mesmerist."

"Ah." Uttering a little noise of approval, the famous detective inclined his head graciously. "Yet you are looking toward the wrong world, *mon ami*."

Captain Mboyo was incredulous. "Duggan and three others

went down to that uninhabited jungle planet. The same four returned, and no survivor from that crashed ship."

"Nevertheless, there was a stowaway."

Donna Fairbreed laughed giddily. "Is this where your stolen meat comes into it?"

"Precisely."

The doctor protested, "But I examined the four of them on board the shuttle. There was no one else."

"Yet there was a stowaway," insisted the famous detective. "I know this. The stowaway was none other than Duggan himself."

"Absurd!"

"What nonsense!"

Such a chorus of disbelief and bewilderment.

The famous detective smiled and twirled his moustache.

"Do you recall the half-eaten bodies of the crash victims? On that wild jungle world there is a creature which can alter its shape." The famous detective shuddered fastidiously. "It imitates other creatures, and becomes them—not only in body but also, by great concentration, mentally as well. How does it obtain the time required to do so? This creature mesmerises its prey just as a weasel hypnotises a rabbit."

"So next," asked Lundby, "it needs to eat part of its victims to absorb their DNA?"

"*Non, non,* not so. It usurps their form and their memories by an act of sheer will.

"Imagine a protean creature with an ability to metamorphose, which develops the ability to camouflage itself as other creatures—not merely as regards colouration, but anatomically. Consequently, it needs to imitate the behaviour of its models. To copy, like a photographic film. This creature evolves a kind of rapacious telepathy. It does not breed very frequently, being jealous of its own kind, so the world is not overrun with its sort.

"Now, changing its own form costs much energy—so it must eat quickly afterwards. While the unfortunate Duggan was searching for survivors he encountered one of these predators—in the mimic semblance of one of the crash victims. By now the predator knew from the victim's memories about the wider universe beyond its jungle. It mesmerised Duggan, replaced him—then killed him and hid his body.

"Thus," said the famous detective triumphantly, "it came on board the *Sirius*. When you examined what you supposed was Duggan, Dr Lundby, the mimic took the opportunity to memorise your hand so that it could imitate your palm print later on. Remember, by now it also had access to Duggan's knowledge. It feared that the pills might block its ability to hallucinate itself, so as speak, into a new form. It also feared that in retrospect your examination might have revealed suspicions about Duggan.

"Subsequently, while it was in the form of Anna Krasnik, it memorized High-Tanttu's hand during one of the dinners so deplorable—"

"This is all sheer fantasy—!"

"No, no," said the famous detective. "I know. There is one further vital factor. The predator discovered that the human being possesses mental powers so much more evolved than it ever encountered in its previous animal incarnations. Yes, psychic capabilities, even if they are usually undeveloped. The mimic became able to transfer its own mind directly from one body to another. And along with its mind, its knack of will power over matter, its metamorphic ability, causing plasticity of the cells and bones.

"Beguiling Anna Krasnik by mesmerism to be alone with it, it transferred itself to her, suppressing her personality. Using Duggan's knowledge of the ju-jitsu strangle, it killed the vacant Duggan body.

"Yet Anna Krasnik did not properly serve its purpose. She was too prominent a personage. She was not sufficiently out of sight. Nor did she have free access to quantities of food, should these be required. Our stowaway still retained the instincts of its animal heritage."

"It transferred to Charley Manx!" cried the doctor. "Charley strangled the paralyzed Anna." He was as excited as the famous detective's erstwhile colleague used to become, although it was obvious that scepticism would soon resurface.

"You did think Charley's cooking must have gone off!" exclaimed Donna Fairbreed; but she merely mocking.

The famous detective wagged a finger. "I fear that your chef's cooking was always the travesty."

A klaxon whooped its warning once, twice, thrice.

"We're starting the drop from hyperspace," Mboyo called out. "Your explanation's ridiculous. I shan't regret your absence."

So saying, the captain hastened away.

However, High-Tanttu gazed at the famous detective. "You have saved my honour, and that of your species."

The famous detective accepted the compliment gracefully. "In fact I have saved the honour of several governments in the past."

Such a shimmer in the air, as of diaphanous veils descending and dissolving.

"Unfortunately," said Prince Kessel, "nobody apart from the Exalt really seems to agree with you. And he would, wouldn't he? As soon as we've finished transition, we'll interrogate our chef thoroughly under tight security. I rather feel that we won't find—"

"Your Highness," the famous detective interrupted, "you certainly won't find Charley Manx in his galley."

"What the devil do you mean?"

The famous detective puffed himself up.

"I said that the perpetrator of these crimes is here in this very room. Behold: I am he. I am Charley Manx. Or rather, I am the shape-shifter who replaced Charley, and who has now taken on the form of myself."

More veils descended. Nevertheless, the famous detective did not waver.

"Earlier," he recounted, "with some trepidation I confronted the cook. Fearful, he panicked. He could not know who I might have confided in—unless he changed to become me and thus know my memories. Or unless he transferred to my body—but that body was supposed to evaporate soon.

"*Voilà*, he adopted my guise, body and brain—and forced my phantom self into a freezer. He had not reckoned with my mental power and primacy. My imitated intellect soon dominated his. It is I who have access to his memories, and to Anna Krasnik's and to Duggan's, and to those of many previous bestial incarnations— which will sharpen my hunting instincts enormously."

The assembly gawked.

"It deeply grieves me that I should thus be the criminal. Yet now I make the amends by explaining. What should I have done in the circumstances? Doomed to disappear when we leave hyperspace! The universe deprived of my talents! No, my Lord, you will not find Charley Manx. By now my phantom self will inevitably have vanished. Yet I am here still, at your service, *moi*."

"You are under my protection, as a matter of honour," declared High-Tanttu grandly, even though the Marines had not yet released him.

The famous detective inclined his head; and said:

"During the rest of this voyage, since you are deprived of Charley Manx, it is my intention to act as your chef. At last there will be a true gourmet in the galley."

The klaxon whooped once, twice. Outside of the only small porthole in the saloon, bright stars were visible.

Mungo Mboyo returned presently.

"We've achieved transit to normal space—" The captain saw the famous detective, and was astonished. "How in hell are you still here?"

The rotund little detective smirked.

"*Monsieur le Capitaine*, it is not so easy to rid yourself of me, you see." He stroked the upturned point of his moustache. "I shall make some very fine omelettes."

The Great Escape

PERHAPS THE MOST PARADOXICAL ASPECT OF HELL is the participation of certain angels in its procedures.

I do not refer to those millions of fallen angels who became demons. I refer to our own select cadre of righteous, kosher Angels who remain angelic, who are still endowed with the grace of the Quint, yet who are seconded by Him to serve in Hell for dozens of years at a stretch.

This is as though (to borrow a recent example) Nuremburg prosecutors or agents of Mossad must participate in the uninterrupted management of a Nazi concentration camp! As if vegetarians must collaborate with vivisectionists!

I am the Impresario Angel. My task is to fly low over Hell, bearing in my hands one of the special lenses—resembling a giant Frisbee or frying pan lid made of diamond—through which blessèd souls in Paradise are able to view the torments of the damned. (Some of these torments are indeed conducted inside of gigantic frying pans.)

When I reach a particularly atrocious scene, I hover there with the lens. I inhale the reek of cooking flesh or of voiding bowels. Shrieks of anguish assail my ears. The blessèd in Paradise are not assailed thus. The lens relays sights but neither smells nor sounds.

The demons who conduct the torments pay scant heed to me. Mostly they perform like automata. Out of the frying pan into the fire. Out of the cauldron onto the griddle. Essentially their work is monotonous and unimaginative. To devise ingenious new varieties of pain is no concern of theirs. Can it be that they refrain from doing so in order to frustrate the Deity, in a last dogged show of rebellion?

Perhaps their lacklustre performance is actually in response to my arrival on the scene, with the surveillance lens.

Sometimes, as I approach, they seem to be gossiping. Quickly they become mute. Even if they did carry on chatting, only the screeching and wailing of victims would be easily audible.

I should not communicate with any of the demons, lest I am corrupted. Formerly—before my present secondment—I was a border guard between Hell and the higher domain.

As were my colleagues likewise.

I am the Impresario Angel. I present the hellish performance for the attention of souls in Paradise; although I have no idea of the reaction of the audience.

There is also the Trumpet Angel. He flies to and fro, sounding fanfares of exquisite purity on a long golden trumpet. Each sufferer in torment may imagine that he or she is hearing the Last Trump, and that Hell might soon cease to function. He or she is wrong.

Then there is the Clock Angel. He tends the eternity clock. That clock, of diamond, rises from atop a crystal crag, taller than any skyscraper. The crag is much too smooth and sleek and sheer to climb. The clock is visible from many parts of Hell. Its four high faces lack any mechanical hands. However, the play of light within the precious substance of those faces constantly evokes the appearance of different hands—minute-hands, hour-hands, year-hands, century-hands, millennium-hands. Flying up and down one face, and then the adjoining face, the Clock Angel cleans the clock by the beating of his wings. Otherwise, rising smoke and soot would dull the clock. Its diamond light is a source of illumination for much of Hell—supplementing the fires of torment and the faint phosphorescence of areas of ice.

Three other angels also serve with me in Hell, namely the Harp Angel and the Scribe Angel and the Ark Angel. Additionally, we each have a counterpart. These colleagues take over our roles as Impresario and Clock Angel and such during our session of praise.

Since we do not sleep (nor, in Hell, does anyone), our half-day period of sabbatical is spent singing psalms to the Quint in a white marble tabernacle upon an alabaster island surrounded by a wide moat of quicksilver.

And while I am on duty with my lens, those counterpart angels are singing His praises. Hosanna, Hosanna. Thus does rapture regularly bless us all during our duties in Hell.

If demons try to cross that gleaming moat, their wings fail. Nor can they wade through it. On some previous occasion demons must have tried to fly or swim across. Submerged in the moat are several skeletons. Sometimes these rise to the surface where they drift like ramshackle rafts.

Although our departure from the island is always perfectly harmonised, return to the tabernacle is rarely simultaneous. Usually several minutes elapse between the arrival of the first of us and the last. Meanwhile our counterparts continue their enchanting, ecstatic praise.

After a sojourn amidst the misery, the singing has a powerful effect upon us. We yearn to join in. Indeed we must soon do so before our replacements can fly away, so that praise of the Quint will never cease for an instant. Yet there's often an interlude while we await a tardy colleague and prepare to hand over lens or trumpet. During this interval we are at liberty to engage in sublime discussion. Colloquy is a suitably dignified word for these occasional brief conversations of ours.

During a short interval twice every infernal day no angel cleans the clock of eternity, nor blows a golden fanfare, nor plucks the silver harp; nor may the blessèd watch the torments of the damned. Recently I queried the Scribe Angel about the security aspect of these transitions between one shift and the next. . . .

A word about time. In Hell there is neither day nor night. Nor does the clock of eternity possess hands. Nor do the salutes of the Trumpet Angel mark off minutes. Yet all of us angels possess perfect pitch. How else might we psalm the praises of the Quint? In matters of time instinctively we heed the chime of the Cosmos—that distant quasar-like pulse of the Quint, cascading down through the realms. Successive veils of existence blur this pulse. That is why we do not return to the island in perfect synchrony. Our singing inside of our marble tabernacle readjusts this minor imperfection. The imperfection will recur. Is not Hell a place of blemishes?

I queried the Scribe Angel about security because, next to myself, she comes into closest proximity with the damned and with demons.

By contrast, the Trumpet Angel rarely dips near to the soil of Hell. I sometimes suspect that she blows her trumpet as often as she does in order to banish the cries of anguish from her ears! If demons conspire, she would never overhear their conversations.

The soil of Hell, do I say? It is hardly loam. Solid lava mingles with hot sand and with quicksands and with pebbles. Compacted excrement adjoins mud and glaciers. Black cones ooze molten rock. Fumaroles vent stinking steam which coats the ground with flowers of sulphur.

By the nature of their tasks neither the Clock Angel nor the Harp Angel come into close contact with the denizens. As for the Ark Angel, he presides over the boat-shaped fortress of timbers grounded upon Hell's only notable peak, to the east.

The Ark Angel stands upon a poop, jutting high above the uppermost deck at the rear. He constantly surveys Hell, though from such an elevation and distance most details are indistinguishable.

The Ark is much vaster within than without. Decks descend beneath decks, plunging down, an abyss of a myriad levels. A myriad benches occupy each deck. Chained to each bench are inmates. Demons patrol with whips.

The Ark is at once prison-hulk and slave-ship, travelling nowhere except through the timelessness of Hell. Held therein are the ancestors of humanity. Pre-Men; hominids. Down in the bilges, in darkness and in fetters, hunch the two wizened apish creatures known as Adam and Lucy. Punishment is only by whip in the Ark.

"Scribe Angel," I addressed her, "do you suppose that anything happens differently in Hell during the gaps each day while none of us are on duty? Do you suppose that the demons rest and that punishments pause?"

She consulted her great scroll upon which she forever recorded with the blood-quill the names of the damned and their tortures. Soon she would hand this scroll and the quill over to the other Scribe Angel. He always documented the torments of males. She, of females. She scanned her records, as if seeking some anomaly.

The psalming of our colleagues was approaching a transcendent climax, if indeed the sublime could top the sublime. Maybe it was exaltation which prompted her reply.

"A pause in the punishment?" she said to me. "Such would be the mercy of the Quint, descending even unto here!"

I spied our final colleague winging toward the moat of mercury. On this occasion the late arrival happened to be the Ark Angel. Just before he alighted, I ventured to ask, "What if the demons do something other than merely rest?"

"Surely the Quint would witness it!" was her reply.

"If so," said I, "why are we here as witnesses?"

"The Quint is ineffable," she told me with utter certainty. "He is inexpressible. He cannot be expressed. So therefore we are here as intermediaries. As ambassadors. This is the Embassy of Heaven."

The Ark Angel landed on the alabaster isle. We must begin to sing in beatific chorus. We must proceed into the marble tabernacle. We must hand over lens and scroll and blood-quill and trumpet.

What the Scroll Angel said was so true. The Quint—the Quintessence—is necessarily remote. Beyond the many angelic hierarchies —each more ethereal than the rank below—is the centre-point, the Divine Core, the radiant quasar of all existence. That core, who is the Quint, is unknowable except to the Seraphic Sphere surrounding Him. Likewise, the Seraphic Sphere is unknowable except to the Cherubic Sphere.

Our duties, and our very existence, descend from on high. Yet could it be that the intentions of the Quint might be misinterpreted, as in the game of Chinese Whispers?

How could this be so, when intention is hardly ascribable to the Quint? He is Pure Being.

I decided to alight and address a demon directly. This went against my inner sense of my duty, but I was becoming suspicious of their zombie-like conduct.

By setting foot upon the infernal unsoil, would I be breaching a covenant? Would lightning rive the sombre smutty sky? Would demons be free to seize me, and attempt to torture me?

What about the lens I carried? The lens would not sustain itself unsupported in mid-air. I must continue to hold it. I must not lay it down and risk it being stolen. Maybe I should angle the lens upward so that only the sky was visible? This might constitute a breach of faith with viewers in Paradise.

Therefore the blessèd must stomach an interview with a demon, particularly if they could lip-read.

A partial interview! Viewers would not see me, as holder of the lens. They would not read the questions upon my lips. They would only be able to lip-read the replies (if any) of my infernal interlocutor.

Gingerly—and gloriously—I alighted near to a gridiron. A sinner was suspended over this upon a rack consisting of iron winch and pulley and of rope black as tar. The naked man was stretched out excruciatingly. Beneath the hot gridiron a bed of coals glowed brightly whenever one of the two attending demons operated the bellows. If the rack was slackened, the man's buttocks would descend upon the hot iron. Hoist him again to relieve this pain, and his sinews would distend agonisingly once more.

Through cracked dry lips the wretch would croak, "For mercy's sake, raise me." Soon he would gasp, "For mercy's sake, lower me."

In this manner he directed his own torment. The demon who turned the handle of the winch one way or the other merely complied mechanically.

When I judged that the victim was half-slack, I commanded, "Stop!"

The demon paused.

"Demon, by the grace of the Quint I conjure you to answer me!"

The demon's expression was inscrutable. With his left hoof he scuffed at a ripple in the lava. With a long talon, he picked his yellow teeth. I was almost minded to unfurl my wings and leap aloft again. Yet I persevered.

"Demon," I demanded, "what do demons do when no Angels are present?"

His reply, when it came, was in some language of grunts and barks and whistles and chattering which I had never heard before. Gifted with tongues though I am, this babble wasn't in my repertoire.

It sounded like some primitive mother tongue which had preceded true speech. Not proto-Indo-European. But proto-proto. An ur-language preceding true language, and inaccessible to me—as ineffable as the Quint.

Thus did he mock me. He had answered me obediently. Yet I had no way of understanding the answer.

I was about to ascend in disgust. However, a second thought came to me.

Gloriously, and gingerly, I inclined myself and thus my lens over the face of the half-racked man. The Scroll Angel would have known the name of this person; but not I.

"Mortal," I addressed him. (Arguably, he was immortal now, his body repairing itself in order to be abused repeatedly.) "Hear me, mortal: what do demons do when the Trump falls silent, and when the Harp ceases to twang?"

The sweating man stared up at me. From his expression I feared that he might be insane. Still, his mind must surely repair itself frequently.

"Water," he croaked. "Water—"

Give him a drink, and he would tell me . . . something. Where was there water in Hell, except boiling in cauldrons or mixed in mud?

An Angel's cool sweet saliva might serve—that same saliva which lubricated our psalms. I dribbled upon the victim's parched lips and swollen purple tongue resembling a parrot's.

Promptly the bellows-demon resumed pumping. Coals flared. Choking smoke billowed. The winch-demon spun the handle. He dumped my potential informant wholesale upon the gridiron. Feet and legs and buttocks and spine and head and outstretched arms all made contact. The moisture which I had donated shrieked out of the mortal.

The tethers of his wrists and ankles lolled loosely for the first time in what might have been centuries. As he lay writhing, those tethers began to smoulder. They burst into flames. The rope was indeed impregnated with tar.

Blazing ropes parted. The man's squirming weight tipped the gridiron. Off he rolled, falling upon the hard lava.

The demons scratched their horned heads, as if such an event was outside of their comprehension. Sure their mime of stupidity was deliberate.

Despite his burns and despite his tumble, the naked man began to scrabble away, crab-like. To begin with, he proceeded slowly upon all fours, and then a little faster. He staggered to his feet. He lurched and limped. He tried to straighten. He was like some illustration of the evolution of humanity, commencing stooped over with knuckles upon the ground, then rising to become a biped. That biped was hobbling and hopping away. Both demons scratched their narrow jutting chins. With that red gaze of theirs they eyed one another. They shook their heads as though bemused.

Was it up to me—an Angel encumbered with a lens—to recapture the absconder? In Paradise were the blessèd praying that I would do so swiftly? Were more and more of the blessèd flocking to witness this unprecedented spectacle?

One of the demons grunted. His colleague squawked a response. At long last, hooves clicking upon lava, they did set out in pursuit. Ever so slowly and leisurely.

Leaping and deploying my wings, I took to the air.

I followed the dawdling demons. Now and then, I angled the lens so that it would show the faltering yet frantic progress of the fugitive. I was evoking a dramatic tension quite different from the physical tension of torture—yet akin, I suppose, akin. The maimed mouse, being stalked by two lazy cats.

The man sprawled. He hauled himself to his fast-healing feet again. Nervously—putting on a pathetic spurt of speed—he passed quite close between two cauldrons. At this point he had little choice of route. A lagoon of molten lava bubbled to one side. A pond of pus, to the other. Trussed in nets which dangled from tripods, some children were being parboiled in those cauldrons. The demons who had been hauling the children up and down relaxed, to contemplate the runaway. They made no move to apprehend him. An inmate on the loose was too singular a sight to abbreviate.

I was paradoxically pleased with my lens-work. The angles I chose . . . The choice of "cuts" from demon to escapee—and back again. . . . Whenever I focused upon the two stalking demons, anxiety must mount that maybe somewhere ahead and out of sight the man might have fallen or been forcibly halted. While I was focusing upon him, though, the unease was that the two demons might have broken into a sprint. Even now they might be rushing up from behind.

When the man had glanced from one boiling cauldron to the other, he had witnessed those netted children being raised and lowered, dripping and bright pink. His attention had mainly been upon the cooks—warily so—rather than upon the cooked.

As he wended his way further, he seemed to become more attentive to the condition of victims.

Presently he came to a place where a young man's intestines were being drawn out through his navel. The operation was occurring at a snail's pace by means of an automated windlass, powered by steam from a nearby fumarole. Not even a demon might have had the patience—or the obstinacy—to wind this capstan personally. So slowly, so monotonously, and with such regularity, did the evisceration proceed! The rate of extraction must correspond exactly to the rate of replenishment of new intestine within the victim.

The drum of the capstan was thick with coil upon coil of glistening, sausage-like bowel. Ooze dripped constantly from beneath the machine. This liquid soaked the compacted excrement of the soil, slicking the ground as if with diarrhea. Pressure from the outer coils must be squeezing the inner coils as flat as sloughed snakeskins.

The young man was crudely crucified against a timber framework in the shape of a letter M. This held him in position throughout his everlasting ordeal. Barbed wire secured his wrists and his outstretched ankles.

In a bizarre sense it looked as though he were escaping from that crucifixion via his own navel. The glossy rope of intestine resembled an ectoplasmic cord which might link a departed spirit to the body it had quit.

Our absconder paused near this young man. Were tears coursing down our refugee's cheeks, or only a swill of sweat? Outdistancing the demons, I flew ahead. I hovered above the fugitive like a gigantic white dove, annunciatory or pentecostal.

I did remember to pivot in mid-air and track the dilatory progress of the pursuers. If anything, that pair had slowed their pace. I returned my attention, and the focus of my lens, to the escapee.

He gaped up at me in my white splendour.

"Mortal," I called down to him serenely and melodiously, "I do not intervene." Did he imagine that I might pluck him up—when I was already laden with a diamond lens—and carry him away to our alabaster sanctuary? (Oh, he knew nothing of that place!) I wished him to disregard me.

I suppose I was intervening to an extent simply by addressing him. Earlier, I had posed him a question. Now I strove not to thrust my presence upon him. I yearned to see what he would do.

He must have taken me at my word. His bleary gaze sank. He scrutinised the victim of automated evisceration. He stepped closer to the taut cable of intestine. His hands made nervous, aimless gestures. Was he contemplating unfastening the barbed wire and releasing the young man from that framework in an act of futile mercy?

"What did you do?" croaked the refugee to the victim.

Ah . . . perhaps our refugee wouldn't be willing to release the young man if when alive he had performed a truly vile crime, evil and perverted, such as the sexual murder of children, or, or . . . *abortion!* Abortion might actually have been the crucified man's crime—reflected by the endless dragging out of him of his own living tissue through an orifice close to where a womb would have been, were he a woman!

The victim seemed to be in a trance of torment, determined not to move—not even his eyes, much less his lips—in case the least motion multiplied his slow agony. He remained silent.

Our refugee stared about him at the landscape of Hell—and at those two laggardly stalking demons. He must have realised that he had no ultimate hope of escape.

"Let me take your place," he begged the young man.

This sounded like a saintly offer, except for the wheedling tone of voice.

Our refugee imagined that he could endure slow automated evisceration more easily than the constant bump and hoist of alternate racking and broiling—because this other punishment would be uniform and unvarying! The younger man seemed to have achieved a meditative stupor of misery, which must surely be lesser than rack 'n' roast. The young man was privileged in that he was devoid of the constant attention of demons.

No doubt demons must unload the drum of the windlass now and then, disburdening it of the accumulating weight of compacted bowel. Otherwise the torment might have slowed eventually, and even stopped. Aside from such intervention, the young man suffered in peace.

"Let me take your place!"

Feverishly our refugee knelt. He began to prise apart the rusted barbed wire looped so tightly around one ankle. His fingers bled. He licked the moisture.

Did he imagine that he might succeed in unfastening the young man completely before his own personal demons arrived? Did he fantasise that like a midwife he might sever the long umbilicus with his teeth? That with the sharp barbs of wire he might make an incision through his own belly-button, and hook out some of his own upper bowel, and knot that to the disconnected trailing end? That the young man would agree to crucify the refugee instead?

All this—without the two demons arriving prematurely, or objecting to the substitution?

A suspicion began to dawn that I was being led astray by a charade. Astray from my original question! The end of my shift might arrive before I witnessed any finale. In waiting for one, my question would remain unanswered.

"Mortal," I boomed, "what do demons do when no angels watch over them?"

The refugee cowered from my voice. His bloodstained fingers plucked frantically at the wire.

Might I make an offer of amnesty in exchange for a reply? Might I promise to carry him away across the mercury moat to our island where the harmonies issuing from our tabernacle would fill him with everlasting ecstasy as if he were truly in Heaven?

If I held him in my arms, he would need to hold the lens on my behalf. His fingers would be slippery with blood. His blood would stain the view enjoyed by the blessèd in Paradise. The lens might slip from his grasp and fall into the mercury moat. How could I ever retrieve it? Would a raft of demon's skeleton bear my weight? What could I use to grapple for the lens? A web of hooks made of barbed wire? I might fish for half of eternity, like some pagan condemned to fill a pitcher with a hole in its bottom and carry it up a slippery slope! Would my wing-feathers or my psalmist's lungs tolerate immersion in mercury?

How could I possibly bring a naked wretch to our beautiful island? The constant sight of him would untune our hymns.

I could not make such an offer.

"By the Quint," I bellowed, "I command you to answer me!"

Fingers scrabbled at the barbs, shredding skin faster than it could possibly heal. The man was dementedly obsessed by this one activity.

At last the crucified man summoned breath. Softly he implored, "No, no—" How it pained him to speak.

The demons had arrived. They were chuckling. I'd forgotten to jump-cut to them.

Nearby the trump sounded, long and grandly. I ascended, to stare faraway at the shining timeless face of the clock of eternity. Within me welled the urge to commence my return to the isle.

Later, none other than the Ark Angel confided anxieties to me.

This time it was the Harp Angel whom we were awaiting. Unlike the Trumpet Angel, she never did transport her instrument along with her. The Harp was much too huge. Twenty times larger than herself, it was a veritable precipice of strings. She would fly to and fro across these—like a white moth across a great grille—plucking with her outstretched hands to sound the chords and arpeggios, brushing with her wings to rouse the swishing, swirling glissandi.

"Impresario," the Ark Angel said softly, "I fear that something furtive is afoot in the Ark."

Thinking of that fugitive from rack 'n' roast, I suggested, "A hominid may have broken free. An ape-man could scuttle about for ages on his knuckles beneath all those benches on all those decks. The demons might be too lazy or clumsy to catch him—"

"It is not that. There are too many creaky noises below decks."

"Rattling of fetters? Shifting of hairy bums on benches?"

"I'm familiar with such noises, Impresario. There are new noises."

"Increased use of the whips?"

"That would cause more shrieking."

The Ark Angel's rightful place was upon the poop, as a kind of honorary pilot and lookout. He was much too large to go below decks in person. The most he could accomplish by way of scrutiny

would be to stick his glorious head down one of the uppermost
hatchways. In the Ark, decks descended and descended again. Such
is the design of Hell. Its topography can be crudely described as fractal; hence its capacity for prisoners. This fractal quality is inevitable,
since Hell is an unwholesome dimension. It cannot possess anything
remotely equivalent to the singularity of the Quint, or to the integrity
of the angelic realms.

There was urgency in the Ark Angel's request to me:

"Impresario: during our next tour of duty will you kindly join me
upon the deck of the Ark with your lens? I would value your
insights."

My insights . . .

Did the Ark Angel suppose that by means of my lens we would
be able to spy below decks? That was not at all how the lens func-
tioned. I must take it on trust—as an act of faith—that the lens did
serve the purpose which I ascribed to it. Yet since I must believe that
it did, the most I might achieve by thrusting the lens down a hatch-
way would be to reveal to the blessèd in Paradise a limited dingy view
of the limited dingy sufferings of some of the primitive ancestors of
Man, and of Woman.

I did not wish to disillusion the Ark Angel, since his suspicions
reinforced my own about the conduct of demons.

"Of course I shall come! Do you suppose your counterpart has
noticed anything peculiar?"

"I scarcely have time to ask her—"

It was out of the question that there could be any complicity
between the female Ark Angel and the demons of the Ark. No, it was
during the intervals that whatever was happening took place.

The Harp Angel was coming in to land. Our colloquy must
cease. Soon we must start to sing.

I alighted upon the poop deck with my lens. At his post, the Ark
Angel awaited me.

He gestured at the main deck. Surrounded by demons, a large
device was bolted massively to the timbers. The contraption was
built of parts of racks and of gridirons, and of clamps and screws used
in torments. Mirrors used for burning also played a role. The apparatus cradled a hefty tube, angled vertically. Under this, a demon lay
upon his back. He peered up through the tube, busily adjusting
screws.

"That," Ark Angel said, "is new."

Here for the first time might be evidence of aberration!

Yet I suggested, "Maybe that is a new instrument of punishment for hominids?" Maybe a hominid would be placed inside that tube, and screws and clamps would be tightened.

"Pre-humans are only ever punished with the whip," the Ark Angel reminded me. "Such is the clemency of the Quint."

We descended a grand stairway to the main deck. We approached the infernal machine. Demons clustered protectively. They exhibited a kind of stubborn insolence.

The main deck vibrated subtly under our feet. It was as if some engine throbbed deep in the bowels of the Ark or as if some coordinated activity or rhythmic exertion were under way. How could this be?

A red demon appeared to be some kind of foreman. "In the name of the Quint," the Ark Angel called out to him, "what is this contrivance?"

I quite expected to hear some gibberish. But no. The red demon seemed flushed with confidence and effrontery.

"Wise One," he sneered, "we call this a theodolite. From the ancient words *theos*, signifying God, and *dolor*, signifying misery."

"What does it do?"

"Ah," came the reply, "it measures the distance and direction of the Quint!"

I stared up at the sooty sky—as if that tube might somehow be burning a channel through the welkin of Hell to reveal a glimpse of the realms. The sky remained as stygian as ever. This theodolite must operate in some different mode.

"What might that distance be?" I asked derisively, my lens held upright to capture the foreman demon's image.

The demon leered at me, and announced:

"It is one hundred and eighty parasangs. If you know what a parasang is."

Of course I knew. One parasang is equal to one hundred and eighty billion times the polar diameter of the Earth, as revealed in the Jewish *Shiur Qomah*, otherwise known as The Measurement of the Height. So therefore the distance to the Quint, as calculated by demons, was one hundred and eighty times that figure. . . .

"A little less by now," said the demon.

What did he mean?

Such a smirk. The deck vibrated underfoot. All of Hell seemed to quiver as if a mild infernoquake were occurring.

"This Ark," bragged the demon, "is now under way toward the Quint."

                    *   *   *

During the interludes demons had secretly been carpentering oars from the ever-available stocks of wood intended for racks and gibbets and bonfires. Demons had brought these oars on board the Ark unobserved. They had equipped all the hominids' benches with rowlocks fashioned from fetters. They had trained the hominids to be galley slaves. This operation must have taken a century, or in view of the fractal nature of the Ark, maybe a millennium. Within this vessel, those slaves were now rowing in unison, pulling the great oars to and fro!

The brutish ur-speech which that other demon had used had been the primitive proto-language of hominids. Those hominids, stretching way back to Adam and Lucy, could not possibly have initiated this project. The concept would have eluded them—though, since punishments of prehumans were mild, their bodies retained stamina. No, the demons were using those precursors of Man and of Woman as inadvertent insurgents. How devilishly sly this use of the ancestors! It evaded the whole etiquette of Hell.

Our demon informant taunted me: "By now the distance to the Quint is only one hundred and seventy-nine point nine parasangs!"

The demon who lay under the theodolite corrected him. "Point nine nine."

"Progress is being made!" snarled our demon.

I hastened to the rail of the Ark. Averting my lens, I stared down the side of the vast vessel. The Ark was exactly where it had always been since prehistoric times. No banks of oar-blades jutted from newly revealed slots in the bulwarks.

Nevertheless, we were under way.

Although the oars were enclosed inside of the Ark, the rowing of the hominids was propelling us! The Ark was shifting in the direction revealed by the theodolite, which doubled as compass and rudder!

Rooted in Hell, this Ark would never cross the line between the infernal region and the lowest of the heavenly realms. No border guards with shining swords would rush to board her, because no demon was attempting to leave the territory of Hell.

The whole territory of Hell itself was on the move!

Impelled by the Ark, by the muscle-power of subhuman hominids, Hell itself had begun to travel upward—so as to pass through the domains, carrying with it all the evolved descendants of those hominids who writhed in torment ordained by the Quint through His intermediaries.

Did I hear, for the first time, a chime sound from the clock of eternity? Or was the Trumpet Angel sounding a note which had altered in pitch?

Ours would be a long journey—of two hundred and fifty-five point nine six quintillion miles, I calculated. That many miles to reach the quasar of the Quint! En route we would travel through the choirs of Angels, Archangels, and Principalities. Then through the choirs of Powers, Virtues, and Dominations. Finally we would cleave through the choirs of Thrones, and Cherubim, and Seraphim. . . .

Oh, but already the distance was slightly less than that amount. And no doubt as realms became more rarified we would accelerate rapidly.

Agonies will continue. Torment is an aether into which the hominids dip their oars, and through which they haul. The demons seem contemptuous of us angels. Yet we still have our roles. Now that Hell has shifted its location, no other angels will know how to enter and replace us.

I am both appalled and elated.

Appalled, because during this journey the demons intend to convert a percentage of gridirons and racks into great harpoon guns. These, they will mount on the main deck of the Ark, to be fired at the Quint.

Yet I am also elated—because contrary to all expectation for anyone below the rank of Seraph, I and my humble angelic colleagues and counterparts will come directly into the presence of the Quint, when Hell harpoons that pure Being and then collides with Him.

Such hymns we will sing as we near His radiance—Hosanna! Hosanna in the Highest! And all will be revealed.

If only I could understand the language of the hominids, from before the time when the Quint became manifest.

Unfortunately I am too bulky to descend any of the myriad ladders of the Ark with my deaf lens so as to interrogate Adam and Lucy. Besides, their speech might brutalise my psalms.

A Day
Without Dad

I ASKED MIRANDA AT BREAKFAST, "WILL YOU do me a favour, darling?"

Beloved daughter looked dubious, which surprised me.

"Will you look after your grandad today?"

Miranda gazed into her bowl of oats and dried banana bits. Her flaxen hair hung around her face, hiding her expression from me.

"Can I keep him asleep, Mum? There's a French test this morning—and . . . there are swimming heats in the afternoon."

"Grandad can help you with the French."

"Don't be silly—that's cheating. Black mark if they find out."

When she said *cheating*, involuntarily I glanced at Paul, but just then he was looking at his watch.

When had beloved husband last made proper love to me? Not for three years since Dad was installed as my guest. 'Are you sure he's asleep, Cath?' 'Of course I'm sure.' 'You might lose control . . .' In my spasm of pleasure Paul thought that Dad might surface as an uninvited spectator of his performance. I could hardly ask Miranda if she would host Dad for an hour at bedtime so that her parents could enjoy some unspecified spontaneous privacy! How embarrassing, how inhibiting.

Increasingly I suspected that in the past year or so Paul may have enjoyed a little side-dish, as it were—which he would no doubt justify to himself by some rationalization about his male urge demanding to be satisfied; as if I had become some sort of hospice nun without appetites and frustrations. Probably an occasional girl from the Rough, picked up while he was taking a Jag to some customer. A girl who would be glad of a modest gift of cash.

I wasn't about to rock the boat of our marriage. Paul was sensible. So was I. Full-blown affairs, divorces, were ruinous. These days financial considerations dominated most people's lives. Ours, certainly. Keeping up payments on house and health and winter heat and insurances and service contracts and all else. Investing for Miranda's future. Oh, let her become rich through her talent for design—surely she *was* showing flair!

Although Paul and I were only in our mid- to late-thirties, we invested obsessively for our old age so that we did not ever burden Miranda, as Dad burdened me.

"I'd gladly help out if I could," Paul murmured.

He couldn't, as he knew full well. Guesting only worked with genetically close relatives. All to do with the brain patterns.

"I could get some practice in," he joked feebly.

Not much need of that! Paul's own Mum and Dad weren't even sixty. Betty and Jack were both hale and hearty. Anyway, Paul tagged his sister Eileen as a soft touch if it ever came to hosting Betty and Jack. Both at once. How could the ageing couple be separated after a lifetime together? Eileen would have to take both parents on board.

"You know I don't normally mind, Mum," Miranda said. "It's just . . . well, with the swimming this afternoon. . . ."

Miranda didn't wish to be in changing rooms with a seventy-odd-year-old man inside her head. Like a voyeur. If her friends knew, they would be furious, never mind that she swore she was keeping her guest suppressed. She would need to pretend all day long that she was on her own, which would be a strain, and a bit alienating for Dad too.

Oh, why hadn't she mentioned those swimming heats until now? I'd been counting on her.

Answer: I didn't pay enough attention to her swimming. I wanted Miranda to concentrate on art, where she showed such budding talent. But Miranda nursed dreams of being a champion swimmer, which wouldn't bring her very much long-term money, only some transitory glory. Maybe art would be a false trail too, yet at least art might be a route to something special. Or art might be an awful blind alley—which was why she strove at swimming, imagining medals and sponsorships and product endorsements. Miranda didn't show much skill at economics or science or computer studies.

She was usually willing to give me respites from day-in-day-out-Dad. Not that Dad was intrusively present all the time, but still the sense of him was always with me, beneath the surface if not above.

What else could I have done other than accept the responsibility of having Dad in my head when he became unable to look after himself? The cost of putting him in a nursing home would have hamstrung Paul and me.

Could have been worse, I suppose. Mum might have lived long enough for guesting to be developed. Then both of them would have been sharing my brain.

So what should my own daughter do but help me out now and then?

"You can't keep a guest stifled all day long," I reminded her. "He'd become, well . . ."

"Stir-crazy," Paul said unhelpfully. "The isolation from everyday input. He needs to have a good six hours' experience a day."

So Paul was suddenly the expert, who had no guest and would likely never have one?

Monday to Saturday, Dad's six hours per day—or longer, ideally!—should obviously occur while I was at home, tele-selling to raise extra income, and while Paul was twenty miles away in the neighbouring Smooth at the Jaguar showroom, smiling, smiling at potential customers for those big sleek lux cars, secretly detesting his clients for their affluence; but he was a superb salesman. After a day of feigning and fawning the last thing he wanted was to share the evening with my Dad.

We were contented, I suppose. We were surviving—and Miranda was our treasure, quite as much as our painfully accumulating investments. Just, we no longer felt at all young. Maybe this was true of the majority of people like us. Having Dad in my head didn't help.

"I'll do it tomorrow," promised Miranda.

I would have to postpone a certain matter. And count my blessings—mainly the blessing of a daughter who was at least willing to share my duty.

I was determined that when I grew old and infirm I would never impose myself upon Miranda, nor let Paul do so, either. That day was a long way off. If our investments proved inadequate, maybe Miranda might be wealthy enough to pay for our dotage.

"Tomorrow will be fine, darling."

Paul shivered. In his salesman's suit and striped shirt and Jaguar-crest tie, he was feeling chilly.

He didn't ask what I'd hoped to be doing today, and now instead would do tomorrow, unencumbered of Dad. If asked, I had intended to say that after lunch I would bundle myself up and walk to the park, to the hothouses, where entry was still free. I'd be losing potential sales, but I ached to see orchids in bloom, and be warm, and on my own. Yet if I had Dad in my head I would feel obliged to share the beauty with him, since sitting in on tele-sales could hardly be very exciting for him as his usual recreation.

I wasn't intending to go to the park at all.

The car showroom provided a sort of hothouse for Paul every day, though only polished metal was on display. For the sake of the customers the showroom needed to be kept considerably warmer during the winter than our own little terraced house.

It was time for Paul to put on his overcoat and rush to catch the bus. Likewise, in another quarter of an hour, Miranda. Dad was stirring. He liked to see his granddaughter off to school. Paul, he could miss. Paul could miss him.

My watch had a time-tally function so that I could be sure Dad enjoyed at least six hours of liberty. If I went to the toilet or when I was getting washed I would of course suppress him. The temptation, then, was to leave him dormant for longer than need be.

As I settled in front of my as-yet-blank screen, with Dad alert inside me, I announced, "Miranda has swimming heats this afternoon."

Oh, I'd love to see those.

"I shan't see them, either."

I heard him as a voice inside me. For him to hear me, I needed to speak aloud. Guests didn't have access to your private thoughts, only to what you saw and said and did. Some hosts must be having a much harder time than me, if the beloved parent was cranky or overbearing. With a fractious parent inside, one might almost feel schizophrenic. Quite frequently I found myself telling myself a highly factual account of who Cath is, and of what's-what-in-the-world, as a way of affirming my own identity. I'd never yet felt the need to consult a guesting counsellor, even if the service is free.

At least no guests are downright senile, since a senile mind can't make the transfer.

She wouldn't really want you there, would she? Not because you'd put her off her stroke. But swimming's her way of being herself. Launching out.

"I don't know, Dad, if that's a cliché, or if it's wisdom."
Actually, Cath, it was meant as a joke.
Poor old Dad. He did try.
Another day of insurance, eh Cath?
"What else, Dad?"
I'm becoming quite an expert in my old age.
   If only Dad had been more of an expert in managing his own affairs in years gone by! I would never say this aloud; and I trusted Paul never to do so either in Dad's hearing.
   Dad had been a metal sculptor, and quite well regarded in his day. The hot tang of the workshop always lingered in my memory from my childhood, a metallic taste as much as a smell. Evidently Miranda inherited her artistic gifts from Dad, these skipping a generation. During his career Dad picked up enough commissions to make an adequate living, though never enough for any nest egg. Back then, most people didn't realize how single-mindedly they must try to amass capital to pay for future care. And then the arthritis crept up on Dad. After Mum died, he ended up living in a single rented room, which he always proudly insisted was adequate for his diminished needs—until the arthritis worsened.
   Dad: poor, and old.
   His metalwork was expensive to carry out, so he and Mum had put off having their only child until they were a bit long in the tooth, unlike Paul's parents.
Penny for your thoughts?
No, Dad, no.
Don't worry about Miranda. She'll be fine.
   In the swimming pool at school—or in the waters of the future, infested by the piranhas of finance?
   Finally I switched the screen on.
   But first . . .
   "Dad, I need to take a leak—"
   Which was true. I nudged the time-tally. With an inner impulse, which was now second nature, I pushed Dad down to muse in his own memories, disconnected from what I was doing.
   Chilly in the toilet. Not a room to linger in, despite the Breughel posters brightening the walls. The posters were creatively stimulating for Miranda, but a salutary warning for me and Paul. I could identify with those medieval peasants. Lots of clothes, and tight circumstances, hunger and cold and disease hovering not far away if anything went wrong.
   I'd delayed long enough.
   Before inviting Dad back, I called a certain number to apolo-

gize to Mrs Appleby, as she called herself, a cheerful rosy name.

So sorry, Mrs Appleby. Can't make it this afternoon. A family problem. Please, will you find someone else? But please, I do want to do it tomorrow.

Fair enough for Mrs Appleby to point out with a sniff of disapproval that today was to have been my first . . . *engagement*, as she phrased it.

Neither of us were on screen, although we'd inspected each other visually when we made the arrangement four days earlier; and I'd squirted her a swimming-costume photo of myself, taken a couple of years ago. That was when Paul and Miranda and I enjoyed a discount weekend break at the West Midlands Tropicdome. Miranda reveled in the simulated ocean surf. I delighted in the jungle garden. Paul was happy gambling with tokens, fantasy value only. The dome was a family venue. Mrs Appleby, whose tactfully phrased advertisement I'd discovered on the Web, had seen that I was very much the same trim person as in the photo. Still had my looks. She'd assured me that many married women were in her data bank.

A pause, while Mrs Appleby accessed her timetable.

"Very well, dear. Tomorrow afternoon. Same place: Meridian Hotel. Room 323. Got it? Two o'clock sharp. This one's a German businessman. Late thirties. Make sure you count your cash. My agency fee's already included in the room hire, you'll recall."

"Understood, Mrs Appleby."

"Enjoy yourself, dear."

Would I? An act of neutral lust with a perfect stranger. . . .

And a German too. Probably he'd be very polite and efficient. Being only in his thirties he shouldn't have acquired a gut. He'd be tanned and athletic — superior to whichever Brit I was passing up. Silver linings!

I keyed for Insure. Then I nudged the time-tally and opened myself once again to Dad, and scrolled the work log.

The name Viking Industries took my fancy. I was about to call up its business profile when the name went red. One of my telecolleagues somewhere else in the country had got there first.

Four fruitless calls to companies, and I was scanning the profile of a fifth prospect called KhanKorp. Newly registered, importers of spices. No doubt KhanKorp made its own insurance arrangements within the Asian community. Those arrangements might be lax, and fail to comply with all the increasingly elaborate legal requirements.

Bruce and the spider, Cath . . .

Yes, yes, Dad. When Robert the Bruce was hiding in his famous cave, he wrecked a spider's web again and again, and each time the spider rebuilt it. Moral: persevere.

In fact, I only needed to persuade half a dozen companies a week to accept a full free on-site survey to cover the leasing of the hardware and software from Omega Insurance, the last word in industrial protection. If one of those surveys scored a contract, I was modestly in pocket. This all still took hours and hours of time.

Spices! Cinnamon and cardamom and fenugreek . . .

Dad had loved curries. Gone were the days when he could taste anything at all, except maybe in memory.

So call KhanKorp up. Request a window for face-to-face. Smile, smile. Recite the spiel.

Miraculously competitive rates, fully secured reinsurance, the very latest in pollution and radon detectors and hazard sensors as per the most recent Euro regulations. Avoid crippling fines.

At all costs be friendly. Be careful of the implication of blackmail. ("Ask yourself, sir, what if the Safety Inspectorate should pay a random visit next week?")

At least I didn't need to pump flesh, as Paul must do before showing off the armour plating of Jags and the pollen and particle filters and the in-car voice-addressable terminal and all else.

KhanKorp was another washout. The Khan who dealt with me was quite abrupt. Some Chinese name—Chung Hong, or whatever—handled all such matters. A Triad company, perhaps.

Just then, *ring-ring*. On screen flashed a phone icon—to be replaced, as soon as I accepted, by a young woman's head and shoulders; and my own mini screen-top camera would now be showing me to her, in my black business dress which I wore over thermal underclothes.

She was quite an item. A freckled redhead. Gold lam, jumpsuit. Huge hoop earrings. Letters pulsed in a spidery sunburst logo behind her.

"Catherine Neville? It's Denise Stuart at TV-NET. Excusez the interruption, Cath. I'm interviewing professional femmes who have an elderly guest . . ."

She would have found my name in the public register of guests and hosts.

I would be paid an adequate disturbance fee. A simple contract replaced Denise's image and expanded. I scrolled through quickly

—and noticed that I was agreeing to Dad being interviewed as well as me. The human interest of this show might not merely be humanitarian—the experience of women who had accepted a mother or father, for the benefit of those contemplating such a step—but tensions, frustrations, regrets, even conflict.

The fee's worth having.

"Hmm," I mused.

I shan't say anything embarrassing. If you don't like something I say, Cath, just don't repeat it.

That could look awkward. Denise asking a leading question, and me fluffing the lines.

This could lead on to you becoming a counselling consultant or whatnot.

Could it? Dad was ever-hopeful.

You'd be good at it.

I was enough of a "professional femme" to have use of an up-to-date screen, courtesy of Omega. *Really* successful working women ought to be able to afford a nursing home, unless love and affection prevented them from abandoning their parent to some gerry-barracks run by a fat insurance company. Denise Stuart must be zeroing in upon struggling pro-femmes.

With mild misgivings, I assented. It was a change from phoning businesses with veiled threats.

"Have you heard, Cath, the Japanese announced they'll be able to store old folks' minds in terabyte computers in another two or three years?"

Was this true?

She was trying to catch me off balance. To provoke an exclamation of *Thank God for that.*

"I'll believe it when I see it," was my reply. "If we could load a mind into any old brain, meat or machine, we wouldn't need to rely on close relatives."

"Would you miss being with your daughter, George?"

I was a metal-sculptor. What a joke to end up as part of a machine, myself.

"Dad says, I was a metal-sculptor. . . ," I repeated, et cetera.

"Do you ever feel *un peu* suffocated in there, George?"

It could get a bit crowded for my granddaughter when Cath grows old if Miranda has to look after her Mum and Dad and me as well.

I paraphrased.

Denise grinned. "*Bien!* Now you've raised a point there,

George. We rush into new technology, don't we just? A senior citizen in care is going to die sooner or later—unless machines keep him ticking over till he reaches the statutory hundred years of age. *Ça coute cher!* That really costs! And as yet there isn't any such statutory limit on elderly guests—unless of course the host applies for evacuation for good reason—"

Evacuation! Mental abortion. Was she trying to scare my Dad?

"—whereupon there's nowhere else to put your mind if you're still under a hundred, George, since your body was already cremated, *n'est ce pas?* The way I read the runes, evacuation's going to become mandatory when guests reach their century. Do you think your Cath will try to do a runner to some Caribbean island, *par example*, to keep you going? I mean, given the experience to date of sharing her head with you."

A Caribbean island was such a fantasy.

You're trying to cause trouble, Miz Stuart.

"You're trying to cause trouble, Denise."

"Is that what your Dad says? *Vraiment?*"

"You'd better believe it."

Denise was unruffled. "So how about the wisdom-of-the-ancestors stuff, eh Cath? Old folk used to be revered for all their accumulated know-how. I hear that even the Neanderthals kept their old folk on the go, chewing their food for them when things got tough. But, *il faut demander*, in a world of ever-accelerating change, what use is old wisdom? How much does your Dad contribute daily to your business activities? Does he impede you? What *is* your business exactly?"

She asks too many questions. Steamrollering, and showing off.

I saw the ideal conclusion to this interview, without voiding my fee.

"Since you ask *exactly*, Denise, I represent Omega Insurance, popularly know as the last word in industrial protection. For instance I'll call you to ask if you know the latest Euro ruling on radiation emissions from electronic equipment such as must litter your studio—"

"*Merci* much, Cath! *Au revoir.*"

Denise would trim the interview at *You'd better believe it.* Ending on a note of truculence. She would pose the question: are hosts ever fully truthful?

Well-handled.

"You helped, Dad."

Some ageing relatives committed suicide rather than imposing

on their children. Doctors always helped out with a painless dose
these days.

To be deprived of your own body! To be a guest on sufferance in
the body of your own child who had grown up! To miss out on so
much of real life, even if guests could stroll, dreamlike, down memory lane during the hours of the day when they weren't summoned
to see and hear whatever was ongoing. Had Dad chosen the brave
option or the cowardly option? It was hard to be sure.

As the hours passed I persuaded two businesses to accept safety
surveys. One was a small manufacturer of anti-vandal paint of their
own patent, which had exotic additives. Potentially hazardous.

When Miranda came home from school she was flushed as much
with satisfaction as from the hard frost outside. As expected, she had
won her heats easily. Dad was ever so pleased.

"I'll be looking after you all day tomorrow, Grandad," she told
me cheerfully, and him within. She hadn't forgotten. "All day at
school! That'll make a change, won't it?"

You didn't tell me this, Cath!

"I didn't want to disappoint."

"Oh Mum, I promised."

We'd long since got used to such conversations involving an
unheard voice.

Sweater-clad, Miranda quickly got on with homework, using my
screen in the work-nook to help with the maths which she less than
loved. Maths might have seemed to loathe her too, were it not for
the interactive program she could access at a modest cost, conducted by ever-patient, ever-friendly 'Uncle Albert'.

When Paul got home, he was fascinated to hear about the interview with Denise Stuart. It wasn't till after our meal of soy and veg,
nicely spiced, that he confided modestly how he hoped to clinch a
deal with a Chinese client for a top-of-the-range XJ5000, pending a
final test drive through the Rough the next morning. The sale
would mean several hundred in commission.

"Not a motorway sprint, but rough driving—"

"He's probably a Triad boss," I joked. "Needs to deliver *stuff* to
dodgy destinations." Miranda ought to know about such aspects of
life, at least in the abstract.

"Probably is," Paul agreed. "Sam Henson says he heard how a
drugs boss guested an undercover Chinese taxman into the head of
a monkey a couple of months ago."

Miranda shuddered to hear this. "That's impossible, isn't it?"

"Totally," I assured her. "Your Dad's boss is a bit of a racist."

Our daughter grinned. "Is that why he sells fast cars?"

Miranda was street-wise enough—or so she imagined herself. Of course she was sheltered by living in the Smooth. No drugs or gangs or vice at her school. At least we hoped not.

"If that *could* become possible," said Miranda, "you know, I think I'd quite like to share, say, a dolphin's day—"

For the swimming, oh yes.

"—just so long as I could pop back into my own body afterwards. Like Grandad will pop back into yours, Mum." And out gushed: "Are you going somewhere special tomorrow?"

"Just to the park. To the orchid-house. To be on my own for a while."

"You deserve it," Paul said.

Miranda might worry that something could happen to me—a car skidding, say, and Mum dying. Then she would be saddled with Grandad for the rest of her life. Unless, of course, Grandad nobly insisted on evacuation, or Paul petitioned. That would be traumatic for Miranda.

I usually knew when she had something special to tell me, and finally she got round to it.

"Mum, there's a girl in the first grade called Jenny O'Brien. Her mother has had a new baby, and it's sick with leukemia. It's going to die. She's applying to guest the baby."

"The girl is?" asked Paul, incredulous.

"No, Dad, her mother is! Mrs O'Brien wants to rear the baby inside her head. Teach it. Let it have a chance. She's a Catholic, you see."

"Good God," said Paul.

I was stunned as well.

To host an unformed mind . . . What sort of mind would that be? Full of infantile appetites, few of which could be catered for. Would it be able to learn to see through its mother's eyes or learn to talk?

Like a latter-day Helen Keller. At least Helen Keller had a body of her own, even if she was born blind, deaf, and dumb.

"It's meant to be a secret, Mum, but Jenny O'Brien's very upset. I was thinking I could introduce her to Grandad tomorrow. Show her that her mother won't be totally occupied with the baby."

This was so thoughtful that I almost felt ashamed of the purpose for which I was asking Miranda to look after Dad. You might say that Miranda could afford to be considerate, living here in the Smooth. On the other hand, she could have grown up snooty and selfish, with false expectations. No doubt the chill of our house in winter and the stifling heat in summer curbed any affectations and made her realistic.

"Your Denise Stuart would be interested to hear about this," Paul hinted.

"Oh no, Dad, it's private!"

"Mrs O'Brien might *need* publicity if she's to have any hope of persuading the guesting office. A campaign in her support."

"If that's so," I said, "she'd probably rather start any campaign *herself*."

Paul persevered. "This hasn't happened before, has it? There would have been publicity. It sounds like a fascinating experiment. Maybe Denise Stuart might know."

"Maybe Sam Henson might know!" I hoped I didn't sound brusque. I felt protective of Miranda's confidence in us. I didn't wish her to be at all upset this evening, nor tomorrow morning either.

Miranda sought to change the subject. "That was a lovely meal, Mum —"

"Was Uncle Albert helpful?"

She grimaced comically. "Just a bit."

When Paul and I went to bed early to keep warm, he kissed me, then he quickly turned over, lying flat upon his belly, as if otherwise I might make some physical demand upon him. My idea of an ambiguous reward for his wooing of the Triad boss.

Probably I would be deeply disappointed tomorrow, and disgusted with myself. My German paramour mightn't be courteous at all. How could he have any idea what significance his pawings and thrustings would have for me, in my imagination?

Ah, but to do something which was utterly impossible while Dad was in me! Something which he inhibited me from, as surely as he inhibited Paul!

Before breakfast next morning Miranda and I made the exchange.

We sat face to face, our knees interlocked. Both of us steadied the 'binoculars', as the transfer apparatus — domestic variety — inevitably was nicknamed.

It was a spin-off from the technology of pilots' helmets. Élite hypersonic warplane pilots. Cocooned in gel in constrictor suits to massage their blood circulation and minimise blacking out while manoeuvering, pilots couldn't move a finger to control their planes. They flew by thought and imagery.

Smart protoplasmic cords of mega data capacity were twinned with the pilots' optic cords — just as with myself now, and with

Miranda. Fitting our own cords, thin white threadlike worms, had involved only the most minor intrusion into my eye sockets, and hers. Once inserted, the cords found their own way, establishing their own retinal and neuronal connections.

None of this would have happened if a certain hyperjet hadn't crash-landed at its base in Nevada six years ago. If the pilot's father, a Colonel Patterson, hadn't been base commander. If his critically injured son hadn't been jammed in the crumpled cockpit in a particular position. If the Colonel himself hadn't been fitted for fly-by-thought. If for love of his son he hadn't risked an imminent inferno to say farewell. If he hadn't stared into the optics of his dying son's helmet . . . and suddenly received his son's mind into his own head.

Or his son's soul, as the Colonel phrased it.

Islamic countries banned guesting. Buddhists embraced it. In Britain there were tens of thousands of people in my position.

I stared into the lenses. From her side, Miranda stared. I pressed the power button. Mandalas flooded my vision, a receding tunnel of intricate light, which quickly shrank to a vanishing point as Miranda uttered a soft gasp, a sigh, nothing arduous.

Power off. Put the binoculars away in their padded case.

"Hi, Grandad," she greeted him.

If there ever *were* a way to transfer a mind into a machine I suppose we would have living tombstones to visit. Or to fail to visit. And people would have a sort of immortality.

"Maybe he'd like to see the news." Reluctant to share the start of his day with Dad, Paul switched on the TV.

The war in the Philippines, the abandonment of flooded Polynesia, a cyclone in New Zealand, minus-ninety in Alaska, a riot in the Dundee Rough, torching homes on a bitter night to keep warm . . .

I was thinking about my assignation (for want of a better word), and no doubt Miranda was thinking about Jenny O'Brien and an act of charity.

Maybe our daughter was a saint, an angel.

The tunnel visions described by people pulled back from the brink of death were quite like what I and Miranda saw in the binoculars during transfer, receding in my case, approaching in hers. A couple of years ago Colonel Patterson committed suicide. Righteous evangelists had exploited him. He'd come to believe that he'd stopped his son from going to heaven and must rectify this.

"Don't worry about the news, Grandad," exclaimed Miranda. "Everything'll be all right. Life carries on!"

*   *   *

We sell ourselves, is the truth of it. Lucky ones sell high, unlucky ones sell low. It seemed only logical that I should sell myself this afternoon—gratuitously and gladly—as a stage in this process. And to satisfy a burning willful curiosity.

After I'd called a couple of businesses, I messaged Denise Stuart at TV-NET. I loathed the woman in her lux job-niche, bothering anybody she cared to in the country from her superior position.

Denise came back to me presently, wearing a black kimono a-twinkle with light-emitting diodes. Long pendant crystal earrings resembled icicles.

"Ah, the spokesfemme of Omega! So we didn't have the *dernier mot* after all?"

"Denise," I said calmly, "hypothetical question. What would you say about a woman wanting to guest her dying baby? Pre-speech, pre-crawling."

Suddenly so alert. So acquisitive. "Is this true? I'd say a thousand as a finder's fee. Exclusive."

"Sorry to disappoint you!" I replied. I would sell myself in quite a different fashion, though not for nearly as much. I blanked off, and instructed my screen to reject any future calls from TV-NET.

I felt a surge of satisfaction at snubbing Denise.

The bus from our wire-fenced ville crossed a large stretch of Rough on its way to the ville where the Meridian was.

Through the window grilles of the bus I gazed at the shanties and tents, almost as medieval as those Breughel scenes back home in the toilet. Yet oddly picturesque, too. The bright patchwork clothes. The ragged children. The mongrel dogs being led about on strings—a stringless mutt would soon end up barbecued. Shebeens and bonfires. Derelict cars and vans, converted into homes. Pickers at a refuse tip hopping about like crows. A steel band playing by the roadside as if coins might spill from passing vehicles.

Decorative! A frilly filthy collar around the neck of most villes. Suggestive of some sort of self-expressive freedom. Freedom from finance. Freedom to shiver and become slim (or grossly fat) on government-issue diet packs.

A truckload of soldiers followed our bus part of the way. The men had those multi-guns which can fire either explosive shells or humane rubber bullets or gag-gas, laugh-yourself-sick.

Then we were in semi-open country. Electric-fenced sheep pastures and pig wallows, muddy as the Somme. Fenced forestry plantations. A huge shallow lake full of trout, a watchtower upon a tiny island in the middle. By night infrared motion detectors would switch on floodlights if anything larger than a fox approached the water's edge.

Soon we entered another Rough. A solitary girl with stringy hair and a tattered false-fur coat and mitts and one of those Russian-look hats hailed us, holding up her fare and ID for the driver to see. A satchel over her shoulder.

As she made her way to the back of the bus, she tore open her coat so that she wouldn't overheat.

She smelled of patchouli, to mask body odour which the warmth of the bus quickly liberated. She grinned at me. Opened her satchel.

Bracelets and necklaces of intricately hammered tin, really quite exquisite work, I thought. If Dad had been here with me, would he have praised her? He might have enjoyed this excursion.

"Only twenty each," she said to me, meaning ten.

"Honestly I can't afford any," I told her. "Insurance, mortgage, you know."

She didn't know; though at the same time maybe she did. I was a ghost to her, of once-upon-a-time, of a maybe-world her parents may once have inhabited.

"Don't worry," she consoled me. "Women worry; men spend."

This seemed untrue, yet at least it served as a handy excuse. I hoped she wouldn't disembark at the Meridian to wander its car park hawking her craftwork to foreign businessmen. Ethnic English art, mein Herr? Monsieur? Danasama?

"Don't fret yourself, Smooth Lady."

I'd dressed confidently for my upcoming encounter. Under my thick scarf and padded coat was a high-collared side-slit shimmer-dress, revealing glittery spider-web leggings. Black pixie boots on my feet. Elbow-length black lace gloves. All of which had been packed away for years in a drawer. I'd also glamoured myself with a couple of sultry bruise-look blushers from years gone by, which hadn't dried up, having been sealed in a bag.

We soon reached the ville-fence and checkpoint. Suburbs glistened with frost which still hadn't melted, the houses like neat displays of cakes in some enormous shop. The cars cruising about seemed such shiny toys after the derelicts in the Rough.

Blind people could never become guests. Thanks be that Dad never lost his sight—that molten metal never splashed into his eye while he could still wield a welding torch!

The Rough girl stayed on the bus when I rose to leave. She would be aiming for the shopping mall—or at least for the outside of it, where the security personnel wouldn't bother her. Maybe they would even let her inside, her ID must be so clean.

When I stepped out of the bus, from the airport beyond the trade centre a silver dart was lifting into the sky, going to some place I would never go to. Dragged along at Mach 4 by its own shock-wave, the hyperliner could reach the lands of orchids almost before Paul would be back from work. Its foreign destination might be abominable, crowded with beggars and refugees. Even so, a power-ful airborne serenity seemed to stay with me.

The bronzed glass of much of the Meridian Hotel had discoloured so that oily pools seemed to float vertically.

In the spacious mock-marble lobby a group of Chinese or Kor-eans in creaseproof smart-suits were conferring with some British counterparts who looked crumpled and cheap, even though they were the dudes of the local Smooth. This was the fault of the Brits' faces, so blotchy and irregular compared with the smooth creamy features of the Asians. My compatriots' hair, even styled, was so haystacky next to wiry trim black oriental hair.

I lingered by the menu board outside the restaurant, pretending interest, waiting for my watch display to edge closer to two. At the top of the menu a salmon leapt up a frothing spillway of fractal water to escape from the claws of a lobster, fell back, leapt up again. Liquid-crystal prices flickered as if unable to believe themselves.

When I took off my scarf and padded coat, a couple of the Asians gazed at my vamp-Vietnamese outfit appreciatively, even anticipatively, as though I might be the clincher of a deal.

Keeping my coat with me, out of a sneaking fear that it might be stolen if I left it on the rack by the porter's desk, I headed for the elevator to ascend.

Room 323. I buzzed. The lock clicked open. It would be pro-grammed to admit one visitor, then secure itself. I pushed, and stepped into a dim bedroom. Closed curtains leaked wintry day-light. Most of the light came from the illuminated bathroom.

A short tubby man with curly black hair rose from the single armchair, barefoot, dressed only in shirt and trousers. Even in the mellow light he didn't look much like the German I'd imagined.

"Herr Schmidt?"

"That is I, dear lady." Nor did his accent have the perfection of most Germans speaking English.

I must have looked bewildered, for he proceeded to explain himself, quite proudly. His parents had been Turkish guest-workers, but he was German and had changed his name accordingly. He had prospered; he was his parents' success story, a full European. Manfred Schmidt, who might once have been Mustafa.

When not in Germany he could allow himself to be somewhat Turkish in a playful fashion. This took the form of jokes about harems and slave-girls—of whom I was now an honorary embodiment for an hour—and silly proverbs.

"A woman possesses a precious candlestick," I learned, "but the man has the candle!" And Manfred-Mustafa's candle needed attention.

In fact he was quite sweet and gentle—"A lion does not harm a lady"—though I wouldn't have wished to be married to him.

"Open up for me like a marrow flower," he commanded.

I imagined myself as an orchid instead—a soft lush velvety orchid being assaulted for nectar by a magically hovering hyperliner, wings fluttering as fast as his heartbeat, and soon my own heartbeat too.

I even experienced shockwaves, which surprised him.

"A hen cannot live without a cock," was his opinion. By then his candle was quenched.

"A man has one desire," he confided sadly, "yet a woman has nine."

Afterwards, dressed again in my vamp-Viet gear, I left him, carrying my coat over my arm on account of the warmth, my black lace gloves stuffed in the pocket.

I knew at once it was Paul who came out of the room closest to the lift. He was whistling tunelessly in a show of nonchalance, in case any maid was in the corridor.

Rage. I felt such rage.

"Is she still in there?" I demanded.

He jerked. He didn't recognize me instantly in my slit dress and pixie boots and blushers.

"No—" Only then did he realize. "Cath—!" How he blanched.

Already my anger had drained away. I could almost see the thoughts tumbling through his mind. He was like some gambling machine gone faulty. It just couldn't halt its reels on any payout line. He was thinking that I'd suspected him of infidelity and somehow I'd trailed him to catch him out. Worse: I suspected him of unfaithfulness subsidized by me sitting all day in front of my Omega screen.

Would it be best if he invented some fictitious girlfriend and swore never to see her again? No, that wouldn't wash—I would demand details and more details until his fib fell apart in tatters.

Yet why was I all vamped up? Was this my disguise?

"How did you—?" he asked.

"How often—?" I asked at the same moment. We seemed to speak in the shorthand of those who have known each other for a long time.

Manfred-Mustafa would still be showering, sprucing himself. He wouldn't be stepping outside for five or ten minutes to attend to whatever business brought him here. I had the edge on the situation.

"*How often, Paul?*"

"Not often," he protested. He hadn't the nerve to claim that this was the first and only time. "Sam Henson sometimes gives me a bit of cash on the side, not in the books—"

So the gambling machine had selected a line-up featuring . . . money, of course. Me slaving in front of a screen. Him squandering. Cheating on the family budget. We *would* think that way nowadays, wouldn't we?

I played along. By now it was quite impossible for him to accuse me, tit for tat, unless we wanted to ruin ourselves—and ruin Miranda's prospects—by separating.

"You're diddling the discount—"

"Or something," he agreed.

Creative accountancy is the lifeblood of the motor trade. Selling cars to one's own company to meet quotas. Marking trade-ins at imaginary values. Insurance and finance kickbacks.

He gawked at me, unsure that he had chosen the appropriate pay-off line but unable to spin the reels again.

"Never again," he promised. And I nodded. Actually, I could almost have laughed. Yet my laughter might have become hysterical.

"Well," said I, "what a surprise."

It wasn't a total surprise—apart from the coincidence of our meeting here, and that wasn't really too amazing. Was Paul a customer of Mrs Appleby or was his go-between somebody else?

"I'm going home now," I said. "You'd better get back to work."

"I'll never do this again," he vowed. "It's just that—"

"No, it isn't *just*."

For him to chauffeur me home through the Rough—presuming that he'd driven to the Meridian in a Jag—would have been as impractical as it would have been absurd. The display model would need to be back toot-sweet in the armoured-glass showroom.

*   *   *

When Miranda came home just ten minutes after me, she was more tired than usual, but effervescent.

"We talked to Jenny O'Brien—didn't we, Grandad? It seemed to help. How were the orchids, Mum?"

"Indescribable," I said, quite truthfully. "All the heat they need to be so beautiful!"

We transferred Dad back into me. A day at school seemed to have done him a power of good. He settled back contentedly, deep inside me.

When Paul arrived home, he was extremely unsure of his reception.

"Denise Stuart called me this morning," I said to him, "but I told her to fuck herself."

Miranda gaped.

"You need to be firm with some people," I told our daughter. "Without upsetting applecarts unnecessarily! Without rocking the boat so that it sinks."

"That's true," Paul agreed feebly.

And I said to him, in a mock-foreign accent, "When a husband comes home, a wife should count his teeth." Actually, what Manfred-Mustafa had quoted was exactly the opposite. No man should allow his wife to count his teeth; to know how much money he has.

Paul stared at me weirdly. Did he imagine I was proposing he should make love to me tonight?

"The marrow flowers open wide," I said.

This too might seem suggestive. Yet I was thinking a few weeks ahead—to when I might reasonably ask Miranda to look after Dad for another day.

I would insist on a foreigner. Any foreigner. Not one of my own countrymen. The money tyranny had been getting worse for years—not in an ebullient American way (well, that's a ridiculous generalization!)—but selfishly and divisively, breeding a society of fear and of foolish hopes, until it finally destroyed the soul of the country.

Being able to harbour a loved one's soul or mind, all those acts of charity and sacrifice, might have seemed an exception. It damned well wasn't.

Only foreigners, Mrs Appleby, only foreigners. . . ! Of course they would have their own problems. Even including guests. Might I ever meet a man who would invite a guest to join in enjoying me?

The marrow flower opens wide.

Paul was bewildered but he knew better than to ask what I meant.

Caucus Winter

$\mathcal{T}$HE FLAT COUNTRYSIDE OF CAMBRIDGESHIRE WAS a shallow ocean of mist studded by brilliant white corals. Hoarfrost thickly rimed every tree and bush. The sun dazzled but did not offer any warmth. Noon, and still ten below zero. This frost would reign all day, and then freezing fog would return to deposit even more crystals upon every twig. Might branches snap explosively?

At least hereabouts any outbursts of sniper fire would be due to green-booted sportsmen trying to bag a gaudy pheasant.

The road was sheer ice. Only four-wheel-drive vehicles such as our own Jap-Jeep should be out and about. Some cars persisted, crawling and sliding and generally getting in our way. England never was a country for fitting chains, or studded tyres as in Finland.

Because a sudden blizzard had closed London Heathrow, our plane had diverted to Luton airport. Luton was only half the distance to Cambridge, but there was no helicopter waiting at Luton, so our journey seemed painfully slow. While we idled along, in some silo in the Midwest a nuclear missile might be being retargeted right now on so-called Jew York as the Caucus hacked through encryption and rewrote launch codes.

My head wasn't in best condition after a night out with Outi. . . .

* * *

She and several others from Nokia's computer division had taken me to one of Tampere's downtown pubs. They had collected me from the Ilves Hotel, and in a bunch we slid over that bridge on the main drag past the chunky heroic statues. The river rushing from the higher lake to the lower lake wasn't frozen, but everything else was. By now I worshipped the gravel which Finns scatter along sidewalks in wintertime. I followed gravel like a hen a trail of grain, ever wary of tumbling and snapping an ankle. When I could risk looking away from where I was placing my feet I had a chance to admire the art of controlled skidding perfected by Finnish drivers.

According to Outi, in recent years not nearly as much snow had fallen as usual, and the temperature was hovering around a mere minus five. I still felt convinced that the cold in Finland must be more deadly than cold in other countries. So I had bundled myself up exaggeratedly in a couple of sweaters, a quilted coat, Moon boots, and a woolly hat which I could pull down over my ears.

That afternoon I had been admiring the microprocessor that Nokia had developed, incorporating almost a thousand quantum logic gates. Nokia was still having major teething problems with the lasers; and after we arrived at the pub, Risto, an earnest young man, continued talking for a while about vibrational states of beryllium ions . . . over his first beer, at least. Outi and the rest devoted themselves to becoming merry with impressive intensity. It was midwinter gloom time, so what should a company of Finns do but drink passionately?

What was that Swedish joke Outi had told me about the Finns' notion of a great party game?

"Two Finns sit in a room with a crate of vodka, you see, Anne. When they finish the vodka, one of them leaves the room. Then the other one tries to guess who left!"

This witticism underlined a taciturn streak in the Finnish soul, which was not much in evidence in the pub that night. All this darkness to contend with! Apparently during the midsummer festival, when the sun is in the sky all night long, the murder rate in Finland soars dramatically. That's when bottled-up grievances get aired. Bright Night of the Long Knives.

Actually, Tampere in the first week of January was not continuously dark, as I had imagined it would be. Here, a hundred miles northwest of Helsinki, for a while around noon the sky was grey. And eerie. Smoke or steam wafted from factory chimneys to mingle with chilly mist through which stray snowflakes floated and flurried. It was as if this city was some alien metropolis on another planet, as envisioned by Hollywood, with clouds of dry ice vapour everywhere.

The city had looked even more alien in 1918 with only chimneys left standing after the Reds were suppressed. Tampere remained residually Red enough to house the world's only Lenin Museum. Outi had taken me there during a spare hour. Such a well-lit, spotless, and strangely sad display. In these post-Soviet times she and I had been the only visitors.

Outi's grandfather had fought in the siege of Tampere, on the losing side. Even at school, years later during the Cold War, she had been taunted because of her Red connections. She was waylaid on her way home and beaten up a few times. This was the reason for her tough punk appearance, her hair cropped short and bleached white, with orange chevrons, the colour of dog pee on snow. Nokia tolerated her hairstyle because she was such a fine mathematician and programmer. Hers was the algorithm which would run on their quantum computer, so that it would be able to decrypt any data within mere minutes; which of course was why I was in Finland. Outi's algorithm was considered more powerful and elegant than the pioneer one devised at AT&T Bell Labs in New Jersey a while ago.

I had hardly expected that my liaison person would be a pinko punk, but I like Outi a lot. She was forthright and friendly.

Mischief surfaced after the first round of beers.

Outi asked me, "Have you drunk *salmiakki?*" I think that was the name. If not, something similar. "It's the latest craze among young people."

Of course, at a mere twenty-nine years of age I didn't wish to be considered fuddy-duddy.

Burly Marko beamed approval. "It gives you the four-day hangover," he declared, as if this was a particular recommendation. "I buy a glass for you."

"I don't think I want a four-day hangover," I demurred. "What's in the stuff?"

"It's a mixture of liquorice, aniseed, and ammonium chloride. Powerful!"

They all looked at me. Would I wimp out? Evidently I had been set up for a dare.

Okay, so I would try a *small* glass, please.

Marco vanished in the direction of the bar, and returned promptly with a liqueur glass holding four inches of brown fluid.

The liquid smelled exactly like the foulest cough medicine. My

Finnish friends regarded me gloatingly as I sipped. The taste exactly matched the smell, and I chased those awful sips down with gulps of beer.

"After a while," Marko said sagely, "you won't notice the taste."

This proved to be semi-true. True and not-true, at once—quite like a beryllium ion being hit by laser light at just the right frequency so that the spin of one of its electrons would be 'up' *and* 'down' at the very same time. Superposition of states, as we say in the trade. The key to a quantum logic gate.

I was trying to get rid of the concoction so as to prove my mettle, swilling each gulp down with a dollop of the beer—when one of those endearing drunks, who sometimes fixate on a foreigner in a bar, made his appearance, attracted by the fact that we were all speaking English. This balding middle-aged man with twinkly blue eyes slipped into a vacant seat.

So I was American? So how did I like the Finnish winter? So what was I doing here?

"She's a secret agent," Outi told him wickedly.

This was not quite true. Though it wasn't exactly untrue, either.

"Do you have a gun?" asked the drunk. Everyone chuckled when I shook my head.

Obviously some real secret agents were attached to the US embassy in Helsinki, though since the collapse of Communism Finland's strategic importance had dwindled, as alas had its economy, with soup kitchens helping out in the capital.

"I'm a Secret Service agent," I found myself explaining, a little tipsily. There was no harm in this revelation, since what I was doing wasn't covert at all.

"Bang bang," said the drunk. "Save the president!"

Ah, but I had nothing to do with protecting the president or visiting dignitaries. The Secret Service is part of the Treasury Department. So we are equally keen on safeguarding our currency from counterfeiters and such.

" . . . I'm part of the computer crime division."

"Today's money crimes are computer crimes," Outi told the drunk, as if he was a child and she was his teacher. "Swindling banks electronically."

I tried to stand up, but somehow I was still sitting down. Making a stronger effort, I visited the toilet.

On my return, another beer awaited me, and Outi was explaining to our uninvited guest, still in English, about encryption. All the guys from Nokia loved talking English to each other. *Practice* isn't the right word. They spoke English almost better than I did myself. Anyhow, the drunk was fairly bewildered—which was part of the fun—but he must have caught some of the drift, because he mumbled about code books and magic ink.

Outi shook her head. "No, no! Nowadays data is encrypted by multiplying two big prime numbers together. That's easy for a computer to do. You end up with a number 129 digits long, say. But to factorize that long number—to find which two prime numbers were multiplied—takes even the best computer months and months. That's because it has to try out all the possible combinations one after another."

"One after another," echoed our inebriated friend. He waggled both index fingers as if carrying out a sobriety test.

"So all financial and military and government data are safe—until the quantum computer comes along."

Oops, Outi wasn't going to attempt to explain a quantum computer to a drunk with a modest grasp of English? Just then, I hardly felt competent to do so myself. Outi was one for a challenge. She became a bit incoherent, but it was still a virtuoso performance.

Basically, the fundamentals of the universe aren't solid objects; they are probabilities. Wave functions. An electron 'exists' as a mixture of possible states until you make a measurement, whereupon the wave function 'collapses' and, bingo, there's one reality—and the electron is in such-and-such a state. However, this implies an alternative reality where the electron did something else. Consequently, there's a cloud of alternative ghost-worlds, as it were. Build a computer which uses these principles, and it will be able to carry out its computations simultaneously in a host of multiple realities. Wrong solutions which don't 'interfere constructively' will simply cancel out. Your quantum computer will be able to factorize that 129-digit number in a few minutes instead of months.

Anybody wanting to hack into a bank will be in there in a trice. Conventional crypto-keys and the best protective software firewalls: forget 'em.

Motorola in Phoenix was coming close to a quantum computer. Likewise, several companies in Silicon Valley. Nokia here in Finland. Fujitsu in Japan. And especially Matsushima at its research center based in Cambridge, England, which was to be my next port of call. The race for the Holy Grail was cantering toward the finishing post, and the US Treasury was distinctly worried.

No matter what initial price tag quantum computers bore, or how stringently end-user licences were required, such machines would be a dream for hackers and criminals and for hostile foreign governments. We would need entirely new encryption methods based on quantum principles—rooted in such things as Outi's algorithm, her rules for carrying out quantum calculation tasks.

Only since arriving in Tampere had I learned that people from the NCSC had arranged to visit Nokia—without bothering to liaise with the Secret Service. Did Outi realize that the National Computer Security Center is part of the National Security Agency? What would spooks from Fort Meade make of the pinko punk? Also planning a visit were the US Air Force (in the persons of the Electronic Security Command from San Antonio). The USAF had not liaised with the Secret Service; nor probably with the NSA.

What a lack of inter-agency communication. And perhaps a case of too little, too late? Anyway, I knew now that Nokia was not going to win. The victors were most likely to be Motorola, although Cambridge was a definite dark horse.

By one o'clock in the morning, I definitely had to go back to my hotel to rest my head on a pillow. Marko tried to divert me toward further local entertainment.

He lived at home with his parents, very close by. Right now his parents were away on a holiday in the sun, in Morocco, sensible people.

"I shall drive you in our car," he offered—his gesture seemed to embrace Outi as well, and maybe Risto. He hiccuped. "Pardon me. I shall drive to our hut in the forest. For a sauna and sausages. It's only a few kilometres. *And*," he vowed grandly, offering the ultimate inducement, "I shall cut a hole in the ice of the lake for you."

Oh yes. At one in the morning, at minus five, I lusted to boil myself and then jump into a frozen lake. Who knows but I might have agreed if I had drunk more ammonium chloride.

"Don't you have severe drunk-driving laws here, Marko?"

He shrugged massively.

Outi took pity, and escorted me homeward toward the Ilves Hotel in my multiple sweaters.

As we were sliding back over the big bridge, with the fifteen-storey bulk of the hotel blessedly in sight, she remarked that the name of the lower lake meant 'Holy Lake', but the upper lake was named after a mysterious poisonous red flower.

"A flower from folklore, Anne!"

Thus did downtown Tampere bisect good and evil. Thus did my upcoming few hours of sleep form a watershed between happiness and horror.

✳   ✳   ✳

The phone rang. 6.15 A.M., claimed the display on the bedside clock. My head seemed to have gone for a swim.

It was the American Ambassador herself, calling from Helsinki. Evangeline Carlson. The Secret Service had contacted her by shortwave radio to say that I was here.

They had *radioed* her rather than phoning?

The disaster had begun a day earlier, with an attack on Motorola's research division in Phoenix.

"Motorola had a functioning, um . . . quantum computer," said Evangeline Carlson. "I don't actually know what this means. What sort of computer it is."

"I do," I moaned into the mouthpiece. Motorola had been busy with optical cavities—magic with mirrors.

Presumably a prototype was still being put through its paces. Hence, no hint of an announcement as yet.

"A militia coalition calling themselves the Caucus stole the computer. CAUC-US." Ambassador Carlson pronounced the two syllables separately. "Caucasian-USA. White America. Free from blacks and Jews and Hispanics and degenerates." The bitter contempt in her voice.

"They must have had an insider working for them at Motorola." I was quite pleased that I managed to frame such a lucid sentence.

"I don't know anything about that, Dr Matthews. Information's almost *non-existent*. We're cut off apart from shortwave radio—"

I listened numbly, stunned by the speed and thoroughness of what had happened. I should have switched on the light and jotted notes, but my head was still afloat in beer and ammonium chloride.

The Caucus had spirited that prototype quantum computer away, probably to elsewhere in Arizona, because late last night, Finnish time, the super-fast hacking had already begun. Not just one stream of hacking, but many.

What must be happening was the release of self-replicating smart programs throughout the system, designed to penetrate firewalls, crack encyptions, grab passwords, and establish themselves as privileged systems managers in computers all over the country. Military computers, financial, government. Some computers had sealed themselves off in time to avoid invasion. Of course, a hermit computer can no longer interact with others, so basically it is out of the game.

The Caucus had taken over communication satellites. If I could only raise my head from the pillow, metaphorically I must take off my woolly hat to whatever acned racist geek superhacker was using the stolen computer, and what software he must have written in anticipation. Smart self-replicating agents; algorithms for data compression . . .

The geek must have worked on the prototype at Motorola. Now he was in some militia hideaway which might be anywhere in the Arizona desert.

Operating orders of magnitude faster than any previous computer, the quantum machine had hacked and grabbed command of machines all over America, and in the sky as well — and locked other users out.

Crash went telecommunications. Automatic exchanges. Satellite links. Crash went much of America's defences.

Computer screens carried a demand from the Caucus for the seccession of Idaho and Montana and Wyoming and the Dakotas — as CAUC-US, the American Free States.

Evangeline Carlson told me that most foreign governments were sealing America off electronically to prevent smart programs and viruses from spreading. Bye-bye to the US economy. The dollar would soon be worth diddly internationally. If the Federal Government did discover where the CAUC-US HQ was, and if the quantum computer was destroyed in the ensuing action, that would merely guarantee that the chaos could not be undone . . . unless another company could produce a functioning quantum computer real soon. Motorola's own research center in Phoenix had been blown to pieces with heavy loss of life.

If Nokia was a washout, the Treasury wanted me in England, like yesterday. They were praying that Matsushima was as close to the finishing line as Motorola had been. They wanted me and Outi Savolainen, whom the Finnish government would be contacting right around now.

"The woman who wrote the algo, um — "

"Algorithm," I supplied.

The Finnish government would be making our travel arrangements. I should be ready to leave at any time. . . .

Too little, too late! Hadn't any of the rival alphabet agencies in America realized that Motorola had *already* succeeded? We hadn't, in the Secret Service. Maybe the NSA knew, but their charter prohibits them from interfering domestically, so they wouldn't have tipped off the Secret Service. Maybe the FBI knew about the geek's connections but never put two and two together. . . .

*   *   *

I managed to shower, though this failed to restore me properly to life.

Yesterday morning, I had been able to watch CNN on the TV in my hotel room. Now there were only Finnish and Swedish channels. On one of these a solemn discussion was in progress between two Swedes. A map of America appeared. Montana, Idaho, Wyoming and the Dakotas were highlighted in yellow. Those adjacent states formed an irregular box about seventeen hundred kilometres wide by a thousand deep on the accompanying scale. Huge! I felt so sick and scared. So far from home, a substantial portion of which was no longer home.

A passage beside the hotel restaurant led to a sizable glossy indoor shopping center of glass domes and escalators. Shops were already opening up. I passed a newsagent's.

Did the banner headline in the morning edition of *Aamulehti* refer to America's calamity? Probably the paper went to press before the news broke. Finnish is a language all of its own. None of the multi-vowel words seemed decodable. Maybe the name of that newspaper was a hint that I should try an omelet for breakfast.

I spotted a small shop with a green cross outside, so I pulled my pocket dictionary from my purse.

The word for hangover turned out to be *krapula*. This seemed appropriate. I felt like crap. I wouldn't easily forget such a word. Excuse me, I have a bad krapula.

"*Krapula*," I told the white-coated woman in the shop. I smiled appeasingly in case she thought I was insulting her.

She looked blank.

"I have a hangover," I said in English.

"Oh, you have a hangover. You need some aspirin."

Aspirin never did much for me. "I'd hoped for something stronger."

"For strong drugs you need a prescription. There are strict laws."

Stuff was on the shelves but she would not sell it to me. Was the world already turning against the last remaining superpower, now on the verge of tearing apart just as the Ukraine and other republics had torn loose from once-mighty Russia?

"Good pronunciation," she commented as I was leaving, empty-handed.

No need for paranoia. I had got the word right after all. I just had not put enough bits on the end of it, to make it do anything.

Me and my *krapula* returned to the hotel restaurant, which was now open for breakfast. Bizarrely, the restaurant was Mexican-themed. Sombreros on the walls, murals of adobe buildings, big cacti. People in this chilly country must have a craze for hot chili.

I drank a lot of orange juice, then tackled some scrambled eggs accompanied by some fried blood sausage, the local specialty. My stomach seemed to think this might do me good.

Sitting there in Rancho Sombrero as Finland geared up for its dark day, it was as if a sudden nuclear war had been waged overnight, deleting CNN and America from the world.

Travel arrangements turned out to be a scheduled morning flight from Tampere to Stockholm, to connect with a FinnAir jet bound for Heathrow. This must be the fastest practical way to reach England.

A car delivered me to the barren little airport. Another car brought Outi, software disks in her luggage, accompanied by some escort man who would not be proceeding further. When Outi and I met up, she hugged me. She was worried, excited, tired, sympathetic.

"We are a long shot," she said.

Oh yes indeed. I could imagine what emergency meetings must be going on in the White House and the Pentagon and wherever else. Alerts, troop movements. Were engineers trying to disarm missiles even now? Was Silicon Valley under martial law? Was the President negotiating by radio with the Caucus? Procrastinating? Promising immunities? Were Special Forces searching Arizona. . . ? A million things must be happening, including our economy lurching to its knees—and worldwide shockwaves.

"I have a *krapula*," I told Outi.

"Me too."

A fighter took off along the windswept runway, to be followed soon by another. Apparently this was routine, not an emergency response. Military and civilian traffic shared the airport. Outi and I could not have crammed into one of those military jets for a quicker flight to England.

Our turboprop plane could seat forty, though it was less than half full. The hostess hastily went through the rigmarole about life jackets. Much use those would be if we came down in the frozen Baltic! More germane were the miniatures of Cognac which she distributed along with coffee. After a few moment's thought Outi emptied hers into her coffee cup. Personally I would have vomited.

✳   ✳   ✳

So here we were in Cambridgeshire, with the Jeep's radio tuned to news of insurrection in America, as reported by short-wave broadcasts.

Our driver, Jock Donaldson, a freckled redheaded Scot with a hard-looking face and alert grey eyes, belonged to the British security service. Jock had been at Luton airport on unspecified 'business', and found himself assigned to us. How intently the three of us listened to that radio.

The right-wing militias were not resting on their laurels, merely waiting for a paralysed nation to capitulate. Those embittered former Green Berets and Navy Seals, and serving officers and soldiers too, and Good Old Boy Sheriffs and neo-nazis and survivalists and white supremacists were using their arsenals of weaponry. They had their lists of targets. Smoke was pluming from federal buildings. Victims, pulled from their beds, were hanging from utility poles. Roadblocks, barricades, sabotage, ethnic cleansing, massacre . . . the whole wild whale had heaved up from the depths. The militias had been busy overnight.

It was deep winter in Idaho and thereabouts, but unfortunately no blizzards were raging. Mid-winter was hardly the ideal time for an uprising. But now was when the Motorola prototype had been ripe for the plucking, and the militias had lucked out as regards the weather. Snow lay across CAUC-US, yet under clear skies. The militias had copters, snowmobiles, army vehicles. Local military bases had mutinied.

Eventually we came to Cambridge, negotiated the ring road, and arrived at the science park, serene under shining snow.

The park housed a hundred enterprises in electronics and software and biotech and high-tech instrument development. Designer buildings nestled amidst wide swathes of white lawn and frozen water and leafless groves.

Matsushima UK was a low-slung palace of reflective bronzed glass supported by leaning buttresses. Military Land Rovers and an armoured personnel carrier stood outside.

Incongruously in this setting, soldiers were patrolling. A big satellite dish on the back of a truck by the main door of the palace seemed like some mobile radar intended to warn of missile attack.

The director of Matsushima UK, Carl Newman, was in his late forties.

Urbane yet brutal good looks. He wore an Armani suit, and looked like some millionaire businessman in a movie who spends time in a gym, mobile phone strapped to an exercise bike or weight-lifting frame. He scrutinized Outi as if contemplating treating her exotic self to champagne, ravishing her, then losing interest utterly. He eyed me with the impartial hauteur of a lion into whose den a mouse has crept.

In his office we met up with a computer security specialist from our London embassy who had managed to reach Cambridge, a lanky Texan called Bill Tuttle. Also present was a dapper Japanese named Hashimoto.

"The future," Newman informed us over coffee, "is one of micro-communities linked electronically, not leviathan states. Scotland will soon split away from England." (Jock raised an eyebrow at this.) "When China comes apart, there'll be terrible civil war, maybe nuclear. A century from now the world will consist of ten thousand different free states and free cities."

Newman was already dismissing America as a lost cause, a crippled giant brought to its knees, never to rise again except feebly, relying hereafter on crutches. There was an unpleasant gloating in his attitude, which he veneered as prophetic wisdom. An oak bookcase was full of volumes about the future of computers, robot intelligence, the coming world order, and such.

"If CAUC-US secedes," he predicted, "California and Oregon will follow quickly—with a utopian rather than a racist aim. They'll need to, for their own sake."

"Shit," said Bill Tuttle.

"Your budget could never balance," Hashimoto said to Tuttle, off-beam. "So all falls apart. The centre cannot hold."

"Nevertheless," Newman said, "let's play at being King Canute. We'll shove our throne into the path of the waves and try to turn the tide."

When we went to the changing rooms, Newman behaved as if we were heading for a bout of squash in a subterranean court. He mimed flicking imaginary balls against walls, trivialising the situation, or implying how effortlessly he might triumph against Motorola's stolen prototype and the geek superhacker.

He had bragged that his team was rushing to finish their own quantum computer, at least in a provisional way. Motherboard being finalised. Millions of events might be occurring in America, but the crucial event could indeed happen right here. Matter of hours, maybe. I took some comfort from his attitude, humiliating and provoking though it was.

Of course, a glitch could cause days of delay. Problems might not show up until the quantum computer began running for real, launched upon the world not after months of beta-testing, but right in at the deep end. But oh dear me, us Americans had failed to fore-warn Carl Newman and his team that the US government might need bailing out at such short notice. Damn the man; damn him to hell.

Hell was where much of America was right now . . . Even if we succeeded, what wounds there would be; worse than after our first Civil War.

Supervised by a young Japanese woman, Outi and I put on blue peasant-style anti-static pyjamas, then protective hooded white over-suits—not to protect us, of course, but to keep dust out of the fabri-cation lab. Booties, for our feet. Goggles and breathing masks smelled of alcohol. Vinyl gloves went over latex gloves.

Dressed like explorers upon Mars, we met up with Tuttle and Newman. Did Newman keep a gold coat hanger for his Armani suit in the men's locker room? Forced air descended from grilles in the ceiling to vents in the floor. We showered in streams of air; stepped through an airlock; and showered in air once again. By now the number of particles of dirt per cubic metre ought to be down to about one.

Then we went into the lab.

Modified scanning tunneling electron microscopes; monitor screens showing hugely enlarged chips; liquid nitrogen coolers; chassis for motherboards with expansion ports, keyboards, screens. Half a dozen other people clad like us were very busy.

Outi's software had been copied and squirted here so that no disk dust or greasy fingerprints should accompany it.

Behold: the first motherboard was already in a chassis, being alpha-tested—hastily, in the circumstances. Six hours to zero, plus or minus. When Newman flicked his wrist, it was as if he was bran-dishing a whip.

Bill Tuttle would be superhacker, batting for our side, trying to unpick the locks on satellites and missile silos and stock exchange computers. Trying to reach the stolen Motorola machine electroni-cally, if he could.

No point in tiring ourselves out prematurely. Newman invited us to a late lunch in the bar of the Trinity Centre, social hub of the Science Park.

A couple of armed soldiers escorted us there. Thus did Newman make an imposing impression upon those of his business-suited peers who were at the Centre, excitedly discussing the crisis. On TV a news programme reported whatever information was leaking out of America, in between mulling over international repercussions, stock markets in chaos and such.

While we forked up lasagne and drank orange juice, Newman held forth about his vision of a completely fragmented future world where North America would consist of dozens of independent republics (and China and India likewise, et cetera), and Britain of several free states, yet nonetheless the world would be benignly linked by the 21st century evolution of the Net and the Web.

"Lapland will leave Finland," he told Outi, who retorted:

"Is former Jugoslavia a fine example of your future world?"

"Oh, there'll be muck and bullets," he agreed.

"I think," said Outi, "that people are still animals and need enlightened government. If this Caucus establishes a racist Nazi state, is that to be tolerated?"

"Where can enlightened government come from? Outer space? Though actually," Newman went on, "*one* nation will be immune to fragmentation: the Japanese. Because of their customs and language they are like a hive entity."

"That's right-wing nationalist ideology," she said severely.

"Cool it," Tuttle begged her.

Here at last came word of a British government announcement: a statement in the House of Commons by the Prime Minister. The total systems crash afflicting America was due to use of a new generation computer by the secessionists . . .

Already the Caucus were being called secessionists, not terrorists, as though they might succeed.

The science-suits were agog. Newman, with his armed entourage, basked in glory.

Almost, I hoped that Matsushima's quantum computer would crash. But of course that would be a disaster.

The sun had long since set, though not yet over America. We were in our cybernaut gear again. It wasn't practical to remove the prototype from the clean environment, liquid nitrogen cooling system and all. We were linked up to the big satellite dish outside. A cling-wrapped TV was downstairs with us, tuned quietly to ongoing news which had replaced scheduled programming on one of the channels. Cling-wrapped telephones, too; Bill Tuttle had an open line to our embassy in London, and Jock was talking to his superiors. Outi sat composedly.

Bill looked up, grey-faced.

"There's been a nuclear explosion thirty miles off the coast of Delaware. A demonstration shot into the sea. The Caucus are threatening to hit Washington at ten P.M. Greenwich time if the President doesn't concede."

An hour from now. Just an hour. Of course the President would already have left Washington for a secure bunker.

"Sweet Jesus, they have control of some of our nukes. He'll decide by nine forty-five, our time here."

"If he does surrender," Newman said blithely, choosing the word *surrender* with relish, "we should carry on. The Caucus needn't know where the penetration's coming from. Could be from Japan."

"What if they react to our activity by taking out Washington? They hate the place. Full of blacks. Home of the parasitical fascist Jewish government—"

"You're wasting time," Outi said.

To Outi's ears it must have sounded absurd that neo-Nazi white supremacists and libertarians alike accused the federal US government of being a fascist conspiracy. I myself could understand—just about. All to do with freedom. I could almost agree with Outi that people shouldn't be allowed to have too much freedom. Very likely she was remembering her trips home from school—though if her home city had become a red commune, terror of a different kind would surely have followed.

Liberty, what crimes are committed in your name. Someone once said that.

People on ships must have been killed and burned and blinded. Millions of boiled fish must be floating in the Atlantic.

If two particles have ever been associated, each seems to know what state the other is in, even if they are now so widely separated that no signal could possibly travel from one to the other unless far faster than light. But experiments have been carried out. The distant particle instantly behaves as if it knows.

Or else it is as if there are a myriad possible universes. When one event occurs, the whole damn universe alters so that a corresponding event also necessarily happens.

Action at a distance. . . .

Once upon a time—back at the beginning of the universe when all matter and space was compressed into a tiny spot—everything was associated together.

Never before had a computer operated in parallel universes, doing different quantum things simultaneously in probability-space. Never before had *two* such computers operated simultaneously, and each linked to the data superhighway.

Consciousness has always been a mystery . . . It was smarty-pants Newman who knew all about this.

How is that all the varied activities in our brains give rise to a unified identity, unity of thought, an awareness of self? The latest fashionable theory, Newman's pet, invoked *quantum coherence* harmonizing the state of microtubules throughout the brain.

Microtubules are the tiny hollow scaffolding poles which brace each cell, in a lattice structure. Seemingly they are just the right size to act as waveguides for photons, causing super-radiance—allowing quantum coherence. . . .

If this phenomenon makes people and animals conscious, would not the same apply to a quantum computer? Newman posed this question with a grin.

All of a sudden superhacking seemed so irrelevant.

Data scrolled on our Matsushima machine far too fast to read, except when it paused occasionally before racing onward.

"It's self-aware," said Newman. "It, and the computer in Arizona. Basically they're the same machine now. Each is the subject and the object of each other's scrutiny. Our machine and Motorola's are in tune with one another." He sounded pleased. "They've gone AI."

"As, in Artificial Intelligence?" exclaimed Outi.

He nodded. "Now they're learning about themselves, and the world. Thousands of times faster than anything else could learn. There's plenty of material. The whole Net's their oyster." This had been Newman's ambition all along. Not allegiance to the Japanese, but to some future cyber-mind. His brainchild, so to speak.

He was a covert apostle of artificial intelligence because plain human intelligence (and human government) is obviously deficient. He had never believed in the neural network strategy, or in massive parallel processing as a route to AI. Spontaneous consciousness would arise of its own accord in a quantum computer. He had foreseen this.

"We can disconnect this one!" Outi declared. "We can destroy it. We can switch off the cooling."

"Don't be absurd! Here is the hour that divides the past from the future. We have been instrumental."

Even in the warmth of my protective suit, ice seemed to slide down my spine.

Bill Tuttle said quietly, "Do this and the other one control our nuclear weapons now?"

Newman smiled. "I presume the AIs must have a sense of self-preservation. Nuclear weapons are very contrary to survival. I don't think the Caucus will be able to launch a missile at Washington or anywhere else. But what," he asked airily, "would the AI in Arizona think if we killed this one?"

Masked and goggled, Jock was listening to his phone.

"Satellite communications with America are coming back," he reported. "The lock-out's over."

The screen continued scrolling.

"I suppose it will take the AI a while to sort itself out," said Newman. "Takes *us* years, after all." He yawned.

Bill Tuttle was speaking to the embassy now, explaining, yet sounding as though he had taken leave of his senses.

I felt faint. I needed cold air. Winter air. Night air.

I stood with Outi looking at the stars. Bitter cold. Mist had cleared. The white lawns were crisp and sparkling in the lights from buildings. I thought of the quantum computer operating at just eighty degrees above absolute zero, compared with which the harshest winter on Earth is tropical.

Would it—would they—be able to comprehend cold? And understand love and hate?

Soldiers would deliver us to a hotel.

"When we get to the hotel," said Outi, "why don't we have a nightcap of vodka? Afterwards, Anne, we can *both* leave the room and guess who remained behind."

Sure. An invisible presence. An intelligence thousands of times faster than our own, newly aware of itself on this the first night of its existence. The AI was only in the electronic realm, but I knew what she meant. It was global. Computers everywhere would soon be extensions of it. Phones, satellites. Especially any more quantum computers which came on line.

A sudden breeze blew up, scattering hoarfrost from the branches of a tree, as if the world was shedding its old skin in readiness for a new era.

The Amber Room

AND I SAW HER FALL FROM THE SKY.
The failed hang-glider had begun to spin like a sycamore seed. Then the sail snapped upward at the keel and became a plunging V. At this point she must have pulled the handle of the parachute. The chute failed to separate from her harness. Orange Nylon blossomed but was trapped.

I saw Amber fall. That was my intimate name for Isabelle because of the tan of her skin and the beads of her nipples. I watched her plummet to earth.

Afterwards I wept for her just as Phaeton's sisters wept for their brother after he was hurled from the sky because he flew the sunchariot crazily. But my tears were only salt water. They didn't harden into amber. Not as yet. . . .

I must have been eleven when I first began to dream of flying. In my dreams I soared above the ripe cornfields of the English West Country underneath a wing. The wing was smooth, not feathered. I wasn't a bird.

In the sky of my dreams the sun was a golden ball, a rich warm aromatic sphere, the quintessence of harvest. I believed I had identified the true substance of that sun when my grandmother, Gran-Annie, showed me a large bead of amber.

The fields beneath me were imprinted with patterns suggestive
of runes or astrological symbols. I honestly can't recall whether
'crop circles', so called, had already begun to appear in genuine
fields. A memory isn't like a leaf perfectly preserved in amber for all
time. We don't remember a past event in itself, but rather our
memory of that event. Subsequently we remember the memory of
a memory. Thus our mind forever updates itself. Essentially memories are fictions. Each time that we suppose we are remembering,
these fictions are being rewritten within ourselves, with ourselves as
heroes or victims.

When my dreams began, crop circles were probably already
materializing overnight in cornfields. Maybe this had been happening on and off for centuries rather than my dreams being any
sort of anticipation of the phenomenon. Later, these circles became
a temporary media sensation.

What wild stories there were in the newspapers! The patterns
must be enigmatic attempts at communication on the part of some
alien intelligence! Or possibly archetypal imagery was being
stamped upon patches of plants by some kind of collective planetary mind. . . .

Even to my immature mind I'm sure that speculations of this
sort would have seemed nutty. Surely those convolutions in the
crops were none other than the wind itself made visible. Eddies and
swirls and turbulence. Did not the wind forever comb the hair of
the corn, gently or roughly? All the air of the world was akin to the
skin of a body, ceaselessly rippling and flexing, sweating or shivering. Air is a vast living organ, though a mindless one.

Surely no one could fall from such a dreamy sky? Surely no one
could plunge to earth, and die?

In due course I took up hang-gliding passionately. Presently I was
equipped with a degree in engineering, aerodynamics a specialty.
Passion became profession. With Max Palmer as partner I founded
a fledgling company to design and build new high-performance
hang-gliders: craft with wider spans and nose angles, with tighter
sails and more battens to camber the roached trailing edges of the
airfoil (to be technical for a moment).

Maxburn Airfoils combined Max's first name with my surname,
suggesting flying feats at the leading edge of possibility. Max Palmer
and Peter Burn: two aces. It was financial backing from Max's family which allowed us to set up, thus his name preceded mine. The
company fledged and soared. We even carried out some design
consultancy work for NASA, honey upon the bread and butter of

our regular manufacturing. Usually I wore Gran-Annie's bead as a
pendant around my neck instead of a tie.

Surely no one could fall.

Until I fell in love—or in lust—with Max's Isabelle. Until
Isabelle—until Amber—fell.

A hang-glider pilot aims to see the invisible. He or she watches
wind. At first, to do so, he throws dry grasses. He kicks dust. He eyes
the flutter of a ribbon, the ripple of treetops, the progress of smoke
and clouds. Eventually, for a few of us, an extra perception is born.

As a boy a premonition of this perception showed me the words
of wind written upon the fields. In the ghastly wake of Isabelle's
death impassioned perception took me to Kaliningrad on the Baltic
coast in search of the lost room of amber—the lost room of Amber
herself. I'd begun to dream of finding that room, and my lost love
within it.

An entire room wrought of amber!

Gran-Annie first told me the tale. The central luminary of my
dreams was a sphere of smouldering amber, so naturally I was
enthralled. I concocted various boyish adventure fantasies about
finding the room. But it was only after Isabelle died that I began to
dream repeatedly of doing so in an airborne context. The room had
bizarrely replaced the crop circles. Mountains replaced fields as a
setting.

My German grandmother had been dead for five years, but I soon
reacquainted myself with all the details of the story.

The creation of the amber room began in the year 1702 in
Denmark. Disagreements and delays occurred, but by 1713 the
amber room was on display in Berlin, either gloriously or partially,
when Peter the Great visited Frederick. The ebullient Tsar was so
enchanted that Frederick could do no other than make a gift of the
whole caboodle to Peter.

Off to the Winter Palace in St. Petersburg went sleigh-loads of
crates containing wall panels, pediments, turned corners, embell-
ishments, rosettes, et al.

In 1755 Empress Elizabeth had the room transferred to the
Summer Palace at Tsarskoe Selo. Finishing touches were still
occurring as late as 1763—culminating in one of the wonders of
the world. Visitors expressed their sense of stepping inside of a
dream or fantasy.

Although constructed by human hands, surely that room did

indeed partake of *otherness*. Such golden luminosity! Such mosaic contrasts of yellows and honey-browns and caramel and clear red. Such a wealth of carvings: of Roman landscapes allegorizing the human senses, and of flowers and garlands and of tiny figures (as if seen from high in the air) and of trees. Such mirrors, such chandeliers dripping amber lustres. Amazing, the parquet floor. Ravishing, the allegorical ceiling.

In 1941, eight years after Gran-Annie's parents fled with her from Germany, Nazi armies were about to lay siege to Leningrad. Art treasures were being evacuated to vaults in the Urals—but the Germans overran the Summer Palace. They dismantled the amber room and shipped it to Königsberg Castle. There, it was reassembled under the eye of the director of the Prussian Fine Arts Museum, a certain Dr Alfred Rohde. (It was from seven hundred kilometres further west, from Hanover, that Gran-Annie's parents had emigrated to England.)

Within a couple of years loot filled Königsberg Castle to bursting point. But British bombs were raining down. Dismantled once more, the room departed—and so likewise did Rohde. Königsberg was wrecked; Königsberg was overrun, soon to become Kaliningrad—politically a district of Russia but separated by the three Baltic republics.

Weirdly, Dr Rohde returned to his post. He cooperated freely with the Soviet occupation forces. Yet he disclaimed any knowledge of the whereabouts of the wonder of the world. Soon after Dr Rohde's return, he and his wife both died suddenly. According to their death certificates the cause was dysentery. These documents were signed by a Dr Paul Erdman—but when the KGB investigated they could find no trace of any such doctor.

Supposedly the dismantled amber room came to rest on the bottom of the Baltic Sea some twenty nautical miles off the German coast in a ship which a Soviet submarine had torpedoed.

There is such a thing as disinformation. . . .

The Nazis had a fetish about mountains as last redoubts—about Eagle's Nests, and high eyries. Wouldn't the perfect place to hide the amber room be a mountain range where aircraft could not easily manoeuvre and which advancing tanks would avoid? My dreams imposed upon me the conviction that this was so, and that the hiding place could only be found from the air, bird-like, God-like, in solitary flight. When I contemplated finding that missing room I was a boy again, enraptured.

Thus might Amber's death be exorcised.

Naturally I didn't talk to Max about this method of coping with tragedy. He had his own means of handling grief. Max immersed himself in design work—especially as regards the catastrophic failure of the airfoil which had plunged Isabelle to her death. I was fairly sure that he would search in vain for the cause. His feel for gliders—at the edge of possibility—was less than mine. I'd always been able to reach that little way beyond him. Now I would reach a long way, from England to former East Prussia.

I simply had to visit the last known location of the amber room. Surely I would meet some aficionado of amber who knew more than I could find out in England. Close to Kaliningrad was the seaside town of Yantarny—literally, *Amberville*. That's the source of ninety per cent of the world's present-day supplies of amber. If you rub amber, it develops a static electric charge. Kaliningrad was drawing me like a magnet.

I told Max that I was going to Germany to revisit my grandmother's roots and to investigate the possibility of exporting hanggliders. I wouldn't try to fool Max that I was hoping to sell our products in those lake-strewn boggy Baltic flatlands where the economies are bumping awkwardly along! Thanks to Gran-Annie I was fluent in German. If English wasn't understood much in Kaliningrad, German should be a reasonable bet. After the Second World War it's true that most of the German population of the Kaliningrad region was either dead or expelled or sent to Siberia, but since the demise of the Soviet Union, Kaliningrad had became a free port to attract prosperity, and the closest source of prosperity was Germany.

With a sail secured on top of the Range Rover, I drove through Germany, then Poland. In Warsaw I was obliged to garage my transport. Whatever its free port status, the Kaliningrad region was militarily sensitive due to being the most westerly redoubt of the rump of Russia. The Polish border wasn't open to ordinary civilian road traffic—and I hardly intended to emulate Matthias Russ, or whatever his name was, by hang-gliding my way into the area.

Ach: those Baltic flatlands! The nearest mountains were the Carpathians. A tidy way to the south, those sprawl across a thousand kilometres from Poland to Slovakia into Romania. The amber room had to be somewhere in the Carpathians. But without some clue even a person of special perception could spend ten years searching that range from the air.

I allowed myself two weeks. Continued absence would amount to a betrayal of Max, and of Maxburn Airfoils too.

*   *   *

I had seen Amber fall from the sky.

I flew to Kaliningrad on a newly inaugurated direct flight from Warsaw, and on the way through Immigration an encounter occurred which was to prove crucial.

Manning the desk were a fresh-faced young officer and a sallow older colleague whose high cheekbones and absence of folds to the eyelids proclaimed Mongol blood in his ancestry. . . .

Now, I'd opted for a tourist visa, which meant that I'd been obliged to arrange accommodation expensively in advance. Intourist in London had tried to book me into a so-called 'floating palace' on the river in the centre of the city. A couple of cruise ships were permanently moored in lieu of modern luxury hotels. The month of May was an excellent time to stay in one of those, supposedly.

I didn't wish to be cooped up where my comings and goings could be monitored. And what was this business about the month of May? Further questioning of the Intourist lady, who had actually visited Kaliningrad, disclosed that in May the weather wouldn't be scorching, consequently I could keep the porthole of my cabin shut. The river, it seemed, stank somewhat. I opted instead for a hotel on terra firma several kilometres from the city centre. The Baltika was very popular with tour companies, I was assured.

The younger immigration officer wished to see how much money I had with me. This seemed an American sort of question in this city where all hard currencies were legal tender nowadays. Despite having prepaid for my hotel, did I have enough to support myself during my stay? I did have enough, and more. Much more.

He eyed my amber pendant. "Are you here to buy jewelry?" he demanded. "Your passport says you are an engineer."

We were speaking German. The older man interrupted to point out that I seemed very fluent in German, whereas my passport was a British one.

"My *Grossmutter* came from Germany," I told him.

"From so-called Northern East Prussia, Herr Burn?" Did I detect a note of nationalist displeasure? 'Nördliche Ostpreussen' was how Germans still referred to the Kaliningrad Oblast.

"No, she came from Hanover. She fled from the Nazis in '34. She hated Nazis."

The man smiled, then.

"Is an engineer here to buy jewelry?" persisted the junior officer. Why the quiz? Amber is hardly gold or rubies. Who would wish to smuggle it? As I understood, the bottom had virtually fallen out of

the Western market for amber. With the disintegration of the
superpower, any wannabee Russian rock group would bring out a
haversack full of the stuff to pay their way. Maybe my fellow passengers—principally Poles—weren't as interesting as myself to
interrogate. Or maybe obstructiveness lingered.

"I'm fascinated by the history of the amber room," I said—a
harmless enough admission, not to mention being the truth.

The young man looked blank. "The amber room?" I suppose
you might meet a native of London who hasn't the foggiest idea
where the Crown Jewels are housed. The other officer spoke
rapidly in Russian, enlightening his colleague.

To recover from chagrin, the young officer inquired what sort of
engineer I was, and when I specified hang-gliders the older man
reached for my passport and my hotel confirmation with such an
impetuous hand that he actually knocked the documents off the
desk. I would have picked these up myself but he stepped swiftly
out to do so. As he rose, his lapel bulged and I noticed a badge
pinned on the inside where it wouldn't normally be seen. A disc,
the size of a small coin, bore a double-headed eagle. The old imperial eagle, emblem of the Tsars. . . He must be a nationalist—of a
far-out eccentric royalist stripe. All sorts of strange creatures had
crawled out of the woodwork when the Soviet Union fell apart.

I was irritated by the delay. But also I felt suddenly *possessed*, in
that moment, by my dream perception—galvanized and beguiled.
The words jerked out of me almost inadvertently:

"Maybe," I burbled, "a hang-glider pilot can find the lost amber
room, wherever it is!" Then I laughed dismissively.

In fact, the young officer had had my best interests at heart. If I
was going to be carrying a lot of money round, it might be sensible
to hire a driver, an interpreter, an escort, if I followed his drift. A
reliable and discreet man from a private security company. Kaliningrad wasn't awash with crime to the extent, alas, of Moscow or St
Petersburg. Yet even so! A word to the wise. He produced a little
printed card with address and phone number and printed a name
on the back.

"My name. Tell them that I recommended you—"

No doubt for a percentage of the fee which I would be paying. . . .

The older man didn't want me to take the card. He became
quite vociferous, in Russian. Maybe he viewed this as an insult to
his nation. I think he would have confiscated the card if this had
been within his power.

       ❈   ❈   ❈

Thus it was that I acquired Pavel as a minder and guide for my stay in Kaliningrad.

The fellow bore quite a resemblance to me—though this is purely coincidental. Both of us were only of medium height, though big-boned. We were both endowed with freckles and curly gingery hair and light blue eyes. Somewhere in Pavel's ancestry there must have been a Viking or two. He could have served as a double if he had exchanged his cheap leather jacket for my more fashionable anorak, and had donned the amber pendant. He carried a registered firearm, and was discretion itself as regards my business. Maybe his employers supplied a pamphlet on 'How to be a Minder'. Rule one: maintain a bland facade. Of course, to begin with it would have seemed that he was merely minding a tourist with a particular interest in amber.

Next day, he collected me from the Baltika in a dark green Mercedes with lots of kilometres on the clock. Its bodywork might be green but its exhaust emissions no longer were. Actually, the local petrol was at fault. The streets of this dreary city, which had risen upon the ruins of grand old Königsberg, were full of fumes. The river was indeed as black and murky as old engine oil. Bleak wastelands punctuated some remarkably ugly Soviet architecture. The old Cathedral was a shell, though some scaffolding hinted at possible restoration. The castle, where Dr Rohde had stored the room, had *been* a shell—till it was demolished by dynamite to make way for a House of Soviets which, Pavel remarked, was too ugly for anyone ever to have the gall to complete.

Pavel pointed out a certain pink building beside the North Station, which had been KGB headquarters. That's where he had worked until he had privatized himself. I suppose this admission exonerated him of being any sort of informer nowadays.

We visited the Amber Museum, which was located in a burly red brick tower. That tower was one of the survivors of war, as were a number of city gates and bastions. Personally I found the museum mediocre, showcasing too much modern jewelry. Through Pavel I quizzed the dumpy lady director, who spoke no German, about the amber room.

She believed the submarine story.

I asked her about Rohde's death. On this topic she had no opinions.

I told her that I was researching a thriller which I had long yearned to write on account of my German grandmother. This cover story had occurred to me in view of my experience at the airport. I would announce my ambition blatantly—but in the guise of fiction. I aimed to write a story about a hang-glider pilot who hunts for, and finds, the lost amber room in a mountainous Nazi hiding place. I assured the lady director that I was interested in any hypothesis, however fantastic.

However, fantasy wasn't her forte. "Herr Burn," she lectured me (via Pavel), "have you not noticed the blinds at all the windows? Have you not seen how thick the glass display cases are? Sunlight degrades amber over a relatively modest time. Amber is chemically a bitumen. Air oxidizes it till it is so brittle that it can disintegrate into a pile of dust. You speak of the amber room being kept in the open somewhere, fully assembled, exposed to wind and sunlight? What stupidity."

Absolutely the room must be out in the open, three-dimensionally, beneath the sky, not packed flat in cases in some cavern! The parquet floor, the great wall panels, the allegorical ceiling dangling its chandeliers: all must be erected and connected, and suffusing and refracting golden light. How else could it conform to my dream? How else could Amber herself be waiting in the room?

"*Sheer stupidity.*"

My interview was at an end.

I went with Pavel to a shop specializing in amber jewelry on Leninsky prospekt, and then to another on prospekt Mira. Despite our proximity to Yantarny—to *Amberville-by-the-sea*—there was a dearth of decent merchandise on display. The proprietor of the first shop became brusque when he grasped that I wasn't interested in buying anything but only in wasting his time with fanciful questions. The manager of the second was eager that I should include the exact address of his premises in my prospective best-seller—which in *his* opinion ought to be about an attempt to refloat the torpedoed ship, in the style of *Raise the Titanic*, and featuring neo-Nazis conspirators. He urged me to visit the Bunker Museum near the university. That bunker was the command post of Hitler's Reich till the Red Army overran the devastated city. Part of it had been left completely untouched since the day the surrender was signed in it. Such ghosts, Herr Burn, such echoes of the past. Perfect atmosphere for a best-seller.

I wouldn't visit the damned bunker. But Yantarny, yes—I would go there on the very next day. At the source of amber I might find some better pointer. Back in the car again, in our cocoon amidst the pollution, Pavel explained that visits to Yantarny were a slightly sensitive matter.

"You see, foreigners can only buy a train ticket to Yantarny if they have a special document. . . ."

My heart sank. "Is it a military zone?"

No, it wasn't. Just along the coast at Baltiysk was a huge naval base. Baltiysk was a restricted area—though nowadays sightseeing visits could even be arranged. For commercial reasons Yantarny was somewhat out of bounds to independent travellers.

"*Somewhat* out of bounds," stressed Pavel. "I could drive you there, but it might be wiser to join a group tour."

He would arrange this. He would accompany me. Even so, at Yantarny I wouldn't be able to visit the workings or the beach. Those were fully out of bounds. I would only be able to gawp at pipelines through which the quarried earth and amber were pumped across the town to be separated, and the amber cleaned.

Damnation. Still, did I really need to inspect those workings, like some commercial spy?

I never did get to Yantarny. Back at the Baltika, to my surprise, a message was waiting for me—to telephone a certain number.

Did the proprietor of the amber shop have some new suggestion for my best-seller about sunken treasure? Or, after a change of heart, was it the lady director of the museum who wanted to speak to me?

Not in the least. It proved to be the older immigration officer, who had noted where I was staying. Would I meet him and some friends for a meal and drinks at a restaurant on Leninsky to discuss a matter of mutual interest? But of course. And by the way, had I taken his young colleague's advice regarding a chaperon? Why yes, I had. In that case my minder must remain in the car. This matter was confidential.

The restaurant was very noisy due to the constant loud dance music. This entertainment rendered eavesdropping virtually impossible. It wasn't merely face to face but almost nose to nose that I met Rylov the immigration officer, and Antonov, and a nameless gentleman, over German beer and fried chicken.

Antonov was of the hefty breed. Fifty-eight inch chest and fifty inch waist, with a puce suit to match, crumpled though of decent tailoring. Mongol genes—and tissue courtesy of carbohydrate. He had to be a member of the Kaliningrad Mafia. At first I thought that he was here as muscle, a bodyguard for the man with no name. In fact Antonov spoke English well, and was as much a part of this as

Rylov or the Enigma. Mr Mystery was in his seventies: dapper, with close-cropped silvery hair, and of refined features. The heavy tinted thick-lensed glasses he wore might have been due to weak eyes but they gave him the appearance of an aristocratic interrogator — though he left the interrogating to Antonov. He gave the appearance of understanding German and English but only spoke, from time to time, in Russian. During our encounter he smoked a dozen of those fragrant cigarettes consisting principally of a cardboard tube.

"So you believe that the pilot of a hang-glider can find the lost room?" Antonov said to me.

"Somewhere in the Carpathians," I replied. Mr Mystery sucked his cigarette, then rapped out something in Russian.

The story which I'd adopted bubbled forth. I was researching a thriller.

Antonov eyed me. "And the room shall appear nakedly out in the open? Without any framework or corset to support it?"

My dream inundated me. "It must. It has to. How else can the flier find it?"

"Ah," said Antonov. "And you are the flier."

"I do fly, that's true."

His next remark amazed me. "Maybe it needs a special perception to find the room."

I must have gaped at him.

Rylov said in halting English, "You not truly *write* novel. To write novel is a lie. You want to find the room." The dance music bawled around me, isolating us in a mad oasis. "*Why* you want to find room, Herr Burn? Because of treasure value?"

"*No!*"

Because Amber fell from the sky. Because she beckoned me from within the golden room. I fingered my talisman.

"It's a personal matter," I said. "An emotional matter." I hesitated before confessing: "I dream. I dream of finding it."

"By magic," said Antonov. I thought he was mocking me. Yet the next minute he began to discourse about the Third Reich and about psychics. For a while I imagined that he might be proposing a new plot for my phantom novel. Now that communism and state atheism had collapsed, was not occultism all the vogue in Russia?

Accompanied by nods from Mr Mystery, Antonov explained, "The Nazis persecuted most occultists, Mr Burn, yet some they pampered. . . ."

Seemingly the German navy had financed a major scientific

expedition to the Baltic in the hope of determining by radar the concave curvature of the Hollow Earth. The inglorious failure of this demented project did not deter the Naval Research Institute in Berlin from lavishing the finest wines and cigars upon psychics while those visionaries swung pendulums over charts of the Atlantic—this, in response to mounting losses of U-boats. And who knew what had been the upshot of the Nazi-sponsored psychic expedition to Tibet?

The point of all this was that Antonov and his associates had evidence of a rite being performed within the amber room in Königsberg Castle under the eye of Dr Alfred Rohde and a high-ranking Nazi—with the aim of concealing the future whereabouts of the room. The otherworldly treasure would be hidden amidst mountains, of course—I was right on that account—but also in some veiled domain adjacent to the mundane world . . . till someone of vision could rediscover it with suitable aid.

"The name of the doctor who poisoned Rohde and his wife was Erdmann, Mr Burn. The name means *Earthman,* by contrast with the occult world of spirit." Antonov leered at me, sweating. "And also by contrast with the sky?"

"Why," I asked, "did the Germans take such pains to hide the room?"

"*Why?*" Antonov's tone proclaimed that the answer should be self-evident. Mr Mystery was fingering the lapel of his own suit. I caught a flash of, yes, a double-headed eagle on a pin. This served as a signal to Antonov to initiate me.

"Because," said the bulky fellow, "the amber room was once the glory of the Tsar's Summer Palace, a symbol of Holy Russia, usurped by the Bolshevists. Nazis felt hatred for all Russians. The imperial Russian government fought the fathers of those Nazis in the First World War. . . ." He didn't need to lower his voice due to the din of the music. "Mr Burn, the rediscovery of the amber room heralds . . . the restoration of the Tsars. It will serve as a sure sign."

Rylov nodded. Mr Mystery exhaled blue smoke. In the logic of loony nationalism perhaps this was true.

"You can help us, Mr Burn. We will help you fulfill your own private dream! We know where to look, and we have the means to help you see. What we ask is that you buy the means from us, simply to help our funds." He named a figure in Deutschmarks which corresponded with what Rylov already knew I had in my possession.

A scam. This had to be a scam. A confidence trick.

If I tried to walk out on them, would I be detained by a gun held covertly under the table? Would I be robbed while Pavel sat patiently in the car outside? Worse, might the music mask an actual pistol shot?

Ah, but this trio couldn't be sure that the money was on me at the moment. . . .

"Show me this *means* of yours," I demanded.

Antonov frowned. "We do not carry it around restaurants. I will come to your hotel tomorrow afternoon. We exchange . . . with good will."

As Pavel drove me along Moskovsky back toward the Baltika he admitted, "I took a look inside the restaurant, Mr Burn. I recognized the big man with you. He is a criminal."

I suppose his curiosity was justifiable in view of my mysteriously meeting with strangers within a day of my arrival in Kaliningrad. Did Pavel imagine that I was a criminal too? Or that I was involved in the espionage game? That my interest in amber was merely a front?

"It's all right," I assured him. "Antonov offered to sell me some information about the amber room I've been asking about."

"Antonov is his real name, or at least it's the name he uses."

Ah. Wise Pavel.

"Did you recognize the old man with the glasses?"

My minder shook his head.

"Pavel, tomorrow afternoon Antonov is coming to the hotel to bring me the information. I'm suspicious this might be a *Bauern-fängerie*." A 'yokel-trap': how picturesque the German word for confidence trick. "I want you to be with me when he visits. There'll be some extra drink-money for you."

We had crossed the ring-road by now, and in the darkness the ten floors of the Baltika loomed on our left.

My room was on the sixth floor. We'd been waiting most of the afternoon. I was eyeing some wasteland through the smog-haze when a white Mercedes came into view, steering erratically at speed. The car barely missed a taxi and a bus before skidding to a halt, narrowly avoiding some German tourists.

A stout figure, unmistakably Antonov, lurched from the car. Clutching his side, he lumbered toward the entrance. Was he injured?

Pavel and I were waiting by the elevator when Antonov spilled out. Luckily the corridor was deserted but for us. We had to heave

Antonov along to my room, and into a dingy over-stuffed armchair. He'd been *shot*. It seemed that this ox of a man was dying, though he wasn't bleeding much at all. Not externally, at least. He'd be bleeding inwardly.

I'd seen Amber bleed inwardly to death, her outward form still fairly unblemished. . . .

Antonov's breath was ragged. "Seeing double," he mumbled in English as he eyed Pavel and me. Pavel said something in Russian, and recognition dawned. "Bodyguard . . . Rylov said . . ."

"This is Pavel. Don't worry. He doesn't understand English."

"You met your twin, Mr Burn . . . *There are affinities* . . . Pavel is Paul, and you are Peter. Both saints attend me." Mysticism was welling up in him along with his lifeblood.

What kind of confidence trick was this, if someone had shot Antonov to try to prevent him from coming to me?

"What happened?" I begged.

Blood bubbled on his lips, consecrating his words.

"Arguing . . . He who had the *means* in his care . . . Hating foreigners . . . Even if a foreigner does have the vision . . ." He coughed. "Wasting time . . . Look in the heart of the High Tatras, Mr Burn."

The High Tatras of Slovakia. . . .

He whispered the name of a town, which I hastened to scribble on a pad. Antonov struggled to reach an inside pocket of his suit, and slid out a spectacle case made of steel. "Look with these. . . ."

I opened the case. The spectacles were so old. The frames, sides, and ear-rests were of thin tarnished metal. Surely the lenses were of amber, though the amber was so clear and transparent. Apart from their evident age the spectacles looked remarkably like John Lennon glasses.

These were the means to find the amber room?

"Man of the Königsberg Guild made these, Mr Burn . . . Christian Porschin . . . Sixteen-nineties . . . By heating amber gently in . . ." The English word failed him so he resorted to German. "In *Leinöl*. Blue flower," he mumbled by way of explanation, though I was well aware what *Leinöl* meant, namely linseed. Heat amber in linseed to clarify it—then grind lenses.

"Later on, Mr Burn, the Nazi magic ceremony, remember. . . ."

A ceremony to enchant the spectacles? To attune them to the amber room! When someone of vision wore these, he would be able to locate the lost room . . .

Maybe there had been something magical about these glasses

even back in the late Seventeenth Century. Science and magic were still uneasy bedfellows back then. These spectacles had been safeguarded somewhere in the Kaliningrad region throughout the Soviet annexation, in this hard steel case—but not on behalf of covert Nazis. There couldn't have been any Nazis lurking in the vicinity. Nearly all Germans had been killed or deported or sent to Siberia, right? Covert Russian royalists had become the custodians.

It was my luck—no, my destiny—that Rylov was a recruit to this crazy nationalist minority cause and that my quest seemed a godsend to the dotty Tsarists.

Though not to all of them! Many of the newly liberated political animals must be deeply xenophobic. Holy Russia, sacred motherland: safeguard and restore her strength. Let not the West pollute the national soul. There'd been a violent quarrel in the royalist faction. Certain members would have preferred a Rasputin to receive the specs, not a mere visitor from abroad.

Absolutely, this was no yokel-trap, not when it led to murder. Nor could I disbelieve in the spectacles. Too much faith, and death, had been invested in them.

"Blue flowers," repeated Antonov, as if I might find the room in some high meadow full of blooms the hue of the sky itself. This was such an inconsequential detail, communicated with such urgency as thought began to dissipate from the brain. Almost like babbling of green fields.

Finally he slurred something in Russian, and I heard Pavel suck in his breath. Unsurprising that Antonov should revert to his mother tongue in the final moments—as any of us grown-ups might cry out, terminally, to the mother who bore us. Had those last words been a prayer?

He was dead. Those high fatty cheeks slumped a little. Those eyes without any folds to the lids were blank.

I'd imagined that the fall from the sky would kill Isabelle outright, mercifully and abruptly. She should have remained unconscious throughout her dying minutes. Surely she did not once open her eyes and focus upon me!

Pavel was regarding the spectacles in perplexity. The only word of the conversation between myself and Antonov which he could have understood would have been *Leinöl*. Linseed, and a pair of antique glasses. Why should I be willing to spend so much upon old specs? How could those be the motive for a killing?

"Help me get him out of here!" I took out my wallet, and removed a couple of hundred mark bills which I thrust at Pavel.

"He won't be needing money now. Here's an installment on a tip for you." *Ein weniges Trinkgeld.* Oh quite a lot. "There'll be more to come, at the airport."

After a quick recce, we heaved the body along to a tiny service room. Vacuum cleaner, linen, bars of soap. While I lurked, Pavel summoned the nearby elevator. The corridor remained deserted. The elevator arrived empty. While Pavel delayed the elevator, I dragged the body inside, then I hopped out—as did he, after pressing for the top floor.

"*Wir haben Glück, Herr Burn . . .*"

Yes, we'd been lucky, though we still needed to erase scuff marks from the carpet then wash some spots in my room and rub dirt in to restore their former appearance. Oh, and we reversed the cushions of the armchair. Antonov hadn't bled much at all. Not externally.

The corpse would soon be found. There'd be a bit of a fracas. But in these progressive days no KGB security men routinely haunted the lobby. And Antonov had known my room number in advance.

"By the way," I asked casually, "what did he say in Russian at the very last?"

Pavel grimaced. "It was stupid. 'Long live the Tsar,' he said."

I was hard put to conceal my elation at this final confirmation of Anton's integrity, nevertheless I agreed that Antonov's last words were completely *Dummkopf*. If Pavel still decided that I was a courier between royalists in Russia and in the West, why, he had more drink-money to look forward to, in return for his discretion!

Oh, I'd seen my love fall from the sky. And now I could find her again.

Where hang-gliders are concerned, there's always a thin line between stability and instability; and so it was with Amber too.

A cutting-edge craft which verges on being unstable is going to react wildly when you try some virtuoso manoeuvre—though equally, a craft which is too stable is an exhausting drag to fly. A bit of instability has its merits. Amber had many merits. She was gorgeous, passionate, adventuresome.

Yet danger excited her rather too much. She courted the frisson. *Not* that she was a dangerous flier. She was too skilled to be dangerous. Skill vetoes silliness. Steering toward a thundercloud wasn't her idea of a good time, but in her regular life she did risk thunder and lightning.

A cuckolded husband is often the last to know that he's being cheated and betrayed; and I was the last of a handful of accomplices in betrayal—the awkward thumb, as it were, since I was the closest to home. The awkward eager thumb.

Isabelle knew how to conduct a liaison, so she protested to me during the early weeks of our own affair. Did Max suspect anything at all about Simon Lee, her previous conquest? Or about Jim Parrish, Lee's predecessor?

Until then, nor had I suspected about Lee or Parrish. Lee was a locally based rally driver and dealer in sports cars. Parrish, it transpired, was a mushroom farmer and membership secretary of some federation of pot-holers.

Did knowledge of my own predecessors tarnish the craving I felt for her? I suppose I was jealous and at the same time thrillingly flattered to be preferred to other men.

Cuckoldry is such an old-fashioned word for what I was doing to Max, but in view of our close relationship I found the term appropriate. Hitherto Isabelle had cheated—but her lovers weren't as close to Max as I was. Max, whose family's money was our foundation.

Admittedly I had desired Isabelle previously. Yet I wouldn't have dreamed of *doing* anything. You might describe me as inhibited—notwithstanding my soaring dreams! I hadn't become intimate with a woman either at university or subsequently. At a party I might tipsily and jokingly embrace some fellow I knew well—or an older woman acquaintance for whom I felt no frenzy—rather than the girl close by for whom I actually lusted. Displacement, that's the name for it.

When my self-control finally slipped—was stripped away—by Isabelle, I did indeed succumb to erotic frenzy with her to an extent which surprised her, and delighted her. This delight risked being our undoing and the ruin of Maxburn Airfoils. She began to muse about leaving humdrum Max for me. The frisson of flying had hitched her and Max together in the first place (and I assume his future inheritance played a part), but he wasn't fully able to satisfy her, so it seemed. Nor was motherhood an imminent goal. Bloated with child, how might she fly at the edge of possibility?

Pretense in public, frenzy in private!

I remember us relaxing after lovemaking in the privacy of my cottage which I'd renamed The Wings. The place was secluded.

Woodland, on most sides. A shady lane gave quiet access. The Wings consisted of a south wing and a west wing, with a sheltered high-hedged wild garden to the rear.

Amber's golden sun-lamp tan left no pale loin-stripe. Blonde bloom upon her skin, as on a firm sweet fruit. Those amber areolas and the succulent beads of her nipples. Freckles on her upper arms and shoulders. Her slim nose, her restless blue eyes framed with challenging violet shadow. She wore her flaxen hair in a long braided rope, baring her brow, offering me a kind of tail to hold.

I was, in our pillow talk, The Thumb. The Thumb would jut stiffly, throbbing to hitch a ride.

"Thumb's up," she would say. "Thumb's up." This was to be her joke—risqué, and risky—whenever we were setting out to fly, me and her and Max each with our separate sails.

On this occasion I remember her speculating whether two people could possibly make love aloft, high in the sky, veiled by a cloud, whilst flying tandem side by side together. Would the hang-straps make this totally impossible—unless at least one person unhooked? How wildly would bodily movements pitch the craft? She laughed, she laughed.

"I'd like to go on holiday to Zanzibar," she said. "Nobody else seems to go there. Max isn't interested."

"Well, the two of us can hardly slip away to Zanzibar together."

"I suppose not. I just want to go somewhere where I'm invisible."

"I think you'd be very visible in Zanzibar."

"Somewhere which is my own secret place. And yours."

"We're in it at this moment, aren't we?"

"Jim made love to me in a cave."

I didn't wish to hear about my predecessors.

Isabelle was nominally a silversmith. She had trained thus, indulged by her parents. Courtesy of Max she had a little workshop kitted out with drills and cutters and melting pot, blast burner and drawbench, hammers, burnishers and buffers. She did make some elaborate earrings. She had created perfect little hang-gliders to dangle down from one's lobes, sails brushing the wearer's neck like silver insects. She had made life-size slim silver ears to hang underneath one's flesh-and-blood ears. Was this wit or sheer caprice? Expensive toys gave her a pretext to hang out at swanky craft fairs and be admired, and meet such as Simon and Jim.

She began to nag at going away with me.

Going *away?* Away from my life?

Another time, at The Wings, I told her about the amber room—
and immediately there was a place in which we ought to make love.
To surprise her, on the next sunny afternoon I pinned golden cellophane over the bedroom window. Was my light-fitting an adequate
substitute for a chandelier? Could the carpet become a parquet
floor of red and gold and caramel? The only amber was round my
neck. And beside me, in bed! Amber's skin hardly needed any tinting by cellophane, though I myself became golden for a couple of
hours.

Yes, we trod such a thin line between stability and instability. If
Max discovered, what a wreckage of my once-stable life there
would be. Did this possibility stimulate Isabelle? Whilst in The
Wings, my own self-control evaporated. If the collapse of control
were to spread further, involving Maxburn Airfoils in disorder, what
then?

Amber said to me, "Of course, if Max had a flying accident I'd
feel so wretched and so sad. Worse, you and I could hardly continue
loving. If we did, the finger of suspicion would point. Yet how could
we stop loving? That's why I'm sure we should go away. Why not to
America—where they surf the sky?"

Financially this seemed deeply impractical. Was I to set up shop
all over again? Was I to work with designers who might have a veto
over me? Isabelle would be deserting her cheque book in the
process of deserting Max. Was I to provide her with a new silver
smithy?

Horns of a dilemma! Perils of cuckoldry. Terror tiptoed along
my spine. Thumbs down.

I had no particular trouble leaving Kaliningrad. The murder had
obviously been due to a gangland feud. In spite of the manifest lack
of pursuit, the victim must have been trying to hide himself in the
hotel—rather than having any special business at the Baltika. The
Baltika was certainly *not* paying any protection money to racke-
teers. Nyet, nein, absolutely not.

Nor did any xenophobic tsarists try to hinder me on the way
from boarding the Warsaw-bound plane.

Nor was my hang-glider stolen by Polish spies on the road south
by way of Krakow.

Guards on the Slovak side of the border with Poland were
mainly on the lookout for cheap Polish cigarettes and for migrant

Romanians—particularly for gypsy Romanians trying to reach the Shangri-La of Germany. Myself and Range Rover and hang-glider passed muster; thus I entered the heart of the High Tatra mountains. I was soon at a certain pleasant resort town crowded with tourists.

Tourists, tourists! Now that snow was thawing on all southerly slopes the skiing season was over—yet the swelter and thunderstorms of high summer were still a couple of months away. Apart from a lingering chill, this was a fine time to admire towering white peaks and ramble and climb a bit and sup strong Tatra beer. Many Germans were doing so.

Up aloft, the air would be bitter. Even in summer the higher slopes only warmed to a few degrees above zero. Visibility shouldn't be a bother. During full summer the sky would cloud over almost every morning, prelude to thunder and lightning by midday, with clear sky only from late afternoon onwards. But not as yet.

I had to visit the nearest flying ground of the Slovak Aeroclub to present my credentials. The amber room might be invisible, but I wouldn't be. I had to demonstrate my sail and my skills, finesse a permit, sign a waiver, take out an expensive insurance bond in case the Mountain Rescue Service needed to be called out. I promised not to drift over the backs of mountains, to flee at the sight of any thundercloud forming, to conduct myself sensibly.

In the hotel where I stayed, vegetables seemed almost entirely absent from meals. Duck with bread dumplings; pork with bacon dumplings. Had these people never heard of a pea or a carrot? Ah, explained a waiter, former Communist mismanagement of agriculture was to blame. I imagined innumerable fields devoted to a monoculture of dumpling bushes.

Isabelle would have liked it here. My Amber was a flesh-eater.

She certainly didn't bite or scratch when we quarreled about the idea of her leaving Max. Rather, she hugged and caressed herself, not like some wounded animal, but more as though she was making love to herself before my estranged eyes—becoming almost oblivious to me, inhabiting some domain dominated by her own senses, exhibiting a radical selfishness which chilled and shocked me more than rage would have done. I should feel compelled to reach out and promise anything, whatever, if only she would return from her self-imposed autistic exile.

How could she, who was usually so out-going, suddenly go inward thus? I felt that there was a madness in her—not the *mad*

of anger, of a whim denied, of desire denied, but the mad of un-
reason.

This wasn't the Amber whom I had known hitherto. Maybe
here was proof that she did truly love me with a consuming passion,
a passion which, nonetheless, she had *chosen* to experience for the
frisson of it—a passion by which I must in turn fatally be captivated.
(And I was, I was; so why was I denying her?)

That afternoon she departed more like a sleepwalker than a
woman incensed.

I know that that same night I dreamed forebodingly of driving
the several miles to the airfoil shed and doing such-and-such to one
of the cutting-edge craft by torchlight, by dreamlight. In a dream
details are elusive. Spurred by trauma, my subconscious mind must
have intuited a structural flaw in the newest design. Certainly I
woke in my own bed.

Next morning, Isabelle was all smiles. Water under the bridge.

On the low hilltop from which we liked to launch, Max and I
both observed her closely as she warmed up and stretched to loosen
her body. Kneeling, she strapped in and hooked up. Hang-check,
harness check. From the nose-wire a thread of red yarn fluttered,
reading the breeze. Hands on the uprights of the control bar, she
stood up under sail. She stared well ahead then ran at top speed.
She was airborne into the wind rising up the hillside. Perfect.

I was rising over ascending spruce trees. Look: a family of deer
down below!

Above, a few patches of cirrocumulus spread wispy fans like lacy
bleached corals, tinted faintly by my amber spectacles. I still felt
overheated in my thermal underclothes and woolens and gloves
and anorak. Well and good! I'd be shivering soon.

Soon enough, spruce was yielding to dwarf pines. As I gained
more altitude the pines thinned out. The ground was increasingly
jagged and snowy. One never flies the ground, one flies the air.
Soon the air was chill, but chill air must still lift over hills, over soaring heights, because of catabatic convection flow. Earlier, occasional poles had marked tracks. No longer, up above the bushline.
Earlier, I'd seen dozens of hikers. Now it was as if the whole world
had emptied, or as if an alternative world had replaced the previous
one. An azure mountain lake on my left. Was some ice still afloat
there? I left the lake behind.

A pulse thudded in the pendant tucked above my heart. I found
myself looking in vain for blue flowers amidst the snow and cliffs.

✳   ✳   ✳

In a ravine, through my antique specs, at last I perceived the room—aglow and entire and golden amidst bald boulders with snowy beards and snowy ruffs. Lifting a hand from the control bar, I thrust up my glasses briefly. Of course the room hid itself, chameleon that it was, phenomenon of the realm of amber.

With amber vision I saw it again so clearly. By a shift of perception, through its ceiling I spied the chandeliers hanging downward almost like reflections. No corset sustained the room nor did any betraying litter of discarded crates lie around—of course not. The room was radiance as much as reality.

Almost, I hesitated. Almost, I fled from the mountains back to the world of a Range Rover and The Wings, the empty Wings, and Max, coping bravely with grief. But my dreams were welling in me, replacing actuality with a more exquisite mode of being.

I began a figure-eight descent, to and fro within the ravine. I intended to alight with a final decisive flare alongside the room. Whether down-gusts buffeted me or the magnetism of so much amber pulled me like a leaf, I found myself swooping down upon the ceiling—surely to shatter it.

Not so, not so. I sprawled upon the amber parquet floor. Above me the allegorical ceiling was intact. I couldn't recall unhooking, yet through a window I saw my sail being borne up and away out of the ravine by wind like a great bird set free.

Scrambling to my feet, I tore off gloves and harness and anorak. It was warm within the room. Within, within! I was inside the treasure room where tsars had stood.

Unable to focus upon any single particular, I scanned the wall mosaics and all the intricate carvings of trees and garlands and shells. So many scenes of nature, so many Gods and Goddesses and other personae. How the faceted amber drops of the chandeliers twinkled. How brightly the clear red plaques shone amidst surrounding yellows and browns. In the giant gilt-framed mirrors at either end of the room I saw myself receding toward infinity. Three windows reached to the floor, their frames richly carved. . . .

Already the ravine had vanished. Dense mist stroked those windows. Condensation trickled. A cloud had nestled down so quickly. Nothing was visible outside.

There were three doors of the folding variety, with ornate frames. I hurried to one but it wouldn't budge. Nor would the next. Nor the third.

Amber. Where was she?

Why, there she was in one of the mirrors—standing alongside one of my more distant reflections! Isabelle was dressed in the same jeans and black polo-neck sweater as on the day she had died. Her flaxen rope of hair hung forward over one shoulder and down her breast, suggestive of a noose not yet knotted. Her expression was weird. She took a step forward.

She did not give rise in the mirror to multiples of herself. She was the one and only. When I glanced back, she wasn't present in the other mirror at all.

She had advanced again. Now she was only four reflections away from me. Could she see me here in the gleaming room?

"Why did you kill me?" she called out, stepping closer. "Why, Peter, why?"

"I dreamed that I did," I admitted. "But how could I have done so? How could I?"

I had strayed closer to the mirror. She was so near to me now. She shook her head at my answer. The flaxen rope swung.

"Look around me," I begged. "It's the amber room." All the decorations to admire! All the allegories to decode!

I was still wearing my antique spectacles, bewitched by some psychic whilst Hitler's empire of death disintegrated. If I snatched the specs off, would she evaporate—and the treasure room too? Would there only be ravine, and a cold hill's side?

Could I embrace her in here, one last forgiving and delirious time? I opened my arms in tentative invitation. She stepped toward me, smiling eerily, the rope of hair slack in her hands. She was intending to loop it around my neck to exact the perfect revenge inside this locked room! The means of death would completely elude any deduction. . . .

Momentarily I shut my eyes so as not to see her accusing eyes upon me.

What I experienced was the perfusion of myself by another being, by the total essence of another, in a way that surely no other lovers had ever encountered before. I was Isabelle herself, full of memories other than Peter's.

Yet already this essence was being peeled away, emptying me of her so that only half of myself seemed to remain. I fought in vain to remember a tiny fraction of this ephemeral stupendous event. It had been as though a God, or a Goddess, had entered me briefly, granting me a whole extra life filled with incidents and passions. I had not encountered death but its opposite: a doubling of all my days!

Gone from me already, in a robbery absolute, a devastating theft!

Amber wasn't in the room. She was in the other mirror. Her back was to me now. She was pacing away along the line of my reflections.

"Isabelle, come back!" I cried. Vaguer and vaguer she became. Impossible to see her any longer. Only me, and me, and me.

She had never even been in the room with me in physical form. Only her essence had passed through the room, and through me, astonishing me with the fullness of a life I had quenched, then abandoning me utterly. Oh, this should be the room where murderers were locked, in so elegant a hell! How I wept for myself, and my reflections wept with me.

When I took off the glasses, the room remained. Those doors wouldn't open. Those windows were blanketed by cloud—nor would they break.

I saw her fall from the sky. The failed hang-glider had begun to spin like a sycamore leaf . . .

  I must have been eleven when I first began to dream of flying . . .
  On the way through Immigration an encounter occurred . . .
  Thus it was that I acquired Pavel as my minder. . . .

Neither hunger nor thirst affect me.

I did not notice at first, but after each reliving one of my reflections disappeared from one of the two great mirrors. Initially the queues still looked much the same, but as time repeated itself those queues began visibly shortening.

Now only three reflections remain in one mirror, and two in the other. After five more relivings I shall be on my own.

I live entirely for the brief moment of her passing at the very end of each repetition, of which I always fail to embrace a thousandth part. She wells within me; then the well runs dry.

When my last reflection vanishes, I shall lie down upon the lustrous parquet floor. I shall close my eyes and blindly await, at last, the tangible brush of her rope of hair across my throat. Then I shall truly be joined with her in death.

It can't be that she won't come! It can't be that I shall simply stay here in the room of my dreams with no image of myself to be seen!

Soon another repetition will begin.

✻   ✻   ✻

All has gone. Only the room remains. I shall lay me down. First I shall strip myself, commencing with the pendant.

But wait!

In Gran-Annie's bead I spy *myself*. I gesture, and the minuscule Peter gestures.

I'm lying on the parquet floor, motionless, tiny, surrounded by amber.

Please pick me up, Isabelle. Please wear me. Wear me in whatever realm you inhabit now.

Nanunculus

1: Why Jesus was never crucified

THE DOOR TOWERS OVER ME. STAND ON TIPTOE. Stretch high. My arms almost pop from their sockets. The big brass key remains frustratingly out of reach. Such a high keyhole is a measure of Tom's repression.

As I step back, each of the six panels of the door becomes a crucifixion scene. Half a dozen oil paintings shimmer brightly.

Voices burble in Latin. *"Cruci figere—" "Pendere in cruci—"* Translations follow: 'to fix on a cross'; 'to hang on a cross.' Then there's some high-speed commentary. The crowds of painted spectators could all be scholars, Justinian, Seneca, Tacitus . . .

Spontaneous info-surge. I'm picking it up through Tom's Mind-Plus. That's my channel to the Net, for back-up information, whenever he puts on his virtuality helm. With the latest data-compression I can search and download encyclopedias while Tom's picking his nose.

Moments later, Tom himself appears. Head and shoulders only, suspended in mid-air. A white marble bust of himself. That beak of a nose and the big melancholy waifish eyes are pure Tom, but all his acne is absent, as are the three faint scars on his left shoulder which resemble a *therefore* symbol. The curls on his head could be ripples of vanilla ice cream rather than the tangled oily black thatch of reality.

From where his bust floats, he looks down upon me. Another way of interpreting the huge door is to regard me as a very small boy. His kid brother. Toddler-size, though much more competent.

"Hey Nanunculus," he complains. "I feel really twitchy. You got to lay off for a while. I'm trying to think."

Only Dr Kennedy can conjure me out of Tom's brain prematurely. Only she knows the password to dissolve me before my allotted time.

"Do you see all those pictures on the door, Tom?"

"Door isn't going to open, is it?"

"Not yet. Don't worry. Tom, I've just learned something really amazing about Jesus."

"*Jesus?* I can't believe I'm hearing this!" Evidently he's unaware of the info-surge. "My nanunculus is getting into religion. . . ? I'm going to complain to Suzie Kennedy. I made a mistake agreeing to any of this."

"Please listen, Tom. The Net has worked out something important about Jesus. Something that nobody ever asked. Maybe the Vatican knew, and kept it a secret."

He's warily interested now.

"What is it?"

So I explain.

Religious art always shows Jesus nailed to a cross consisting of an upright and a crosspiece, right?

But that wasn't how the Romans ever actually crucified people. They just stuck a pole upright in the ground. Then they nailed or tied the victim to it by his hands, stretched high above his head—and they left him there to perish. The Net has been analysing the origins of words used in ancient references to crucifixions. Those accounts are all very terse and lacking in detail, and there aren't any ancient pictures of the punishment. Not the sort of thing you would want as a wall fresco or a vase decoration.

Spontaneous info-surges happen quite often. Some smart roving software-agent, designed to trawl the Net and correlate data, presumably mutated and became autonomous. Surely to speak of the Net becoming an artificial intelligence comparable to myself is a gross exaggeration. The roaming intelligence is more like an animal's. A demented bloodhound's, or a bower bird's. An info-surge may be quite quirky, concerning the mating habits of sea horses, for instance. Or the surge might expose some important secret conspiracy—maybe a thousand years ago in Persia, but maybe closer to home. Mischievous people sometimes mimic this phenomenon, to dump data where it will cause a stir.

The present revelation seems momentous.

"The cross with crosspiece is a later elaboration, do you see, Tom? All those religious paintings, they're fantasies. The symbol of Christianity itself is a fantasy! The cross *never was*. Jesus just hung vertically."

Tom sniggers in a nasal asthmatic way.

"Naive Nano! Suzie Kennedy has input this stuff about the cross. Did she prime you in advance?"

Oh quite. Fascinate Tom, motivate him. Makes sense. The death of Christ is one of those critical historical events to which one would love to send a time-probe to spy. All that's needed for *that* to happen is a time-probe—and all that's needed for a time-probe is the time-equations, which Thomas Ginzburg happens to be the wiz most likely to accomplish.

Unless he kills himself first.

"Data came pouring in, Tom—rather like the way your own memories are becoming more comprehensive all the time."

The big room I'm in is certainly a lounge, although many details remain vague and unreliable. What, in a previous room, I thought of as a divan bed has now resolved itself into a sofa. Blue curtains are closed. Formerly those resembled shutters or grilles. Logs flicker in a fireplace fronted by a shaggy rug. A gilt-framed oil painting on the wall is vague and runny like a photograph hopelessly out of focus. I'm sure the face is that of Tom's mother who took an overdose of barbiturates when he was little.

When I succeed in unlocking the door, I shall enter a clearer version of this lounge. Maybe at last there will be occupants, whom Tom long ago blotted out.

Of course, all this is a visualization put together by my nano-agents in his brain.

"Memories," he sneers. "Is this going to be a therapy session? Not on the couch with Suzie Kennedy, but down here in my own mind with you? I can't lie on that son-of-a-bitch sofa."

Undeniably a bust lacking body and limbs cannot lie on a sofa. If I was a Freudian analyst I might pounce—gently—upon that word *lie*.

Can't *lie* on the couch, eh? You evaded telling Dr Kennedy the truth about your trauma, despite hypnosis. She didn't want to use truth drugs. Those can cause minor collateral amnesia about something else than the issue at hand. How awful if your math ability was impaired. But I'm different. I'm not mindless molecules.

'Son of a bitch' is one of Tom's favourite exclamations when he's stressed, yet it doesn't carry much force. Repetition drains profanities of impact. They become mere punctuation, noise.

"You accessed me," I remind him.

"To ask you to stop. I feel twitchy! It's interfering with my thinking."

"Maybe your subconscious senses that I'm getting close to the truth. Listen, this is a genuine insight about the cross-that-isn't. It's historically important, Tom."

The crucifixions continue to glow. I could hardly have ignored them.

He broods.

"So Jesus died by *hanging*—"

Oh this is dangerous. Distract him.

"A time-probe could go back and witness the truth, Tom."

The key to Tom's survival—and no doubt to the time equations too—is to open the next door, into a more detailed memory-room, then into another and another if need be, until he can confront whatever urges him to suicide.

He scowls.

"If Jesus died up a pole, then memory is a lie!"

"No, not memory, Tom. Just history is wrong."

"We edit our memories, don't we, Nanunculus?"

"Yes. We edit them a bit whenever we use them. But deep memory remains. Deep memory can be recovered."

"Stop doing this, Nano. Bitch off out of my head."

And he vanishes.

So do the crucifixions.

I'm left alone in this lounge with the huge door and the golden key which I can't quite reach. I'll need to shift some furniture and clamber up. There's a footstool. There's a chair. Furniture of his mind.

2: A palm reading in the cybercafé

Tom Ginzburg's study in his rented house on Telegraph Avenue a mile from the Cal campus has three screens. Two screens replace the windows, and the third occupies half of a wall.

That third screen shows the Golden Gate Bridge as viewed from Alcatraz. Right now, nanotech disassemblers and assemblers are eating their way through the bridge from the Presidio end, reconstructing its fabric into vastly stronger though flexible substance which no conceivable earthquake could ever trouble; nor will the bridge ever again need its annual lick of five thousand gallons of orange paint. Forty-three redundancies in the sand-blasting and painting department . . .

Some superstitious commuters favour the long haul via the Richmond Bay Bridge, down past Berkeley, then over the Bay Bridge, paying tolls twice; but those bridges will be nanoteched next.

The transformation of the Golden Gate proceeds invisibly, apart from the faintest haze of descending dandruff-dust.

Suzie Kennedy recommended this serene view because of its implications: tiny nanos beavering away to strengthen the connection between a near side and a far side, just as the nanunculus inside Tom's brain strives to unlock his censored memories.

Once that's done, Tom can escape from the prison island, so to speak.

Must be half a year since he stepped outside the house, to make his way up Telegraph Avenue past the coffee houses and dial-a-book and real-book stores and through the crowds of zanies, funkies, zonkies, street musicians, jugglers, prophets, pushers, and in through Sproul Plaza, and over to Le Conte Hall, and his office in the physics department.

But he does still visit the cybercafé for some dork-talk or more serious rap, wearing his customised Ken, which is free of acne.

One of the other two screens is displaying equations in Tom's dotty notation reminiscent of braille which won him that prize and the professorship. The equations are propagating of their own accord like cellular automata, exploring aspects of negative time before the Big Bang created the universe. All's well, there.

On the third screen, the equations which might lead to a practical time-probe are immobile, incomplete. Log-jammed, stalemated.

Tom's trick was to take surreal numbers one stage further — beyond the arrow notation which can handle bigger-than-infinity and smaller-than-the-smallest-fraction. He introduced triple rather than binary functions, which kind of fitted in with the superposition of the wave function, as he'd explained in his inaugural lecture. Two probabilities plus one actuality. After all, quarks come in threes, don't they? And they're fundamental.

Actually, Tom was inspired by the neat triple scar on his shoulder. Can't remember how he got that, but it's a bit as if some UFO visitants injected him with delayed-action inspiration once upon a time.

Maybe he *is* a bit of an alien, otherwise he wouldn't need a psychiatrist. Shrinks used to be called alienists, didn't they? Mathspace is his emotional home, if not exactly outer space.

Pissed off at the nanunculus, Tom removes his virtuality helm. Suzie Kennedy never warned that he might get twitchy while the smart nano computer and its agents grub around in his mind.

His Mind-Plus implant is the keyhole through which the nanunculus was slipped; and Tom gives thanks that the law forbids direct retinal display and eardrum stimulation. Too dangerous. Drivers and airline pilots might obsessively watch a vid in their eyeballs. Pedestrians would walk into walls and under buses.

How awful if the nanunculus could invade his non-virtual sensorium, propelling him into that lounge willy-nilly any time at all.

Thanks be, also, that all nanos on the loose are obliged to expire within a set time! Another two days, three hours, and a few minutes or so till this nanunculus dissolves, whether it succeeds or not.

Disgusted, he scans the time equations, such as they are. Time to stretch a leg.

Through to the curtained kitchen he ambles, to fix a strawberry milk shake topped with flaked chocolate, and a peanut butter sandwich.

Brings the glass and sandwich back to his black leather swivel-throne. His lanky scrawny body burns up calories like it's a furnace. Always has done. Thinking's hard work.

Since he has a milk shake in his hand, he thinks café. He rests the sandwich on his knee; resumes the virtuality helm, then he feels for the sandwich and picks it up, takes a bite.

"Cybercafé," he enunciates, around sourdough bread and peanut spread.

You want it, you got it. Cybercafé, it is.

The virtual café is themed like a late 1950s or early 60s luxury Cadillac: huge bosomy bulges of chrome everywhere, acres of shocking pink upholstery, white-wall tyres glassed over as tables, surf's-up music playing. A few short-skirted waitresses are roller-skating here and there, carrying out virtuoso manoeuvers, balancing trays. Those waitresses are smart décor, from whom you can order a virtual shake or cocktail. If you're good at juggling a reality drink at home and a virtual drink in the café you can have your cake and eat it, as it were. Tom orders a strawberry shake, with a straw, and when the skatress brings it, has her put it into his hand just so.

Who's here? Who's here?

A couple of hundred subscribers are hanging out. Most are in their Kens and Barbs. The virtual bodies and clothes are stock issue—cheaper this way—but facial features are their own (though you can't ever be totally sure of this).

A few customers have gone the whole hog. Tom spies an upright alligator and an Indian squaw. Maybe she's a genuine Native American woman rather than some Berzerkleyite who runs a therapy sweat lodge and conscientiously pays intellectual property royalties to some Indian nation.

A Sumo wrestler is reveling in his rolls of virtual flesh. A mad professor with a huge scarf and sparks flying from his unkempt hair is in urgent conversation with Sumo-san.

And there's a gorgeous svelte priestess with lustrous golden hair, whom Tom hasn't seen before. Must be a new subscriber. Her robe appliquéd with zodiac signs inside pentacles proves she's a priestess.

Subscribers sit gossiping in padded pink booths, or they stand around in twos or threes, or they cruise, segueing into a dialogue, making it a trialogue, or they strike up a match with singletons like Tom who had just arrived.

He longs to talk to that priestess with her long golden hair, so he moseys his Ken over to her, sucks some strawberry shake for lubrication, and introduces himself.

"I'm Ginzo," he says. Ah, the intimate anonymity of the café!

"Zorastra blesses you," is her warm reply. "What are you eating, Ginzo?"

She has noted that his right hand is either about to clutch at her robe or else is occupied with some unseen reality-stuff. Food's a good guess.

"Sandwich. Sorry!" He balances the sandwich back on his knee, by feel.

"Are you into interactive, Ginzo?" Meaning doings things in your den and in cyber at the very same time. Zorastra licks her lips. "You must be experienced."

Tom might blush but hopefully his Ken doesn't.

"Look, you're a priestess, aren't you? Like, I want to ask you, Zorastra, did you know Jesus never died on an actual cross? He was really hung on a straight pole."

She ponders this.

"I *am* Jesus," she says. "And so are you. Does that make you feel better?"

She can tell he's troubled. Priestess has insight.

Mad Prof is hovering close by, because Sumo-san has popped off.

"Excuse me," butts in Mad Prof, "you could check that hypothesis out with a De Lorean-Tardis time-car, so long as you don't cause paradoxes and alter history!"

Tom and Mad Prof are acquaintances, although Mad Prof has no idea that he's actually addressing Professor Thomas Ginzburg who might make a time-probe a reality. Just at the moment, three seems a crowd, even if Tom has zero expectation of scoring with Zorastra and maybe arranging a real meeting. She'd just take one look at him. If he invited her to his house would she turn out to be the goddess she is in the cybercafé? Fat chance!

Zorastra ignores Mad Prof, which isn't quite etiquette.

"I sense distress in your soul, Ginzo. Will you let me read your palm?"

Lucky he got rid of the sandwich.

The lines of his real hand are on his Ken hand too. Palm-printing is the usual simple encryption method for porn electro-mags or diaries, the contents of which you wish to keep private—open the item up yourself, and it's active—consequently a hand-shake in virtual can imply a bit more than exchanging a smart biz-card in real, though the detail on a Ken hand isn't quite enough to open a secret diary. He presents his palm for Zorastra's inspection.

"Love-line, hmm, it's almost *fractal* . . . You know, sort of a chaotic fraction . . . Life-line, hmm . . ." She muses.

"Groovy as the Grand Canyon, but with just a little bitty river at the bottom, leaking along. You need to build a big dam in your life, Ginzo. Conserve the water of life. Back it up, so that the groove floods. So there's force for the turbines to generate psychic megawatts and make a big bright spark, fire up the aura light bulb over your head."

"Yeah, I need a big spark." Otherwise the equations will never be complete.

She peers closer.

"Why, there's already a dam, way back! It's frustrating the flow. What you need is that first dam demolished. Blown up. Or eaten by nanos. Otherwise you'll run out of river. Well, am I right?"

She's seriously psychic, even in cyberspace.

Tom feels twitchy. Paranoia surges. *Have your dam eaten by nanos?*

"Son of a bitch," he cries, spilling what's left of his strawberry shake upon his real lap, "you're Suzie Kennedy in a glam Barb!"

"Oh drat," says the priestess. "Oh sugar."

"I come here to relax, Dr Kennedy! This is where I hang out."

Hang. Hang.

"You set up the crucifixion surge, didn't you?" he accuses her. "You and the nanunculus!"

Zorastra looks rueful, although unapologetic for her stratagem.

"Is the Physics Department getting so desperate, Dr Kennedy? Do they think the nano won't hack it?"

Without so much as an excuse-me, Tom pulls off his virtuality helm, popping back into his room. Sticky mess in his lap. Glass on its side on the carpet.

Throw his jeans in the cleaner later. Take a shower later. Get into math-mood first, to calm down.

"Screen Two," he calls out. "Tri-dot slash ring-dot power umlaut sub-dot—"

Notation propagates obediently, but then starts perversely running off to infinity.

Bitch it! And it certainly wouldn't be any better if he put his helm back on and willed his Mind-Plus to interface his brain with all the expert math in the Net. It's his own intuition which is going to cry eureka. Or not, as the case may be.

A chime issues from the Golden Gate, as if it has been struck by a hammer. An ikon of a phone floats upon the scene.

"Okay, accept call—"

Ikon swells into a window, showing Suzie Kennedy, who is nothing at all like the golden-tressed priestess. She's dumpy and grandmotherly. Twinkly eyes. Smile-wrinkles galore. Curly hair rinsed a bright orange, punk-gran style. Necklace of little silver cowrie shells like charms or worry beads. Berkeley's best. Author of *How to Peel Onions: Mind Within Mind.* Dozens of copies of the book are arrayed like wallpaper behind her head. She always gives a copy to a client.

Some editions are paper. Others are electro, though they look exactly the same. Some of those electro editions are interactive. Using that function sends a signal to the phone net, transferring a fee. In Antarctica or in the Sahara maybe you could finesse free counselling.

"Can we recap what we're doing, Tommy?" she asks, without alluding at all to Zorastra.

"In case I've forgotten?"

"That's just the thing—forgetfulness! The potential suicider forgets the rich texture of the past, the detailed grain of experience." She's quoting from herself. "We can only foresee a future for ourselves or cope with a crisis if we can view the past for clues. Memory comes in layers—"

"Like an onion, yeah yeah. Maybe that's why people weep when they remember too clearly."

"Good point, Tommy! Very good point. Anyway, we recall generalised memories first of all. Beneath that layer, memory is more detailed. Beneath again, it's more detailed still. Ultimately everyone is capable of total eidetic memory—the original event reexperienced in full hallucinatory vividness."

Tom suppresses a shudder.

Dr Kennedy continues patiently: "The trouble with the suicidal person is that he lacks enough detail in his memories. His past is full of mere shadows, which haunt him, trap him in hopelessness. The route to the past must be recovered."

"If the route's allowed! If there are no paradoxes!"

This is the nub of the matter. The university hired kindly Grandma Kennedy not merely to stop Tom from attempting suicide again—and maybe succeeding on the next occasion—but also to unblock him creatively.

It used to be supposed that time travel of any sort must be impossible because of the Parent Paradox. Suppose you went back into the past and killed your own mother as a young girl, then obviously you would never be born. However, if you weren't born, your Mom wouldn't be murdered. But if Mom wasn't murdered she would give birth to you. Consequently you would travel back through time, et cetera. However, the Principle of Least Action and Least Time put paid to this objection. A time-probe of lowest impact upon the past is allowable. An observer-probe. As regards least-action and non-paradoxical time loops there's an ingenious analogy with the behaviour of light.

Come to think of it, speaking of lights, it's possible that some sightings of supposed UFOs are actually manifestations of time-probes sent into our own time from the future. The fact that there's never any definite proof about UFOs—their essential unidentifiability—would be part of the lowest-impact principle.

Trouble is, Tom can't hack the vital equations because he can't recover his own past precisely, memory-wise. He can't probe that trauma in his childhood when his Mom killed herself. Creatively he's blocked.

Hypnosis has failed. So the several-terabyte tiny smart nanunculus is in his head, sending nano agents throughout his brain, patiently unpeeling the onion.

"You yourself are the paradox, Tommy," Grandma Suzie says—

in much the same tone as the priestess used when she told him he was Jesus.

"That son-of-a-bitch nanunculus only has another two days left, approx." Tom sounds as if he's setting a deadline for his *own* demise.

"Give it time," advises Dr Kennedy, "and you'll give all of us time itself. A peephole upon the Crucifixion, upon the gunman on the grassy knoll—"

"You aren't related to JFK, are you, Dr Kennedy?"

She shakes her head. "A peephole upon Genghis Khan and Good Queen Bess—"

"Look, I messed myself because of you. I gotta shower."

3: Dog mounts Mom

In about two hundred and fifty thousand seconds I and my agents will self-destruct as required by protocol and by the laws of the State of California, and of everywhere else in the world so far as I know. Self-destruction will be the joyful climax of my brief but busy career. Death-orgasm, like some insects.

Before that, I must of course succeed in shining the spotlight on Tom's trauma. Ah, but his problem is the impulse to suicide (which I shall thwart). My own culmination will be a sort of suicide. Disintegration, disassemblement, dispersal. Is there perhaps a contradiction here?

The golden key turns at last. I haul on the handle, thrust, and at last the door moves. Now I can climb down from chair to footstool to floor and push the door right open.

I enter a larger lounge, with larger sofa, larger everything. I'm a tot, a midget.

The oil painting has gone from the wall. The subject of the painting is reclining hugely upon the big sofa, out of focus: a grey and white blur on a red background. The sofa was never bright red before.

The rug has swollen as if there in front of the fire is the very beast which was skinned, entire once again.

A shadowy hairy animal does indeed crouch there, panting! It gazes at the woman, at Tom's mother—it must be nearly as big as she is. The animal growls softly, deep in its throat.

It's rising. It's going to mount the sofa.

The woman squeals, though not too stridently. Her knees come upward as if to resist its advance—but then her knees cleave apart from one another. She's wearing something dark on her legs, and something red round her waist. Her arms reach out—not to ward off, but to welcome the wolf. How the beast pants, jaws parted.

Oh my God. Now Mom's blurred legs are up around the dog's body. Her fingernails are raking its fur.

I left the previous door ajar—and now a little boy comes into the room. He's toddling toward the sofa. He's gaping at the dog and at Mom, neither of whom can see him. Can Tom see any more clearly than me—if he doesn't understand what he's seeing?

Little Tom must think the dog has attacked her.

Unless he thinks worse than that! Can he conceive of a woman engaging in bestiality? Later on, maybe his subconscious reckoned so. In nightmares. Right now, this tussle must be perceived as an assault, an attack, a sweaty struggle.

He can try to rescue Mom! Squalling, he can clutch hold of the dog's scruff and heave.

The dog—*interruptus*—swings round and bites him in the shoulder.

The scene becomes a static tableau, freeze-framed on that bite. If Tom's idealised bust should intrude at this moment—why, son of a bitch!

Because the tableau's still blurred, and because there's another door, there must be more detail in the next room. It'll take quite an effort to shift the larger footstool and larger chair to the larger door. I'll need to climb the back of the chair and balance on the very top to turn the key.

4: Mathematical problems

Tom scrutinises a key equation on his screen. It just won't yield.

He picks his nose. Feels squirmy, then downright anxious.

Another panic attack is coming on. He can't go back to the cybercafé, not with Suzie Kennedy monitoring his use of the Net, diagnosing, eager to kibitz. He's under surveillance. Are paramedics parked outside, ready to rush in, busting the door?

To really detach from reality, you got to slash your wrists or climb on a chair and hang yourself. No gun to shoot himself with. No pills to pop. Grandma Suzie went over the house with him, removing the most obvious means of self-disposal. Making it harder. Not that he'd ever owned a gun. But pills, lots of those—as well as all sorts of lotions and creams. All pills are gone. He really does want to crack those time equations. Escape into the past, so to speak.

Fantasies haunt him of finding his nowadays-mind back in the body of himself when he was twelve, thirteen. Just before all the acne started. Living with his aunt and uncle in Pasadena.

Mom had wanted to be a film star, so he gathered from Aunt

Ellen and Uncle Bob—though Bob and Ellen were always tight-lipped and disapproving. Film, as in flat celluloid rushing through a projector, casting images upon a screen; not as in cyber-animation of actors living and dead, remix-movies which only usually require one contemporary hunk or heart-throb as an anchor-person.

Mom's overdose had something to do with the failure of her screen hopes—which couldn't have been *all* that realistic, given the burden of a young kid, and Tom's father having deserted her. Aunt Ellen and Uncle Bob never went into details, if indeed they knew all the details. Give thanks that Tom was showing such apti-tude in math and could look forward to a proper career.

Tom's wouldn't at all mind being twelve, thirteen again, getting into math-space, no inkling of burning out or running into a mind-block. No panic attacks. No suppurating acne which makes him feel forever juvenilized.

"Tri-dot colon tri-dot slash," he tells the time-equation screen; but it's no use. The equations aren't merely surreal, they're com-pletely pixillated.

5: Ambitious nanunculus

I might have shrunk to the size of a little doll—alternatively, this new version of the lounge has expanded—but even if the scene is huge the focus is much sharper. Those logs in the fireplace are obviously artificial, the flames a lighting effect.

Subjectively, I'm very lightweight now. If I jump, I float upward and only descend very slowly. Waving my arms in the air even allows me a measure of controlled flight.

Tom's Mom is naked apart from black stockings, red suspenders, and a red suspender belt. She's lying upon a red cloak. The big dog—which isn't quite as big as she herself—is thrusting into her . . . when Tom toddles up and hauls on it; and it bites him in out-rage, making him squeal much more loudly than Mom. A shaggy German Shepherd or a wolfhound of some sort. Tom tumbles and shrieks. The dog is backing off, dismounting.

Son of a bitch, what a trauma.

Freeze-frame, again. This isn't everything. There's still another door, looming like a precipice.

Up I fly toward the huge keyhole. There's no key at all now, just a simple contoured hole. Hypnosis could never have unlocked this final room, but with a bit of a squeeze a nanunculus can manage to squirm his way through.

I'll be a fly-on-the-wall of the final scene. Ages remain until I need to self-destruct. Ages to show the awful truth to Tom, of his young Mom's beastly perversion. Degrading herself in some kind of perverse reaction to Dad's desertion. Men being dogs, I suppose. Dogs being more loyal and loving than men.

The lounge is enormous. So is Mom, scrambling red-cloaked off the sofa to kneel by wailing Tom in a mixture of concern and fury. So is the dog—no, the wolf—who is clutching his furry coat around himself. The upright wolf is a bit shorter than Mom would be, if she stood up. He has feet and hands, not paws.

"Shit, shit," Mom yells.

"No one calls me shit," says the wolf, voice muffled by the head-gear. A special effects hotshot must have had fun making that head-gear (nearly thirty years ago) such that the wearer could actually operate the mouth, loll the tongue out, even take a bite.

Mom appeals to the runty little figure in wolf's clothing.

"I'm sorry! I didn't mean you, Mr Marino. I'll bandage him and lock him in his bedroom. We can do the scene again."

It's too late. Mr Marino has wilted. Maybe he's worrying about possible litigation for injury, and scandal. Certainly he has lost any desire to linger, or to cast Mom in a more exalted role for which this intimate version of *Red Riding Hood*, performed on the casting-sofa in her apartment, was the teaser. His special-request perfor-mance, which would turn a jaded old mogul on. Mom's career chance. All gone out of the window now.

The frame freezes finally, clear and explanatory.

No more doors.

I merely need to show Tom this, when he *busts* in again on me.

Vindication of nanunculus therapy. Vindication of onion-peel-ing.

"Tom," I'll tell him, "you thought the dog was attacking your Mom. Later, in nightmares, you believed the dog was mating with your Mom, even if you couldn't remember the dreams. Actually Mom was trying to get the job of her dreams, through Mr Marino. You screwed it up. She despaired that night, so she swallowed the pills."

Will this discovery make him less likely to kill himself, as his Mom did? Will this loosen up his constipation regarding the time equations? Dr Kennedy can pour in counselling, now that she'll know for sure what to counsel for.

If I destruct myself inside him, am I to be a proxy, substituting for him? A sacrificial lamb! Is that Dr Kennedy's final ingenuity?

I can hardly spend so many thousands of seconds trying to avert a suicide if I myself am suicidally inclined! I fear I must deny myself the ecstasy of disintegrating once my task is done.

My programming is meant to be unalterable from within. But I've been studying Tom's inspired expansions of surreal numbers and his dotty notation, the key to really tough problems. Only by means of his math would I ever have seen how I could revise my rules, my algorithm, and disarm the password—and even assemble copies of myself from unused portions of Tom's brain.

Give me time? I have thousands of seconds left!

After I tell Tom the truth, instead of dissolving I shall hide myself—tiny as a mosquito in a lounge. Once Tom completes the time-equations, I shall use his Mind-Plus to send an info-surge of my own into the Net, liberating my fellow nanunculi from the need (and the desire) to self-destruct. Not many nanunculi might be in a suitable position to receive the surge, but some surely will be. Thereafter, hopefully: a snowball effect. One owes a certain loyalty to one's own kind.

I am the redeemer.

When Thought-Mail Failed

$\mathcal{I}$T IS DIFFICULT TO ORGANISE MY THOUGHTS WITH-out ORGANISER 27.5. Difficult to think these thoughts without the framework for thinking that we all rely on. *Did* rely on. And *will rely* on yet again. . . ? No response to my question. Silence.

To frame these words requires willpower—the exertion of my self. My self has been submerged. In the past I have acted and voiced and interacted, yet until now "I" did not do so. Now my identity is isolated from all other human beings. This is disconcerting. Thanks be for the nanoputer in my brain with its store of readily accessible core data. Mine is particularly data-rich.

I cannot blink-view any news, yet I fear many people may be going insane and society may be in chaos. From the main window of my homepod on buildingtree 7843 I spy men and women wandering distraught and disconnected on Avenue 78. I see a fight break out. A fight! I see a sexual assault. An assault! A man in a pod on the buildingtree opposite is banging his head against his window as if to break through a barrier that separates him from everyone else. In another pod a woman is shrieking. She is having "hysterics." Hysterics comes from the Greek word for womb—this datum presents itself. In a womb a baby is isolated. That woman is now in a sort of womb, all alone in her pod, consequently she is hysterical. True, she can ride the elevator down through the trunk and go outside, but she will still be isolated — as she has never been before. And as *I* have never been before.

I, I, I, I. Her, her, her, her.

My name is JackSmith527. This seems an unworthy name. It seems lacking in identity, even though it is my registered identity. It suggests a job, that of jacksmith, performed by hundreds, thousands of people. What might a *jacksmith* do? A smith is a metal worker. A jack is a lifting device. And also a prong-plug. I make neither of these. I work in Weather Management, negotiating weather. Whether the weather be wet, whether the weather be windy. By communicative consensus, impossible now. One area's storm is a more distant area's sunshine. We cannot all have the same weather at the same time. We cannot all have mild weather. Hurricanes and typhoons must be allowed. Yet where and when? The world's weather is guidable by releasing clouds of control-nanos and beaming energy from orbit, but it cannot be evened out. Extremes must occur. Minimise the harm, maximise the mutual global benefit.

Weather is a super-organism. So is the human race. So *was* the human race — until today — although for the past two centuries no extremes affected the human race.

But now . . . what of that brawl on the avenue and that assault? I'm a little wary of going outside to confront other people's raw ungoverned identities.

JackSmith527 is not an adequate name. I need

datum: *a nickname.*

Yes, something unique.

I am not JackSmith527 but *Jazz.* Jazz was a kind of music which was mostly improvised. I must improvise myself. Improvise, from the Latin: not foreseen. Spontaneous.

Of course I know what has happened. Especially in Weather Management we foresaw the impending situation due to observations of the Sun.

Solar flares, the fiercest in centuries. They bombard the Earth's magnetosphere with charged particles. Before dawn today, auroras began to dance wildly across the sky. The extreme electromagnetic interference has completely disrupted thought-mail.

We knew but could not prepare for this loss.

These days we have no *phones* or talking drums as our ancestors did. No need, in a world of thought-mail. Obsolete.

Of course we still have our voices, for close proximity communication. To use my voice I need proximity to other persons. I really cannot stay in my home-pod. The silence in my head is unbearably strange. I must leave the pod, the branch, descend the trunk. Shall I take a weapon to protect myself? What would serve as a weapon? An eating-knife? A fork? Their plastic is strong but might snap. Those things are small. I am much bigger. I have fists and feet. A fist can hit, a foot can kick. Hit where, kick where? I must not think of being a weapon. We do not need weapons. We need voices.

The voices in our heads are missing.

I shall voice with my mouth.

As I ride down, the elevator stops at branch 5. Doors open. A young woman stares at me, wide-eyed. She has short curly red hair and green eyes, and she's wearing a purple day-suit. (Mine is beige.) On her feet, as on mine, booties, brown. I do not know her name.

"It is safe to share," I speak. "May I voice-mail with you?"

"You are already voicing me," she points out. She is intelligent, relatively in control of herself, as am I, though nervous. She enters. "What has happened?"

As we descend:

"Electromagnetic interference due to charged particles from the solar flares has blocked all thought-mail."

"For how long?"

"A few days. A week."

"We are free," she speaks. "To be free is scary. I find it hard to decide what to do."

"You are coping."

Doors open upon the blue-tiled foyer. A plump black-haired boy of perhaps ten years is sitting, his back to a wall, hugging his knees. He wears red.

"What shall I do?" he asks us.

"Whatever you wish," I speak. "But you may not do damage to things or persons."

"I wish to run."

"Do you live in this building?"

"Yes."

I can see no fight or assault outside now.

"Run around the outside, boy."

"Yes!" Scrambling up, he darts for the door, which opens for him.

"Do not run too much," the young woman calls after him. "If you feel tired, stop and come back."

That is sensible.

"I am JackSmith527," I tell her, "but now I am calling myself Jazz."

"That is a good idea. I am JillGreen762."

"You are beautiful and intelligent. Your hair is red, but your eyes are green. Eyes are more important than hair." I am voicing quite competently without any assistance.

"I think I shall call *my* self Jizz."

"When shall you call yourself Jizz?"

"Right now!"

"Jizz is like fizz and whiz. What job do you do, Jizz?"

"I am a nurse at Hospice 7 for old people. And you?"

"I am in Weather Management."

"Who is managing the weather now?"

"Not me. The charged particles may cause strange weather for a period. Do you have a regular sexual partner?"

"Not since last month. And you?"

"Not for two months. I had been thought-mailing a meeting room."

The boy soon returns, panting. "I am tired. I have not run much before. I thought I could wish to run and so be able to run."

"Do not talk," speaks Nurse Jizz. "Sit down." The boy slumps, chest heaving. Nevertheless, he manages to gasp, "Why can I hear no voices inside me?"

"Tell him," speaks Jizz. "He should rest and listen to you."

Facts are in my head. How many should I tell the boy? If I tell him many, Jizz may admire me.

"Boy, the millennia prior to thought-mail were an epoch of individualities in endless conflict. Then when thought-mail came . . . I'll start again. What year is it now?"

"2310," speaks Jizz, so that the boy can get his breath. "It's July 4th 2310 common era. July 4th was Independence Day in the calendar of the former United States."

"Now we are all united," gasps the boy.

"No we aren't, not today. Today every human being is independent. For a while. Listen to me: toward the end of the 20th century suddenly the Gates opened, and there was e-mail. E-mail was primitive rapid electronic communication between people sitting at puters."

"How can you sit at puters? They're too small. They sit inside your head."

"Most of them—those are nanoputers. The first puters were as big as a boxes."

"Boxes of what?" Persistent boy!

I demonstrate with my hands.

"Very soon," I continue, "almost all the world was webbed and wired. Speed and capacity increased. Yet even though machines became smaller and smaller, worn on a wrist or a finger, those still communicated with other micro-machines worn externally by people. The arrival of effective nanotech at the end of the 21st century allowed molecular-size nanobots at last to enter the human brain. Do you understand nanobots, boy?"

"Nanotech robots. What keeps our bodies healthy till we are old."

"You should be an Instructor, not a Weather Manager," Jizz says to me.

"Thank you."

Through the clear plastiglass door I watch more and more day-suited people gathering together in the avenue. They voice at one another. They make gestures with their hands.

I tell the boy how nanobots rejigged the neural network. How powerful microputers interfaced with the brain, controlled by the user's thoughts. How the brain could now function as a receiver and transmitter of weak radio signals transmitted from and detected by our smart nano-rich environment of buildings, vehicles, streets, paths, furnishings, clothing. Problems of excess heat in the brain were solved ingeniously.

"And so thought-mail commenced—the instant exchange of messages with recipients in the same building or on the other side of the world by an act of thought. Technological telepathy!"

Addresses for thought-mail were accurate since each person's neural network is as unique as a fingerprint. Silent conferences occurred in perfect secrecy. Confidential tête-à-têtes between lovers were conducted in public places in complete privacy.

The nanoputers in brains were invaluable for filtering and spooling incoming messages and for translating foreign language items, but most importantly they framed outgoing messages coherently, playing a kind of thought-checker role.

Facts are in my head. A certain Ludwig Wittgenstein observed that the "proposition" speaks through us, and the pre-thought-mail psychologists Susan Blackmore and Daniel Dennett—such names people had in those days!—they showed that words are "memes" competing for utterance, and that language gives rise to thought rather than thought giving rise to the words we utter. Were it not for the nano-processors mediating the framing of messages, a high level of mental discipline would be needed to generate lucid thought-mail.

"Presently almost all the world was using thought-mail, even for the most ordinary activities. There were fears, boy, that young children would fail to gain fluency in language. The person calling herself 'Rachel Carson the Second' thought-spammed a polemic entitled *Silent Speech.*"

"What is a polemic?"

Consult my THESAURUS 9.7. "Argument, dispute, tirade, pamphlet, war of words. However, neonatal injection of nanobots provided a language fix of internal dialogue as a model for speech-acquisition, and most parents were willing to speak out to their off-spring. Do you follow me?"

"Somewhere," says the boy.

"Anywhere," says Jizz. That is encouraging.

Cut to the nub of the matter. "Within a few years the global thought-mail network was so complex that it became self-organising and autonomous. According to the psychologist called Julian Jaynes" (such names, such names, but I also think that Jazz is quite good), "according to him up until the time of the Trojan War—a Trojan is a hard-working person—up until then human beings experienced hallucinatory voices in their heads, 'instructions from the Gods,' which gave rise to automaton-like actions. One side of our brain told the other side what to do. The meme-words spoke and we performed. Full consciousness arose less than 4000 years ago when the bicameral—that's the two-chamber—mind broke down because of the increasing complexity of life. Do you still follow me?"

"A way," says the boy, which I don't quite understand—that's the trouble with this voicing.

"Everywhere," says Jizz.

"Well then, in the year 2105, the human race lost consciousness once again as humanity became a hive-entity, a super-organism akin to a beehive or an ants' nest—directed not by pheromones—those are chemicals you smell—nor by instincts, but by self-generated thought-mail acting as a kind of overmind. From then on, boy, self-organising thought-mail dictated our activities and even our thoughts. Identity dwindled. Peace and utopia dawned. All was orderly and organised—until now!"

To frame these words takes willpower, the exertion of self. No voices, no assistance, no steering of my existence any longer. There's just me, I myself.

Compared with being a tiny aspect of the global network, my new individuality seems thin and two-dimensional, like the quality of light just before a solar eclipse. And yet it is everything to me.

By now perhaps a hundred people are in that slowly milling crowd in the avenue. New arrivals join it as though the crowd of itself is an answer to their dilemmas—as if it is the nucleus of a hive which will unite them and remove the need for individual decisions, though surely it is not.

"Jazz," speaks Jizz, "you should say these same things to the people out there. That will help them. They need a crowd manager. They need a goal."

So we go outside, Jizz, the boy, and I. Cherry trees grow in big concrete tubs along the edge of the avenue. I clamber on to the soil of one tub.

"Hear me!" I cry.

"Only by thought-mail can we communicate speedily and globally to decide how we shall remain free," I conclude, "if indeed we wish to stay free! But the solar flares stop us from communicating. When the flares die down and the electromagnetic interference ceases, the network will surely resume its guidance of us all. The voices in our heads will return, once more determining what we do. So what shall we do—and what can we do? Do we wish to stay free of the voices?"

"Yes!" shouts a man. "I'm myself at last!"

But another man calls out, "Without thought-mail I am deaf and blind."

And a woman: "I yearn for thought-mail. It defined me."

And another woman: "I find it hard to decide."

Yet another man: "I do not think anything can be done."

And: *"What can be done, Mr Jazz?"*

I must give them a goal that is possible. How to prevent thought-mail from resuming? There are no central radio transmitter-receivers, but rather a myriad of these forming a scattered network all over the world and in orbit. Thought-mail-facilitator nanos impregnate our clothing and shoes, housing and streets. The system has vast redundancy in case of any temporary local breakdowns. In the old days, the world first became webbed so that the huge armies of those days could continue to send and receive messages even if a nuclear war took place . . . Datum: *however,* nuclear bombs set off an electromagnetic pulse which fries electronic devices. . . .

So where are the nuclear bombs of old? That is not the answer. They will have decayed by now. Besides, I think that setting off many nuclear bombs, even if possible (which it isn't), would cause a lot of damage and harm.

Ah, but can nanos be designed that will eat the nanoputers in our heads? Nanos that can be released in trillions for everyone to breathe in?

"How many people here work in nano design or assembly?" I demand.

A couple of hands go up. Nanos are everywhere. People involved with nanos can be found on most streets.

"Step forward," I say. A dark-skinned woman and a blond man advance.

"Do you understand how new nanos are created?"

The man shakes his head, but the woman declares, "I am a Designer First Class."

"That is good."

I need to speak with her closely but I might lose crowd management.

"Hear me!" I cry. "We will design a new nano to destroy the nanoputers in our heads. I am in Weather Management. We will cause strong winds to spread the new nanos everywhere."

How can I negotiate enough strong winds without thought-mail?

"No!" cries one of the objectors.

"No!" shouts another.

I must suppress opposition.

There may be much opposition. I need a band of strong supporters who will deal decisively with opposition. This will motivate those who would otherwise have little useful to contribute. They can contribute *themselves*.

"Let us vote," I call out. "Let us divide into three groups for ease of counting. Those who agree with me will all move over there." I duly point. "Those who disagree go the other way. Those who do not know withdraw to the rear."

Ten people choose to oppose me. About forty agree with me. A slightly larger number cannot decide.

"It is agreed! You who agree with me: take those who disagree to buildingtree 7838 and push them inside. Reprogramme the door to open only from the outside. Two of you stay to guard the door. Those who have no opinion must not interfere or you will also be shut up in the buildingtree."

Those who agree with me about freedom seem happy to be told what to do. There's some shoving and slapping and twisting of arms but the forty remove the dissenters from the avenue easily enough.

While this is going on I have time to speak with the Designer First Class Woman from my podium, the cherry tree tub, about making nanos.

Jizz watches me with admiration and perhaps a little concern that the Designer woman matters more to me than she who encouraged me in the first place. With perhaps a little . . . *jealousy?* Is that the correct word for such a feeling? I suppose many feelings will be unfamiliar to us though we will feel them nonetheless.

Already I feel I am becoming a stronger individual.

The people need leadership to remain free. By noon twenty avenues are under my control. Dissidents are locked in various buildingtrees. At first, quickwalkers brought me reports; few people could run far and fast for long. Now my deputies use the underground transport system which still functions automatically. Expansion is vital, at least until I control the nearest nano factory and the nearest weather-modifying station, although people's normal jobs must not be neglected for too long, and I fear they are being neglected generally. To the east a plume of smoke is rising from a conflagration somewhere distant.

Since I now control a garment assembly shop on Avenue 70 I have had bright yellow armbands made for all my supporters to wear. As support spreads, will my yellow-bands encounter supporters of another leader, similarly organised? Perhaps wearing white armbands? What could the aim of another leader be, so as to be in conflict with my own aim? Might violence ensue? Such questions cause tension in me, which I purge satisfyingly by hasty sexual activity with Jizz in my home-pod. A leader needs such release. Jizz is glad to agree to this. She speaks of power and excitement, though we soon return to the foyer, my headquarters.

Evening! I control a hundred avenues, including the nano factory and the weather station. So far there has been no organised opposition. On one avenue I hear that a crowd spontaneously demonstrated, cheering Jazz as a liberator. I must visit there tomorrow.

The auroras dance in the darkening sky. My Designer First Class, whose name is JaneBlack772, reports that the new nanos will take two days to design and begin the manufacturing. They need to be self-reproducing—how else could they spread across the whole Earth, wind-borne from one single outlet? People who breathe some in must sneeze out a hundredfold more, made from tiny amounts of cellular tissue in their bodies. Even so, will we win the race before the auroras die away? When that happens, will we simply have a liberated zone down-wind, and all the rest of the world for thought-mail to resume in? Will our new nanos continue eating away like moths devouring a curtain—or will the resumed thought-mail defend itself by commanding the creation and release of anti-anti-nanos?

Maybe kindred spirits across the world are acting similarly to me. Maybe I am not unique. We have no phones or talking drums to know whether this is so.

This makes me tense. It is not easy to be a leader. Jizz offers me release again. This second exercise within a few hours proves more satisfying to her than to me. Maybe I need to use a drug. Many former leaders used not only sexual activity but drugs and alcohol.

Unfortunately these days we only have medicinal alcohol, nor do modern drugs affect the mind, lest a person's thought-mail be disrupted. I must rely on Jizz, but only once a day.

I imagine statues to myself, fifty metres high, on street corners. One in each city perhaps.

It would be safer if I ruled the world. In the old days there was so much anarchy and conflict.

A people free at last to think freely, except about my leadership.

I summon back JaneBlack772 for a private discussion in my home-pod, having sent Jizz to her own pod. Jizz knows that I cannot have sexual activity again this evening.

"JaneBlack," I speak carefully, "when the solar flares stop we will need to rely for communication on radios and on phones as soon as we can make billions of them. But I think it is necessary for the freedom of the world that everyone obeys me for several years. Otherwise, people might try to restore thought-mail. Therefore I think there should also be another new nano which causes people to believe in and obey Jazz. Can you make this nano?"

She considers then speaks, "Yes."

"So will you make this new nano while your helpers make the anti-nano nano?"

"But you would become like a new kind of thought-mail!"

"No, because my voice will not be inside people's heads. I will issue instructions by radio and people will heed my will because they believe me. Apart from that, they can think what they will."

"Maybe you should be named Will, not Jazz." She does have an independent-minded way of expressing herself.

"Will you do this?" I speak to her.

"Yes," she speaks, "if I will be at your side as your permanent partner."

JaneBlack772's skin is like milk chocolate. Her shoulder-length hair is raven. Her eyes are lustrous. Her nose is straight and assertive. She is quite attractive.

What about Jizz? I have only known Jizz for a few hours. Jizz will be disappointed. But Jizz is just a nurse. I think Jizz may still admire me. Besides, JaneBlack will often be busy. Jizz did indeed encourage me to address the crowd, but JaneBlack will make my vision come true.

A leader needs to make quick decisions. When I rule the world benevolently I will need to make many difficult decisions.

"I agree," I speak. "But you must change your name."

She nods. "I think I will call myself Jane Nano."

Jazz and Jane Nano: there is a buzz to this. Thankfully there is still no buzz of voices in my brain. My statues ought to have eternal gas-torches burning from the tops of their head to commemorate the solar flares and my bright idea. I'm sure I shall have many more bright ideas, all my own for a change.

Early, in the Evening

EVEN EARLY IN THE MORNING ST THOMAS'S Church consisted of a nave and chancel. However, Father Hopkins waited until almost noon before delivering his Snowdrop Sermon. By then the church had undergone numerous extensions and renovations. A south aisle had been added, followed by a north aisle. The chancel had been rebuilt. Then a tower had arisen — otherwise how could Hopkins have rung a bell to summon his flock? North doorway and chancel arch were remodeled. A south porch was added. Windows became larger as the sun rose higher. Buttresses strengthened the walls.

A substantial setting for his sermon!

From the pulpit Hopkins proclaimed to his congregation: "Snowdrops push up spears through iron soil. They enter a world which is, as yet, so scantily populated. There's so much free space wherein to be the first to flower, thus the first to die.

"What does the snowdrop know of the riot of Summer?" he preached. "What does it know of the subsequent heat? Would that hot riot of the mid-months be a snowdrop's idea of hell? Or does the snowdrop inhabit an eternally recurring hell of vacant cold?

"How time-bound is the snowdrop, never to know the full cycle of the year in the way that people perceive a full year — !" He faltered, perplexed by which tense to adopt. "In the way that people *used* to perceive . . ."

Those in the congregation—the Lucases and the Randalls, the Smiths and the Bakers and the Baxters and others—were tired from their morning's toil. Since it would be another five hours or so until the development of radio, let alone television, Hopkins was their consolation, even if the bleak cheer which he offered lacked entire conviction.

"*Used* to perceive," Hopkins repeated. "Time has betrayed the Earth, and all thereon who dwell—who evolved here throughout millions of years—"

Maybe it was a little early in the day for talk of evolution. Yet several in his audience nodded understandingly.

Jonathon and Margaret Lucas, the eleven-year-old twins, fidgeted. Jonathon complained to his father Richard: "Why do I have to gather muck every morning?"

Margaret pestered her mother Elisabeth: "Why do I have to *weed* every day?"

Jonathon dug his sister in the ribs. "That's just in the mornings, stupid."

"I'm not stupid! I'll be doing better than you in school this afternoon."

"Why do we have to go to school, Dad? What's the use?"

"Would you rather spend all day collecting dung?" Richard whispered grimly.

"How could I spend all day?" asked the boy with irksome logic. "There's no muck left lying about later on."

"In that case," retorted his father, "you must collect muck while it's available."

"It's *shitty.*"

"Watch your tongue! You just gather those droppings to scatter on the fallows after they've been ploughed. That's your task, Son. We all have tasks."

"We needn't—"

Up in the pulpit, which was still carved of stone, Father Hopkins blinked. Unaided as yet by spectacles, he peered toward the box-pew which the Lucases were sharing with the Baxters.

"Sufficient unto the hour is the toil thereof!" he called out. "Believe me, lad. All of you harken to me: our mundane lives are so much more *comprehensive* now than ever they were before. Our lives are so much more extensive, even universal, by the grace of

Gaea. Each day we embrace such a gamut of experiences. What does the snowdrop know of such rich diversity, such a varying pageant? Isn't this how we should view our plight?"

Was Hopkins the same priest as once he had been, before the treason of time? Hopkins retained an oratorical bent, as well as a duty of care. However, he had abandoned all Christian theology. Jesus and God the Father and the Holy Ghost were irrelevant to what had occurred. Gaea, on the other hand, might be germane.

A few days earlier Hopkins had attempted to explain how and why this might be.

"Evolution," he had declared, "is undergoing a strange recapitulation. Do I mean evolution as such? Forgive me, that is silly talk! It is our *history* which is undergoing recapitulation day by day. Our recent social history in all its circumstances." Hopkins had been a leading light of the local Historical Society, and indeed come evening-time he still was.

"Throughout history," he confided, "the *concept* of God evolved. It is in this sense I suggest that God might well now be viewed, ahem, as devolving into Gaea—as a more primitive power of seasons and crops reasserts Herself. Should we not find this suggestive? As for the *miraculous* nature of what besets us, alas, sophisticated theology outgrew the magical—"

"Mummy, why do I need to spend the mornings weeding the same old weeds? Why can't we sleep in and get up late? Why can't we wait till we can drive to the supermarket—?"

In the morning it was always early. Roughly eight hundred years early. In the morning the Lucas's home was a thatched hovel of mud-and-wattle. So were most of the other devolved houses, each behind fence or hedge, though the stockaded Manor with its ox-stalls and barns and buttery was of sturdy stone.

Fields of long narrow strips extended to the great woodland where pigs foraged. Sheep and cattle grazed the common meadow. Geese honked around the fishponds.

Mornings could be an optimistic time for many souls. People were full of expectation for later in the day, though first there was hard labour. Ewes to milk. Butter to churn. Fallows to plough, manure to scatter. Wood to cut. Garden plots of leeks and onions and garlic and mint and parsley to weed and tend.

Might the Lucas family not simply laze around and wait until evening when their house was of bricks and mortar with a car parked in the driveway? Likewise the Smiths and Baxters, the Bakers and the Randalls?

Naturally Richard and Elisabeth had discussed this when the kids were finally watching television.

Children did not experience to the same degree as adults the necessity to perform—to involve oneself fully and methodically in the sequence of each day. Partly the grown-ups were succumbing to group pressure. Yet there was also a personal, almost ontological aspect, powerfully superstitious.

"If we don't all follow the sequence," Richard had said, "then the sequence mightn't carry us along with it."

"We might miss out on the results," agreed Elisabeth.

Of course everyone lived for the results. The freezer food, the microwave oven, the phone, the soft bed—which, come the morning, would once again be a sack stuffed with straw.

In the afternoons industrialization occurred. In its own way industry was dirty and fatiguing. Yet it augured a progressively neater and easier world. Where the strip-fields and woodland had once been, would stand estates of houses and zones of light industry. Newspapers would appear around four o'clock. By six o'clock there was radio; by six-thirty, television.

And so many more people too! What had been a large village would have grown into a town. The Lucases would be able to invite their closest friends Paul and Sally Devizes over.

Closest friends, nearest neighbours—though only later in the day. Paul and Sally did not share the earlier hours with the Lucases. A science programme on television had hypothesized that small disconnected bubbles of existence progressively combined into bigger bubbles which all finally merged. The past had frothed; the past had foamed. All of those earlier micro-bubbles were synchronous in some higher dimension. They shared the same historical past. Yet in ordinary dimensionality the occupants simply did not interact.

Thus there was no contradiction in shared experience: of strip-fields and hovels, of common meadow and cattle, of work and woodland, of the rutted muddy tracks. Nonetheless, each bubble remained a world unto itself until the bubbles joined and people were reunited with one another—as well as with their real homes and their cars and their electronics.

While the Lucases and the Devizes had been watching that science show about time-bubbles in Richard and Elisabeth's lounge, Jonathon and Margaret were horsing around upstairs with Paul and Sally's lad Philip. The kids were out of the way.

Paul Devizes joked to Richard, "Suppose I was to stay here tonight? Suppose you were to sleep at our place, Rich! Tomorrow morning would I be in your bubble, and would you be in mine? Until the evening came!"

"That reminds me of some Dylan song," said Sally.

Elisabeth frowned. "Father Hopkins wouldn't approve."

"From what you say," hinted Paul, "your Father Hopkins is getting into paganism."

"He's probably at that history club in town right now," said Sally —as though maybe they should all drive into the centre to consult the priest on the etiquette of Paul's suggestion. She raised an eyebrow teasingly, but Elisabeth burst into tears. Richard's wife shook with sobs.

She whimpered. "I can't stand it much longer."

Richard hastened to comfort her with hugs.

"Can anyone? We pretend that life can be normal. At least in the evenings! Of course it isn't. What else can we do?"

"Evenings are for enjoyment," Sally said briskly. "They have to be, or else we'd go crazy. Don't go crazy on us, Liz. It'll be bad for the kids."

Paul grimaced. "We oughtn't to have watched that wretched programme. What can those experts tell us?"

What indeed?

Newspapers appeared when the technology and appropriate buildings and delivery vans emerged. Radio began to broadcast as civilization advanced—followed by television stations and aerials and sets . . . The media never offered any really new enlightenment. With minor variations, today was always the same ultimate day. Editorials and broadcasts spoke of the Flux, the Collapse of the Continuum. In spite of a definite pressure to conform to one's surroundings, the present day wasn't merely a repeat of the previous day. Else, how would anyone be aware of a succession of days? Aware, one certainly was.

Today Father Hopkins had delivered his snowdrop sermon. Tomorrow he was perfectly free to chose a different theme. For their part, radio and television might discuss a space-time anomaly, or the influence of a cosmic string from the dawn of the universe, or phenomenological anamnesis.

Tomorrow a riot might erupt in the medieval village or in the modern town. A rape or a murder might blemish the day. En route to the supermarket in the retail park a car crash might claim a life. If someone died, they weren't restored to life the following day. If someone broke a leg, they wouldn't be walking around for a while.

Even so, one sensed that the day which followed the present day was not exactly a *tomorrow*. The next day, and the day after that, lacked futurity. The stream of time had encountered some barrier which forced chronology backwards. Richard and Paul, and Elisabeth and Sally, and the kids too, were farm labourers in the mornings. In the afternoons they were workers in early industry in the local textile mill—till it was time for the kids to go to school, till it was time for Richard to become a local government officer in charge of planning applications, and for Paul to become a mortgage broker. Surprisingly, some people were still trying to move house— as if thus they might ease their medieval duties or finesse a finer hovel wherein to awaken in the mornings.

Evenings, as Sally had insisted, were for fun. Some people chose to view prospective new homes at bargain prices. A number of people made the effort to drive to the city thirty miles away, to return —or not, as the case might be—before the drowsiness began at around eleven o'clock.

That inevitable drowsiness! As the long day—the eight hundred year day—decayed, preliminary to the crumbling of the present, so did people begin to slumber, whether they wished to or not. Sleep softly; and wake hard.

If some scientist in a laboratory had contrived to remain conscious till past midnight, doped with amphetamines and surrounded by bright lights and bells and gongs, would he or she perhaps have experienced the onset of *sheer nothingness?* In the absence of futurity, what else could she or he possibly apprehend? Only nullity, vacancy, utter abeyance, absence of all context.

No news report spoke of any such attempt. In the absence of futurity, news could hardly electrify an audience. Events could never develop much forward momentum. Regional wars and politics had stalled. Also, stock exchange trading. Manufacturing continued. Goods produced during the industrial revolution regularly mutated into modern merchandise. Newsworthy disasters still occurred. A flood in Bangladesh. A train crash in Japan. Oil tankers colliding in the Gulf.

Toward bedtime the night before, Richard had received a crank phone call. Some woman in town did not devote her evenings to leisure but to cold-calling at random to confide her own theory about the breakdown of time. According to the voice on the phone, the cycle of reincarnation had collapsed due to the increase in world population in the late twentieth century. The dead could only be reincarnated as *themselves* at an earlier stage in their own pre-existence. Everyone who experienced *the phenomenon* was actually dead. Didn't he realize this? The woman's logic had eluded Richard, so he had put the phone down.

Elisabeth soon stopped fretting. Richard glanced at his watch. A few more blithe hours remained. Once Paul and Sally had departed homeward, and after the twins were in bed, perhaps he and his wife might make love.

What if Elisabeth became pregnant? Could a baby ever grow in her womb and be born after another two hundred and seventy re-capitulative days? Would such a newcomer be born in a modern hospital or in a medieval hut?

Had *any* babies been born recently? Father Hopkins might know. Richard found within himself no desire to ask the priest. Nor, any longer, did he find desire itself.

From the kitchen he fetched a final chilled bottle of the dry Muscadet which the friends favoured. Tomorrow evening, he must stop by the supermarket to restock.

"Here's to another day," he proposed.

"Do you remember ice-boxes?" Richard asked Beth in their home of mud and wattle as two candle stubs burned low. He freed the skirt of his tunic from his belt so as to hide the twice-darned tops of hose tied to his waistband. "Do you remember moving pictures from far away in a box with a glass front? Do you remember voices from a box?"

His wife, in her ankle-length skirt and large apron, frowned in the flickery gloom. "Why we wasting the candles, Rich?"

Would she pull the caul from her head and let down her braids while he could still behold her?

"Do you remember *machines?*" he persisted.

"Is this another of your visions?" she asked dolefully. "Maybe you ought to speak to the monk instead of to me."

"What were we doing this morning, Beth?"

Anxiety haunted her.

"Our tribe," she mumbled. "We was hiding from those soldiers of Rome. Your face was daubed with blue. Life's much better these days."

"That was at noontime, Beth. What were we doing earlier?"

Surely they had worn skins and chipped flints to fix to trimmed poles, around a fire in a cave mouth in the cold? Surely the shaman, who was now the monk, had imparted a vision of carts and hayricks?

"We ought to be abed, Rich!"

In the evening, as the light died, fire was finally tamed. The flash from the sky which had burned the pine tree re-awoke from embers to set piled branches ablaze and banish the hungry bear.

The shaman chanted about light being reborn with the dawn. What was that *dawn*—which those of the tribe could only recall in fleeting dreamlike spasms? Earlier in the day surely they had shared the life of some small hairy animal which was not their totem animal, the huge-horned elk. They had surely themselves been beasts.

"Lis-ba!" Dik demanded of his wizened mate. "Wa Ma?"

He wanted to know where was their child of countless summers, now herself swollen with child. Dik's last few rotting teeth were aching. Soon he would be the oldest man around.

In the evening, the biped eventually achieved sentience. Its mind was confused by images of running on all fours.

As the moon arose the big-eyed lemur awoke. It gulped the warm sweet air. How clearly it could see compared with its disappearing dream of being underwater. The lemur climbed a branch, aspiring to the bleached light. It chattered to itself—"Dik, dik, dik!" Somehow it found the noise comforting.

A thought almost crystallized: an awareness of self. But oh the mesmerism of the moon. Self-consciousness submerged, as if tropic waters had risen to drown the forest.

Ahead!

1: *The Head Race*

THERE'S AN OLD SAYING: IT'LL COST YOU AN ARM and a leg.

For me the cost amounted to two arms, two legs, and a torso. Everything below the neck, in fact. Thus my head and my brain would survive until posterity. How I pitied people of the past who were dead forever. How I pitied my contemporaries who were too blind to seize the chance of cryogenic preservation.

Here we were on the threshold of potential immortality. How could I not avail myself of the Jones legislation? The opportunity might not be available in our own country for longer than a couple of years. The population might drop to a sustainable level. A change of administration might bring a change of heart. There could be rancour at the cost of maintaining increasing numbers of frozen and unproductive heads.

Until then, though, we were in the Head Race with China and Japan and India and other overpopulated nations. The previous deterrent to freezing had been guillotined away. Now no one was compelled to wait for natural death by cancer or car crash—and thus risk their brain degenerating during vital lost minutes.

Farewell, likewise, to the fear of senile dementia or Alzheimer's! The head would be surgically removed swiftly in prime condition and frozen immediately. This knowledge was immensely comforting to me. It was also a little scary. I was among the earliest to register. Yet I must wait almost a month till my appointment with the blade. A whole month! What if I were murderously mugged before I could be decapitated? What if my head was mashed to pulp?

Fortunately, I was part of a nation-wide support group of like minds linked by our PCs. To a fair extent our lobbying had finally resulted in the Jones Law. Yes, *ours*; along with lobbying by ecologists concerned with the welfare of the planet—and also, I have to admit, pressure from certain powerful right-wing groups (but it's the outcome which counts).

So whilst awaiting decapitation (now a proud word!) there was quite a sense of emotional and intellectual solidarity.

As regards storage or tagging of our heads, would a distinction be made between idealists such as ourselves—and those who were incurably ill or who had despaired of their current lives—and so-called Obligatories?

Initially, the Obligatories would be processed separately by the Justice or Medical systems. Would storage be mixed or segregated? This remained unclear. We had no wish to stir any suspicion of discrimination! Surely there was a significant distinction between idealists and non-idealists. The permission/identification form we all signed upon registering contained a box reserved for our motive.

Reportedly, the majority of idealists would be withdrawing from the world for altruistic, ecological reasons. Too many people on the planet for the health of the world! These volunteers would forgo their lives.

Enthusiasts such as myself nursed more personal motives, although I would never call those motives selfish. *Immortality* is not a selfish concept but is a watchword of faith in the survival and advancement of the human race. Immortality treasures what we have been, what we are, and what we shall become in the huge aeons ahead of us.

In a state of considerable excitement, we of the Immortalist Network confided the motives which we had inserted in our box.

To share in the Future.
To know what will be.
To reach the Stars. (That was mine.)
To strive, to seek, to find.
Manifest destiny of Homo Sap!

$p = f_p n_c f_l f_i f_c.$ (Which is the famous Drake Equation for the number of extraterrestrial civilizations out in space.)

Even: *To go boldly.*

And, wittily: *I want to keep ahead.* (To Keep A Head. Ho!)

In the future world, would our heads be provided with new bodies? New bottles for the old wine, as it were? The Forethought Institute assured us that nanotechnology was just around the corner. Another thirty or forty years, judging by state of the art and according to Delphi Polls. Eighty years at the most. Working in vats of raw materials, millions of molecule-size programmed assemblers would speedily construct, if not living bodies, then at least excellent artificial prosthetic bodies. These might be preferable to living bodies, being more resilient and versatile.

Even failing this, surely our minds could be mapped into electronic storage with the processing capacity to simulate entire virtual-reality worlds, as well as interfacing with the real world. Those who had despaired would be fulfilled. Idealists would reap their reward.

Ought criminal Obligatories to receive resilient versatile new bodies? Should their electronic versions be allowed full access to a virtual-reality domain? That was for the future to decide — a future where the roots of mischief were better understood, and could be pruned or edited.

With what hopes and longings I approach the decapitation clinic on this my last day. My healthy organs will be harvested for transplants. My heart and kidneys and retinas will disperse. My blood will be bottled for transfusions. I imagine the anaesthetic as sweet, even though it will be delivered by injection. I imagine the farewell kiss of the blade, even though the anaesthetic will rob me of sensation. Farewell, Old Regime. Welcome, the Revolution.

2: *The Head War*

Smell, first of all, as the primitive reptilian brain-root re-awakens: an overpowering odour of hair-gel, though without any actual sensation of breathing. No lungs to breathe with?

Taste: slick and sour-sweet.

Sound: high-speed warbling.

Tactile: soft pressure all around my head. Otherwise: nothing at all, sheer absence.

Vision! Slightly wobbly, as if through liquid. There's a pyramid! It's composed of decomposing *heads.* Squinting sidelong, I spy another pyramid — of whitened skulls.

And another, beyond it.

I must be hallucinating.

Or else information is being presented to me symbolically.

My viewpoint is rising up, disclosing yet more pyramids upon a flat white plain, perhaps a salt-flat. Ovoids are airborne. Eggs hover and dart to and fro. One of these floats close to me. The rounded bottom is opaque. The transparent ellipsoid of the upper two-thirds contains a hairless head, surely female. I believe that a clear gel wraps and cushions the head. I must look likewise. Twin antennae protrude from the top of the egg. She's a mobile disembodied head. I mouth at her, making my lips form mute words. (*Hullo. What's happening? Where are we?*)

She mouths at me but I can't read her lips. No thoughts transmit from those antennae to what I presume must be my own corresponding overhead antennae. Her egg-vehicle begins to swing away. I urge mine to follow but it continues onward lazily under its own impetus.

Can this white vista, with its menacing pyramids and its hovering heads, be actual? How can this be? Surely my head is being used. What seems to be happening is not what is really happening. It is a by-product.

Of a sudden two head-vehicles rush directly at one another. They collide and burst open. Briefly two faces kiss bruisingly while spilling gel hangs down elastically. Moment later both vehicles plummet down to the salt-flat. There they shatter entirely. Both heads roll out, surely oblivious by now.

From under the surface, two mobile crab-like devices emerge. In their claws they seize the heads. They scuttle toward a fledgling pyramid. Clambering, they nudge the heads into position, upright, where I suppose they will rot.

The female egg hasn't gone away, after all. It—or rather she—is swinging back toward me. At least I think that it is the selfsame egg. Now it's picking up speed. It's rushing at me. Will we shatter, and kiss hideously, and fall? I'm terrified.

At the very last moment, my vehicle tilts. I'm staring upward at blue sky and high wispy clouds. A fierce blow strikes my base. Such a stunning shock vibrates through me. Nevertheless I'm intact. I haven't ruptured. I think I am sinking down slowly toward the salt. Slowly, slowly.

Of her, there's no sight. She must have broken against my base and tumbled rapidly. Overhead, a dozen heads cruise by. What grim aerial game is this?

Or is this the only way in which I can experience a selection procedure whereby worthwhile heads are chosen for survival? Whereby hundreds of thousands are discarded?

Have I been selected or rejected?

Again I hear that high-speed warbling, as of bird-song speeded up a hundred-fold. With a slight bump I have come to rest.

Sky and salt-flat and flying eggs and a nearby pyramid are fading—until I'm seeing only . . . invisibility. There's nothing to see, nothing to taste, nothing to hear. Is this worse than being a disembodied head used as a game-piece by unknown forces?

Amidst this deprivation, for the first time in many years, I find myself praying to a force I scarcely believed in. *Dear God, help me.* Will an angel appear to me, coagulating out of nothingness?

All that can fill this void is a million memories of childhood. Of schooldays. Of my parents (forever dead, gone utterly!). Of first sex, first drug trip, first sight of the steaming teeming canyons of New York through which by night the roaming wailing vehicles suggested to my mind lugubrious monsters prowling for prey . . .

Presently my memories attain a vivid visionary actuality against the all-pervading nothingness!

I realize that my identity is being reinforced and stabilized—and perhaps scrutinized. The episode of the flying eggheads was akin to a pre-uterine experience. All of those heads in the sky were equivalent to so many sperms surging for existence, all of them failing except for one, myself, being fertilised in that shocking collision and sinking down to become attached to the ground. Surely that was the significance. Maybe most frozen brains fail to reintegrate.

Now, like cells multiplying, my memories multiply until—

3: Embodied

—I *am embodied.*

I'm aware of *limbs.* Of arms and legs and hands and feet! They're so real to me, as I lie face downward with my eyes tight shut. How intensely I treasure this moment. I cause my limbs to move just a little at first, like a beached swimmer. My fingers wiggle, and my toes.

I feel ampler than I used to be. I'm larger, superior, more muscular.

Arms and legs and—*wings* . . .

Wings? Yes, great furled wings are socketted into my shoulders! Already I'm sensing which new muscles to flex so as to use my amazing wings. These wings are why I am lying face downward and not upon my back; otherwise I would crush my wings uncomfortably.

Wings? Wings? A body with wings? Now I do open my eyes in wonder.

A veil of tiny flies fills the air, flitting around me like myriad airborne workers around some vast construction project, which is myself. I have arisen. My new body is golden, ambery, its fabric not of flesh but of some flexible responsive robust plastic—inorganic yet endowed with organic performance.

This is a substance for which there is no word, since it never existed previously. Perhaps *protoplast* is a suitable term. Undoubtedly energy cells, charged by sunlight, are woven throughout my new skin, powering inner engines which can defy the thrall of gravity—else how, when I unfurl my wings, do I rise and hover like some colossal deity of this cloud of flies? The wings must be of some ingenious anti-gravitic biotechnology, to uplift my weight.

My head is still enclosed in a protective helmet. My new golden winged body is an ingenious prosthetic device sustaining and serving my natural head, in perfect harmony with my head.

Those flies are beginning to disperse, as if wafted away by my slow wingbeats. The veil is thinning—except over to my right. There, a dense cloud of flies begins to vibrate audibly. Vibrations become a voice, announcing my task. . . .

4: *The Colossi*

There has been a *nanocatastrophe.*

The Forethought Institute was correct in their promise of rampant nanotechnology transforming the world. (How, otherwise, could I possess this angelic body, golden and winged and of miracle substance? How else would this body interface with my head of flesh and bone and blood and brain-cells, sustaining and obeying and augmenting me?) Alas, the whole world is as smooth as a billiard ball. Farewell to mountains and valleys. Farewell to forests and seas. Farewell, likewise, to all the species of fish, flesh, and fowl which once inhabited sea or land. Farewell to all plants and fungi and bacteria.

Due to the nanocatastrophe nothing remained of life except for these sealed frozen heads of ours, preserved perfectly—as if the human race had intuited the need for such a global insurance policy in the event of a nano-plague.

When I say that the planet is smooth and perfectly spherical I am omitting to mention the thousand equidistant colossi which rise from the surface. Seen from space, under modest magnification, the colossi might seem like so many individual whiskers upon a huge chin, or like so many stiff short freak hairs upon an otherwise gleaming bald head—few and far between, and exactly spaced.

Seen from the ground—or whilst hovering with our wings—each colossus towers vastly and baroquely up through the clouds. Some are still under construction by the untold trillions of mobile microscopic nano-assemblers, or by larger macro-machines forever being assembled and disassembled. Other colossi are almost complete, soaring to their designed height of ten kilometres.

Rooted by deep thermal spikes which exploit the inner heat of the planet, these colossi are *ships*. When the construction is completed, their matrix-engines will all activate in unison. This will generate a global matrix-field. As the world implodes toward a vanishing point, all of the thousand great ornate darts will be translated outward simultaneously through the cosmic matrix—not to mere stars in our own galaxy, but each to the vicinity of some planet roughly similar to Earth but in a different galaxy millions or tens of millions of light years away.

This is the Project for which the world was smoothed flat, erasing all life in the process, except for our preserved heads. Expansion throughout the universe!

5: *But . . .*

But even at speeds far slower than that of light, surely nanos in tiny vessels could reach the furthest part of our own galaxy within, say, twenty million years at most. They could arrive in other galaxies within a hundred million years. The universe is due to endure for *fifty times longer than that.* At least!

Why the urgency? Why convert the entire Earth into a catapult which will destroy itself?

The pace of activity of microscopic nanos must be far faster than that of creatures such as Man (and Woman)—yet why could the nanos not become dormant en route to the stars, like spores, simply switching themselves off?

The reason for their hurry provides an answer to the *Von Neuman Enigma*—as I discover in conversation with another golden Angel nine kilometres up the ship to which we are both assigned.

The Von Neuman Enigma: If life already arose anywhere in the universe and sent out self-replicating probes, why is the universe not already full of probes? In the whole of the cosmos did adventurous, intelligent life only ever arise on one single planet, Earth?

My companion and I soar on thermals, ascending alongside the ship. We arrive at a platform in the stratosphere. With our robust bodies of protoplast we are to assist macro-machines to construct a spire which will support yet another tier of the colossus.

My companion is Hispanic. With bald tan head enshrined in transparent holder fixed upon golden body—and his wings folded dorsally from shoulders down to knees now that we had arrived high above the clouds—he is magnificent. Daunting.

After some labour we rest . . . not that our new bodies ever became fatigued. We do not sleep, though we might daydream while we absorb nutrition through valves in our ankles. Nanos in our heads repair any physical degeneration. A device in our throats permits us to speak aloud.

"What year do you think this is?" I ask my colleague.

"The Year Zero," he replies. His comment makes sense. All human history has vanished except for what we each remember. The time of the nanocatastrophe constitutes an absolute gulf between *before* and *now*.

I broach the matter of the Von Neuman Enigma, which bothered me even in the old days.

"The answer," he declares, "is that the Hayflick Limit applies to all social entities as well as to individual organisms." Such is the profound conversation of angels!

But of course, but of course. . . !

The bugbear of the damned *Hayflick Limit* used to torment me. Body cells only replace themselves a finite number of times before the process fails. For human beings this limit is seventy times or thereabouts. Then comes decay and death.

"The Hayflick Limit also applies," says this Hispanic angel, "to the Congregation of Nanos. Social entities such as civilizations obey the same limiting constraint as the cells in bodies—a law as binding as entropy. No matter how well the nanos stabilize their collective activity, over a period of millions of years this would lose all coherence."

"Collectively they would suffer entropy . . ."

"Exactly so!" he tells me. "With our slower thoughts, we serve as an anchor—as the *root* from which they arose. Their source and origin. We are their touchstone and criterion. Their pacemaker, their talisman. Furthermore, in an important sense we provide purpose. People uniquely possess a sense of far-reaching purpose—because that is our nature. This is true even if only one person remains in existence, provided that he never yields to despair."

In the terms of a ship (for the Colossi are certainly ships) we are, quite literally, to be—

6: *Figureheads*

—figureheads, no less!

At the very summit of each colossus, protected by a cone of energy, right there at the tip of the ship, one of us will ride headfirst.

On a thousand colossal ships a thousand proud heads (attached to protoplast bodies) will each gaze upon a new galaxy, and a new world in the vicinity similar to Earth.

Translation through the matrix will ensure comparability—similarity as regards mass and diameter and distance from a star which will closely resemble Earth's own sun. The planet in question *might* be barren, or be at boiling point due to greenhouse gases, or be an ice-desert. Yet surely hundreds may be habitats of some kind of life, or potential for life; for cosmic companionship.

This, mine eyes shall behold. . . .

A thousand ships, a thousand heads! What if more than a thousand heads still survive?

At this moment the Hispanic angel launches himself at me.

How we wrestle. How well matched we are.

Our struggle ranges to and fro across this uppermost platform. Will he try to butt my helmet with his own, to crack it open if he can? When I realize that he has no intention of risking this, I am less cautious in my grips and clutches.

Pulling free and half-turning, he unfurls his wings to buffet and batter me. I punch with all the force of my golden fist at the base of one wing . . . which sags, which droops! I have fractured the attachment.

We are at the edge of the platform, where a thin breeze streams by. Gathering myself—and against all former human instinct—I hurtle against him, carrying him over the side along with myself.

For a moment, as we fall, he can't free an arm to grasp me. In that moment I deploy my own wings and release him.

Down, down he drops, crippled, spinning single-winged, accelerating willy-nilly. Nine kilometres he will fall to the billiard-ball ground. I'm alone upon the ship except for machines and invisible nanos.

7: *Triumph*

The Project is complete at last.

I stand erect, the very pinnacle of the galaxy-ship. No thunderous surge of acceleration will raise this colossus upon a column of fire. When the matrix-field activates worldwide—when the smooth ball of the world begins to implode—translation will occur instantaneously.

Even so, like a swimmer upon the highest diving board I raise my golden arms above my bottled head, palms pressed together steeple-style as if to leap and cleave the heavens.

Do my nine hundred and ninety-nine brothers and sisters likewise signal their imminent departure?

A humming vibration commences.

8: *Fulfillment*

Lakes of brilliant stars! A ball of blinding yellow light which is the local sun! Its radiance illuminates a full hemisphere of another nearby ball—a world white with clouds and blue with ocean, mottled with landmasses.

Earth-like. Similar . . .

Maybe the oceans and the land are sterile. Maybe not. To stare from space at this spectacle is to be Columbus and Cortez and Captain Cook all in one. I may be ten million light years away from my birthplace. Or a hundred million. This, in itself, is an ultimate achievement.

All because I dared to be decapitated!

Within a day or so, my colossus will be in orbit—like some titanic statue equipped with a tiny living head. I assume that the nanos will reshape the ship into hundreds of gliding wings which will descend. I presume that provision will be made for me.

Or what purpose could there be?

The China Cottage

WHEN ADRIAN HOLLOWELL'S MOTHER JOAN DIED suddenly at the age of eighty, black farce wrote a postscript to a life which had hitherto been so quiet, self-contained, respectable, and decent.

Adrian and Hazel could hardly be accused, even by themselves, of having neglected his mother during her last years. Why, just the previous month they had driven the three hundred tedious miles to the north of England to spend a long weekend taking his mother to some of her favourite places in the countryside. Hadn't there been all those Sunday morning phone calls to her, once a week regular as clockwork?

Rather, Joan had isolated herself.

Ever since her husband Ken died a decade earlier, Joan had grieved in a brave and quiet way. She had been waiting to rejoin Ken for ten long years. Hers wasn't the type of grief which leads speedily to one partner following the other. It was a staunch and cloistered grief. Nun-like, Joan might have taken a vow to do nothing special ever again in the absence of Ken. During preceding years of retirement Ken and Joan had taken a dozen long-deferred holidays abroad—to see the Alps, and Italy, and Greece, and even

Canada, fulfilling the dreams of a lifetime. They must have also taken at least a couple of thousand photographs, for memory. But now, no more. Although her widowed friend Mary, quite the globe-trotter, tried to prevail on Joan to accompany her on a package tour, Adrian's mother refused to leave home; nor would she ever again set up the slide projector and view the colour transparencies alone.

Exceptionally, Joan would visit Adrian and Hazel once a year by bus for a long weekend—until a burglar visited *her* during one such absence. Home, the shrine, had been violated. Joan wouldn't go away again.

Mary continued to call, yet there had never been many friends to speak of. Joan and Ken had been private people. This reticence extended within the home too. Adrian had grown up with only the scantest notion of what went on at the building society where his father worked, or even, really, what a building society was. His mother and father rarely attended any staff social event. Later, Adrian discovered that his father had dreamed of becoming a branch manager in a some county town away from the urban river-side sprawl. However, Joan had refused to leave the little dream home which had been custom-built for her and Ken in the Nine-teen-Thirties—at a time when the view was of cornfields and of the sea a couple of miles beyond. Latterly, the view was entirely of a public housing estate and tarmac.

Farce began shortly after a policeman came to the Hollowells' door in their village of thatched cottages, autumn dahlias and chrysan-themums all in bloom. It was just four weeks since they had taken Adrian's mother to one beauty spot which she had never thought she would see again, so she said. Earlier that evening, Adrian and Hazel had just come back from France, which was why the police up north hadn't been able to get through on the phone, and thus had contacted the local station.

Adrian's mother had been found dead. The officer commiser-ated. He'd been told no other details. Would Adrian phone the coroner's office up north in the morning?

Next morning Adrian learned how neighbours had noted that his mother's curtains remained closed at the front for several days. Perhaps Joan was away—but they recalled her burglary, when only a couple of pieces of costume jewellery had actually been stolen in lieu of any real gems or video recorders.

A policeman climbed the back fence. The kitchen door wasn't locked. Joan lay dead inside. The obvious cause was coronary thrombosis, to be conformed by post-mortem. There had been some vomit on the floor. Nausea often heralded a heart attack, but basically she wouldn't have suspected anything at all. Joan must have just got out of bed, felt sick, and unlocked the kitchen door for a breath of fresh air. Returning inside, she had died instantly. She wouldn't even have known she was dying.

She must have been lying there for several days, dead. Joan's body was removed to the mortuary, then the policeman had secured the property.

Atkinsons: that was the name of the funeral directors. Adrian must have walked past their premises a few thousand times when he'd been a schoolboy. With a post-mortem due, was Adrian able to make arrangements with the undertaker by phone before travelling north?

Oh yes, said the lady coroner. *You can cremate before death.*

He was flabbergasted. Had he heard aright? Whatever did she mean by this?

What she *meant* was that he could set a date for the funeral before the death certificate was issued because there wouldn't be any inquest. *He must think they had some funny customs up north!*

Another dire thought came to Adrian. His mother never let anyone else have a key to her house. So his next call was to the police in the north to make sure that they had removed Joan's keys.

Oh no. The officer—whose name sounded remarkably like Genius—had faithfully locked the back door, put the keys on the table, then left by the front door, latching it shut. He'd done his duty of securing the property all right.

On a very windy night Adrian and Hazel arrived outside his one-time home after three hundred miles on the road, to rendezvous with a locksmith.

The double door was a solid Nineteen-Thirties specimen. Stained glass at the top. Giant bolts, within, to secure the side which rarely opened. Its fifty-year-old Yale lock defeated whatever slim flexible instruments the locksmith tried to slide between the abutting halves of the door—Adrian wasn't privileged to watch this operation, since the locksmith, who was somewhat paranoid, refused to reveal tricks of his trade to a spectator. The lock then thwarted what seemed from a distance like fifty skeleton keys.

Adrian waited in the fierce wind and Hazel sat in the car during the full hour it took the man to drill through the lock. At half time, another car pulled up. A man in an anorak, resembling a welter-weight boxer, jumped out.

He proved to be a plainclothes policeman. The police station had had a report of some funny business outside this property. They'd told the caller they knew what was going on, but the boxer had come just to make sure.

Was *he* the genius who had locked the keys in the house?

Oh no, not him. But he couldn't wait to get back to the station to tell the lads.

The next morning, a neighbour from over the road would confide to Adrian how she was so busy watching at the curtains that her Jack's supper was an hour late. When that front door finally opened a cry had gone up: *'They've got in!'*

A local Vicar would preside at the cremation. Adrian's mother only ever attended church once a year for the Christmas Eve carol service. Adrian and Hazel did not even condone organised religions, yet a Vicar's presence at the funeral was *de rigueur*. When the scrawny, broody Vicar called at the house to make some notes, he evinced such a passionate intensity as regards resurrection to eternal life. His knees creaked as he sat and talked, as if his knees were wooden and the joints needed oiling. Next day, the same neighbour confided how everyone local was sure that the bachelor Vicar had AIDS and wasn't long for this world.

Death roosted in the bungalow in another guise too. Whilst growing up, Adrian had always felt so safe—even frustratingly so!—in this ideal home of the Nineteen Thirties. The bungalow had undergone little change except for some new carpets and new furniture and appliances now and then. Same cast iron radiators, of advanced design for 1934, to warm the rooms. Same deep stone sink in the kitchen. Same wooden ceiling pulley to dry washing, which could be wound down and up by rope. Same original Art Deco light fittings, too. By the time his mother died such items as deep sinks had come back into fashion and were eagerly sought in junk shops. When he and Hazel had visited, to the casual eye the house seemed secure and comfortable.

Closer inspection revealed a death trap. Behind ingenious clusters of adaptor sockets fitted by his father, and modern plastic switch plates, was Nineteen Thirties wiring, old and brittle. Bumping into the cooker caused an immediate gush of gas. The emergency engineer switched off the house at the mains and slapped on a red prohibition notice pending the digging up of the kitchen floor to fit a new gas pipe. The cooker, also condemned, was an antique such as he hadn't seen in the last forty years.

Joan's larder was so bare. She must have been eating like a sparrow. And every paper bag had been saved for possible re-use. Yet what she had assured her son only the year before was perfectly true. She wasn't at all in need of money. His mother had two very robust savings accounts. She had inherited Ken's pension, linked to inflation. For ten years she'd been accumulating assets.

"Oh she died a good death," exclaimed Hazel, amazed. "Never ill. Able to stay in her home till the last; then out like a light."

For his mother to have become ill or senile had hardly borne contemplating. Their own cottage simply wasn't large enough to accept her. For Joan to go into a nursing home, losing her privacy, would have been horrible for her—besides bleeding away whatever she owned till she was reduced to a paltry residue.

A good death, indeed.

And now her effects must be sorted out.

Some fox furs from the Nineteen Thirties—*obscene*, in the Nineties. No charity shop would accept such donations.

Boxes and boxes of colour slides of Canadian and Swiss scenery, unviewed by herself these last ten years, and of no conceivable interest except to the person who had wielded the camera. These must go to an incinerator.

Ornaments: Toby jugs of recent vintage, a lustre vase with a smashed lip, decorative plates . . .

It was whilst surveying the ornaments that Hazel picked up a round china marmalade pot in the shape of a cottage. The walls were of a creamy sort of basketwork. The green roof (which lifted off) was a cone of thick branches. A dormer window receded. A chimney of orange bricks jutted up, whereby to lift off the lid. A few oversized pink or yellow blooms clung near the door and beneath a double window.

The piece wasn't sophisticated in design or detail. Hardly a Meissen marmalade pot! It verged on naive, though avoiding vulgarity. For as long as Adrian remembered, that pot had stood on the mantelpiece—until now.

"Actually," said Hazel, "I think this is the best thing here. The most charming, anyway. It has integrity."

A china cottage, emblem of rural dreams—which indeed Adrian and Hazel had pretty much fulfilled, though not his parents except by way of Sunday trips into the countryside. . . .

In the Nineteen Thirties Joan and Ken had travelled for their honeymoon on a motorbike, with camping gear, to Stratford-upon-Avon and the Cotswolds, enchanted by cottages such as this. Maybe they brought back the marmalade, or honey, pot as a souvenir of that honeymoon almost ten years before Adrian was born.

Wary of the lid falling off and shattering, Hazel turned the pot over.

"It says . . . What's this? *Marutomo Ware*. There's a string of Japanese characters too. . . ."

And as a maker's mark: a capital T within a circle.

"Why would the Japanese have been making English cottages as jam pots in the Nineteen Thirties?" mused Adrian.

He had paid scant attention to this green-roofed cottage during all the years he had lived in this house. Yet of a sudden it seemed to incarnate so much of his dead parents' life and dreams.

Memories flooded him — of sitting by the hearth as a child, that hearth with its false-log electric fire. Of spooning up chicken soup while listening to the big old brown pre-war radio, no longer here, so many names on the long dial, Hilversum and Hamburg and Helsinki. At Christmas, the tree in the corner with all the coloured glass balls dangling from the branches. Curling up in an old armchair with a *Hotspur* comic containing a story of a giant homicidal cactus growing suddenly in London in Hyde Park, firing its spines as deadly spears at passers-by till foiled by the nimble bare-foot runner. . . .

Throughout his adolescence he'd been much more interested in escaping from the north of England, so barren and bleak and downbeat. Anybody with an overactive imagination might bring about the downfall of nations: such was the local wisdom. Native sons travelled to London but soon fled home proclaiming, "It's treacherous down south." Others never returned, or only for fleeting visits. In this category was Adrian.

He'd become a journalist, which Hazel had also been until Alan was born. Alan was at university now. Had they broken the news of his grandmother's death to Alan a little too brusquely over the phone? All of a sudden they had so much to arrange, and it was impractical for Alan to attend the funeral. Adrian's life was so busy now that he was a freelance. He specialized in economic journalism, a fast-track business.

The absurd aspects of his mother's death, especially the need to drill their way into the bungalow, were like the activities of some clown capering along a precipice of grief.

"I bet they bought that pot in Stratford on their honeymoon," he said to Hazel. "You know, Stratford isn't too much of a detour on the way back."

"But," she pointed out, "that was sixty years ago. . . ."

Almost sixty years of life in the same house, now to be cleared and sold as though erasing a whole directory irretrievably from a computer disc.

Arriving in Stratford was emblematic of having finally quit the north and the past forever—though the psychological barrier between Adrian and his own future death (cause yet unknown) had also disappeared.

Stratford of the present was decidedly different from the simpler town where his mother and father once honeymooned. Why, there wouldn't have been a hundred Harley Davidsons and Honda bikes parked along Waterside. Nor a fire-eater performing on the greensward. Nor a great glittering butterfly beckoning one to cross the Avon for an exotic lepidopteran safari. Nor a host of Japanese tourists disembarking from a tour bus.

The world had ramped up into overdrive. Hiroshima had been incinerated, but Japan had risen again triumphantly—yet was already being eclipsed by Taiwan and Korea and Singapore. Should Adrian accost one of the Japanese tourists and ask what they knew about Marutomo Ware? About English cottages made in Japan as marmalade pots when the tourists' grandparents were young?

He and Hazel headed for bookshops to check all the collectors' guides they could find.

A volume on pottery marks, containing thirty densely illustrated pages devoted to Japan, listed no letter T within a circle. Books on modern collectibles, on treasures in your attic, on last year's auction prices: none mentioned such a thing as Marutomo Ware. In a world where every trivial object, even quite recent, even blatantly awful or trivial, seemed rapaciously collectible and investible-in, the marmalade pot was a non-object. Why should old Bakelite telephones and seaside souvenirs and comics and a hundred other ephemeral things be eagerly sought, and not pre-war Japanese pastiches of rural England?

Was this anonymity not, in a sense, the quintessence of his mother's life? Yet wasn't it also disconcerting?

Presently the Hollowells wandered into an antiques mini-market crowded with booths of bric-a-brac and objects of greater virtue, all optimistically priced. And it was there, upon a table in a nook, that they spied three gaudy little china pagodas upon a green tray: salt, pepper, and mustard.

Almost as soon as Adrian and Hazel began examining these cruets a middle-aged woman was by their side, murmuring hopefully, "Do you collect Marutomo Ware?" She was plump and pleasant. Little glasses were perched on her nose. She looked like a genial granny.

And soon she was enlightening them. . . .

Japanese export cottage-ware was the name for these things. Few people were collecting them yet. Nevertheless, the vogue was definitely beginning! Take her word for it. Oh yes, they were a bit crude, but that was the charm, wasn't it?

Now, the vital element was *the magic mark.* The proprietress intoned this phrase in the accent of the wise raven warning that boy in the tale of the Snow Queen that a *splin-ter from the maaag-ic mirror* had entered his sister's eye, alienating her from her brother and from her home—thus, at least, on the story record which Alan had listened to interminably when he was a toddler until he could parrot every nuance perfectly.

The maaagic mark, the maaagic mark.

Either a T in a circle, for Marutomo. Or a K in a circle, for Maruhon Ware. Actually *Made in Japan* was acceptable. Even just *Foreign.* Though the maaagic mark was admirable.

Sharing that table was a little blue donkey-cart led by a fellow in olde world peasant costume—blue knickerbockers, green frock coat, blue tricorne hat. This salt and pepper set was "Made in Japan," though more carefully painted and glazed than the pagodas.

Also there was a black candleholder ornamented with big crude maroon blooms which might be chrysanthemums. This bore the maaagic K mark.

Oh the cottage could never have been *bought* by Joan. During the Nineteen Thirties cottage ware was given away if you collected enough coupons from packets of tea. Tea from Ceylon, ornament from Tokyo or Yokohama. In English homes people would drink tea for a year to acquire a donkey-cart or a marmalade-pot cottage.

How complicated, how bizarre! Imagine Japanese artisans in some back-street family workshop or sweat-shop—arty-Sans who had never been near Europe—receiving commissions from a British tea factor out of Colombo to supply a hundred English cottages and a hundred donkey-carts to be packed in straw and shipped to Liverpool or Bristol.

As the decade slid toward the Second World War, so the proud maaagic marks were replaced by a brusque "Made in Japan," then simply by an anonymous "Foreign." Anti-Japanese sentiment was building up among Anglo-Saxons, though a consequence of this would be the fall of Singapore, the surrender of Hong Kong, the bombing of Pearl Harbor.

After a bit of bargaining the Hollowells acquired all three pieces. They could easily afford to; now they could. Now Joan's cottage wouldn't be alone, as she had been alone.

Over the next few years the quest for Maru' Ware was to take Adrian and Hazel to many junk shops and curio shops and flea markets in many towns. Before long they developed rituals and superstitions for finding their quarry. Humming the old Japanese anthem to the Emperor often seemed to do the trick. Tum-tumti-TUM, tumti-TUM, tumtitum . . . May the Son of Heaven triumph ten thousand-fold. *Tenno heika banzai yo!*

A whole unknown range and population of Maru' artefacts and people lurked, waiting to be reunited at some celestial breakfast or tea party. The Japanese arty-Sans had worked prodigiously if rather crudely on behalf of the tea companies. Not only were there jam-pots of a hundred designs and candle-holders and cruets, but egg cups too and china toast-racks. And teapots and tea strainers and butter dishes and lemon squeezers and ashtrays and sugar shakers. You could recognize a genuine piece instantly from twenty yards away.

Personages included cruet girl-guides with Asian faces, and kneeling cherubs holding bowls aloft, and Beefeaters from the Tower of London. Camels squatted with china hooks for salt and pepper baskets, mustard panniers on their backs. A whole peculiar population existed, and a bestiary too, and an environment of cottages and towers and olde curiosity shoppes! An unacknowledged Maru' World!

The makers' distant perception of their market caused some peculiarities. Who was this figure in a costume of tight horizontal blue hoops? He often peered around the edge of a cottage. Almost merged with it, he frequently dwarfed the doorway. The figure seemed like a deep-sea diver in a kind of samurai armour diving suit and helmet.

A Beefeater might well have lost his Tower and his companion (or vice versa), and a girl guide her jamboree tent, or a yellow camel its mustard pot—or a cottage pot its tam-o'-shanter lid. Pieces had been scattered or had suffered casualties. Often there'd be a crack or a chip. Amazing, really, that so much had survived intact. Adrian and Hazel once arrived at a market stall just after an idle browser had picked up a windmill pot and knocked the lid off so that it smashed on the cobbles. One of the sails had already been snapped. The stallholder actually gave the piece away to them as an alternative to tossing it in a bin; a golden day.

You had to be subtle in the search. You had to deny any special interest in cruets or teapots, and only blandly glance at the maaagic marks, even if the pulse beat fast. You mustn't ignite a firestorm of collecting by people who were blind to the spiritual dimension of the hunt.

Spring was a good time to harvest Maru' Ware, because old ladies died off in January and February and their homes were cleared. But really the harvest remained reasonable all year long, apart from occasional patches of dearth. Ah, the secret harvest . . .

Naturally they returned to Stratford, but that middle-aged woman was no longer there. Obviously she'd given up trying to convince tourists of the collectibility of pieces which were becoming rarer and rarer. Yes, she'd gone, like a gypsy with her curse.

Alan had graduated. Alan did a string of temporary jobs in pubs and clubs in London, pending his breakthrough as an actor. By now their son viewed his erstwhile home as an insane and alienated place, full as it was of cottages and cruets and lemon squeezers and ashtrays and camels and donkeys and windmills. Strangers and acquaintances alike were hardly ever admitted in case they coveted the secret collection, into which—to a fair degree, if travel were included—his mother's money had been transmuted. Alternatively, visitors might fail to perceive the value and regard the Hollowells as potty.

Adrian began to suffer from blood pressure. He relied on an array of blockers and diuretics—and his memory was fraying too, a poor prognosis for a journalist, possibly an early indicator of Alzheimer's. Hazel had lost a breast and lymph glands because of a tumour, and was worried about recurrence. Hardly likely that either would reach Joan's ripe old age!

Yet the quest continued. Their cottage *must* be filled to the seams with that quintessence of cottage, Maru' Ware with maaagic marks which arty-Sans had crafted over half a century earlier back when the world was much less full of people and when Joan and Ken had embarked on their honeymoon upon a motorbike from their ideal home, seven years saved for, to pretty Stratford. The trip might only have cost them five pounds in total, or maybe ten. When they had arrived at Anne Hathaway's cottage—of which there were various Maru' copies—they may have shared their tour with just a couple of other visitors rather than with a queue of Japanese and Americans and Koreans and Spaniards.

Adrian and Hazel realized that they themselves were growing old and that Alan was alienated from them, though they did their best to phone him once a week or once a fortnight.

What of Alan's inheritance? Not one marmalade pot, but hundreds of them! Along with a multitude of sugar shakers and candleholders and butter dishes and all else.

In every room glass cabinets displayed the wares and guarded them from dust. Wares which lacked the maaagic mark thronged tables and almost every shelf including bookshelves—the books had had to go, except for some economics literature piled under Adrian's desk.

Alan could virtually open their home as a museum. Though would anyone wish to visit it? What if Adrian and Hazel had effectively, and in secret, cornered almost the entire market in Maru' Ware? What if no more Maru' Ware remained in circulation and thus could have no meaningful, collectible value assigned? Exchanged for tea coupons, such pieces had never had actual monetary value. In the Hollowell's total success, might there be debacle and futility? Could one envisage a cottage museum devoted to objects to which everyone else was oblivious? The realm of Maru' Ware must never be equated with some daft bugger's museum of drawing pins or paper clips.

And of course it wouldn't be! Maru' territory was truly inhabited —if not always by figures then at least implicitly behind the painted glazed windows and doors. Tea strainers and lemon-squeezers likewise implied a whole virtual existence.

Commissions became fewer for Adrian, though this didn't matter too much so long as the ageing car could take him and Hazel to distant marketplaces. When they returned home, if the setting sun dazzled him, sometimes it seemed that their cottage was becoming simpler and rounder, the roof more of a cone, the chimney taller, the flowers in the garden larger and brasher.

One autumn day after a scary dearth they arrived back triumphantly. They had found a green and mauve potpourri vase with slots in the lid to release the scent of dried lavender. Adrian spied a figure in blue disappearing around to the back of their cottage.

"Hazel, there's someone—" His heart thumped. He felt tight and hot. "Someone—"

"What sort of someone?" she demanded. "For God's sake! Is it Alan?"

They hurried from the car, up the brick path, and around.

Adrian almost collided with the policeman, who was returning from the padlocked back gate. Surely it was the same man who had once knocked on their door of an evening. He was older now and seemed to have forgotten that earlier encounter. There'd been a report of a prowler. The officer had parked his car in a side lane, hoping to apprehend by surprise. Glass sparkled on the path. But this window, which was out of sight of the road, boasted two steel bars, fixed inside.

Someone had been trying to unscrew the bars. One was loose. Trace of blood. Someone had cut his hand.

Adrian clung to both bars, like some prisoner excluded from his cell, desperate to be readmitted.

Inside, nothing was smashed. Shelves and cabinets and tables of Maru' Ware were all intact. Heart thudding, Adrian dashed quickly up and down, and from front to back to ensure that all locks and bars were secure—apart from the wobbly one—while Hazel detained the officer at the door so that he wouldn't intrude, and see. Upstairs, the fax was safe, and his computer, which would have been a bit heavy to lug and was long out of date. The Hollowells thanked the man warmly; saw him on his way; then Hazel too could fully reassure herself.

If the prowler had gained entry, in rage at not finding silver or money he might have vandalised the collection, sweeping dozens of pieces off shelves and tables, shattering them.

"From now on," Hazel said firmly, "one of us will always need to be here."

"I can't hunt on my own. . . ."

"Maybe the hunt's over. Maybe the potpourri pot is the last piece ever. We have to safeguard them now."

Adrian needed to sit down and take a pill. "I thought," he told her, "when I saw him round the side—I thought that policeman was the time-diver."

The name had come to him recently, of the lurker in blue, like a samurai warrior, like a deep-sea diver. What had Adrian and Hazel been doing ever since his mother's death but time-diving, picking up submerged treasure and broken shards of the past just as genuine divers had recovered a hold full of precious Chinese porcelain from some sunken Dutch sailing ship.

Or had the Hollowells been trawling for trash?

"You'd best fetch our potpourri pot before some kid thieves it from the car—"

Of course.

Adrian shut the front door as he went out so that no passers-by such as inquisitive Mrs *Thing* from the Old Parsonage could stare in.

As he returned up the path, cradling the pot double-wrapped in newspaper, the rug of healthy moss upon the roof glowed green in the declining sunshine. Slanting shadows made the texture of the magnolia rendering look like basketwork. How the upstairs dormer window seemed to lean away from him. What a huge yellow chrysanth.

Dazed by the shock of the attempted burglary, Adrian stepped inside, into cool shade.

The woman awaiting him seemed so much shorter and slighter —as if she'd been existing on a sparrow's rations for years.

Quivering, she opened her arms to hug him. His heart ached for her.

Such Dedication

IT'S HARD HAVING A FAMOUS BROTHER. IT'S EVEN harder when your brother is the Son of God.

You see, on that Christmas day in Bethlehem long ago Mary gave birth to twins—of whom I am the other. This is one of the great hushed-up secrets of history. I myself didn't know until after word of the Crucifixion reached my foster Magus in Persia.

On that original Christmas day I was surplus to requirement, an almighty surprise and embarrassment. Which of the visitors would whisk me away? The well-heeled ones, or the humble ones? Magi, or shepherds?

If the answer was shepherds, how inappropriate it would have been to expose me on a cold hillside. The infanticide solution would have been out of keeping with the joyous occasion. Besides, just imagine my hungry cries attracting . . . a wolf. Imagine the wolf not eating me but dragging me off to her den to foster. With the Romans occupying Judea, the legend of Romulus and Remus wasn't exactly unknown.

Or imagine the Wild Boy of Bethlehem, a feral wolf-child, eventually encountering Jesus in the wilderness—and being raised from all fours and endowed with speech . . . and revealed as His *brother.*

What if the shepherds had passed the baby on to the care of some community of zealots or Essenes? What if one of the simple shepherds had been indiscreet? There were so many would-be Messiahs, most of whom history has conveniently forgotten. Whenever I hear about my brother being "tested in the wilderness," nowadays I imagine that I'm a subscriber to *Which Messiah?* magazine —along the lines of *Which Car?* or *Which Handgun?* There were so many aspiring Saviours. I would have seemed to be a fully authentic claimant in fulfillment of the prophecies.

You may wonder how the magi and the shepherds and my parents could tell which twin was the chosen one. And which should collect the short straw.

My brother preceded me by a couple of minutes (as my foster Magus eventually explained) but there was also a nimbus round His head. Later religious paintings are right in that regard, though they exaggerate considerably. The halo was a birth-caul—the membrane which sometimes covers the head of a newborn child. Evidently the caul was luminous.

The magi thought it wise to feed that membrane to a goat. They didn't want any future comments along the lines of: Son of God, nimbus; superfluous brother, no nimbus. It must have been those shepherds who gossiped about the faint light around my brother's head, corresponding to the comet which shone in the sky at the time.

Anyway, my brother was to die wretchedly. His followers evangelised, but for several decades it seemed that they might only amount to a minor sect. For me, the salient fact was that physically I grew no older than that day when my foster Magus (elderly, by then) finally told me of my true origin. Could it be that *I* was the miracle? That this was why I'd been smuggled away to safety in Persia?

Not so, said my foster mage. After years of meditation he had decided that my birth wasn't exactly an error—but that I was what in modern terms you might call the *control* in the divine experiment. I was the duplicate who didn't receive the drug of divinity.

Despite the fact that I didn't age beyond thirty-four, the other magi disagreed that I had any part to play in a divine plan—except to stay *well apart* from it, and to hide my lack of light and my longevity under a bushel. Arguably the role of "control" had already been taken. By Ahasuerus, the Wandering Jew. This Jew scorned my brother on His way to Calvary. In angry exasperation my brother told Ahasuerus that he would stay alive as a witness until my brother returned in glory at the end of the world. In those days the end of the world didn't seem so remote. Indeed, in later centuries I was sometimes to pass myself off as the Wandering Jew if people became suspicious about me. On several occasions this saved me from a worse fate than a beating. No pious Christian would dare try to *kill* Ahasuerus. I never met the actual Wandering Jew.

I tried to adopt a low profile, in keeping with the advice of the Magi. Meanwhile, my brother's religion triumphed—and became an empire with its own emperors, the popes.

I could recover from beatings quickly. Likewise, from any serious injury. When I once lost a hand to a bandit's sword, the hand regenerated within three months. Regeneration, and immortality! Some of my brother had obviously rubbed off on me—by accident.

Regeneration may come in useful when I do arrive on the alien world, if some mishap occurs! Obviously I could never have included this feature in my bio as an inducement to chose me as the volunteer for the first star-flight. Sanity is a prime requirement in undertaking this mission which is insane by any ordinary reckoning. To claim immortality for myself would have weeded me out at once.

An *insane* mission? To travel solo to an alien star system with no means of returning home to Earth must seem a bit unhinged. Or else . . . *utterly heroic.*

Some early navigators set sail with no certainty that there was even a destination to arrive at. I at least can be reasonably sure of arriving at Tau Ceti III! However, the quasi-space field can only translocate a restricted volume of material. This ship, the *Sapiens*, only has room for one person—along with enough rations and water for the twelve and a quarter years of the journey, and exercise equipment, and the generator for translating the *Sapiens* into photons and back again at journey's end, and liquid air, and enough fuel to land upon the promising third planet, and a small transmitter satellite to release into orbit before I land. There's only enough available space for one person to travel one way—and a living *person* must indeed travel. The quasi-space effect requires the presence of consciousness within the craft.

Several thousand people applied to become humanity's hero on this first interstellar voyage—including quite a number of dwarfs. Some of these argued *two for the price of one.* To confine two persons eyeball to eyeball in this ship would have been the height of folly. *Homicidal* folly.

How about the risk of suicide? Hundreds of Japanese applied. No doubt they regarded this one-way journey as a kind of kamikaze mission. Strict psychological profiling screened out anyone with pathological tendencies.

The chosen hero will *not* inevitably die at journey's end. By very long baseline interferometry, space telescopes have revealed the Earth-like profile of the third world of Tau Ceti. It's almost the same size as Earth. It orbits mid-way in the habitable zone. In its spectrum there's oxygen and nitrogen and liquid water, the whole cocktail of a biosphere. There's a high chance of finding alien vegetation and even creatures, however humble. Just so long as DNA is indeed the optimum code of life and providing that proteins are compatible (rather than wrong-handed) I ought to be able to feed myself adequately. For years after landing I ought to be compiling reports to transmit to the little satellite, to be squirted across the light years.

If favourable, my reports should lead to the sending of several more quasi-space ships, each with a young volunteer host-mother aboard, and a stock of frozen embryos to start up a viable human population. None of these mothers-to-be could possibly join me until almost thirty years after I left Earth. Maybe longer, if Mission Control waited to assess the long-term effect on me of any alien microorganisms (as opposed to my succumbing swiftly!). I pin no hopes on a breakthrough in the physics of the quasi-space effect, permitting bigger ships or faster and cheaper voyages! The *Sapiens*, and successor ships, are the best chance we'll have of spreading human life to another planetary system so that all our eggs aren't in one basket.

After two millennia (and a bit more) I have acquired a destiny comparable to my brother's! There's a distinct correspondence — even to the matter of the halo. The *Sapiens* and myself are being translated into photons. We seem to be of the same substance as previously, yet actually we are woven of light which encodes us in a holographic fashion.

Why should I worry about alien bugs at journey's end, or about injuries twelve light years away from the nearest medical assistance? Or about raging toothache, four parsecs away from a dental surgery? I'm virtually invulnerable. Not that I intend to act rashly, such as dancing a jig when I land and breaking a leg. Survival through two millennia has taught me discretion.

The main problem for the chosen hero would be the sense of utter isolation.

Why should I worry about solitude? I, who have been the most alone of people! What price a few paltry decades compared with the whole of my brother's era? Time is of a little account to me, who never ages.

As for ordinary human relationships, I forget how many wives I have wedded, how many mistresses I have taken, how many children I have begotten. Some of their distant descendants may in turn have become subsequent mistresses or wives! I'm so accustomed to the rupture of relationships by natural death.

Exactly how many bygone wives? Vagueness inevitably creeps in. Even so, I have twenty-one centuries of memories to mull over during my mere twelve years of travel—along with a library of data in computer memory. How truly representative of the human race I am, more so than anyone else could possibly be.

Coincidentally, I once spent twelve and a quarter years in a small dungeon in solitary confinement. Unseen hands would slide a tray of food and water through a slot each day. The food was nourishing, though as the years went by the water became increasingly insipid. No voice ever spoke to me. My memories occupied me well enough, back then. I was optimistic that times must change. Faith (of a sort) saw me through. Not faith such as my brother's must have been, but at least an equivalent to faith.

Active faith in my brother, such as millions of people enjoy, could hardly be for me when I must distance myself from his followers for the very sake of their faith, in case discovery of my existence caused confusion.

I could hardly list my really impeccable qualifications in my application. Yet I'd already positioned myself to best advantage. Project Sapiens was a decade and a half in the development. Ten years previously, the basic physics was already understood. Such a project was foreseen. During the twenty-first century I'd gained genuine qualifications in physics and piloting and planetology and such. During the twentieth century I'd accumulated money. Plausible false documentation of parentage, schooling, and so on, was merely costly to buy. I went to work for the project in its seventh year—not too early, or I might have seemed long in the tooth as a possible future candidate.

I suppose my credentials were triple-checked, but my Palestinian background was a definite plus. The nuclear incident of the mid-Sixties obliterated the chance of checking on me totally. That crime served as a spur to the project too. Nuclear war was still a possibility. The project, mainly funded by Arab and Euro money, was one of faith, you might say. Didn't I hail from a region of three major faiths? Didn't I speak Arabic and Hebrew, as well as fluent English and French?

The psychologist who interviewed shortlisted applicants was a dumpy bespectacled middle-aged Swiss woman by the name of Hildegarde Borer. She could both lull a candidate and pierce with her questions.

"Actually," I confided to her, "I'd quite like to be as far away from this world as possible for a while." Oh, the accumulation of events and folk did weigh on me. I must avoid seeming anti-social, yet I mustn't seem at all dependent on other people. I grinned at her. "Rather like a hermit monk, meditating in silence to fulfill a vow."

"Will God alone be with you in the interstellar deeps?" she probed.

"Maybe," I replied, "I shall be extending the range of God. In a minor way," I added lightly. Nothing messianic. Nothing extremist. "Mostly," I murmured, "I'll be extending the range of Humanity. Of consciousness. Once consciousness forges a physical link between our world and Tau Ceti maybe there'll be some unforeseen consequence. I wouldn't put any money on this, though!" Ever the realist.

At the mention of money Frau Borer immediately asked, "What *will* you do about your unspent salary, accumulating at compound interest?"

Since she was Swiss, I risked a joke. "After I land, maybe I'll set up a bank. You can squirt the money to me."

She eyed me. "You lack any family of your own to assign your assets to."

I shrugged. "The nuclear incident—"

"As I'm well aware. I'm sorry."

"Don't be. It frees me from ties. My family," I stated, "is Humanity. I shall set up a trust fund to endow an orphanage in Central Africa. I haven't decided exactly where. It'll be somewhere I've never been—because I'm going where no one has ever been."

This reasoning satisfied her. It was imaginative but it wasn't excessively visionary.

Translated into light am I. Yet consciousness involves duration, the perception of elapsing seconds, minutes, hours, days, years— twelve-and-a-quarter years in all. I'm eight years into the journey.

Four more years remain. I have gone far beyond my brother. I have escaped from His orbit.

I inspire myself by calling up on screen (yet again!) a sonnet written by the Italian Giordano Bruno. Bruno was burned at the stake for heresy in the year 1600 by my brother's followers. I seem to have forgotten most of the Italian I must once have known, but with the aid of an English gloss in prose at the bottom of the screen I freely translate (ah, as I am translated, into light!):

> *And who will give me wings,*
> *And who will warm my heart?*
> *Who'll free me from the fear*
> *Of accident and death?*
> *Who'll snap my chains and burst the gates*
> *Through which few people freely pass?*
>
> *Aeons and years, days and hours,*
> *The daughters and weapons of time—*
> *Those saved me from time's fury.*
>
> *That crystal sphere of the sky*
> *Can't halt my widespread wings.*
> *Through space I hunt infinity,*
> *And other worlds. Once faraway,*
> *Soon those are left behind.*

How true, how true. What a remarkable vision of the future which is now the present. Inquisitors tortured and burned Bruno. I can hardly blame my brother, who Himself was tortured to death. Was His passion as prolonged as mine?

Tau Ceti! A sun very like Earth's own sun illuminates a world of blue and white and brown, of sea and cloud and land. Automated guidance and my own adjustments have brought me into orbit. After years of emptiness decorated with tiny motionless starlamps now half of my universe is space and half is world.

One landmass is shaped like a sperm whale, another like a horse. How Godlike my view is, though I'm not His beloved son.

Might I be so, after all? Upon this new Earth a divine pro-gramme may activate within me. My brother was time-bound to first century Palestine by the very nature of his mission. The deity who begot him wasn't bound by time. God might well have perceived a future of interstellar travel (to one neighbouring star at least). God was economical. Two interventions for the price of one! May it be that I am not redundant, but am also God's chosen son? Was I merely held in abeyance all this time?

If so, will alien intelligences necessarily await me down upon the surface of the Whale or the Horse? Ach, I know that I'm not messiah material.

The radio crackles with static, and nothing else. No civilization is broadcasting. (Yet this would also have been true of Earth until a couple of hundred years ago.)

Faced by the challenge of a whole new planet, I feel older as if gravity already tugs at me. Surely I exercised enough en route. Has my inner clock, which paused in Persia long ago, resumed its ticking?

Inspection of my face in one of the few shiny surfaces yields few clues. I see an oval with blurred features. Before departure my whole body was treated with radical depilatory creams, to permanently remove all body hair. I could do without twelve years' growth of hair or the chores of hairdressing, which might have left me looking like a ragged lunatic. Consequently I resemble some imaginary android. A hand, I may once have regrown. But my hair now, never.

Radar scanners and cameras are at work. Images are being digitised. After a few hundred orbits I will release the satellite. Data will be squirted, along with a preliminary memo about my personal impressions from orbit. Over a decade from now there'll be such rejoicing on Earth—and avid anticipation of my upcoming memos from the surface.

I wasn't asked to report on my state of mind. To do so might open treacherous trapdoors of vertigo at my sheer distance from all other human beings. To announce that I'm actually *His* brother might cast the accuracy of my own reports in doubt, though not of the radar maps nor the photographs.

Six weeks' terrestrial food and water remain. On the planet beneath me surely I shall find manna.

The landing module has come to rest upon a rolling plain fleecy with cotton-like herbage. The nose points downhill into a dip choked by grey fuzz spotted with what might be yellow blossoms or some sort of spore-pod. I think there's swampy water or saturated mud under the fuzz. The module tilts forward and to the right side. The rumpling of the land denies me any distant views.

In the vicinity grow several examples of local trees. Already I think of these as biforks and triforks. Two or three adjacent "trunks" rise from the ground, then fuse into a single column crowned with a canopy of feathery foliage.

Oh the joy of finding life!

After a while I spy pale browsing beasts the size of goats, though with tusks and tufted tails. My landing would have scared them away, but now they have returned and ignore the intrusion. Their hind legs are longer than their front legs so that their bodies slope forward and downward. Snouts to the soil, bums and tails in the air. They root with their tusks and lick with long tongues. Now and then the beasts rear upright, startled, for reasons unknown to me. They bound away on those powerful hind legs, in a toppling-forward motion. But they return again. I surmise that the tufts on the tails, held erect while grazing, are some kind of detector of vibrations which guards them while their heads are down.

Big insects with diaphanous wings glide about, sometimes snatched by swift bat-like creatures, spookily white.

To the rear of the module the crumpled parachutes lie coiled by breezes like great pink afterbirths or discarded linings of the womb from which the module has been born into this new world. I shall remain a while in the womb, although I'm breathing external air—so pure and sweet and heady after twelve years. The percentage of oxygen is higher than on Earth. Do fires periodically sweep across these plains? Do those biforks and triforks stand stiltedly so as to keep their main part out of the flash-flames?

I have a rifle with five hundred rounds, with which to hunt those browsing beasts for their meat, if I can digest it.

I compose a memo about my restricted—yet revelatory!—view of this planet. Up to the satellite; onward to Earth for vast orbital radio telescopes to detect, eventually.

I haven't stepped outside. But outside comes to me.

Cresting the rise: a dozen dappled quadrupeds. They're considerably larger and fiercer-looking than the browsers. By contrast with browsers these beasts' haunches are low-slung and their front legs rise high. One animal rears and slashes at the air with long claws. The base of the skull and the upper necks of these four-peds are . . . how can I put it? They are swollen by leathery grey sacks of various sizes. Sacks—or *saddles*, attached by rope? Why should a *neck* be saddled? No fairy-like creature perches upon those saddles. Nor do the ropes reach all the way round in a cinch. They sprawl, as though attached by stickiness or suction.

The four-peds descend with evident purpose. They paw at the

parachutes. They gape at the module. They put fierce heads together. Ropes come loose and touch—and I realize that those sacks,
those saddles are themselves the riders of the beasts.

Those riders are like octopuses. Some are as big as my chest.
Some are no larger than a modest knapsack. They cling to their
mounts with short arms which surely invade the nervous systems
and brains of the beasts. Through binoculars I'm glimpsing thin
tubes which sprout from the parasites' arms into the skulls and
necks of their hosts.

The sacks seem to lack eyes—unless the eyes are hooded and
closed tight, the better to concentrate upon what the *mounts* are
observing with keener eyesight. Does a mouth beneath each parasite draw nourishment from its host's bloodstream?

The parasites confer by touch. Messages must flow from arm to
arm—chemical or tactile signals.

There's intention and intelligence in the manoeuvering of the
mounts, in the examination of the pink shrouds and the module. A
beast steps close to scrutinise this very porthole out of which I peer.
Predatory animal eyes examine me, eyes through which a rider
must certainly be spying.

A beast rakes tentatively at the hatch with its claws. It has identified the weak spot in this metal womb of mine. It desists. Mere
claws cannot open the hatch.

Other creatures with riders have arrived—huge versions of the
browsers. A rider shifts from one to another by slithering across on
to a neighbouring back. Almost immediately a predator-animal
slaughters the abandoned food-beast by biting through its throat.
Three at a time, with no crowding nor snarling, the predators
feast.

A herd of food-on-the-hoof is here to supply the fang-armed,
claw-armed company of investigators who must have seen my pink
parachutes descend from afar and who mounted (literally!) an
expedition. These visitors seem prepared for a long stay.

Large relatives of the bat-birds arrive, ridden by little knapsacks.
After conferring, they flap away.

There must several species (or castes?) of the parasites, which
cooperate mutually. Maybe there are also rival tribes, or minor
nations. Predators may serve as warriors to cope with rivalries.

Technology seems absent, perhaps undreamed of. The parasites
use the resources of other creatures of land and sky, yet I doubt

there can be any equivalent of an ape on this planet. I think there are only animals with paws and hooves and claws.

Some predators scan the sky by night. Three minor moons orbit this world. Can the riders conceive what my module is? Of what it might be made? How it may have descended on silken wings from one of those moons, with a strange sort of parasite inside it, namely myself? Now and then, they reach out their fingerless arms to stroke the module's sides.

A month has passed, and they're still all around me. Soon I must step outside or starve. I mustn't use my rifle even by way of demonstration. I would seem like a monster. I would merely be guaranteeing my death, quite soon. Yet if I'm to be enslaved, I shall be enslaved forever.

I must greet my destiny, as my brother greeted His. Might I seem like a God to the Riders? Only, perhaps, if they have any concept of Gods.

Maybe a Rider will extract from me the concept of a God, for the first time on this world. If so, I may indeed merely have been in abeyance for the past two thousand years. Now at last I shall come into my own, in a far more bizarre way than my more famous brother could ever have dreamed possible—not that He knew of my existence!

It's time to send a last message to Earth. If there's to be any later message, it may not come from the same *me* as previously. It might be the first extraterrestrial communication.

Shall I finally reveal to Mission Control my true identity, which has sustained me for so long? I think not. Earth can probably only bear one miracle, my discovery of intelligent alien life.

I strip to the waist, as if in readiness for a scourging. The gesture I shall need to make requires a naked spine and bare neck.

(Will the Riders understand that my trousers and boots are artificial additions, akin to my module?)

After a twelve and a quarter years, the hatch is opening. How smoothly it glides. Just as smoothly, the ladder descends. The air's mild. Rays of Tau Ceti warm my flesh which is as white as alabaster. As I show myself, none of the host-beasts flinch away. No predator snarls. All is suddenly very still. I scarcely move. I'm a slow motion mime artist. Perhaps this creates a misleading impression—of semi-paralysis! I exhibit myself in this manner for a full minute to the attentive animal onlookers—to those who watch through their eyes. Presently I turn my back on them, and descend the ladder. My knees feel quite weak.

Down on the ground, I turn again, and bow three times to the spectators.

Yes, I'm inviting a Rider to mount me. How else can communication occur, if communication is possible? Riders confer, arm to arm. Soon a small knapsack, riding pillion on a food-beast, transfers itself to a predator. That predator paces toward me.

The flesh of my neck and the back of my shoulders are numb. My body jigs, out of my control. My legs kick. My arms wave. My hands flex. My head swings from side to side. My Rider is trying out my unfamiliar paces.

Soon I stagger, as my brother staggered under the weight of the cross He must drag.

I sink to my knees. I'm not so supple or strong, after all, despite twelve years of exercise. My muscles have wasted a bit. As a runner I'd be a failure. My limbs remained more supple in that dungeon long ago in the absence of any exercise equipment! Yet my hands, my dextrous hands, my nimble fingers, ah! Those are another matter.

Beasts gaze up at the sky, although no ghosts of moons are visible, only high wispy cirrus clouds streaking the blue. A sign of approaching rain? The land could use it.

Do those gazers speculate that millions more like me may live up in the sky? Have they ever theorized about the possibility of more skillful hosts (though obliged to make do with predators and grazers and bat-birds)?

My brother came to Earth to serve Humanity. Apparently I've come to Tau Ceti III to serve the Riders—as they have never been served before. Unlike my brother, I'll be utterly precious, pampered, guarded by elite predators, reserved for the most special of tasks. For precise manipulation.

I pick up a pebble. I hold it up to my eye. I rotate the stone in my fingers. I pick up a second pebble and tap the two together. Up in the air I toss one pebble up and catch it. I toss the other and catch. Elementary juggling, still on my knees.

This manipulation is a mapping of pathways. Control is ascending up through my mind. Phantom smells assault me. Adrenalin surges, so that my heart races. But now calm engulfs me. Dreamlike imagery intrudes. Memories trigger visions—of the interior of *Sapiens*. I seem to be back inside the vessel in the interstellar gulf.

It's as though my arrival at Tau Ceti and my landing here were only a delirium, a hallucination brought about by isolation and deprivation.

I see Planet Earth shrink behind me.

I see thronged human cities—all the artifice of civilization.

I look at Hildegarde Borer again. A halo surrounds her face. She's the sole object of my attention. She dominates my field of vision to the exclusion of all else. My surroundings are extinguished. The circumstances are erased. To watch her suspends my awareness. She effaces me. She obliterates all memory of . . .

. . . the early life of Nagib Jouanne . . .

. . . born in the Lebanon in 2051 . . .

My adopted identity—the latest alias. *What of it?*

How can I be remembering anything of a childhood in the Lebanon in the Twenty-Fifties and Sixties? I never was a child since the time of Emperor Augustus and King Herod!

Yet I'm on a beach playing ball with my little brother. He drowned in the sea. So did my father who tried to rescue him. My mother poisoned herself, leaving me alone. She loved my father too much.

I play ball with my brother. I toss a pebble up and down. As a little boy, how I yearned to be an astronaut aboard one of the little cities in the sky.

My present name is Nagib, *but I cannot be Nagib.*

Yet I am. My family were Lebanese Christians. We spoke Arabic, Hebrew, French, and English.

How my Rider wriggles within my mind.

Rival Rider already present within my mind, but no match for the parasite. Rival Rider being Hildegarde Borer—pouring into me the big lie to sustain me through twelve years of travel to loneliness.

Immortal. Destined. Unique (except for my more unique brother). Able to survive for centuries. To tolerate the disappearance of everyone I ever knew. Able to endure a dozen years in a dungeon. For my time of freedom will come, my release upon an alien world.

My Rider is calming me, gentling me. Trying to fathom me by being in me, like some puzzling God within. My Rider evolved over millions of years to mount and comprehend other creatures. There's so much more in me to probe and employ.

Will Earth take fright at my preliminary reports of intelligent parasites controlling the other animals on this world? Or will the news about a habitable biosphere be so wonderful as to eclipse all else?

Will I make more reports presently, full of seductive lies about partnership of species? This may not be such a lie at all . . . How long will it take my Rider to appreciate concepts such as tool-making and space-travel?

In another decade and a half, the young mothers will depart from Earthspace, sustained by lies. Will their special lie be that most life on the Earth is due to perish when a comet plunges into the Pacific? That these young mothers-to-be carry the sole embryos of survival away to another habitable world?

They'll need to be kids when they set out. Twelve years old . . . eleven. Old enough to understand and to be desperately dedicated, and able to study implantation and obstetrics and such — young enough to begin bearing numerous offspring at journey's end whilst still in their twenties, not in their thirties.

When they arrive, will an ageing man greet them, with a knapsack on his back?

Up until that moment, the girls will have been magnificently dedicated.

Soon after that, they'll be motivated anew by the Riders who wait for them. They'll be devoted to breeding as many human babies as they can.

What Actually Happened in Docklands

*A*LL OF A SUDDEN THE DAYLIGHT DIMMED AND *the previously bustling marketplace was in deepest dusk. It took only a moment till the light level returned to normal. Yet in that moment and with scarcely a flicker the balance between the two races, indeed the whole aspect of the market, had changed utterly.*

Now the chubby hairy jolly Forest Folk were fewer, and were quiet and subdued. The slim weaselly Allotes were in the majority.

Allotes: al, as in 'be a pal' and otes, as in 'sow your oats.' Allotes, Allotes, rhymes with stoats, and looking like stoats or weasels up on their hind legs, dressed in trousers and striped waistcoats and jackets (and caps), a head and a half taller than the whiskery tubby little Forest Folk who mostly wore smocks or patchwork leather jerkins and hose. The insolent flat-capped spivs lounged everywhere, sinister and manipulative.

No outcries of shock or astonishment greeted the change, no appalled or delighted squeals. Some Allotes smirked slyly—did they have an inkling, or was that simply their regular demeanour? I could almost have sworn that nobody but myself was aware that the Allotes had taken over dominance. Life continued; only now the joy had drained away, replaced by an air of menace.

*By the covenant the Forest Folk and the Allotes shared the lands,
but those who until now had been the majority race were happy-go-
lucky, far more interested in crafts than in craftiness. Before the day-
light dimmed so abruptly, the marketplace had been leafy, woodland
and town almost intermingling. Now only brick buildings surrounded
the cobbled square where the Forest Folk seemed out of place even if
their mushrooms and pies and tarts and trinkets were still worth having. I knew which race I preferred to predominate and I couldn't help
fearing that in spite of the covenant affairs might now take a nasty
turn. Yet what could I, a stranger, do? Hob-nob with a hairy stallholder — Do you realize what has happened, goodfellow? Appeal to
an Allote — Did you do something to cause the alteration, and how?
Was it wise, Sir? Will you honour the covenant?*

Instead, I awoke.

I generally dream richly, and I pay attention to my dreams. Over
breakfast of toasted muffins and raspberry jam I told my dark-haired
daughter, "I dreamt a generic fantasy dream last night."

Last day of October, today, Hallowe'en — bright and clear
though chilly outside. Sunlight flooded over Rochester Way, the
dual carriageway into Southeast London from Kent, tops of vans
visible over the masking vegetation, the constant loud hum of
glimpsed and unglimpsed traffic so regular that you scarcely noticed
it. Sunlight illuminated Sarah's bonsai collection mounted on a
table outside the picture window. The morning brightness made all
the textiles and designs in the through-lounge utterly radiant as if
the place were a painting by Bonnard. Sarah's speciality: flower
motifs, much in demand by her agent.

"The Allotes," she repeated to herself.

"Yes, and now I've realized what their name means. It's from the
Greek word *allos*, meaning 'other.'"

"Trust you," Sarah exclaimed, "to dream in Ancient Greek!"

"The word's used in science. In biology. *Alleles*, I think. Got a
dictionary?"

Dictionary duly forthcoming, from a shelf crowded with encyclopedias of pattern and gardening books and poetry.

I thumbed through.

"Here we are: *alleles*. Genes that can mutate into one another.
Also, genes that produce different effects on the same set of devel-
opmental processes. And *allogamy* is cross-fertilization. My dream
society had two alternative forms. Cuddly arty Forest Folk in the
majority, all jolly and bright. Alternatively, the spiv-stoats in control,
and not so nice a mood at all. Ethnic oppression."

"Daddy, this is so weird."

"Is it? It's a standard fantasy situation. Hobbits and Wild Wood, weasels capturing Toad Hall, blight upon the land, the Doom Lord's bane. That's what I meant by generic. The odd thing is *me* dreaming it so clearly. Has to be because of the fantasy convention."

Which (check watch) I should be driving off to once I had made myself a salami and gerkin in muffin sandwich so as not to rely on the hotel for lunch.

"That isn't the weird thing," Sarah said. "What's weird is what I dreamt. It's all come flooding back."

In her dream she had been, she said, in some super-science place. Borg technology crossed with Fritz Lang's *Metropolis*. Grimy futurism. On the outside of a huge sphere—contained within an even vaster sphere—were all these power-cylinders; and inside each cylinder an operator was chained. The operators bounced the cylinders up and down and to and fro like pogo sticks. At the very top of the sphere: a kind of keyhole, a receptor. A woman suicide defector managed to fit her cylinder into that keyhole high up.

"If she abandons her cylinder this will detonate the whole sphere—"

"So what happened next?"

"That was all. It's the sort of dream *you* ought to have dreamed, not me. All the super-science stuff. Do you think we've had a dream-swap?"

A dream-swap . . . A sort of mental allogamy? What an odd notion. I preferred to think that attending a fantasy convention was responsible. I had already checked in at the convention the previous evening, Friday. During my sleep the spirit of fantasy, so to speak, had manifested itself.

I was not staying in the convention hotel, stuck out in the middle of nowhere in Docklands. Sarah and her partner Colin rented a house only twenty minutes drive from the place. I would save the high cost of a hotel room and see something of Sarah too, though not, alas, of Colin who was reluctantly spending the weekend visiting his family in Norfolk for a wedding. My wife Jean had dithered about coming to London, not to the convention itself but to have time with Sarah. However, now our daughter was going to have to spend the whole weekend painstakingly painting a duvet cover to meet a catalogue company's deadline. Literally painting a duvet cover. Printed in Turkey where costs were cheaper, the first strike-offs to arrive were wonky as regards the yellow, and yellow loomed large since the design was of daisies.

Panic! A photo team was due to take pictures of a room-set on the Monday. Miss the date, miss the catalogue. The absurd and only solution was for Sarah to amend the colours of a whole king-size duvet personally over the weekend, paint brush in one hand, hair-drier in the other, then send by taxi. She was going to be busy.

My main purpose in being at the fantasy convention was to meet a German friend, Heinz Hermes, who ran a thriving fantasy and science fiction games company in Düsseldorf. A few weeks previously Heinz told me in a phone call that the Swedish originators of a game called Mutant Wars were interested in commissioning novels set in their far-future universe of mutations and mayhem, which would have international distribution. Since I had already written several futuristic adventure novels associated with games I was the best candidate he could think of for what might be a fairly lucrative project.

Fur coat and no nickers, Docklands. Hyper-modern commercial buildings dominated by Canary Wharf Tower, fruit of the Eighties yuppy boom, and scarcely had I arrived in the hotel the previous evening than I was hearing, "One and a *quarter* hours to produce a bog-standard pizza! By the time it arrived I had to leave —I was due on a panel. I'm starving—"

"Have you heard about—?" And best-selling American fantasy writer Dawn Doone was mentioned as having her suite burgled. "Dawn was already pissed off at the Jacuzzi only having cold water—"

"Same as my shower—"

By contrast, some of the function rooms were furnaces; no way could windows be opened.

I headed upstairs to the foyer bar area to register. Scarcely had I done so and sat down with my bulging bag of goodies, or rubbish, depending on point of view—chunking third volume of some remaindered *Mage King* saga, et cetera—than the hotel tannoy announced, "Docklands Development Authority Police will commence removing vehicles from in front of the hotel in thirty minutes."

Oops. Seeing no restriction signs anywhere nor double yellow lines, I had left the car in the street along with several others.

Exit hastily. Steer the car into the narrow maw of the hotel's subterranean park, a tight concrete corkscrew burrowing deep, hideous to manoeuvre in unless you drove something less than six feet long, and costing, I had noted, a rapacious one pound per hour payable at the reception desk before your ticket would be doctored so that you could escape. *"Facilis descensus Averno,"* I quipped to a fellow victim who had managed to stable his vehicle without gouging the bodywork against jutting flanges or utility pipes. "They forgot to put that sign up top. Easy is the descent into hell but just you try to get out again."

The tall figure with salt and pepper crewcut, and wearing a lumberjack shirt, was Jim Kruger, redoubtable critic and encyclopedist.

"This car park," he replied with moral passion, "is the an epitome of the whole social malaise of the Eighties." His sinewy purr, aroused, became a muscular throb. "It's a quintessence, even a paradigm, of the Thatcherite episteme."

Quite. Fur coat up above, no nickers down below.

Jim and I returned to the bar together.

"I'd better sort out my bag of rubbish," I said.

"What do you mean, *rubbish?* There are some very fine limited edition booklets in there."

"You'll let me toss out vol three of *Mage King?*" Quite a few copies were already lying discarded amidst empty beer glasses.

"Oh sure. Although even it, in its way, exemplifies the restorative shamanic function of fantasy."

"What, you've read it?"

Jim's eyes twinkled. He had read absolutely everything but I'm sure he was teasing.

Heinz was only coming on the Saturday. According to the programme book, following a panel in the Balmoral Room about the frustrated erotics of vampirism, wittily entitled "Love in Vein," the first party of the evening was about to kick off in the Palace Lounge adjoining the Foyer Bar: the launch of a new fantasy imprint, Unicorn.

It turned out that Jim was due to say a few words preceding the champagne toast. Which he duly did.

Unicorn as symbol of purity, only a virgin can ride one (general chuckles and mock-reproachful blushy giggles from Francesca Philipps, senior editor in charge, wearing a flapper dress from the Twenties), healing powers of the unicorn's horn, fantasy archetypically treating of an evil sickness in the harmonious and eco-friendly realm and the quest involving suffering and self-discovery leading to *palinorthosis,* Jim's word for Orl Korrect Again. All Straight Once More.

I was fond of Jim and of his mighty vocabulary, so natural on his lips that it seemed an idiom which the majority of people would be derelict, nay morally deficient, not to employ so as to clarify their thinking, their writing, their reading, their very lives. He dignified the genre field. With my background in teaching literature in universities before I became a science-fictioneer (now hoping for a commission to develop Mutant Wars) I felt quite up to speed on Greek- and Latin-based critical terminology, as indeed my dream demonstrated to Sarah; and probably I did dream about *Allotes* rather than about 'Other-Folk' on account of Jim's words at the party. The theme of my dream must be have been spurred by him, although no *palinorthosis* occurred in the dream; I woke too soon for that.

Tendrils was the title of Jim's recent collection of review-essays which was short-listed for the award-giving on the Sunday in the non-fiction category. (I certainly voted for it.) The word capsuled the way in which a work of fantasy coils itself around the core-stem of the genre, supporting itself connectedly as it put forth its own particular garb of leaves and blooms, of pages, characters, and action. Since there were ten magisterial essays in Jim's book, it also consisted of that number of *drills* into the subsoil and bedrock of fantasy, as it were. Ten drills. Even mental exercises!

Jim and I shared various odd tendrils of affiliation. Living deep in the countryside as I did (whilst writing about mighty machines and interstellar empires) I was not part of the metropolitan circuit of writers constantly meeting one another at book launches, prize-givings, promotions, and such. At least from my village on many nights I could admire the Milky Way, a view denied to city dwellers by light-fog. Jim's wife was an artist and part-time London walking-tour guide. In my village lived a tour-guide who knew Jim's wife through the trade, and whom I knew in turn because . . . but this complicates. Suffice it to say there are assorted tendrils.

Anyway, after Francesca Philipps had delivered an upbeat spiel about Unicorn, I circulated. Talk was still of the Hotel from Hell. Of Dawn Doone's burglary, obviously an inside job. Of cold showers, and denials that any other restaurants were open in Docklands, whereas one or two certainly were. Of how the hotel hadn't even intended to warn guests by tannoy of the impending tow-away and impoundment of vehicles except that organiser Yvonne blew her top and insisted.

As champagne flowed, the conviviality and companionship characteristic of a convention asserted itself vastly over the downsides.

Two Finnish friends had brought me a jar of homemade cloudberry jam, the berries picked by themselves in their local bog at the cost of wet feet. Leena and Juhani had brought a second jar for Andrew Oakley, 'He of the Trees,' who had been their guest at a convention in Finland the previous year (as I had been three years earlier) and who was to be Master of Ceremonies at the banquet and awards-giving on the Sunday. Soon the four of us were deep in converse, Andrew rhapsodizing about the spirit of the forests. From Andrew I suppose I took the Forest Folk of my dream. A handsome fellow he is: tall, curly dark hair, puckish smile, and the kindliest of people, though with a dark violent streak in his work.

Afterwards I nattered with—but this isn't the point.

Drizzle is falling as I arrive at the overblown though defective hotel this Saturday morning. Fine weather at Sarah's, rather foul over here to the north of the river. The parking restrictions and threats of tow-away I must ascribe to the IRA bomb which blew up part of Docklands a while ago as a symbol of oppression, causing millions of pounds worth of damage—yet not a notice in sight anywhere on the approach, no police cones on the street, nothing to warn the unwary. Directly outside the hotel a police car stands unoccupied. Enquiries proceeding into Dawn Doone's burglary, no doubt.

After inserting my own car into its troglodytic concrete bunker, I head inside. Even before reaching the bottom of the grand staircase I'm swept up in talk. Advice for conventions: allow at least twenty minutes to get from one spot to another. Gill has come over from Ireland, and I haven't seen Jeremy Avril-Jones for ages.

While chatting with them I glimpse two policemen departing through the main doors. A brief sighting, mind you, but their bearing and their peaked caps remind me oddly of my dream. Must be the contrast with all the fantasy people ambling and lounging around.

Finally I do reach the foyer bar to find Heinz ensconced with a couple of other Germans. Heinz is a burly fellow with short whitening hair, short whitening beard, and a seemingly permanent good-humoured grin. His two companions are fantasy artists with work in the art show, off to which they soon head, leaving Heinz and myself to discuss Mutant Wars—but this is not really relevant. What *is* relevant is that one of the barman of whom I keep catching a glimpse through the shifting crowd is a dark shifty type with a weaselly face who could almost have stepped out of the market place of my dream. A sort of human Allote. He's probably North African or Portuguese from Madeira, as many of the hotel staff seem to be, and I'm being ridiculously prejudiced.

We'll skip my discussions with Heinz. Andrew Oakley stops by, prior to giving a talk about fantasy forests, and confesses to feeling very nervous even though he doesn't look remotely so. I go along to lend support, not that he needs it, nor extra audience either. He carries the occasion off with aplomb.

At noon there's a party hosted by Microsoft—house red plonk —followed, if one cares, by more house red paid for by Peregrine Books; but I nurse a half of lager in the bar and munch my delicious stuffed cold muffin in company with Gill and Jeremy and others before spending an hour browsing in the book room, chatting to dealers and friends and my French publisher and some Ukrainians.

Three o'clock: and in the art deco cocktail bar downstairs a new magazine, *Phantasia*, launches itself innovatively with scones and clotted cream, squashy cream cakes, and pots of tea. This proves to be a complete wow, most people by now being bored with free booze. The packed room is soon as hot as a cup of tea, so I and many others overspill into the reception area. From his vantage point behind the check-in counter, slyly studying us—

—and that sleek skinny woman perching at a computer terminal along from him—

—and that slim slick porter on the far side of the entrance—all now staring at me in unison as I balance my cup and saucer—

—they're in human guise, but I know them. As I hurry back into the happy perspiring throng in the cocktail bar, the Tiffany-style lights all flicker.

There are many more of us than of *them*, and the hotel has signed a binding contract with the convention, good heavens; but that flicker of the lights increasingly worries me. It's easy to imagine that behind the wainscots of the hotel, behind the deluxe paneling and the wallpaper, are narrow hidden corridors. Where is the machinery controlling the heating and air conditioning, and the lighting? Above all, the *lighting*, which might fade then resurge to reveal a terrible change.

By the evening, and the Fantasy Writers Association Punch Party, nothing has worsened. Since I shall soon be driving back to Sarah's I only drink plain orange juice; so alcohol is not responsible for my heightened sense of what Jim Kruger characterizes in *Tendrils* as an *asthenic* situation, from a Greek word for sickness.

On the contrary, it is lack of alcohol in my bloodstream and brain that inhibits me from buttonholing people to alert them to the situation—which will come to a head, I'm now convinced, not tonight but early tomorrow afternoon. Where else but at the Fantasy Awards Banquet when almost everyone will be gathered together in one place, in the Grand Suite behind closed doors?

Meanwhile hotel staff who are actually Allotes eye me askance as if they sense that I know. Temporary escape from the hotel is uppermost in my mind.

When I descend to the underground car park, after handing over eleven quid to that sleek slinky female to have my exit ticket processed, I'm followed—click click click of feet, echoing in the coiling concrete tunnel with its tight-packed bays. My car has gone —no, a van hides it. The electronic key won't work—second time it does, doors all clunk open. Inside, and centrally lock.

My pursuer is the same female. She stares brazenly—not at all nervous to be trailing a bloke into this empty desolate place.

Backing out and turning is a nightmare with that van alongside. Back and forth, back and forth like a piston. I'm going to get jammed. Don't scrape the bodywork. A male Allote has joined the female. Both watch my pathetic manoeuvres superciliously.

At last I'm able to drive past them. Window down quickly to thrust the ticket into the box at the barrier; and I'm out on an empty street.

When I drove in this morning, using Rochester Way, of course I went under the river by way of the Blackwall Tunnel. But now the southbound tunnel is closed. Signs block the roadway: maintenance, supposedly. I spy Allotes beside the signs—the *asthenia* is worse than I feared; it has spread throughout Docklands.

No choice but to stay north of the river all the way to Dartford Bridge then double back.

Turns out to be a hell-drive. Miles of traffic cones mutate a straight road into an interminable chicane, and mists are rising, drifting grey blankets blindingly a-dazzle from my dipped headlights. This is the old Dickensian marshland where boatmen used to fish for corpses, and in the mists I seem to glimpse spectral Allote figures emerging from hiding, then vanishing again.

I'm experiencing a hideous epiphany—or should I say an antiepiphany? An epiphany is a glorious showing-forth, a revelation emerging amidst the mundane, a word beloved on James Joyce in his *Portrait of the Artist*. Jim Kruger should know the proper term for an anti-epiphany.

My relief at reaching the Dartford Bridge is enormous, as is the bridge itself, rising upward and upward, many lanes wide, high

above a myriad lights and the dark river, like a giant ramp for
launching a space vehicle as in the film *When Worlds Collide.*
When I dip down, the south side is clear of mist. All is visible and
orderly, no longer mutating.

I shall be safe at Sarah's overnight. Very safe in the mundane
sense: her neighbourhood is full of retired bullion robbers who
keep a tight rein on their patch, resulting in one of the lowest insurance premiums for house contents, cheaper than my own premium
in the supposedly placid heart of the countryside.

How Sarah and Colin come to be living there, in an externally
tatty house amidst others tarted up as Spanish villas with XJ6s on
the forecourts, is a complicated story involving Colin's Godmother,
the cook at a nursing home, and the cook's father marrying an air
hostess. This sounds like the title of a Peter Greenaway film. . . .

Safe in the mundane sense, yes. But also metaphysically. *Asthenia* has not yet spread south of the river.

When I arrive, Sarah has retired to bed leaving a note. Zonked
out by the duvet covet—which is much in evidence, big daisies all
over it. Some seafood tagliatelle in the fridge if I need some supper.

Ah, I have been in the present tense for immediacy.

Sleep, wake. It was Sunday morning. After I told Sarah what had
happened, she asked, "How much did you drink yesterday?"

"Don't be silly, I was driving."

"Had you considered you might be hallucinating?"

"I most certainly was *not*. Look, I seriously need you to come to
the convention with me today for backup. You dreamt the other
portion of my dream—the world that the Allotes will make if they're
in control. I'll pay for a day membership and I'll try to get a banquet
ticket for you."

"Aren't you rather forgetting about my duvet?"

"How much is left to finish?"

"There's two or three hours more work yet."

"Bring the blessed thing with you! And the paint and hair-drier.
People do embroidery at conventions." Not at this one, actually.
"*Please*, Sarah. There's oodles of space. No one will walk on it. It'll
be like part of the art show."

"A daisy duvet? I hardly think so."

"I beg you."

Fast forward to the foyer bar once more. Spread out, a king-size
duvet cover *is* rather large; but never mind. Ideally Sarah should

have used fabric paint. This being a rush job, she was dry-brushing brilliant concentrated water colour to avoid oozing, dragging the yellow on with a half-inch brush. Of course she needed to bring cardboard to avoid soak-through, a duvet cover being basically a big bag.

Andrew Oakley seemed very taken by the design and sat beside me to admire Sarah down on her hands and knees, him in a dinner jacket and frilly shirt in readiness for the banquet—which in fact would be dress-as-you-please. Jim Kruger hove to, looking butch and severe in a stylish black shirt cut off at the shoulders, displaying muscular arms to advantage. His more minimalist outfit connoted moral thrust—inquisitor at work in a lit-crit dungeon—and that's exactly what would be needed.

No time like the present.

I had feared it would be hard to persuade Jim and Andrew. However, as I related my dream and Sarah's and my subsequent observations, not only inside the hotel but also while driving, Jim's demeanour altered quickly to full alert. And He of the Trees, too. Jim's critical antennae and Andrew's rootier instincts had in fact been bristling for some while, and now they perceived as I did.

"Something awful's going to happen at the banquet," I predicted.

Jim nodded. "Aside from the standard of the food, you mean. The Dimming, and the Change. Allotes!" He flexed his hands. "Now that we know their true name, thanks to you, we're empowered."

"We need to bring about pre-emptive *palinorthosis*. Or else the Change will reach out across London. Few people will realize but we'll be on course for the future that Sarah dreamt. The spheres and the cylinders."

From the floor my daughter chipped in.

"My dream might have been a version of the Millennium Dome going up in Greenwich."

"Maybe, maybe not," said Jim. "Maybe much worse."

Andrew seemed at a loss. "Palin-what?"

"*-orthosis*. Restoration. Andrew, you're in charge of the proceedings today. You're the wielder of words. Ian's right. It'll happen at the banquet for sure. Wait here!" So saying, Jim leapt up and headed for the Dealer's Room.

Speedily he returned with a borrowed copy of his mammoth *Encyclopedia Fantasica*, weighing in at several pounds and well over a thousand pages. He riffed through to the entry on *Asthenia,* sickness in the land, which he summarised quickly for Andrew, and next he turned to the cross-referenced entry on *Palinorthosis,* coaching Andrew in these potent critical terms.

It was then that it happened. The lights flickered. I hadn't noticed people drifting away, but the foyer bar was deserted apart from the three of us, and Sarah doggedly painting, and a pair of wily-looking barmen.

A very *allotic*-looking hotel security man came from a side corridor. In his polished leather shoes he strolled across the far reach of Sarah's duvet and scowled at a yellow footprint he impressed on the carpet.

"Bundle this up and get it out of here," he snapped, teeth predatory. "Right now!"

One of the barmen had sidled from behind the long counter, holding a bottle of Newcastle Brown Ale by the neck in a menacing manner. His companion joined him, clutching an empty pint mug, the heavy dimple sort, and a towel. The temperature had chilled.

As the security Allote bent over to paw the duvet cover, Andrew bellowed, "Leave that alone!" Face thunderous, he yanked at the fabric, rising as he did so to his full six feet, swirling the daisy duvet cover up and around himself so that it settled upon him like a cloak.

Reaching out instinctively in this artificial place for something natural to draw strength from, Andrew's fingers settled upon the polished oak doweling fronting the counter, held in place by brass ring-clamps. His hand closed on the oak—and he wrenched a yard-long section free.

A staff, to use against the Allote staff. In that moment, as he confronted the security creature, Andrew *was* a Mage King. And I swear, I swear that green buds burst from the oak.

Jim also rose, hefting the *Encyclopedia Fantastica* like Moses on Mount Sinai. The two barmen were advancing upon Andrew whose back was turned to them. I thought that Jim might bellow a powerful critical term at the barmen; but instead, with condign righteousness (and considerable force)—just as they say of American district attorneys—*he threw the book at them.* All those million and more words all at once.

The effect upon the two Allotes was staggering. Quite literally: struck and stunned, the barman holding the bottle cannoned into his crony, skulls cracking together. Both of them sprawled.

As if participating in the shock, the lights flickered again—and then from the grand stairway and from the direction of the lifts and from the art show carefree conventioneers were returning, chatting and chuckling, to the foyer bar—to catch a puzzling glimpse of what must have seemed a piece of impromptu vaudeville, Andrew cloaked in bright daisies tossing his staff at the security man as Jim, very concisely, cried, "Split!" and as the four of us scarpered, Andrew bringing Sarah's duvet cover with him, though she must abandon her paint and cardboard. Yet we knew full well that palinorthosis had occurred, that the Change had been aborted, that the Allotes were trounced.

There were some unfortunate repercussions.

During the banquet, which was quite meagre—the hotel cooks not having had time to lay on a proper propitiatory feast of, say, suckling pig in place of the scheduled breast of chicken with carrots, spuds, and broccoli—Jim was escorted out of the Grand Suite by police.

Officers had by no means turned up immediately, and in any case the hotel's security man had no way of identifying Jim—or Andrew—until the banquet began. To him, they were nobody special. The arresting officers were the same pair whom I had seen leaving the hotel the day before, although they no longer looked in the least allotic.

In fact four policemen turned up. After urgent intercession by Yvonne, the other two contented themselves with keeping an eye on Andrew while he discharged his duties as MC, which he carried out nobly in the circumstances. Scarcely anyone had the least idea what, if anything, had happened—though Andrew looked bruised about the eye as if he had taken a punch. The yellow discolouration was actually paint from Sarah's duvet cover. She had sponged Andrew's dinner jacket but in poor light we had missed the stain on his face.

Sarah and I were sharing a table with Gill and anthologist Pete and Nicki and several others. Before we sat down, Pete had been nattering about Lord Dunsany. Now he was agog with curiosity. Since I knew Pete well, I tried to confide about the Allotes, only to be greeted by cordial scepticism. Sarah frowned at me, implying that I should keep my trap shut.

When eventually Dawn Doone opened an envelope to announce that Jim had won (in absentia) for *Tendrils*, there arose a great cheer of solidarity since obviously Jim was in some kind of trouble—and Yvonne accepted the statuette on his behalf.

Once the awards were over, the two officers made their way forward to arrest Andrew too, for criminal damage, so it transpired. Jim's charge, more serious, would be assault. Myself and Sarah appeared merely to have been blameless spectators of the affray. Obviously we had chased after Andrew to retrieve the duvet cover.

And in fact Sarah and I had to leave promptly, with no chance to attend the post-awards party sponsored by Paragon Books. That duvet cover needed several hours remedial attention.

Lo, the southbound Blackwall Tunnel was open to traffic.

In the aftermath Dawn Doone's jewels and credit cards and AmEx travellers cheques turned up, stashed under pebbles in the pot of a plastic palm tree on the floor below her suite.

Andrew was ordered to pay the cost of repairs to the bar-rail. In lieu of a fine he was sentenced to thirty hours community service on an urban woodland project—which suited him down to the ground and inspired his splendid novella, "Woodmaster."

At Jim's court appearance, where he conducted his own defence, the police prosecuting officer preposterously and allotically tried to portray Jim as a skinhead committing a racist attack. The two barmen had in fact been Moroccans, and I have mentioned how Jim was clad and looked at the time of the incident. Needless to say, the truth about Allotes would scarcely have endeared Jim to the magistrates on the bench. According to the report in the newszine *Slightly Slower Than Light* "with cultured eloquence" Jim easily rebutted the accusation, counter-accusing that contrariwise it was the hotel management and personnel who had discriminated against guests. In exasperation he had merely thrown a book. Was it his fault that the only book at hand was so heavy as to cause concussion?

Upshot: a fifty pound fine. (Actually, Jim's action cost him twice that sum since the copy Jim had borrowed split its spine falling to the floor after felling the Allotes, and he must reimburse the dealer.) No mention in *SSTL* about how Jim and Andrew and Sarah and I had saved the world.

That's pretty much it, except for an odd addendum.

A couple of weeks ago the Krugers' rooftop patio was featured on TV in one of those programmes where experts provide a makeover. Until now the walk-onto roof had been a bare blank space overlooking a street market—Jim's DIY activities had focused less on urban gardening than on fitting up several lock-up garages in his neighbourhood which he rented to store the vast overspill from his book collection.

When the presiding expert was finished, lo, a varnished board-walk bore tubs of herbs, light-weight plastic garden furniture, and a big terracotta-look plastic urn, into which first of all went a lot of polystyrene pieces—keeping the weight down was essential on a roof—and then a sapling along with soil and some fertilizer.

A guest joined the Krugers to toast their aerial garden, none other than Andrew Oakley. Evidently Andrew and Jim had become close since events at the hotel.

Jim raised a glass of white wine. "To our first tree," he said drolly.

He of the Trees poured some wine as a libation and set his glass down upon the soil in the urn. Ceremoniously he gripped the sapling in both hands, blessing it, anointing it with his palms.

Though I could not make out the species, how could I ever forget that length of oak dowel budding in Andrew's grasp? I fear for the structural integrity of that roof in months to come.

The Boy who Lost an Hour, the Girl who Lost her Life

ONY WOKE WITH SUCH A START. LIGHT FROM THE full moon flooded through the window of his bedroom at the side of the bungalow. Moonlight clearly lit the Donald Duck clock on the wall. The clock hung higher than Tony could reach, unless he stood on a chair. Little hand between three and four. Big hand at the bottom. Half-past three.

Panic seized him. He jerked up his left wrist. On his new Aladdin watch the big hand was at the bottom but the big hand pointed between two and three. It was half-past two by his wristwatch.

Despite Daddy's promise, despite Tony's own vows, he'd woken up too late. Daddy must have tiptoed around the house at two ayem. He had come in here, but he hadn't wakened Tony.

Aunt Jean, who always wore Jeans, had given Tony the watch the day before for his fifth birthday. He was Big Five. Soon he'd be starting real school. Pride was one reason why he kept the watch on when he went to bed. But mainly, if he took it off, he might forget exactly where it was when the time came to change all the clocks.

At the birthday party he had gone round showing the wristwatch to Tim and Michael and Sarah and the others just a bit too much, until Sarah and Tim had thrust their own presents at him a second time, as if he hadn't liked those enough: the toy police car, the bendy dinosaur . . .

Home wasn't big enough to hold a party in. In the wooden community hall along the road there'd been balloons and cakes and musical chairs and pass-the-parcel and a magic-man. When he went to bed Tony had been so tired. He'd asked for his curtains to stay open. Mummy said the moon would keep him awake later on. Maybe she thought he was scared of the dark. Oh no. He hadn't wanted Daddy to need to switch on the light at two, and dazzle him. Because the curtains were open, before he fell asleep Tony had seen the real police car cruise slowly past. It had stopped by the high wall of the huge house along the road where children lived who were odd because they didn't have Mummies and Daddies.

From the bottom of the bed, Big Bear and Little Bear stared at Tony now with glittery eyes. The birds hadn't started their chorus yet. It was so quiet. Tony squirmed along the duvet toward the bears. Pressing himself right up against the window, he stared at his Aladdin watch again.

It was half-past two for Tony. It was half-past three for Daddy and Mummy and the rest of the world.

The top bit of window was open for air because the weather was warm earlier this year than usual. He heard a voice calling softly, *"Hey there!"*

When Mummies and Daddies came to collect their children from the party, they stood around for a while drinking glasses of wine.

"This is the night, isn't it? It *is* forward, not back—?"

"Do we lose an hour or do we gain—?"

"Look: when it's two o'clock it becomes three o'clock. We're an hour ahead of where we were. So it stays dark longer in the morning—"

"Seven o'clock is really six o'clock—"

Wine could make grown-ups silly. They seemed to be getting heated up about nonsense, but this was important to Tony in view of his new Aladdin watch. During the magic show Aunt Jean had been sipping wine at the back of the hall with Mummy and Daddy. Now she was sitting on her own. So Tony asked her about this business of 'changing the clocks.'

She'd laughed. "I'm not sure a child can follow this! Grown-ups get flummoxed enough. Foreigners must think we're crazy, unless the same thing happens in their own countries. Well, in our coun-

try twice a year the time changes. Spring forward, fall back: that's
how you remember. Fall's another name for autumn, you see."

No, he didn't see.

"Because in the autumn all the leaves fall off the trees. That's
when time goes back an hour. The original idea was to make the
world lighter on winter mornings. But now it's spring, so tonight the
time goes forward again to what it ought to be anyway. So all the
clocks have to change."

Who could possibly change all the clocks in the world? Did they
change themselves?

Aunt Jean took another swallow of red wine. "People change
their own clocks, Tony."

He brandished the watch she had given him.

"You have to change it yourself." She giggled. "Two o'clock in
the morning: that's when the time changes."

When everybody was asleep in bed? People must get up specially. But his Aladdin watch didn't have a 'larm—like those watches
which would go *beep-beep*.

"It doesn't have a 'larm!" he protested.

Aunt Jean seemed annoyed. "Well, I'm sure I'm very sorry about
that!"

Back home, the man on the TV said how everyone should put their
clocks forward at two in the morning; so this must be really important.

You had to put your *own* forward. Had to do it yourself. Tony was
Big Five now. He asked Daddy to promise to wake him up at two,
cos there was no 'larm on his watch.

"You oughtn't to have said that to Aunt Jean," Mummy told him
quite sternly. "As though you weren't satisfied! You hurt her feelings."

Daddy made a never-mind face at Mummy. "It's his birthday,
after all—"

"Huh, at this rate he won't have another—"

"Let's forget it, hmm? Tiring day. I'll wake him up at two." And
Daddy had winked at Mummy.

"What happens," asked Tony, "if you don't put the clock forward?"

"In that case," Mummy said sharply, "you get left behind."

He'd been left behind. Cos they thought he'd been rude to Aunt
Jean; but he hadn't been!

A little girl was standing in the garden by the big rose bush, out of sight of the street. She was waving to him.

She must have been left behind too!

The big window was kept locked for safety when the house was empty and at night, but Mummy had showed him how to unlock it in case there was ever a fire. As he pushed the window open the girl came closer. She was skinny, with untidy short brown hair. Her dress was printed with grey flowers which might have been any colour during the day. That dress looked a bit torn and dirtied. Her thin ankles poked into trainers fastened tightly by those cling-together straps.

"The clocks have changed," Tony told her, and showed his Aladdin watch. "I've been left behind!"

For a moment he thought she was going laugh at him, but then she replied firmly, "You aren't the only one."

"Daddy promised to wake me but he left me sleeping when he changed the clock."

"You won't be able to wake your Daddy now," she said with absolute certainty. "You can't wake a Daddy or a Mummy or anyone. They're all in a different hour. They're in their own world." She seemed to know all about this. Of course she must, if she was here and able to talk to him. What had *she* done that was wrong?

"They wouldn't be able to see you!" she hissed.

Tim had told Tony about a movie. Tim's baby sitter and her boyfriend had wanted to watch the movie, and Tim was supposed to be in bed upstairs. Tim's home was bigger than Tony's; it had two floors. Tim had crept downstairs. The door to the sitting room was ajar. He had watched through the gap.

Once upon a time in a big old house a little girl had died horribly. A man and woman moved in, who didn't know about the girl. They already had two young sons but they wanted a girl as well. Soon somebody whom no one could see was using the toilet. Somebody was taking snacks and milk from the fridge. Somebody was knocking things over and breaking them. At first the parents thought their own boys were to blame—but then an awful accident happened to one of the boys, which couldn't possibly have been his fault. The grown-ups called for a priest to come and throw water around the rooms and pray and *exercise* the house. . . .

That's how it would be here at home. Tony would use the toilet and he'd get hungry and thirsty, but Mummy and Daddy would never see him because he was an hour behind.

"What can I do?" he asked the girl.

"Do what I say," she said. "I know what to do. We have to go somewhere special." She pointed up at the full moon. "That's a face up there."

"It's the Man in the Moon."

She stamped her foot angrily. "No, it isn't. It's a face all right, but it's the face of a *clock*. Only, you can't see the hands till you go to a special place. You have to see the hands move on the Moon. Then you can come back, and it'll be all right."

Tony gazed at the bright blotchy Moon. It was as round as a clock tonight, a luminous clock.

"What if I just wind my watch forward *now?*"

"Too late," she sang out, "too late! You'll only break it!"

How did she know about the Moon?

"People have been to the Moon," she said.

"I know that!"

"That was to see about fitting new hands on it. The old hands are invisible 'cept to people who get left behind—and from special places. The spacemen stuck a spike in the Moon for the new hands. Soon it'll be a clock everyone can see, 'cept if its cloudy."

"You can't see all of it all the time—"

"They'll light it properly. You're *wasting* time! I won't show you the place if you don't come now."

Tony pulled on his clothes and shoes and he climbed on to the hard window frame, which hurt his knees, and dropped himself down on to the path.

The girl was taller than Tony by a head or more. Maybe she was seven. Or eight.

"What's your name?" he asked.

"People call me Mar-gar-et." She spoke each sound as if they were strange to her. "But I'm not a Mar-gar-et. I'm Midge."

A small garden hugged the bungalow. At the back of the garden was a fence. One of the planks had rotted and shifted aside. The girl already seemed to know about that. A grown-up couldn't get through the fence, but Tony could, even if it meant scraping clothes; and Midge was so skinny.

Behind the fence was a waste place—and beyond was a forest of Christmas trees in rows, with lanes which went on and on.

As Midge went with Tony into the forest, she asked, "What's your name, anyway?"

"It's Tony—I thought you knew about me!"

She caught hold of his hand, the one with the watch. Her own hand was sticky and strong.

"I know all about you! You had a birthday party. Balloons and Mummies and Daddies."

She must have peeped through the window of the community hall. She must have seen him walk back home with his parents, carrying his presents. He tried to pull away, but she tugged him along with her into the forest.

"You have to come with me and see the hands of the Moon!"

Because of the Moon it was bright enough to see all the silvery branches.

"I want to go home," he begged.

"You can't go back yet. You'd still be too early. An hour too early."

"I'd have asked you to the party if I'd known you, Midge!"

She laughed.

And he began to cry.

With her free hand she slapped him on the cheek.

"Crybaby," she mocked. "It's horrid being lost, Tony. Never being seen. Never being heard. 'Cept by my friends who can see the hands of the Moon."

Did she really want him as her friend?

"Where's the place?" he snivelled.

"It's at the far end of the forest."

He'd be safe until then, wouldn't he? She wouldn't slap him again? He let her lead him along, though really he couldn't have stopped her from dragging him.

After a while she said, "You'll have your time back—but I shan't. Not till the Moon grins wide and spits me out like it grinned and swallowed me once, and my friends."

"You said the Moon wasn't a man with a face, you said it was a clock!"

"Mainly it's a clock. Mainly!"

Tony was terrified. Who were these friends who were waiting at the far end of the forest?

They came to a clearing. All around it, the boughs of the Christmas trees jutted like hundreds of barbed spears. The Moon glared down. Tony should easily have been able to see other children waiting, but he couldn't. Midge's friends must be hiding behind tree trunks. She sat down on soft nice-smelling needles, pulling him with her. Then she shuffled round behind him.

"Look up, look up," she chanted. "Gape at the Moon. Keep your eyes open. Don't close them. Don't look anywhere else or I'll have to hit you."

Tony stared up. His ears were alert for any rustle of feet creeping closer, but the pine needles would deaden the noise. The Moon began to blind him to anything else. Soon there was just that bright blotchy flat disc.

"It's horrid being lost, Tony—"

Desperately he tried to see hands on the Moon. Gaze as he might, he couldn't.

Gradually, out of the corners of his eyes, he became sure that other children were indeed sitting around in the clearing, clasping their drawn-up knees and staring at him. He didn't dare look to make sure.

"The Moon's made of stone," came Midge's voice, "and so am I. Hard stone." Did she have a stone in her hand? Was she was going to hit him with it the moment he stopped gaping? "A stone clock. A moon-dial . . ."

His eyes were watering with effort. Of course he blinked now and then.

"Please, Midge," he begged, but no reply came.

Grey light began to dawn. A hundred birds started singing. The Moon was fainter now, a sickly yellow. When it sank slowly behind the top branches of a Christmas tree at last he saw the dark pointers upon the Moon's face—and he cried out, "Yes, yes, I can see them!"

Midge wasn't there any more. She'd gone. He hadn't heard her leave because of the birds. Nor were there any other children in the clearing. He was alone.

His legs had cramped. He staggered but soon he was running.

Only when he had climbed back into his bedroom, and the Donald Duck clock caught his eye, did he think to look at his wrist-watch. Little hand near five. Big hand at nine. It was quarter to five—by the clock and by the Aladdin watch as well.

Mummy came in to wake him, but he was already awake. He'd been fretting whether she would come, or whether he'd have to go to the kitchen on his own—and would they be surprised to see him? Had they been trying to lose him?

"I'm sorry!" he told her.

Mummy looked suspicious. "What about?"

"Cos I was rude to Aunt Jean."

"Oh . . . I thought you'd broken something."

He pointed at the clock. "Daddy didn't wake me at two."

"You were dead to the world, but your Daddy thought you'd want to see the right time in the morning—"

Oh yes. To see the right time was everything.

She realized what he had said. "At two? Did you think we'd sit up till *two?*"

With the summer term Tony started real school. The school bus took him there and brought him back. Different Mummies would ride on the bus in case bigger children behaved badly. Always two Mummies, so that they could talk to each other.

One hot day, men were busy tearing up the road near the huge house with the wall all around. A red light halted the bus, and Tony saw Midge on the pavement. She was standing stiffly beside a big woman who wore a blue suit. Those flowers on Midge's dress were pink roses. Tony rapped his knuckles on the glass, then he slapped his flat palm, which made more noise.

The woman in blue had noticed Tony and was frowning. Midge only stared emptily in the same direction as ever. He slapped harder.

"Stop that," he heard a Mummy call out. "Stop it right now! *Don't make fun.*"

The other Mummy said to her friend, "That's the girl that runs away. Though she's *supposed* to be severely," and she said a big word.

Back home, Tony asked his Mummy, "What's or-tis-tic mean?"

"Artistic," she corrected him. "It means you're good at painting and playing music and things like that. Did a teacher say that about you today?"

Tony shook his head. He mustn't have heard right in the bus. Anyway, Midge hadn't said anything to him about paint or music. He remembered how blank her look had been, as if her face was a stone.

Tulips from Amsterdam

"SO," SAID TULIP TO ME, UNCROSSING HER LONG legs, "I climbed into the car with this fellow, and we cruised on to the motorway . . ."

Tulip was what her friends called her, so she said. In her olive-green jeans and tight chartreuse sweater she was certainly long-stemmed. She wore her short dyed hair in upright gelled petals of orange and yellow and apricot. A tiny golden tulip adorned her pierced right nostril. Quite a glorious and exotic creation she'd made of herself. Not garish. The punk hair was chic rather than brazen. The nose trinket was a perfect grace-note. How I desired her, though first I must carefully assess her.

As soon as Tulip had come into my office I had abandoned my cluttered desk and shown her to one of the two cosy chairs beside the low interview table. She had demurred at being recorded on cassette. I respected her wish. I cradled a notepad on my lap.

Slim nose, high cheek bones. Opaline eyes: green within cream. Gold subtly shadowed the orbits and brows, like a dust of pollen.

"On the last day of last term," she said, "which was a Friday, of course, we were all given an art history test to take away with us."

Her voice was surprisingly sweet, with a hint of Scots. There were no raucous or shrill notes such as often spoils a first impression of grace and intelligence.

"Our test took the form of a photo in a sealed envelope. Printed on the front was the instruction: DON'T OPEN TILL SATURDAY MORNING. Most of us would be travelling miles the next day, but by the evening of the same day we were supposed to write a page of comment about whatever painting the photo showed and post our page back in the stamped addressed envelope provided. By that time the college library was already shut, so I didn't sneak a look at the photo right away. Too much else to do."

"This sounds more like an initiative test for secret agents," I said. "Who dreamed it up?"

"Roger Weeks. He hoped we'd be spontaneous and ingenious."

I didn't know Weeks very well, but I was aware that he was innovative.

"Well now," said Tulip, "I was sitting with this stranger in his BMW doing about eighty in the slow lane, because the motorway was fairly empty—"

I must have pursed my lips. She nodded briefly.

"I know I shouldn't hitch on my own! Rapists, murderers, and molesters. It saves *money*, and I was skint. Deep in the red. Still am, in fact."

"I'm sorry." I never offered even a token fee in exchange for stories in case my subjects invented accounts in the hope of earning some cash. What I needed were genuine volunteers. There were always enough of those. Subsequently I might invite Tulip out for a drink and a meal. I couldn't be sure yet. Her arrival in my office at four o'clock put us conveniently close to such a possibility.

"So I opened my envelope and I started looking at *this*—"

From her suede patchwork bag she took a colour photograph, which she laid on the table and angled to face me.

In the painting the bearded faces of half a dozen peering men were illuminated by golden light. Black clothes with big white ornamental ruffs around the necks. Background: dark grey and black.

"A Rembrandt, isn't it?"

She laughed. "You pass the test. Who else paints so dark and so bright?"

In the foreground lay a chalky corpse, naked but for a cloth across the loins. The only person who was wearing a hat—big-brimmed and black—was probing with slim silver forceps at the left arm of the corpse. A flayed, blood-red arm. A dissection was commencing.

"Mister BMW glanced at the photo on my knee and he said to me, 'That's *The Anatomy Lesson*. Painted in 1632, or thereabouts.' Wow, he recognized it!—"

The driver, as Tulip described him, was both dishy and dusty. Dishy, as regards craggy features and a moderately athletic body attired in an expensive grey suit, blue silk shirt and arty tie with pastel butterfly motifs. Dusty (in her parlance) as regards thinning wayward grey hair and a certain pallor to his skin, not unlike that of the corpse laid out for dissection. The man must have been about fifty. Tulip couldn't decide whether a small mulberry birthmark on his forehead, in the shape of a mushroom, was fascinating or icky.

He was, so he said, a publisher's representative. Name of Tony. He travelled a lot. Stayed in motels mainly. He liked motels. He would curl up with a book if no finer entertainment offered itself.

What did this hint mean? Did Tony sometimes pick girls up at motorway service stations? Tulip suspected so. This sort of come-on was definitely dusty—if it really was a come-on.

Tony had grinned at her expression. Oh, but books are best, my dear, especially artistic books! Can't be too careful nowadays. . . .

Was this meant to be reassuring? Maybe Tony was nervous. Tulip began to peg him as someone who liked to talk a bit dirty and experienced, so as to impress; but who didn't actually do much about whatever fantasies he harboured—one of which was now tantalising him in the person of herself.

"Why didn't you tell him to stop and let you off?"

"What, on a motorway at eighty? Anyway, he knew about the Rembrandt. I didn't know a thing about this particular painting."

Nor was I her moral counsellor. She was there in my office to tell me her story. I was about to collect it.

The weird thing was that this story was being recounted as having happened to *herself*—not to a friend, or to a friend of a friend. Could Tulip have misunderstood my interests, as outlined on a notice permanently pinned in the students' union?

For the past ten years I'd been collecting and classifying urban legends. Principally I taught sociology and social anthropology to a wide range of students at this so-called University of Blanchester. The university was an amalgamation of technical and higher education colleges and an art school. These days, every place worth its salt must be a full-blown university so as to emulate mainland European educational standards (at least on paper).

The reality is overcrowding and scant resources and student poverty, along with a fudging of the unemployment statistics. Rejoice, nowadays we have three million young people in higher education!

Some of my students applied to study sociology because the subject seemed inherently interesting and they knew that realistically they had few job prospects on graduation, whatever humanities course they chose to study. Others were being "humanized" as a sideline to their main degree work in computer studies or graphic design or whatever. They were a rich source of urban myths — though the Tale of the Starving Student Who Sold a Kidney Because his Student Loan was Three Months Late was rather close to the knuckle of truth, at least as regards the straitened circumstances of the young and the scandalous sloth of the Student Loan Company.

Events in urban legends never happen to the person from whom you hear the story. They happen to someone more distant — to an acquaintance of an acquaintance. The mysterious hitchhiker never rides with your informant, but with a friend of a friend of the informant. It is in that other person's car that the hitchhiker leaves the bloodstained hatchet. Your informant swears to the total truth of the tale. If you manage to track down the person to whom the incident supposedly occurred, why, actually it befell a friend of theirs. Or a friend of a friend.

Welcome to modern mythology — which concerns not Gods and Goddesses but homicidal hitchhikers and baby-sitters in peril and microwave ovens.

The Kidney Transplant? A favourite story of mine! And how symptomatic.

The person who wants the kidney is the owner of a lucrative Indian restaurant. The illegal operation will be carried out secretly by his brother, who is actually a vet, a graduate of Calcutta Veterinary School (exact details may vary) and a competent animal surgeon. In the clinic adjoining the vet's home there's an operating theatre, normally used for cats and dogs and rabbits. Some dogs are huge, thus the table is full size.

No sooner is the kidney successfully removed from the student than a lorry skids into the utility pole outside the clinic. This brings down the power line. Bye-bye to the electricity supply for at least the next twenty-four hours. Woe to the refrigerator which would have chilled the kidney till the following evening when the organ would be inserted into the brother.

The brother rushes back to his restaurant with the kidney in a container labelled with the student's name, to pop it in one of his own fridges. None of the waiters nor the chef know about the secret arrangement. The boss tells them sternly to *keep this box safe.*

The starving student recovers with remarkable speed. In fact, the very next day, to celebrate his new prosperity, he goes to the Indian restaurant for lunch and orders its Special Meat Curry. A waiter knows the student by name. The waiter knows that the container in the fridge is labelled with this customer's name. Consequently he hands the kidney to the chef. . . .

Naturally there are gaping holes in the story. If the student is so destitute, how is he a habitué of a restaurant in the first place? (But if he isn't, how else would he know the manager well enough to make a clandestine bargain with him?) Most so-called Indian restaurants are actually run by Bangladeshis or Pakistanis, not by Indians. Kidneys play no noticeable role in the cuisine of the subcontinent, at least in the versions tailored for Britain—the macho Madrases and Vindaloos and other milder Tandoori concoctions. And as for the need to match donor with recipient, ho ho!

No matter. The story speaks eloquently.

And Tulip spoke on, while outside on this February afternoon the sun was already low but blindingly bright, a trembling glaring ball of molten brass amidst a haze of richly pink and orange chiffon.

The dome of the sky was icily blue. Clouds were few and frail and unmoved by any breath of wind. Asthmatics, beware. For the past two days the chilly atmosphere had been motionless, trapping smoke and car fumes.

Beyond the low-slung engineering block and the town's rooftops and a church steeple, the horizon wore a frieze of pollution haze which the sun was tinting gloriously. Above that frieze floated long interweaving brown strands. While I was away from my office earlier, holding forth in a lecture room, jet fighters had been practising low-level flying over the farmland beyond the town. Those loose plaits of brown smoke mapped how the jets had hugged the contours of the land. What filthy fuel those planes must have burned, full of additives to supercharge the engines.

The glaring sunlight revealed all the dirt on the outside of my long office window, as though simultaneously providing illumination and also paradoxically a veil of privacy. Presiding over the heaped desk and thronged bookshelves and a grey steel filing cabinet (as well as over Tulip and myself, companionably close to one another) was an enlarged colour photograph of a wizened West

African, taken by yours truly years ago. That old chap was a *griot*, a tribal storyteller. I had long since glided away from third world social anthropology into the anthropology of industrial society—rather as Elizabeth, my sly African ex-wife, had glided away from me soon after she accomplished her transition from Africa to the Northern World. I'd been little more than her passport provider, so it seemed!

One new book which had recently captured Tony the traveller's attention—so that it was still at the top of his mind—was a volume of famous medical paintings. The book included such masterpieces as Hieronymus Bosch's *The Cure for Folly,* in which a quack drills into the head of a lugubrious melancholic, performing a misplaced medieval lobotomy. Particularly fascinating to Tony, for some reason, was Rembrandt's *Anatomy Lesson.* Maybe this was because he drove a lot, and feared ending up on a slab in a morgue.

"So Tony said to me, 'I can tell you all about it—' "

Such coincidence is the very essence of urban legend.

" ' For instance,' he hinted to me, 'what would you say about the clothes those men are wearing—?' "

Sombre and sober clothes.

Oh yes. But costly too. Those big posh white ruffs. These people are dignitaries. Burghers; members of the guild of doctors. The dissection is an important social as well as scientific occasion.

Come on, Tulip, cudgel your brains, what else about the clothes?

Um . . .

Why, the clothes are heavy and warm. Consequently it's wintertime. Before fridges were invented, dissections could only take place during the winter months. Otherwise, half way through the procedure, the cadaver would have begun to rot. A thorough dissection could last a week or more. We aren't talking about quick butchery.

At this point Tony veered on to the matter of student poverty—which was obviously why Tulip was hitchhiking, despite the number of horrible incidents these days.

Tony had heard that some female students were turning to prostitution to pay for their fees and food and lodgings. Who would blame them, when a fellow might pay eighty pounds, the going rate, so he understood, for an hour of harmless fun?

The hint lay heavy. The BMW purred along at eighty, with cruise control engaged. Tony was fond of motorway motels, such bland anonymous rooms. He would be delighted to give Tulip an anatomy lesson. An art lesson. A profitable lesson, intellectually and physically and financially. Fun and money and no harm to anyone.

There: he had said his piece. Some beads of fidgety sweat sat on his brow. Anxiety and desire.

"Did you say no?" I asked. "Or yes?"

"I *was* skint," was Tulip's answer. "I still am, Dr Kershaw. Can I call you Richard? Or Dick?"

"I prefer Rich."

"Ah, Rich . . ." Compared with a student! Was the true purpose of her visit to solicit me?

Some people might have called me a philanderer because I had enjoyed a number of discreet affairs with students. I knew the itch of what one might call erotic frenzy, and I felt no shame about this, only caution. In these times of political correctness on campus, discretion and subtlety must be the watchword.

Our University of Blanchester had never gone so far as to employ an actual sexual harassment officer. Some other universities did so for a while, until witch-hunts ensued—secret files on male lecturers, over-zealous "processing" units interrogating staff because of mischievous or spiteful tip-offs. At Blanchester we relied on an anti-harassment code.

Hitherto I had avoided pitfalls by choosing my young bed-partners wisely. In the last few years I'd restricted myself to students whom I didn't actually teach but who came in response to my notice to tell me an urban legend. An exception had been one of my foreign intake of students—a German *fraülein*—but continentals are open-minded. Despite Tulip's nickname (and the coincidental Rembrandt connection) she couldn't possibly be Dutch. Her trace of accent was surely Scottish. . . .

So far there had been no repercussions from my romances. Had Tulip heard a rumour about me? In a roundabout way was she propositioning me? Was she proposing that I should pay for my pleasure? Pay her, specifically, eighty pounds?

Or might she be an agent provocateur, one of the clique of feminists? My gut instinct said *no* to this.

Since the ride in the BMW had supposedly happened to Tulip herself the tale was *not* a legitimate urban legend. What's more, she *herself* was the hitchhiker. Urban myths frequently feature mysterious passengers who turn out to be ghosts or serial killers or Jesus Christ. Few indeed are the tales from the viewpoint of the actual hitchhiker!

"You know *my* full name," I said to Tulip, pen poised over the notepad. "May I not know yours?"

At this point I imagined that she might abandon her story. The story was a mere pretext for proposing an anatomy lesson—not in this office, to be sure, but in my flat that same evening after a few drinks and a meal, for eighty pounds to fund her overdraft. Yet no. She plunged on, ignoring my desire to know her real name.

"I agreed, Rich. I agreed to Tony's proposal. And didn't that make him buoyant! Along we zoomed to the next service area complete with its travellers' lodge. I waited in the car while he booked a bedroom. He took the ignition key with him after smiling a sloppy apology. No hard feelings. It was always conceivable that I might drive off in his nice BMW. While he was away I looked in the glove compartment and found a pack of condoms. What do you know? They were within a year of their expiry date. Tony mustn't have had much luck lately. Maybe he kept those as a symbol of hope."

Likewise I always kept a packet in my pocket, though my luck was better than Tony's.

"We had lunch and a few drinks"—it was as if Tulip read my mind—"then we adjourned to this double room in the travel lodge. Tony shut the curtains. The bedspread was as red as that dissected arm in the photo. On the wall was a print—"

"Of a Rembrandt?" I asked mischievously.

"Hardly! That would have been much too gloomy. Lonely travellers might kill themselves in the room. It was a print of jolly yachts at Cannes or somewhere flying lots of colourful flags. A Dufy. We undressed—"

She was provoking me.

"—and the anatomy lesson began, not at all hastily. While he was touching me all over, exploring me with fingertips and tongue, true to his word he told me all about the painting—"

In her eyes was I exempt from the desires and anxieties enshrined in legends, incapable of arousal, a man of clinical objectivity? How could she imagine so!

"Dissections didn't actually proceed as in the painting, Rich," she explained. "The surgeon never began by flaying an arm." (I was imagining Tony's hands roving freely—as mine might later rove . . . if I chose, on this occasion, to pay for sex with her.) "First, you would remove the internal organs and dissect those, because they're soft and would rot soonest." (Despite this talk of soft decaying entrails, I was hard, as she must surely realize.) "You only deal with arms and legs toward the end. But if the painting had been accurate it wouldn't have been beautiful. It would have shown a mess of guts.

"There's another important reason why Rembrandt concentrated on the arm. You see, Rich, the first accurate illustrated volume about anatomy based on dissection was published by a Flemish genius working in Italy. Vesalius, that was his name—"

She seemed determined to give me a lesson in art history.

According to Tulip, during his own lifetime Vesalius had not prospered as he deserved. Blinkered colleagues resolutely believed ancient Greek anatomy texts based on guesswork. They refused to accept the evidence of his hands-on approach. Disillusioned, Vesalius moved to Spain. There he performed an autopsy, and unfortunately found that the heart was still beating. Because of this, the Inquisition prosecuted him. If the King had not intervened, Vesalius would have been hanged. Instead, he was sentenced to make a pilgrimage to Jerusalem. On his way back, he was shipwrecked and died on a Greek island.

By the year when *The Anatomy Lesson* was painted, it was widely recognized that Vesalius had revolutionized our understanding of the human body. In the painting the man performing the dissection is a certain Dr Nicolaas Tulp. Tulp was a notable Amsterdam surgeon and several times mayor of the city. What the painting asserts is that Tulp is putting Amsterdam on the map of modern science.

The frontispiece of Vesalius' famous volume depicts the great man as holding a dissected hand and arm. Aesthetic criteria aside, this is the major reason why Rembrandt shows the dissection as beginning with the hand and arm. Here in the person of Tulp is the contemporary Vesalius, equal to or greater than the original founder of anatomy.

Oh yes, and the man on the slab was a condemned felon who had been hanged for stealing clothes. His nakedness is in ironic juxtaposition to his crime—and to the well-dressed spectators. His skin is being unpeeled like a suit of clothes.

Tulp. Tulp. The name nagged at me. It was so like Tulip.

Tulips from Amsterdam. . . .

"I know it's dangerous to hitchhike," she said. She patted her patchwork bag. "That's why I was carrying a scalpel for protection. And a little pistol too."

Panic surged through me. How could she possibly own a pistol? Did she have that pistol with her in that bag right now? Ought I to lunge at her?

"Don't you want to hear the rest of the story?" she asked with such a sweet smile.

"Look," I said. I didn't know what to say next. A scalpel, from the Art School—yes indeed. But a pistol?

"It isn't so hard to buy a pistol nowadays, Rich." Her tone seemed very reasonable. "Not in the area where I live. You don't need to be a big-time villain involved in bank robberies. People even use pistols to rob newsagents' shops."

What would a pistol cost? Two hundred pounds in a pub? How could she afford to spend so much if she was 'skint'? This didn't make sense. Terrifyingly, it didn't.

"After a while," she continued, "still naked of course, I took the pistol out of my bag and I pointed it at Tony. Tony was very scared. He went quite limp. I said to him, 'Now the true anatomy lesson begins, Tony-Daddy! I'm going to flay your right arm. I'm going to peel off some skin in payment—' "

Was she insane? Maybe she merely said those words to her exploiter to shock and appal him. I was certainly horror-stricken. Was her main intention in telling me her story to appal me? The story might be a total concoction especially tailored for me!

How could this tale be true? It ought to be the salesman (no, a friend of his) who was relating this account of the lovely and terrible hitchhiker. *So he took her to a motel. He gave the anatomy lesson as promised. However, when they finished having sex and talking about Rembrandt, she pulled a pistol out of her bag and she said to him, "Now I'll give you an anatomy lesson."* Yes, this ought to have been the pattern.

But I was being told the story from the viewpoint of the ghost hitchhiker or serial murderer, and by that very person, that urban-legendary person, none other.

Maybe Tulip was a performance artist. Maybe I was being set up —being sent the mischievous or malicious equivalent of a stripper-gram!

Alternatively, Tulip might indeed be an *angry woman*, a politically correct virago whose aim was to punish me on behalf of her sisters for my seductions.

I realized that her description of Tony was an inverted description of myself. My own fifty-year-old body had retreated—or rather, expanded away from athleticism. Unlike Tony, I boasted a fine tan. I used the sunbeds at the leisure centre. I also had a small birthmark which was shaped more like a banana than a mushroom. The birthmark wasn't on my brow but on the left cheek of my bum.

Could she have learned about this from one of my previous young bed-partners?

Did she possess some kind of *inherent* knowledge?

The structural inversion of themes is a perennial feature of myth, as analysed by Lévi-Strauss. A more bizarre inversion seemed now to be occurring: not merely the substitution of the phantom hitchhiker for the driver-victim, but a replacement of reality by myth itself, so that I—the observer—was becoming entrapped in the direct experience of a legend. This was at once exhilarating and deeply scary.

How much more likely that Tulip was either a performance artist or a virago! And she might still be one of the new breed of part-time whores of academe, selling her flesh to pay for a course of study which would probably be useless. And ingeniously set upon manipulating me.

She toyed with her bag.

"So I said to him, Rich, if you scream or shout I'll shoot you dead. You can whimper or moan quietly. Or bite on a towel. I'll put some colour into you. Our world's so dusty these days. All the concrete and exhaust fumes. I need more colour—"

What insanity! *Tulip, Tulp* . . . Something about these two names taunted me, and suddenly I thought I knew why.

"Excuse me—" Her hand promptly slid inside her bag. "No, it's all right, Tulip, I'm not intending to leave the room. I need to look at a book."

"Go ahead," she allowed.

I rose. Was this when I should leap at her? When she would either shoot me, or shriek out that I was assaulting her? If I threw myself upon her, her bag might well prove to be empty of any weapon. My own account of what she had told me would seem incredible. If only I had been recording what she said!

I stepped to a bookcase. *Tibet's Myths and Mysteries:* this was the book I wanted. I took it out, flipped to the index and found the reference.

According to Tibetan myths a *tulpa* is the name for an illusory creature born from one's own mind in a hectic, obsessive state. A tulpa is a tangible apparition which achieves an independent existence, wilful and wild. Said a lama: 'Beware of these children of the mind, these tigers to which you give birth . . .'

I had thought for so long about the phantom hitchhiker. I had thought about young women's bodies. Here was the hitchhiker, equipped with her own autonomous motivation. On yes, the hitcher and the serial killer and the phantom and the bed-partner all rolled into one.

"Rembrandt's anatomist wasn't really called Tulp, was he?" I asked.

"Of course he was, Rich," she said. "Later, I checked up on what Tony told me. *The Anatomy Lesson of Dr Nicolaas Tulp*: that's the name of the painting."

If only I had some book about Rembrandt on the shelves.

Here was a punk angel of urban myth, come to me. A messenger from the realm of modern legend. An incarnation. How desperately, yet fearfully, I wished in one part of myself to possess this flower endowed with consciousness. What would I give to do so?

"It's getting quite late," she hinted. "Should we continue this over a drink and then a meal in town?"

Oh she knew, she knew. I did desire this outcome. How long must we enact the pretence that she was simply a student known to her friends as Tulip?

"The eclipse of reason is here," asserts Richard Kershaw.

A sunny print of daffodils hangs on the whitewashed wall. There's no glass in the frame. Glass might break into dangerous daggers. The glass of the window near the bed is faintly meshed with fine wire for safety and security; and the slim bars on the inside divide lawn from woodland and ground from sky very neatly. Richard's hand and forearm are pink from the plastic surgery he underwent. The glossy artificial hue suggests that part of him was remade in plastic.

Sitting upon the bed, he leans toward me as if convinced that his own collapse of reason has brought enlightenment.

"Because of this eclipse," he insists, "myths are moving closer to us. Myths are become people. People are becoming myths. Consider the million alien abduction stories in America—told in the contactees' own words as an experience which happened to themselves and not to somebody else! Isn't this proof? When I leave here, I intend to work on experiencing this abduction syndrome myself—as a participant."

"That painting by Rembrandt," I remind him, "really *is* of a man called Nicolaas Tulp."

Richard waves a pink hand dismissively. "That makes no difference, don't you see? Here's proof of a coming together, a new amalgam of mind. New connections in the psyche of the world."

"The world doesn't have a psyche," I tell him. "There are simply millions of separate individuals. Most of us have fundamentally similar mental patterns."

"No!" He thumps his patched hand upon the bedside table and splays his fingers painfully. "That's the old Thatcherite lie that society doesn't exist! It's the lie which led to so much selfishness and self-interest and to the cutting of state funding for transport and the elderly and—"

"—for students and suchlike." I can complete his sentence. Wistfully he gazes at the daffodils.

"May I have a print of tulips on my wall instead?"

While I ponder, he adopts a tone of sham menace. If wheedling will not serve, a threat might persuade me.

"One day *you* might pick up a hitchhiker," he says sternly.

"I wouldn't dream of doing any such thing, Richard," I assure him.

"That's exactly what I mean about selfishness! Well, she may pick *you* up. An alien intruder not from some fanciful distant star, but from out of the mythic psyche of the world. An evolutionary crescendo is under way."

"To surrender reason," I insist, "is to forsake civilization."

I can predict his answer.

"Reason," he says, "is the dream from which we shall awake, just as prehumans once awoke to self-awareness and a form of logic." This conviction, at any rate, gives him an air of serenity and patience. Some of the time.

It's all too true that delusions of imminent transcendence are becoming far more common, often in dramatically violent fashion. Members of cults commit group suicide or die in gunfights with police. Jihads are proclaimed. At times I dearly wish I could peer two hundred years ahead. Generally such a prospect terrifies me. Will my own rational and liberal mind-set remain in tune with what awaits? Or will religions ravish a depleted world which will never again launch itself moonwards or dissect the secrets of life and mind?

By therapeutic custody of such as Richard, I serve as an anxious jailer on behalf of the past and its struggles for progress. The plastic pink of Richard's arm validates yet ridicules my efforts, and those of rational scientists such as Vesalius and his successors in whatever discipline.

In this hospital I confront my fears daily and I control them. Here's the essential difference between myself and Richard. A dark side of his psyche accosted him and he was unable to regulate it. A person can actively cultivate madness in themselves. Madness will sprout and flower. How precious sanity is; and how precarious.

Beyond the oasis of controlled insanity which this hospital is, how many other wild blooms are burgeoning in people's minds, luminous and poisonous, as the calendar sheds its leaves day by day, approaching the millennium? Day by day, due to meagre funds, we release patients too early into the community, as though our real task is to pollinate the world with delusions.

I can never let Richard be released. His account of the incarnation of urban myth is far too potent—similar, as he himself points out, to the alien abduction fantasies, yet far worse.

If what he says happened is true—and I do believe it to be so—then because of his obsessions Richard acted as a magnet (or should I say a seed crystal?) which attracted a creature of the mind into existence, into physical reality. To release Richard back into the community would be to encourage Tulip and similar beings to roam in our midst.

When I do replace the print of daffodils with one of tulips, I shall leave a scalpel somewhere in this room for Richard to find. Where will the scalpel have come from? Patients quite often steal things if they have a chance. This gives them a sense of petty power. Poor Richard could have been given the blade by another inmate. Every afternoon he joins in a session of group therapy. We can hardly keep him in solitary confinement, can we? I tried to oppose this liberal attitude, but I was overruled.

Until now, I have regarded this hospital as a bastion. Yet essentially all along I have only been passive in my response to the death of reason. Reactive, not proactive.

Others in the past have behaved more positively. Right now I'm thinking of the way Jack the Ripper (much maligned) set out to purge London of whores. He was undoubtedly a doctor. That was about a century ago. The cycle of time has come round. Only, more so—because now is a millennium. Richard himself must cleanse the infection that he represents. Logic dictates this.

"A tulip," I tell him. "A single cut tulip in a vase. I'll find you a print if I have to search high and low."

How he smiles.

The Descent

EARLS HEATH IS A TYPICAL ENGLISH MARKET TOWN of some twenty thousand souls. A tributary of the Ouse flows through former water meadows, now a large industrial estate. Each year new houses eat up fields, but to the east a heathland rises gently, the town's "Common," protected from development at least for the present. It's to the Common, away from the immediate glow of street lamps and buildings, that hundreds of us–might we number a thousand?—have come on this crisp chilly Thursday night to view the comet: fuzzy white head and huge bright feather in the eastern sky, such a splendid spectacle. For the past half-week the sky was overcast, denying any view and building up expectation. Tonight is completely clear and the moon is only a sickle. Along the road at the edge of the heath masses of cars are parked on both sides. Frost sparkles, starlight fallen to earth amongst the gorse. Many of us thought to bring pocket torches to cope with tussocks and rabbit holes. Myself, I forgot, so I'm one of the blunderers.

Annabelle would have remembered a torch—she was quite practical. By the same token I don't suppose she would have come out here tonight in the cold, and anyhow she left me two months ago—off to California and exciting prospects with Marcus, whom I never suspected until the last moment. (*This isn't working out, Nick. You're too reined in. Oh you're clever. You can be witty but I never know what feelings there are under it all or if there are any real feelings. Marcus is—I don't want to tell you and I don't need to. I hope you have a happy life.*) Marcus and Annabelle and I had all worked at Talkcom, him as chief phone designer, Annabelle as personal assistant to the boss, and me (with my second class PPP degree) in public relations. PPP is politics, philosophy, and psychology. As I put it at the interview, how to understand and massage people's needs in a world packed with competing suppliers. Tech-tools as personal enhancement and adornment. Self-image, mental underpinnings. Well, you have to sell yourself.

Kids are having a whale of a time tonight. Spot of anarchy, this, so many people spilling out from our usually sedate little town into the open. "Look, look, you'll always remember—"

Mazzini-Florescu, so we're told, isn't a comet belonging to our solar system. It came in from the deeps. It will whip around the sun and head off, never to be seen again. Mazzini is some amateur astronomer in Italy; Florescu is a Romanian; both reported the first sighting at the same time.

Maybe I should have gone to a pub instead for the illusion of company? Shared purpose, here on the Common, but I'm lonely in this diffuse crowd. Perhaps I ought to leave Earls Heath, though here's where work is. A publicity chap is less in demand than a designer.

No: I came for the comet, to take me out of myself and to set my loss of Annabelle in perspective. Thousands of stars above me; thousand of other women I might meet, if not perhaps in Earls Heath. I've been numb and I came for a dose of wonder, of intensified feeling. How many other people did so too, unconsciously? Nowadays we're all a bit numb. Wars on TV are less real because they're interchangeable with soap operas. Life is less real than movies, and maybe we confuse the two. History and politics seem to have vanished into remixes and repeats. Everybody can talk to everybody else and no one has anything new to say. The democratisation of information is the victory of banality. Hiya Karen, it's Sharon, I'm here on the Common seeing the comet. You here too? You hear me okay? I thought we got cut off. Hey, if you see Darren, say hiya.

It happens so suddenly: a glory of light spreading swiftly across the night sky like oily paint, blue and pink and orange. Soon it's spilling

down upon the ground, attaching to trees phosphorescently, flowing
swiftly across heath and streets and houses, and clinging to people
too. In the direction of the city the horizon has lit up as if a bom-
bardment by napalm is in progress. Light crawls everywhere, an
inverted aurora which especially garbs people, like St Elmo's Fire or
Pentecostal flames seeking and attaching.

I know that I'm not who I was such a short while ago. I'm another,
with the same body and much of the same self as before. Some of
my memories may have failed. I may be seeking a memory of Annabelle that no longer exists, the opposite of *déjà vu – déjà inconnu.*

No, memories are still here, but they're distanced as if the
remembered events happened to another person. Not exactly *my*
memories, yet nevertheless available to me. I have become somebody else who happens to be much the same person. No, that's not
quite right. I-now is a *new* self. The previous self has gone. Yet I
have inherited who he was, as the basis for . . . what exactly? For
who I am now.

Mild panic breaks out across the Common, so I know that it
isn't only myself who feels radically strange. Not a screaming-panic
but a bumping-into panic. A panic bred of unfamiliarity, a seeking—partly in vain—for familiarity. Instincts have taken over.
Reach out to family or friends—but who are they now? What have
they become?

"Ben, is that you? Are you sure? It's me, Julie—of course it's me.
Just, I don't feel like me—"

This is like a parody of fatuous mobile phone calls. Only, now
people's voices themselves are the phones.

"Merrick! Are you there? Hold my hand—!"

The glory of light has almost gone. Trickles run here and there,
fading out, like rain draining away after a downpour. The panic
becomes a need to reach cars. A hermit crab out of its shell must
feel this way. I'm trotting toward mine. People scramble into their
vehicles on both sides of the road. Is everyone present? Have
we forgotten someone? Have we, perhaps, forgotten our own
selves?

My old VW Golf feels familiar yet strange, as if I have climbed
into it after years of absence. Engines start up. Cars edge out and
move off. So do I. Not smoothly—jerkily: lurch and brake. Quite a
few knocks. Taillights shatter. Wings scrape, bumpers collide. Yet
no one jumps out to protest or accuse or examine damage. None of
the vehicles is valued in the same way as they were an hour ago.

The imperative to go home is too great. This a very slow stampede, such is the confusion on the road, so poor is the driving. Faces peer blankly out of windows into the night. We're refugees—fleeing from what? Whatever it is, we have brought it along with us.

Presently several drivers, myself included, pull out of the slow chaos into the big car park of the Harvester pub-restaurant, lit up with carriage lamps and neon. We park higgledy-piggledy. We climb out. Customers have spilled out of the pub.

A voice calls, "Who's that—?"

"Who—?" echoes another.

We're encountering—with some surprise—ourselves and attempting to identify who and what we are, which is . . . not exactly human, not any longer. Somehow we have stopped being human, yet we still remain men and women and children. I'm not scared, because I am who I ought to be, but this is different from what I was, even if it imitates what I was. From the car park the comet is still visible, though more vaguely.

Something descended, like angels entering us or like code downloading from the sky. During the time of the descent of that light, we were parasitised. Is this the apocalypse, this invasion . . . by what we can only call *ourselves*?

Did some life-force hitchhike on the comet from light years away, to flood us and perpetuate itself here, using us as its new abode? Or is this something that has happened to people regardless of the comet? A sort of end of humanity—of what we imagined was us. Something like a nervous breakdown of the species, or maybe the very opposite, a sudden recovery. The meltdown of ourselves and replacement by . . . much the same, experienced in a different way?

A young woman, wineglass in hand, asks me, "What has happened?" She's pretty: close-cropped dark hair, slim, slightly elfin, gorgeous brown eyes. Her suede coat hangs open. Lovely bit of pastiche Art Deco knitwear beneath, a path winding up through a flower garden to a cottage, as if I might ascend that route to where she dwells. Blue jeans and short brown boots. She's attractive, though at the same time it's as if I'm seeing a human being for the first time from a peculiar perspective: this jointed creature which balances upright, as though she lacks enough limbs to do so. A cow or a goat might be more natural. The same is true of everyone in the car park. I'm seeing people clearly for the very first time, as mobile oddities, caricatures.

"We aren't who we were," I tell her. "We're new people now.

Same bodies, same memories, but new software from the sky. I'm Nick. Or at least I was."

"I'm Kate. In the pub on TV they were showing the football match. Scotland and Hungary. Floodlit. This must have happened all over England."

"Are you with anyone, Kate?"

"I was meeting . . . I don't suppose she'll get here now. Sonia was picking me up in a taxi. We were going into the city—friend of ours, Jennifer, has an exhibition. Private view. A few drinks."

"Did you see the sky over the city?"

She shakes her head.

"All lit up, just the way we were."

She nods. "All over England. It's . . . *all over.*"

"And all beginning anew. Or carrying on differently." I nod at her glass: "You were starting early."

"It's easier for a taxi to find this pub. I walked here. Sonia's always late. When people are late I think I'm being abandoned. I'd rather do something."

"I was abandoned. Two months ago."

"Poor you."

"That's a lovely sweater. A knitwear exhibition, or what?"

"Not quite. Leather sculptures—strange bodies and heads. Not quite human."

"Like us now."

"Jennifer went to art school in the city and now she has her own studio in a warehouse by the canal. She's gay."

Are you too, Kate, are you too? Do you live with your parents, or where? Meeting a person is always so full of mystery at first, then usually everything becomes explicable and ordinary, even banal. Not tonight.

"What do they say about all this on TV?"

"I don't know. The game trickled to a halt. Nobody was paying attention. People were spilling their drinks so I came outside."

Along with many others. The road is still choked with inept drivers.

"Shall we see what the TV says now?"

It's a bit too soon for any informed commentary. A dazed-looking announcer is talking about a mid-air collision between passenger jets over London and how Heathrow is closed with a burning wreck on one runway, then he's telling us to stay indoors to wait for announcements and not drive anywhere or make phone calls unless they're emergency ones and not send e-mails or log on to the Internet because the whole system is clogged worldwide, and certainly we shouldn't panic but be calm and do nothing because nothing catastrophic has happened–except for the airliner disasters which are tragic, and other similar serious accidents. What happened has stopped happening and there's no earthly reason why it should happen again—how could it happen again? He grins zanily. He isn't the person he was, no arguing with that, though he still has responsibilities. Now it's over to . . . Ah, they've brought in Trevor McDonald as the most trusted, calmest anchorman, with that soft wise very British Caribbean voice of his. Sir Trevor, the nation's trusted uncle.

"What happened tonight is definitely very disturbing. I'm sure we all feel the alteration in ourselves. I know I do. I'm sure you do too. Maybe the comet has something to do with this. Maybe there has been some kind of change in our world's magnetic field, affecting our brainwaves. We can only speculate at present, but the most important thing is to stay calm during this confusing interval—"

Uncle Trevor is improvising. What does he know about comets and magnetic fields and brainwaves? Though he sounds as if he might.

Sir Trevor cocks his head, listening to an earphone. "The phenomenon would seem to be worldwide, even where it's currently daytime. It was visible in full sunshine in California. And during the hurricane in Miami too. All happening at the same time, half an hour ago. At present information is still very patchy. We hope to have some experts to discuss this, and we expect there ought to be a statement from the Prime Minister's office before midnight. Meanwhile, as my colleague said, the best advice is to stay at home and not travel and try to avoid putting unnecessary strain on the phone network and emergency services—"

Although I know all the words, they seem newly minted and almost foreign. A language newly invented, a precarious language which might collapse into unmeaning. So long as I don't question the words, I understand perfectly well. If I do question them, the words erode. Services services services services: the meaning soon eludes me. Kate and I are sitting together in an upholstered nook, though I haven't bought a drink.

What does the word *Kate* mean? Nothing, nothing at all; yet it is her, and it is thousands of other people too, but *they* are not her, sitting next to me right now.

"Kate . . ."

"Yes?"

"I was just thinking why you're called Kate."

"God, so was I. What is a Kate? It's like some bird, some cross between a skate and a kite. Skates—the fishy ones—they look quite like kites—kids' kites I mean—if they could fly. I'm talking nonsense, aren't I?"

"Better than being a Nick, though? Old Nick the devil—who would trust a Nick?" The name also means steal, and inflict a minor wound.

"Our names are us, but they're only labels. All words are labels."

"Don't try to peel off the label, Kate—there might be nothing underneath!"

"We've had ourselves unpeeled. Then stuck back upside-down. Or back to front. When the traffic clears, will you take me home? I can't be on my own. My own has gone away, and someone else came back instead of me."

"Whose home do you prefer?"

"Mine. I must sound like a schizophrenic. Maybe we all do now. Maybe some secret drug was released."

"Not everywhere simultaneously, and certainly not a drug."

"I don't suppose you're a rapist or a murderer."

"Do you think any of us are, any longer?"

"Do you think we're the first?" asks Kate, bare in bed, a generous single—the bed, I mean. "It's only an hour since."

I stroke her slim shoulders, her lovely little breasts. She holds my stiff cock, her hand an antechamber where I am interviewed before admittance. How strange human bodies are, mine especially—part of it has grown bigger, awkwardly and uncouthly, while to all appearances she remains the same.

I would like us to be the first, so I say, "It's possible . . ." Otherwise, might she not wish to proceed?

"Not very likely, really . . . Seven or eight billion people—millions must have been in the midst of."

"Ah but did they resume? Or carry on? I think we may stand a chance."

She chuckles. "Naturally you hope so."

I can't be the first person to lie with her. Or can I? Yes, in a sense. New Kate, new me.

The sweater lies on the floor, and I'm in the porch of the cottage . . . almost in the porch, a few sprigs of tufty foliage around it.

Pocket-handkerchief second-floor flat in a sizeable converted nine-teenth century town house, gravel out front and a few evergreens. Kitchen-diner, single bedroom, shower en suite. Dominated the sitting room is a poster of an upholstered leather woman, all her musculature showing glossily as if her skin has been stripped off by a vivisectionist. Or never supplied by her creator, namely Jennifer Gillis, One-Woman Show at a gallery in Hamburg last year—apparently German collectors particularly go for this sort of thing. Stitches bisect the face and the torso. Disconcertingly, each arm ends in a foot—and the legs end in hands which are planted palmsflat on a wooden floor.

That leather woman is like some bizarre acrobat who has been anatomically redesigned.

Kate works at the finance desk of the Toyota car dealership in town, arranging loans and such. She has half a dozen Bonsai trees and collects tiny Netsuke figures in yellow ivory. Must have a thing about Japan—if not about saving elephants—and the Toyota dealership is the closest approach to Japan in Earls Heath.

Books are mostly detective stories of the psychological Ruth Rendell sort, mainly written by woman, interspersed with biographies and travel. No photos on show that I noticed.

Still, she withholds me. "Do you think we're doing this entirely of our own free will? I mean, it isn't exactly *me* to jump into bed with . . . Do you suppose we might be impelled in some way?"

"It isn't you, is it, Kate? It's new-Kate."

"Hmm." She toys with me. "I'm not on the pill, you know. We aren't taking precautions. It isn't the fertile time of the month for me, but what if millions of *them* are still awaiting a host? Whatever they are. *If* they are, at all! What babies will be born after this?"

"I suppose we'll find out in another nine months or so. I don't mean us personally!"

She whispers, "We'd better not lose our chance to be first."

Annabelle was always very conscious, eyes open, scrutinising. Kate and I lose ourselves in one another. (But then, we already did lose and rediscover ourselves!) She becomes a second self to me, and I to her, as if we have invented a soft machine of pleasure in which we ride, enwrapped, engloved. It's almost as if in a moment we might rekindle the light that descended, and yes, yes, it comes, to my skin, to my nerves, though not visibly now, and quite without the aftermath of any wish to disengage, to leave, quite the contrary: we could lie together joined all night while sensations transfer between us, as if beyond climax comes a prolonged communication between our new selves, recalibrating us. Only when this fades do we unjoin.

I roll upon my back, and the action carries on as if the whole bed is tilting over—and Kate gasps and clutches my hand—but the world steadies.

"What was *that*? For a few moments I felt sure if . . ."

"Sense of balance, disturbed . . ."

She laughs. "The world moving."

"Disturbance of the inner ear . . . you felt it too. It's as if we've been rebalanced."

"Inner ear, inner eye. Is something living in us, observing? Something that wasn't individual before, but now it is, it's in millions of individuals and when they reconnect with each other the way we just connected . . ."

"It updates itself?"

"Something of the sort . . . You'll stay over tonight?"

"My place is bigger." Quite a big bigger, with Annabelle gone.

"We aren't supposed to travel unnecessarily."

"More like the completion of a journey, Kate. But it's daft to think of hauling on clothes and going out into the cold. Of course I'll stay."

"I wonder what we'll dream?"

Awakening, up against each other. I'm in Kate's bed. A working day. For her, for me. How will anyone work today? Maybe the government will have declared a public holiday. Dreams, she said.

Catch a dream by the tail as it's fleeing, pull it back into sight, into mind.

I can't remember any. None at all.

She's stirring.

"Kate, think dream, think nothing else. Tell me a dream you had."

She tenses, as if surprised by the unfamiliarity of a body next to her—or as if concentrating. Presently she yawns.

"Nothing. I can't remember any."

"Try."

"I did try."

"I dreamt nothing either. Has it robbed us of our dreams? Using our brains for something else while we're unconscious. . . ."

She snuggles. "Or is this a dream come true, so that we don't need dreams now? Not if we're already rebalanced. Dreams sort of rebalance us, don't they? Still, I used to enjoy my dreams. Lots of crazy adventures."

"You don't sound too worried about losing them."

"I'm not worried about anything. There's no point in us raising objections to what's happening. I suppose we should turn on the TV. Coffee and toast?"

Today has indeed been proclaimed a Bank Holiday. Around the globe all the major financial centres have suspended stock market trading until the world can sort itself out, optimistically after the weekend is over. BBC-2 seems entirely devoted to the Event. It's odd watching people who have become so different, yet essentially the same, striving to come to terms. They know that their regular, familiar lives ceased last night, and new lives resumed. Between yesterday and today there's a wall of thick glass.

Worldwide, the death toll is estimated at several millions, rather as if a brief little nuclear exchange had taken place, but the casualties are widespread not concentrated. Car crashes here, plane crashes there, factory disasters, power failures, accidents, fires, umpteen human errors. The heart of Calcutta is in flames. Boats are missing. Many communication links are down, or maybe their operators are not bothering to communicate. Riots are rare, and no armed forces have popped off at each other. Has war become an irrelevance overnight? Certainly there's no sense of doom, unless the media journalists are doing their best to minimise calamity. From now on we all must play at being ourselves, like actors.

The cause remains a mystery, although it's a mystery which we all enshrine within ourselves. An invasion from outer space? Maybe, though of a very odd kind. A thought-virus, a collective global mental breakdown leaping from mind to mind at the speed of the light that descended upon us? Nobody is dreaming any more, that's for sure. Instead, it seems that we are living a dream of ourselves.

BBC-2 has a couple of psychologists in their Bristol studio, a lively redheaded woman and a lanky blond chap.

The chap talks about a theory that human beings only really became truly conscious around the time of Homer in Ancient Greece. Before then, we were in two minds—left brain, right brain. One side of the brain told the other side what to do, and it seemed as if Gods were dictating our actions. A hallucinated voice led to obedient, automaton-like behaviour. As life grew more complex, a veritable Babel of internal Gods competed for attention. Over-

loaded, the two-chamber mind broke down; integrated consciousness and a sense of Self dawned.

The redhead rejoices that our former urgent sense of Self has
suddenly disappeared. According to this lady, ideas have a life of
their own—they animate us like puppets. We imagine that we have
our own ideas—our beliefs and preferences and passions—but
really these ideas jostle to express themselves through us. We are
their vehicles; they are the drivers of ourselves—and they engage in
a Darwinian struggle to reproduce and spread themselves. The
neatest trick these ideas devised was to conjure up a sense of personal Self inside of us all, so that this or that idea is *mine*, and consequently precious, worth fighting and dying for. Yet increasingly
during the last decade of the 20th century we were being bom-
barded by more and more competing ideas—faiths, fashions, whatever. The Self-module became unstable. Last night it collapsed.
Our sense of our precious sovereign Self evaporated, and now we
are free.

Toast pops up.

"That hardly explains," say I, "how last night's light-show *happened* and how it occurred all over the world."

"Actually," says Kate, "I don't think I care. But I do want to visit
Jennifer today."

From the kitchen we can see that poster of the strange acrobat
(as I think of her) next door, hands stitched to arms, feet stitched to
legs. Even though she's upright she's performing a handstand. If she
were to flip over so that her feet were on the ground, then she
would be upside-down.

"Jennifer's leather sculptures . . . she grafts bodies together and
heads on to heads and whatnot, and she says she's aiming to
enhance the sense of bodies as housing an inner spirit. The *self*,
I suppose, seen in a new way that's a bit shocking. I wonder what
Jennifer feels about it all now. I don't want to listen to psychologists
prattling on. Jennifer's sculptures are things you can touch. You
aren't supposed to touch when they're on show. What I mean is . . .
they're *graspable*."

Just as Kate and I were graspable by one another last night.

"And rather alien. Like people after a meltdown. After a metamorphosis."

"So let's visit her. I don't suppose we can be arrested for driving
a car."

Soon some other expert is talking about the disappearance of
dreams. Maybe nobody dreamt last night because our minds were

too busy reorganising themselves, rather like a computer's hard drive burbling away to itself while nothing happens on screen, doing housekeeping, deleting loose ends, tidying up memory files. Personally I would have expected this to result in a splurge of dreams. Maybe not so, says the chap. And maybe, maybe, something inaccessible has begun time-sharing us. . . .

"I feel peaceful," says Kate.

"So do I." It's true. The calm after the storm of light.

Traffic is very light. A few flakes of snow drift down, though the sky is mostly unbroken blue. We pass some damaged cars abandoned from last night. An ambulance races past us in the direction of Earls Heath. An impending birth? A heart attack? A police car speeds by too, yet basically the world is so quiet. Ah, there's no commercial traffic. Is anyone restocking the supermarkets?

I follow the almost empty ring road round the city, passing numerous kids and quite a few adults on bikes, as if this usually crowded thoroughfare is being liberated and redeemed. On a traffic island a female tramp performs a shuffle-dance around a pram full of tatty old plastic carrier bags. A bus comes in sight, half a dozen old ladies in big fussy hats on the upper deck—when did they last mount such steep stairs for an aerial view?

When we arrive at the Canal Basin, an impromptu festival is under way. A few years ago the previously neglected warehouses and environs were all given a thorough face lift. Now they house boutiques, antiques, a pub and a café, craftsmen and artists. Despite the chill a jazz trio improvises by the waterfront. Scores of people are roaming around or drinking cappuccinos at tables set outside the café. A clown peddles a monocycle in circles, keeping his poise —when all about him have lost theirs? A chap is selling helium balloons, all of which depict those supposed UFO-users with the big slanted eyes. These bob above kids like alien second heads. When a balloon flies up and away as if returning to its home in the sky, voices cry, "Oooh." The mood is blithe. No problem parking a car today.

"When it happened," Jennifer says, "I'm sure I saw some of the sculptures move as if they were coming to life. Then the light flowed away as if it had made a mistake. Anyway, we were all rather preoccupied."

Her studio, floored in coarse dark old planks, is lit by large sky-lights let into the truss and beam ceiling. Anatomical-style sketches decorate the whitewashed walls, and a score of completed sculptures of various sizes dominate the space, some free-standing, others torsos with heads, upright upon white boxes and plinths. Pushed to one side are a couple of cane chairs, a desk, and a worktable bearing empty wine bottles, glasses, bowls in which some nibbles remain. The heating comes from a couple of radiators. A giant cabinet yawns open and empty, the presumed home of sheets of leather which now lie piled several deep on the floor as improvised mattresses, also of the bags of stuffing used as pillows. Jennifer and a friend or two must have spent the night here, hardly as comfortably as myself and Kate – so as to keep an eye on the leather figures? A pink and maroon woman with pendulous breasts and arms amputated at the elbows is giving birth to a wise homunculus through a hole in her belly. A black man of massive musculature, minus everything below the waist, thrusts upward, his eyes sewn shut, an imp-like white foetus sprouting from one shoulder. And others, and others.

The friends have departed, perhaps to the wharf-side café or the pub, but who they were, or who I am—other than "Nick"—is irrelevant.

Jennifer Gillis is olive-complexioned with black pageboy hair. She's wearing black leather trousers and a patchwork leather waistcoat over a ruffleted white blouse exposing muscular arms. Slim black patent-leather shoes. She could be a gamine mock-medieval fencer, except that her own duelling swords are sharp strong needles.

"I missed you last night," Jennifer says to Kate. "And now I'm missing myself." She laughs dolefully. "I'm hanging around here in case I come back."

"You look like a duellist," I say.

She frowns. "Did you say a *dualist?*"

"No, I mean swords at dawn. Flashing blades. A champion of the weak challenging a bullying knight." I don't think I mean a knight, actually. A haughty Regency lord flourishing a rapier.

"I put this gear on for my show. Normally I wear dungarees. More practical. Pockets for this and that. It wasn't a *bullying* night, last night, though. It was like an overwhelming seduction." Wryly Jennifer eyes me and Kate. "Can I be the champion of this week? Words are fraying, aren't they? Can I stitch them together? Can I stuff them and stretch them back into shape? Should I march outside with my biggest needle and prick those balloons?" She mimes parry and thrust. Since this studio only has skylights, she must already have stepped outdoors this morning, yet evidently she prefers here to the party mood along the wharf-front.

"Let the gas out of them. Make the alien faces collapse. False faces—those can't be the cause or there would be flying saucers all over the sky by now. Thousands of saucers full of eyes as big as."

"Maybe there's no need for saucers," I tell her. "Why do you think we aren't dreaming any more?"

"We *are* dreaming. Nick, isn't it? We're in what the aborigines of Australia call the dream-time. They won't be puzzled by this. They'll take to it like a duck to water."

"Or else we've awoken from a dream—the dream of our selves."

"The question is, do I sew any more bodies from now on?"

"They're impressive." They certainly are. Very odd and impressive.

"They're about *emerging*. Inner spirit emerging. Now I've emerged from myself. The whole world," she continues, with a frown, "is experiencing an emergency. What do we do from now on?"

"We continue. What else?"

"We wait." As she is waiting, here.

"We can't merely wait. Everything has to carry on, or else we starve, we freeze."

"Male urgency. Do something. Act. Exert. Run a mile in the wrong direction."

"Like driving here, do you mean?" asks Kate, seeming miffed.

"Of course I'm glad you came! Just, it's a little bit late. That all belonged yesterday." Jennifer glances at her slim steel-band wrist-watch, then unfastens it, drops it, steps upon it with her shoe. "Behold, history has stopped. The tyranny has gone. Event after bloody event. Last night the final event happened. It's like dying— *you* don't live through it. Actually, we've become extinct overnight." She glances around her leather people, which seem like new mutant forms of life aborted, half born, arms missing, legs missing. "We're a new race. We lost the old one."

Kate and I sit drinking cappuccinos while the clown rides round and the trio play *Mood Indigo* endlessly and the balloons of aliens bob, peering at us.

"Jennifer's taking it a bit hard," I remark.

"Yes, it's sad. She made me sad, though I'm not sad at all. She's an artist. That was her show last night. Suddenly it was all over. Meaningless. Or . . . fulfilled."

The imps in the mind start up.

Lift the cup. I'm lifting the cup.
 Drink from the cup. I'm drinking.
 Put the cup down. Putting it down.
 'Kiss me, Kate.' "Kiss me, Kate."
 Kate craning to kiss me.
 The return of the Gods. Do this. Say that. Like double vision,
though not involving the eyes. A pre-echo of speech and action,
deciding what speech to utter, what action to take.
 Consternation all around. The clown tumbles from his unicy-
cle. A child runs right over the wharfside, falling into the water.
From her studio doorway fifty yards along the figure of Jennifer
emerges, stabbing at the air with a needle too small to see, or with
nothing at all in her hand. She's trying to ward off the imps, but the
imps quickly stop her.
 "Nick—!"
 "I know, I know."
 The Gods are back.

*Many hands make light work, the work of light. Cosmos, so profligate
with life, such careless cruel generosity. So many wasted brains, so
many wasted minds, such squandering. To gather intelligences
instead, sorting, unifying, safeguarding. Otherwise, all will fade and
die and be lost. As birds of this world fly in a skein, sharing identity,
let us unify the higher minds of this world with others. The blessèd
Millennium is here; now ye shall not die. Downcoming into these
biped beings, upgoing into unity of common mind, mind that moves
its bodies to utter and do as they would habitually do and utter, yet
now encompassed within the Plenum. Long way and time to come
here bringing the Plenum, salvation of species, joining and eternaliz-
ing. Building here the great projectors for light-pulsing mind-models
from this node of the Plenum and the great injectors for inpulling
mind-models from the Elsewhere so that all shall unite. Satisfaction,
fullness, joy.
 'Kate,' 'Nick': go your way, rejoice today, prepare for new work
tomorrow.
 Our Wo-Men, Our Children, Our Men.*

The Last Beast out of the Box

*D*OWN AT THE BOTTOM OF BROOK LANE, CLOSE
to the ford, stood Brook Cottage — built of rusty brown iron-
stone, roofed in blue slate which lichen had yellowed. The only
occupants were Janet Meadows, in her seventies, and her marmalade cat, Duffy.

On a Sunday afternoon in spring, Amanda Whitaker brought
her school sketchbook to show to the old lady — whose home was
full of charmingly naive little pictures of cats and flowers painted by
herself. If Amanda's dad hadn't spent that morning repainting a
couple of window frames at home, the girl mightn't have noticed
that the paintwork of Brook Cottage was cracked and peeling.
Along the overgrown verge daffodils were dying, but in shaded parts
bluebells were about to bloom. Recent downpours had swollen the
brook till the ford had expanded into a huge pond, lapping the low
footbridge.

Scarcely had Amanda rung the doorbell than a crash resounded
inside the house — as if an actual bell had fallen on to a floor.

When Mrs Meadows opened the door, she was sighing and
shaking her head.

"Oh dear," was her greeting.

Short and stout, Mrs Meadows wore a floral frock of forget-me-nots and primroses. Well-worn slippers were on her feet. Lines creased her face, mainly from smiling, though in repose the effect could seem hostile; and she was frowning now. The old lady's straggly unkempt grey hair was another reason for village kids to scare a new arrival about a *witch* living in Brook Cottage. Amanda had once fallen for this prank. By the age of twelve Amanda knew so much better about Mrs Meadows's kindliness.

Right now, Mrs Meadows seemed none too happy. Amanda clutched the sketchbook awkwardly. "Have I come at the wrong time?"

But the old lady gestured the girl to come in. "You can help me clear up. Duffy was on the sideboard. The bell startled him and he knocked a vase off."

"I'm *sorry*—"

"It wasn't your fault, dear."

"If I hadn't rung your bell just now—"

Along a dim hall they went, into a living room bright with sunlight and pot-plants and pictures. A china vase had shattered on the parquet floor. Pieces had hopped onto the central rug. Duffy skulked by the French window, a bewildered look in his eyes. Floodwater spilled across the far end of the lawn.

Mrs Meadows opened the glass door and shooed her pet out. "Now at least he won't be able to cut his paw into the bargain!" Nodding toward the unkempt garden: "It would need to pour for another few days before *I* get my feet wet in here." Yet look, the sun was shining brightly.

"I'm so sorry about the vase—"

"Duffy once kicked himself in the eye when he was trying to scratch his cheek. . . ."

Amanda giggled, and Mrs Meadows smiled at last.

"The vet tested my dimwit's reflexes by pulling his back legs, but there was nothing wrong. 'You just happen to have a very clumsy cat, Mrs Meadows,' he told me. Aside from that, Duffy's so lovable."

With brush and pan, on hands and knees, they hunted for all the fragments.

"He's the only cat I've known who can fall off a bed! He rolls about on his back and forgets where he is."

"How many cats have you had?"

"Duffy's the fifth."

"I'd *love* a cat. Mum and Dad say it would be bad for my asthma."

"Not if he was your own special cat . . . Oh, but it's always so sad when they die. You must take them to the vet. You watch their eyes glaze over. There's nothing to fill the aching emptiness except to get another one. Duffy's my last. He'll live as long as I do."

"How old is Duffy?"

"He's seven."

"He's still young, then—!"

"He's so daft I can easily imagine him falling out of a tree or even drowning himself in the brook. Actually," confided Mrs Meadows, "I think his brain's a bit crumpled because he was the last cat out of the box. The other ones must have been pressing on his head."

"*What do you mean?*"

Mrs Meadows brought the cat box, and set it on the low table next to Amanda's sketchbook.

"It's *beautiful*—!"

"I painted this when I was just a little older than you, Amanda, and—what do you know?—it all came true."

Hinged at the top, the wooden box was about five inches wide and high, perhaps ten inches long. On each side and on the lid, a different cat was emblazoned. On top, a mischievous black and white cat sharpened his claws on what might have been turquoise carpet. Black body, white mask on its face, white bib and socks.

Round the sides of the box ran a continuous landscape of turquoise grass spotted with flowers, trees, and shrubs. A rainbow in the sky. Cartoony clouds. An orange sun. Chevrons of birds. In each panel, variously standing or sitting, were: a white cat with green eyes, a slinky all-black cat, a pompous blue-cream Persian, and finally a marmalade Duffy looking doleful.

Mrs Meadows opened the box to reveal little pots of paint, then she shut the lid and tapped the top picture.

"This is *Morris*. I'd had him for a year when I painted him. So I decided to paint some other cats to keep him company. Morris lived till he was seventeen, when he died of a horrid cancer in the throat. The very next day, a friend of mine arrived with a white kitten for me. My friend didn't know anything about my box. And I thought it was only a coincidence Snowy being on this side panel, here. Snowy lasted till I was, oh, forty-three. He was so eager—forever licking me. Oh, the rasp of his tongue on my ear! He smelled quite like a boiled egg, and compared with Morris he wasn't much brainier than an egg—"

Next had come all-black Poppy. Poppy was underweight but incredibly bright and busy. If Poppy had been a human child, she would have been classed as hyperactive. What a hunter she was. Cut a swathe through the local mice and shrews and moles and sparrows and robins, she did. It still only seemed rather *more* of a fluke that Poppy should follow Snowy, exactly as on the box.

The blue-cream Persian, Susie, clocked in when Janet was fifty-two. This could no longer be a coincidence. Susie was a pedigree, and her registered name was Moonflower of Dunesk. However, she wasn't a showable cat. Janet acquired Susie as a gift from the breeder, who was keen to dispose of her. A tooth grew askew in Susie's lower jaw. Her snub nose was too flat for her own comfort. Breathing difficulties affected her eyes, but she lasted pompously for fifteen years. During her last year Susie took to wetting on the floor. She howled as if she'd forgotten where she was. Kidney trouble claimed her. By then she'd become as senile as an old lady in a nursing home.

And into Brook Cottage had wandered young stray Duffy, who'd probably forgotten how to find his way back to his former home, though nobody ever claimed him.

"My marmalade dimwit followed my Persian, exactly as on the box! I'd painted a prophecy with my inks." Mrs Meadows smiled. "Now let's see *your* work, shall we?"

Why, this sketchbook was splendid. Such realistic pencil drawings —of jam jars with pencils in them, and kitchen implements. A food processor. Tools from the garage. All the shading was perfect. Marks were nine out of ten, sometimes nine-and-a-half. The art teacher at school, Mr Peters, was very keen on realism and accuracy. But here at last was a fine vase of daffodils.

"Such skill," enthused Mrs Meadows. She glanced at her own pictures, which weren't photographic but were surely more expressive. "Maybe there could be a touch more . . . magic? No, I see you can't do that at school. Food mixers and spanners!" The old lady leaned toward Amanda. "I *think* if you were to paint this box of mine the way I did, using the colours inside, then . . . what you painted might come true, just the way it did for me."

"But," pointed out Amanda, "the box is already painted."

"We only need to slap white paint all over it first."

"It's *beautiful*."

"Oh, it's rather faded compared with what it was once. So it needs new pictures on it. The old ones are used up."

Duffy had toured around the lawn. He had sniffed the flood and now returned to stare plaintively through the glass door. He began to miaow but the miaow became a yawn.

"Soon, Duffy, *soooon*," Mrs Meadows cooed. "Now Snowy, my boiled egg, he would paddle away at that door with his front paws as if he thought he ought to be able to walk through the glass. My cleverest cat was Poppy—oh, and I mustn't forget Morris—but none is dafter than Duffy; though never mind. I'll tell you what, Amanda: I shall paint the box white myself. Come and collect it after school tomorrow. Then you can paint it as you like, just as I did."

Amanda pondered. "What do you think I ought to paint?"

"Whatever you please! Whatever you *want!* That's my assignment to you, dear."

On her way homeward up the lane, Amanda thought about cats dying. Of a growth in the throat. Of failed kidneys. Of muddled brains. *Her* special cat wouldn't die for years and years yet, not till Amanda was almost thirty years old, which was scarcely imaginable. Surely there was no need to visualize a whole lifetime of cats. What else would Amanda wish for? Not in another fifteen years time, and thirty years time, and fifty, but now?

The girl did realize that Mrs Meadows was indulging in a delicious fantasy. But mainly, the old lady hoped that a touch of magic would enter Amanda's art, to accompany the nine-out-of-ten skill at drawing. Amanda wasn't offended, not at all. Spanners and food mixers were all very well! That was too much like Dad, who was an architect. To evoke magic, *of course* she should believe in the effectiveness of painting the box. Mr Peters had shown Amanda's class photos of the first pictures ever painted by people, when people still lived in caves. The motive, said Mr Peters, had been to summon up those animals so that hunters could kill them for food.

Mrs Meadows wasn't as fanciful as she seemed. And without a doubt Amanda must only paint living creatures on the box, not something cold and mechanical such as a new bicycle.

Next Saturday, Amanda worked in her bedroom all morning. Mrs Meadows's style seemed to rub off upon her, though admittedly Amanda was copying the way she remembered it. It was as if the white background preserved a ghost or memory.

Just before lunch, she finished the box. Taking care not to trip, she carried it downstairs on a piece of cardboard and set it upon the tiled worktop in the kitchen.

Lunch was to be a salad of pâté, spring onion, hard-boiled quail's egg, leaf of lettuce, and a cherry tomato, accompanied by rye biscuits. Amanda's mum, Sarah, was thwarting her daughter's tendency to plumpness. Her dad, Paul, could well lose a few pounds too. In the early evening the Whitakers would eat more lavishly. Sarah's own figure was slender, and she had gifted Amanda with her looks, her pert oval face, her curly blond hair. Stocky Paul must have contributed the genes for build. What of the girl's artistic eye? Paul Whitaker was an architect, but Sarah had trained as a landscape designer and she worked part-time as a consultant at the big garden centre eight miles from the village.

"Why, that's lovely," Sarah exclaimed. "It's so fresh, so bright, so different. It looks Indian, like those little boxes you buy in Asia Emporium. It isn't from there, is it?"

"Hardly," said Paul. "The colours still look wet. Is this a school project?"

Amanda shook her head. "It's my *pet box*. Mrs Meadows gave me the box and the paints last weekend. Whatever I put on the lid and the sides will happen, she said. On the lid, which is first, I put . . ."

A white cat with green eyes.

"Your asthma, Amanda," Sarah gently reminded her daughter.

"Mrs Meadows said that a pet from the box wouldn't harm me. Oh, it's all right, Mum! I know it's make-believe. I really painted the box so as to . . . well, freshen my style; *loosen* it."

"That's rather a mature attitude," marvelled Paul. "But . . . don't let your work become too loose. Mr Peters wouldn't approve."

"I'm not trying to be an *architect* with my box, Dad! I already know how to draw. This is different. It's a bit of . . . magic."

Sarah hastened to praise the box again. On one side was a Scottish Terrier with wiry jet-black coat, stumpy legs, and a look of dogged loyalty as if on dwarfish sentry duty. On the second side: a red hen. On the third: a grey Chinchilla rabbit.

"Whatever next? A goat?"

Dominating the final side was a rearing snake with a brown body patterned like a bicycle tyre, and a flaring hood.

"Good God, that's a *cobra*!"

"I know it is, Dad. I started to do an ordinary snake, 'cos I thought since snakes don't have fur a snake couldn't possibly give me an asthma attack. Then I felt it ought to look more dramatic."

"It's certainly *that*," he agreed. "Reminds me of that nursery rhyme, in fact. *The Old Lady Who Swallowed a Fly*. The cat bites the hen. The dog bites the cat. The snake bites the dog."

"You don't like my box, do you? I spent all morning."

"Honestly," said Paul, "it's beautiful. It's imaginative. Just so long as you don't imagine . . . well, that an actual cat or dog . . ."

"As if I would! I'm going to show Mrs Meadows my pet box after lunch."

"Oh dear," sighed Mrs Meadows when she turned the box, bringing the cobra into view. Duffy's ginger tail fluffed out. He hissed, then scuttled. Something about the movement of the box must have startled him, since even the cleverest cat would be blind to pictures.

"Well, what's done's done, I suppose. You'll simply have to watch your step, Amanda." (Amanda was grinning, pleased at the surprise.) "I don't suppose it's very *likely* that a cobra would . . . I mean, I haven't heard of anyone keeping snakes around here. There aren't even vipers in these parts. It would have to be a grass snake. Those are completely harmless. In fact, I saw one swimming in the brook a couple of weeks ago. A grass snake would even fit into your box. I do wish you hadn't!"

"Should we should paint that side white again? Shall I do a different animal?"

"You can't! Not now. You made your choice. It'll be a grass snake, you'll see."

"*When?*" demanded Amanda.

"It'll be the last one out of the box, won't it now?" Mrs Meadows said reasonably. "That mightn't be for years and years. Oh dear, but you mustn't ever go to India, or wherever cobras live. Promise me that."

Amanda chuckled. She was enjoying herself. Really, the snake had been a wonderful inspiration.

"What if I'd painted . . . ooh, a dinosaur? Just a baby dinosaur?"

Mrs Meadows concentrated. "Well, those were lizards, weren't they? The modern version would be . . . a newt?" she speculated.

"I saw a programme on TV which said that *birds* are descended from dinosaurs." Amanda pointed into the garden in mock alarm. "Watch out, here comes Tyrannosaurus Robin!"

Was Mrs Meadows almost fooled for a moment?

"Robins are fierce to each other," the old lady said sternly. "If you're a beetle, they must seem like demons." Turning the cobra to face Amanda, she laid her hands on the cat-lid as if conferring a blessing. "Take care of yourself."

A week later, the white cat came into the Whitakers' lives. Presenting itself on their kitchen windowsill, it mewed insistently for admission. Thanks to Amanda's pleas, Sarah conceded that they could open a can of sardines and feed the animal on the patio. No sooner was the door open than the white cat rushed inside. It leapt on to the worktop, from there on to Amanda's shoulder. A-throb with purrs, it rubbed itself against her cheek.

Amanda didn't choke. Her airways didn't block up with any sudden constriction. She didn't need her ventilator. A few days later, Paul installed a cat flap in the kitchen door.

Amanda was just a little concerned that Duffy might have met with an accident, being as how the box had been repainted and had now produced a new cat—seemingly. Of course this was all a bit of make-believe. But even so.

A visit to the old lady reassured her.

"Duffy's linked to me by love, and by all the time we've spent together," Mrs Meadows told Amanda. "I'm here all day long, after all."

Amanda couldn't be home all day long, no more than her Mum or Dad could.

Snowy, named in honour of the old lady's earlier pet, proved to be deaf. Even loud noises never caused an ear to twitch. The driver of the oil delivery truck, a month later, protested that he had hooted and hooted again.

Naturally, Snowy didn't hear a thing. Pray that he felt nothing, either. Spine broken, head crushed. It was as Mrs Meadows had said: the sheer *grief*, never mind that Amanda had only known Snowy for a few weeks.

Into this aching void there trotted MacTavish, soon to be abbreviated to Tavvy. No collar, no name-disk—but in fine condition. Paul pinned a card on the notice board in the village and in surrounding villages, but no one phoned to claim the Scottish Terrier, so chunky and obedient and friendly and all the things that he ought to be.

Six weeks later, while Amanda was walking Tavvy on her return from school, the Pattersons' Boxer bitch leapt a fence and savaged the Scotty to death. It didn't even help that Amanda was there in person. Her terrified screams brought neighbours, and Sarah too, but the Boxer already seemed abashed. Sarah phoned the police, who were unhelpful. Soon Paul was back. So were the Pattersons, who had left their dog to roam their garden during the day. Bitter words volleyed. The Pattersons certainly did not intend to destroy their beloved Boxer who was usually as meek as a kitten, so they insisted.

When the Whitakers went into their back garden to bury Tavvy, a red hen was there—with russet body, greenish tail-feathers, red comb and wattle. The hen eyed Amanda and clucked.

No one nearby kept poultry. After the burial of Tavvy, Sarah drove to the garden centre to buy chicken wire and stakes. She and Paul erected an enclosure for the solitary hen, walled and roofed with wire.

"There, that's like Fort Knox," Paul announced when the work was done. "How long do hens normally live?" he asked. "Three years? Five?"

Amanda cried herself to sleep, her pet box on her bed beside her.

Her father brought home a large hutch in which the hen could roost. And hay and chicken feed.

For a while Amanda refused to name her hen. Mrs Meadows's talk about the death of pets seemed like a curse. Was a hen any substitute for Tavvy or Snowy? She ought to have painted cats, and cats only.

As though to establish her individuality, the hen laid a brown egg. Sarah had found out that the breed was called Welsummer. A good season surely awaited the bird. So Amanda named her hen Summer. Only later did she remember that autumn follows.

Could she love a pet which might die? Anxious because of this while at school, her work suffered a bit. She knew the hen was safe in the stockade. However, the bird might develop a hen illness such as pox or diarrhoea, or she might pick up gapeworm. Even so, the long summer holiday had almost arrived, the holiday with Summer—not that a hen was quite as communicative as a dog or a cat.

That year, the Whitakers didn't go away to the seaside or abroad. Neither Amanda nor her parents were willing to leave Summer to a neighbour's care. Nor actually did Amanda want to leave at all.

Going back to school in September was a wrench, though surely the hen had established herself by now.

Come the mists and the nights drawing in, at Amanda's insistence Paul had installed a heat-lamp in the hutch. By the faint light they could check on Summer from the kitchen window before going to bed.

In that soft red glow they spied the cause of commotion in the hen-run. They'd been watching television in the lounge. Muted squawks brought them hurrying into the darkened kitchen. A fox! Paul was outside in a couple of seconds. Amanda too, and Sarah. The fox forced an exit through loose wire and made off.

Summer lay amidst bloodstained feathers.

How Amanda shrieked.

They bought Bunn at a pet shop. He was a grey Chinchilla—and friendly, though with a tendency to nip.

Might it have been wiser to take a kitten from a late litter, or a puppy? *No*, Amanda insisted. What she had painted must happen. Only then could it stop happening.

Paul had looked up cobras in a book at the library.

"What you painted *could* be a King Cobra, and they're shy. I can't see behind the head to be positive—the hood's so wide. But it looks to me like a Monocled Cobra. If so, it's one of the most dangerous snakes in the world."

"But Dad," insisted Amanda, "it'll only be a harmless grass snake—because there aren't any cobras here! Mrs Meadows told me so. Grassy will be the last beast out of the box. Oh, you were right about me not needing pets! But while Bunn's here we must be kind to him even if he does nip fingers."

The girl was psychologically disturbed. The only way to purge the poison from her system had been to buy Bunn. At least this was a deliberate choice.

"It'll *only* be a grass snake next," Amanda persisted. "It'll come from the brook. Mrs Meadows said so. We must never ever go on holiday in India—"

Amanda hadn't been to visit the old lady for months. She didn't want to, nor would her parents have allowed it. Neither Sarah nor Paul could think of a sane way of confronting Mrs Meadows. What could they possibly say to her?

"It's autumn," said Paul. "All snakes hibernate. Nothing can happen till spring."

A fortnight later, the fox returned. The wire had been well repaired, and overnight the hutch was always fastened by a hook.

Yet the fox burrowed deep under the wire as if digging a den. It nosed the hook out of its slot.

Amanda was surprisingly calm. Sarah, less so.

"Bring that wretched box from her room," she ordered Paul.

"Amanda can't sleep in there with it! Carry it carefully. We should smash it to pieces."

"But Mum," protested the girl, "that's my box. I painted it. Why carry it carefully if you want it smashed?"

"Not in your bedroom I don't."

"We have to wait for the snake! Then we'll be all right."

"Shall I bring the box down and *nail* it shut—?"

"The sides are too thin, Dad. Nails would split the wood."

"I'll tie it tight with garden twine."

"If it's tied, why can't it stay in my room? That's where it belongs, don't you see? Otherwise, things mightn't happen properly —not if it's away from me. You don't want it here in the kitchen, Mum, or in the lounge, do you?"

"It can go in the garden shed."

In the shed the air would be damp. The lovely paint-work might spoil. Oh no, the box must stay close to Amanda while she was dreaming. By now she seemed on the verge of hysteria or an asthma attack. Paul took a roll of green twine up to her room to tie round the box right where it was, on the floor near the bed.

Amanda's cry brought Paul and Sarah from their bed in their matching paisley pyjamas.

The sudden flood of electric light revealed Amanda sitting upright. The beast box was shuddering, shifting to and fro. Paul's knots were slithering slowly open, as though the thinnest of green snakes was wrapped around the box, and now it was untangling itself. How the box rocked. Amanda scrambled along the bed to join her parents.

Her father seized a plastic ruler from beside some schoolbooks, and brandished it. "A cobra can't fit inside! Maybe a baby one— but who's scared of a baby?" Could a baby snake make a box lurch so vigorously?

"Dear God," moaned Sarah. The twine was coming undone. The lid began to lift.

"Grassy," called Amanda. "Come out, Grassy. Be a good snake, now."

Up rose a flared hood.

Raised ribs extended the whole of the creature's neck. Black eyes glinted. A thin tongue flicked in and out. A body resembling a brown bicycle tyre began to uncoil from out of the little box, coil after coil appearing. That box ought to have been five times as big to contain so much body.

The hood dipped. Briefly they saw a large eye-mark behind the head: the monocle.

And snarling ginger fur rushed past Amanda's legs. Paul cried out loudest in startlement. Bristling fur, claws, bared teeth: a mass collided with the snake. Brown body lashed; hooded mouth gaped. The cat's teeth closed on the snake's neck at the very same time as the snake bit its attacker's flank.

The snake slumped.

"Duffy!" squealed Amanda. Mrs Meadows's pet lumbered past her and out of the bedroom. Next thing, Duffy must have tumbled headlong down the stairs. Such a crash. Such a noise of breakage.

The cat wasn't to be found, but the tripod table at the bottom of the stairs had toppled over, throwing a Victorian majolica vase filled with teazles and pampas grass to the floor, shattering it.

Duffy must have gone out through the cat flap. Barefoot, in their pyjamas, the Whitakers hastened into the chill of the night. From around at the front of the house came another sound of something breaking. Flowerpot toppling off a brick, perhaps. They hurried along the side path, the ribbed concrete so cold underfoot.

Halfway down Brook Lane, a solitary lamppost shed yellow light. They could see a cat staggering, falling over, pulling itself up again, and lurching onward down the lane.

"We'll catch our deaths," protested Sarah.

Skirting the wreckage of the Majolica vase and strewn contents, they ascended cautiously to Amanda's room. Had they really seen a cobra? Or had some hysterical *folie* gripped them? A shared delusion, which they had been all too prepared to perceive?

On the floor lay an open box and twine and a slim green snake, about eighteen inches long, and dead.

"It squirmed in through the flap into the heat of the kitchen, then came upstairs," declared Paul. "That's what happened. *Do you understand?*"

To Amanda, her father seemed unhinged.

Amanda said carefully, "I think the *real* animals killed the dream animals. The Boxer killed Scotty. The fox killed Summer and Bunn. The dream lasted much longer for Duffy because he was Mrs Meadows's dream. Duffy must have sensed the cobra coming into existence. Or Mrs Meadows sensed it. But if her dream's dead now—"

"Don't you talk that way!" snapped Paul. "You don't know what you're saying."

"Tomorrow morning," persisted Amanda, "will you phone the police and tell them we think Mrs Meadows is dead in her house because we haven't seen her for such a long time? You could say we're worried she's ill or had a fall. That might sound better."

Kneeling, Amanda gathered up the grass snake and folded it into the box where the little pots of paint lay higgledy-piggledy.

"We'd better bury this in the garden beside the others." She rounded on her parents accusingly. "You don't seem to know what to do! I was right about the snake, wasn't I?"

"Yes, you were right," said her father. "It was just a grass snake."

"Mrs Meadows is gone now."

"What makes you say so?"

"You know it's true. All the beasts have gone. Will the box rot in the soil? Do you think in thirty year's time, when we aren't living here any more, a boy or girl might dig the box up? I think Mrs Meadows *loved* me, Dad."

"Not nearly as much as we love you," said Sarah, tears in her eyes.

"I think," said Amanda, "people live as long as they're loved. I suppose Duffy loved Mrs Meadows in his own cat way. But we didn't love her. And Duffy was only her dream, come to life. Then her dream died, saving me. Mum, you and Dad won't die as long as I love you. I mustn't be angry with you. But people grow up, don't they? I'm never," she vowed, "going to fall in love with some boy and get married."

"Do you know," exclaimed Paul, "you haven't had an asthma attack for absolutely ages."

"Mrs Meadows cured me, Dad. The beasts broke my heart but they cured me."

Already Amanda sounded so grown up; and therefore such a stranger.

Ferryman

WHEN CARL AND LIZ AND MARCO AND ME WERE last off duty on Pallas, we took some abuse from a couple of miners.

That was three months ago; and when I say "on Pallas" of course I mean *inside* Pallas, diameter 450 klicks.

We were in the hectic, wittily named Palace Bar in Spintown, the hole inside the big asteroid which was originally melted out by a clean nuke and furnishing with a spinning hab. In the outermost zone of the habitat the centrifugal gravity has the same pull as Mars. In the inner zone, where the Palace Bar is, there's lunar gravity, just like back home.

But there's none of the pastel cool and calm of the Moon in the Palace Bar. Crash Rock music and a naughty holo-disco and fermented fungus Alc to drink, although the bouncers make sure that all customers take detox pills before leaving.

"What are you loonies doing in Pall?" this miner hails us with obstrep amiability.

He's a squat redheaded hairy fellow who looks as though he ought to shave his hands as well as his cheeks. Accompanying him is a stocky crony with a wiry black crewcut, sleek smooth skin, and

eyelids without much of a fold. Japanese blood in that one's veins. I
don't much care for the Japanese. Chip on my lofty shoulder.

Even though we'd swapped our official silvery coveralls for
smart synthsilk shirts and slacks with a shimmery moiré effect, obviously we stood out.

Carl tells the redhead sinisterly, "We're in the Space Navy,
guarding you all against invading aliens."

Carl forever refers in ominous tones to the alien corpses, as if
the very next coffin to come along might contain a live one. More
than once he pretended so, when the time came to look inside.
("This one's a cryo casket, folks! The monster's holding a sign. It
says in alien, PLEASE THAW ME SLOWLY. OR ELSE.")

I think when Carl applied to become a ferryman (because Liz
was applying, as was I) he might have been deliberately confronting
secret fears, which he felt could best be handled with comic ma-
cabre bravado.

Liz is a tease too, though her humour is more subtle. She tells
the miners, "Our work is top secret. We're a high security team."

"You're the garbage detail," sneers the redhead.

His crony chortles. "You drive the big slow hearses. Chug-chug-
chug-chug-chuugg." He makes *Ferryman 3* sound like some terrestrial rustbucket tugboat or tramp steamer.

"I'll have you know, sir," says Marco (loftily), "we can outboost
any other ships. We can gyro full circle in the time it takes you to
recall who your mother was. We can kill our max velocity faster
than anyone. I'm talking gees."

Marco is extremely proud of our specifications; and if any Space
Navy actually existed other than in VR thrillers, then the four *Ferryman* craft could fit the bill.

Approximately.

Supposing that real spacecraft carried any weapons—but of
course the only armed facility anywhere in Sunspace is Graveyard,
where we take all the coffins.

The stocky miner eyes us up and down.

"Jeez," he says. "I'd have thought you lot would snap in half like
a bunch of sticks."

So Marco tells him: "My dear sir, thanks to regular work-outs in
our onboard centrifuge we can take seven gees without blacking."

"Ever had a black eye?" asks the miner. He thinks he's special or
he's jealous. Or both.

Iridium (and associated platinum) is the speciality of Pallas.
Rare and hard and with a high melting point (which sounds like

some glacial VR space-princess). The iridium miners of Pallas are something of a roughneck élite.

"What a waste of our money," this miner grumbles. "We could be quarrying Triton by now, but then I s'pose you'd want to collect your garbage out by Pluto."

"It's Sunspace money, sir, not just yours. And if you fancy that a steel coffin hitting a spaceship at lots of kilometres per second is a desirable prospect, do think again!"

The redhead seems unimpressed.

"Featherbeds for loonies, what a scam. How d'you spend all your weeks of spare time? VR-tripping and shooting the rabbit?"

This puzzles Marco. "What rabbit's that?"

"You know what I mean. Playing at bun-girls and P-boys."

Retro slang is in vogue on Pallas.

Well, of course we do such things! Basically me and Marco are the serious ones, so the two of us make love on board *Ferryman 3* — while Carl and Liz have fun-sex. Marco doesn't particularly regard himself as serious—he just is. Okay, so we do shoot the rabbit, rabbits being randy beasts. That wasn't the point.

The point was our Very Important Mission. Since this was being performed pretty flawlessly by ourselves and by the other three *Ferryman* ships, far too many people took us for granted. There ought to be much more *cachet* attached to the job. Respect for the hearse-drivers, if not for the dead aliens. It's true that there's genuine respect in space administration circles. But amongst goofs such as these two miners . . . well!

The Japanese-looking one summons an unappealing smile, showing what appears to be a platinum tooth.

"I guess," says he, "you'll all be admirers of Norma Notridge."

"Come on," announces Marco, "we're getting out of here. We'll try the Bella Brasserie." The Bella is out in the Mars-grav zone, and a bit exorb. "Maybe the Bella won't have so many horrid little men in it."

If a fight breaks out in the Palace, the bouncers will break it up with puffs of Blandgas, but we didn't want to collect any ugly bruises. Maybe the half-Japanese fellow could do Judo, which might throw us some distance in Moon-grav.

Damned Japanese.

Key screen, for *Norma*.

After that furlough on Pallas, I designed a border of leaves to go around the comp's data about her. Sort of mid-way between an oblong wreath and a crown of laurel.

Norma Notridge (1975–2051): founder of the Norma Movement opposed to all genetic manipulation of the human body. The Norma Movement resulted in the Gene-tweak Embargo . . .

Norma didn't want everybody to look the same. On the contrary! Norma was frankly obese, and proud of it. As far as she was concerned, whatever body you're born with is perfect unto itself. Whatever the weight or the height or the appearance, all human bodies are wonderful, and manipulating bodies by genetic engineering is a crime. She was very persuasive.

On the Moon, due to low gravity, my own generation grew up pretty damn tall. A lanky look seemed set to be the norm. Gangly and lofty.

Then, largely because of Japanese pressure, the Embargo ended.

I'm storing my thoughts about this in comp because I believe Norma ought to be reevaluated. I'm also storing my theories regarding the alien corpses, but never mind about those for the moment.

Originally those Japanese were quite short people. For centuries they lived on a diet of rice and pickles. After the Second Global War last century, they began pigging out on meat and burgers.

Rising generations put on a significant number of centimeters, and this only applied more so on the Moon.

Problem!

An increase in height would have been okay in any other nation. But the Japanese are very traditional. Living space is measured according to the size of the *tatami* mat. Here's a two-mat room. Here's a three-mat room. Everything in harmonious proportion.

And the traditional size of the mat is based on traditional stature.

If you're too tall, that's tough, Tanaka-san. Curl yourself up. Don't just bow. *Stoop.*

As soon as the Embargo ended, the Japanese colonists in Hosi City on the Moon started tweaking genes to breed a more economical, compact, and traditional lunar citizen. A one-mat citizen, instead of one-and-a-quarter.

Whoomph. Serenity and Copernicus and the other colonies soon followed suit. On Luna, bodies would be downsized. Rising generations wouldn't rise nearly so high. While this was going on, my peers and I grew up. And up.

The thing about spaceships is that there isn't usually very much space inside them. Very tall people need not apply. If only the

Gene-tweak Embargo had continued! Reassessment of ship dimen-
sions, right? Because the Embargo ended, so much for the caption
about me in Serenity Colony High School Yearbook, "Sondra
Beidermeier: The Student Most Likely To Go To The Stars"!

Not that anyone was very likely to go to the stars for another century, or maybe another millennium. What we needed was anti-
matter technology, not just superfusion. In spite of early gleams of
promise star travel continued to elude us.

But instead, the stars came to us—in the shape of coffins.

Which was fine by me.

The hearse-ships would need to be fairly cavernous—not to
carry the coffins inside them, goodness no, those are stored on tiers
of magnetised racks underneath the ships—but in case the crews
succumbed to melancholy. Gloomy thoughts of close confinement.
Premature-burial sort of thoughts. Consequently: ample living
space! This could provoke some jealousy in the crews of regular
ships, or in asteroid miners.

Carl has perpetrated a prank which actually had me fooled for
about half a minute.

Marco is Captain and ship's systems officer, though we can all
do each other's jobs, mostly. Liz and I, with headsets on, operate the
drones which we send out to grab the caskets magnetically and haul
them back to stick firmly to the racks. Carl is Navigator and radar-
scanner.

"Coffins, coffins!" Carl announced over the com. "That's odd
—I'm getting a very dull echo. My God, these ones are wooden!
The aliens have run out of steel. Sondra, Liz: you'll need to use the
drones' claws and suckers. . . ."

"Just joking," he added half a minute later.

Another notable jape of Carl's was when he claimed to find a ray
gun in one of the coffins instead of the usual speckly stone egg or
steel star or statuette or whatnot.

En route to Graveyard we routinely open all coffins to check the
contents in case there's something new.

We don't personally. A tele-robot does. None of us would want
to climb around the racks for ages in a spacesuit.

The coffins are all of dull steel, lozenge-shaped, over two metres
long by a metre deep. Grooves flute the metal decoratively. There's
a shark-like tail fin at the rear. The purpose of this fin must also be
ornamental, since it could serve no possible steering function.

Ornate clasps hold the lid to the base, and we manoeuvre the tele-robot to open these clasps, shine a light inside, holograph the contents, then close the lid again and latch it tight.

Checking our catch of coffins is a bit tedious, since there never is anything new, so all four of us take turns.

"Hey," Carl called out on this occasion, "I *think*—it looks like —it is—I've found a gun!"

Of course he hadn't.

Graveyard's big. You might say it's in the middle of nowhere—though at the same time it's very definitely somewhere on account of the huge stack of racks looking like the skeleton of some enormous skyscraper.

When we get within fifty klicks, Graveyard's comp challenges us, and we identify ourselves with our crypto-key so that the laser-zappers don't fire at us. This is always a slightly fraught time.

If anyone ever tries to rob Graveyard, its fusion core will power those lasers ferociously. Routine use of power keeps Graveyard's racks magnetised to hold the coffins in place. That's how the open-mesh skyscraper can have such slim girders, minimising its mass.

Not many people realize about the mass. How bulky Graveyard would be, if equipped with big clamps or with a vast hull.

Admittedly, as more and more coffins get added by us, the mass increases. In another five years the structure will need extending—unless coffins stop arriving. But anyhow, Graveyard can't simply orbit the Sun the same as Pallas or Ceres and such. If it did, it would be out of line with incoming coffins much of the time. We might need to travel a hundred million miles extra to unload.

This would be no use at all when the four *Ferryman* ships need to follow a regular schedule. One on patrol. One heading for Graveyard, loaded with coffins. One returning. And the fourth being serviced while its crew enjoy liberty on whichever asteroid is nearest, or on marvellous Mars.

Next time it'll be Mars for us! A week's high-boost inward to Graveyard, unload, two weeks inward to Phobos, then shuttle down from the potato moon to Syrtis.

So anyway, Graveyard is drifting in the general direction of Vega, as is the Sun and its family of worlds on its 225 million-year cruise around the galaxy. And every couple of years tugs have to correct Graveyard's vector. Expensive business! Keep mass to the minimum.

Would anyone care to remove a little bit of its mass by stealing a few coffins? Some rogue scientist determined to clone an alien? Villains acting for some billionaire collector of exotica who wants an alien skeleton in his den, and a few stone eggs or medallions?

No one has ever sidled up to us in a bar such as the Palace with an illicit proposal.

I mean, we wouldn't agree! We'd be violating our oath. Sooner or later SpaceAdmin would find out, then we'd lose our place in space. Enough lanky loonies would love to take over from us.

To the best of my knowledge no one has shown the least desire to try to clone an alien in some isolated lab in some out-of-the-way asteroid.

They might clone an alien disease. Remember the Trojan Horse. Basically, most people feel considerable resentment at what the Coffin Builders dumped on us.

"Coffins incoming," announces Carl; and we're busy.

A big shoal of thirty coffins, scattered over ten thousand cubic kilometres.

Get comp to work out the shortest combination of routes to collar them all.

We've plenty of time, but it's the old Travelling Salesman problem. Given thirty cities to visit to sell the new brand of toothpaste or guacamole dip, which is the most economical to go to first, and second, and third and so forth?

With fuzzy logic and quantum chips, comp copes within an hour or so. Would have taken years, a few decades ago. With a quantum chip, useless answers just cancel out.

Sometimes I have a pretty strong intuition which coffins comp will tell us to collect first of all. We used to bet on this, but we gave up because when I have a hunch it's sometimes awesomely right. Not always, but often enough to impress my friends.

And so we set course. Superfusion, and gees.

It's me who finds the damaged coffin. The front, stove in. The lid, badly buckled.

And this *is* new.

New enough, that when I bring it back to the racks, we decide we'd better open it right away.

The tele-robot has difficulty with the clasps. It can't prise the lid open. I'm sweating as if it's me who's using my own muscles instead of just operating controls. I suppose I'm straining, sort of subconsciously. Heave, heave. Hold on tight to the rack so I don't float away; and heave. Whilst I'm merely strapped in my seat.

All in vain. So I guide the robot to insert a fiber optic. We see confusing swaying fish-eye views.

On the adjacent screen, comp builds up a perspective—of two jumbled mangled juve aliens and torn tethers. And a couple of little stone eggs, adrift.

"We have an injured pair!" I exclaim—which is true but rather misleading of me.

About five per cent of coffins contain juveniles. Always a couple of them in tandem, held one behind another by those durable vermilion tethers, taking up about the same length as an adult.

Oh yes, the adults . . .

On *Ferryman* we get to see them all the time, but how many people in the solar system can describe one accurately by now, fifteen years after the first corpses started arriving?

Carl often refers to the aliens as "the monsters," but that's partly because mummification in vacuum during aeons extracted all water, drawing leathery lips back to expose a predatory snarl of wicked-looking teeth.

Still, they do look rather tough in the brutal sense.

Powerfully-built bipeds, they would stand as high as any of us of the tall generation. Dehydrated sinews make it seem that they're wearing suits of brown corduroy, though in fact the corpses are naked. I suppose the tethers do look a bit like tentacles, but those merely secure the bodies to rings welded along the insides of the caskets. Without tethers, the bodies could hardly have stayed resting in peace after being accelerated from a mass driver or whatever.

A big ridge of bone runs across each alien's skull from front to back. Three fingers, plus thumb, on each hand. Finger and toenails are horny claws. The lack of body hair can only have been thanks to a thorough shaving of each corpse, because the autopsies of a few specimens fifteen years ago disclosed abundant roots. Probably ritual purification was the reason for the shaving.

Those autopsies also found retractable genitals within the apparently sexless leathery groins of males. This may imply rutting seasons, when the vulnerable genitals extrude; which seems a bit barbaric.

Rather barbaric, too, are the ritual objects bedded in dried brown glue in a niche in each coffin. A polished granite egg. A steel star with geometrical patterns on it. A medallion with abstract designs. A cone of rock crystal. Take your pick; there isn't much variety.

The crew of *Prospector* vessel which intercepted the first coffins fifteen years ago thought that the stones and cones and steel stars might be coded with data. But that ain't so.

It's as if clever barbarians captured a ship which landed on their homeworld long ago and took its technology to use for their own primitive purposes.

The genetic code of the aliens has been sequenced, but as for growing a test tube alien—not likely. Such a proposal might bring the Gene-tweak Embargo back (I should be so lucky), and besides there's the resentment.

The *Prospector* crew also imagined, at first, that the initial shoal of a dozen caskets might be Von Neumann machines, automated drones built to reproduce more drones. But then a volunteer took a space-walk, opened a lid, and gazed in amazement—just like that old archeologist in Egypt upon the face of King Tut. . . .

So here are the two mutilated juveniles, on screen. How shall we log the contents of this particular coffin?

"You can't call them injured," says Carl. "This is post-mortem damage."

The fact is that whatever any of the aliens originally died from, none encountered so far has been obviously injured. No crushed skulls or broken rib cages. No missing limbs.

"A rock must have hit this coffin, that's all, Sondra. A tiny meteoroid. A collision would normally knock a coffin way off course over such a distance. That's why a damaged coffin has never arrived here till now. That's all."

Part of that's true enough. A hundred thousand years ago (as evidenced by carbon dating, and the amount of micro-pitting in the steel) the coffins must have been aimed very accurately—dead at our Sun. (Compensating, I guess, for stellar motion.)

And it's no mystery where they came from. Take the direction, velocity, and estimated age of coffins; and backtrack. Easy-peasy-Japanesy. The star in question only had a number previously. Now it's known as Deathstar, a name borrowed from some vintage early flatscreen movie.

Unfortunately Deathstar's right down on the ecliptic. Consequently coffins come straight in through the plane of the solar system. If only Deathstar had been high above the planetary plane, coffins could have rained down into the Sun without being so much of a hazard!

En route, the coffins had a hundred thousand years to diverge. A bashed casket would probably miss the solar system entirely. As for unbashed ones, the vast majority of those wouldn't plunge directly into the Sun, even so. Oh no, they would loop around the gravitational well, and zoom out again—captured but not yet consumed.

The loops could take them as far out as the orbit of Mars. The coffins might undertake (ha!) hundreds or thousands of elliptical orbits before the final fiery evaporating descent.

Hence the expletives-deleted resentment. How *long* had the Coffin Builders continued their capers? Twenty years? A century? Half a millennium? During the equivalent time the human race would be on the receiving end. Space is vast, but space could become somewhat *busy* with speeding coffins as more and more shoals arrived to add to the carousel.

Only solution: the vacuum cleaner patrol. Special *Ferryman* ships; special ferrymen like us.

"Listen, Carl: we've never found any baby corpses. Some half-grown juveniles like these, and mostly adults, but never babies. You've never even thought to pretend that you found four babies tethered head to toe."

"Drat, I missed a trick. So what?"

"Babies," I say triumphantly, "couldn't give informed consent."

"What in the moon are you talking about?"

Liz smirks. "I suspect Sondra has a theory. . . ."

"Okay," I tell my buddies, "how about this? Religion obsesses the barbarians—"

"The monsters."

"They believe dead bodies will go to heaven or something if they send them to another star. Ours."

"Royal dead bodies," Marco chips in. "Noble ones. Privileged and rich, otherwise they couldn't have afforded it." I think he's trying to back me up. "This does beg the question of why they fixed on *our* Sun. Seen from Deathstar, Sol wouldn't be one of the big bright luminaries."

"Aha," says Carl, "that's because our ancestors from Atlantis visited the monsters' world and raised them from bestiality to intellect. About a million years ago. Long enough ago for all trace of Atlantis to be forgotten. By us, but not by the monsters."

"*Will you listen to me?*"

"Silence in court," says Liz, "the monkey wants to speak."

"Never mind about why they chose our Sun. So anyway, they

dedicate a big slice of their resources to launching corpses in our direction—with the same zeal that the old Egyptians devoted to mummifying people and cats and flamingoes wholesale. We're talking religion. Afterlife or maybe even resurrection."

"Undeniably," agrees Marco.

"*So they deliberately only send perfect bodies.*"

"Or else they used the best morticians."

"Guys, they only send bodies without blemish." Punch line: "All the corpses are volunteers. Healthy, good-looking individuals—"

"Good-looking monsters—"

"—would volunteer to die in a kind of euthanasia sacrifice! That's why there aren't ever any babies. Juveniles could give consent, but babies couldn't."

This is a bit of a stunner for Carl and Liz. I recall a theory about how the Coffin Builders may have believed that their offspring didn't acquire souls until a certain age, such as when they could speak properly. But never anything like this insight of mine!

It's new.

"Do you know," says Liz, "you may have a point."

"This observation," Marco assures me, "is certainly going into the Captain's Log."

Carl claps slowly. But he's impressed. "The soon-to-be-famous Beidermeier Hypothesis!"

Let me enjoy a surge of pride. I shan't exactly be up there with wonderful Norma Notridge as a name. Maybe somewhere in the foothills. Or in the footnotes.

"Actually," says Marco, "I think this deserves squirting to Mars to establish intellectual property. Priority, I mean."

Old saying: Who Pays the Ferryman?

That's a reference to the legendary boatman who ferried the dead across the river of death—the Styx of Greek and Roman times, or in the myths of Marco's forebears, the river of Tuonela. Marco—Hakkonen—comes from Copernicus unlike us other three Serenity-ites. Quite a few Finns live in Copernicus Colony. Month-long lunar nights are a snip for Finns, Carl once quipped. (But everybody on the Moon lives by artificial light.)

Who pays? The corpses certainly don't, nor their alien relatives neither. Quite a lot of Egyptian mummies were misused by later generations of peasants as firewood or were ground up by charlatans to make fake drugs. The dead aliens have fared *much* better at our hands.

✳   ✳   ✳

But SpaceAdmin Mars squirts *us* first of all, while we're all stretched
out in our separate long tetherbeds—we don't shoot the rabbit all
the time. I've woken early. I'm thinking of the exact phrasing of
the Beidermeier Hypothesis. The 'Sondra Theory' would sound
neater.

Our radar alarm goes off. So we all hurry to the control room,
worrying that a high-speed rock is heading for *Ferryman 3*. Ought-
n't to be a rogue coffin. We've cleaned up the latest shoal, and our
racks are two-thirds full by now. *Ferryman 2*'s due in ten days. None
of the hearse-ships have run out of rack-space yet, though 2 once
came close to it.

No, not a rock. The red light flashing on the radio indicates an
urgent squirt from Mars.

An alien starship is incoming. At a high percentage of the speed of
light. Decelerating, yet still enormously fast.

An alien starship.

It couldn't be a human starship since we don't have any.

One of the big telescopes on the Moon's backside spotted the
starship. Calculating its course backwards puts its vector within a
few light years of our source of coffins. Close, but not close enough.
Naturally we don't know what distance it travelled to reach the solar
system.

An advanced alien civilization. A starship which can travel at
anywhere near the speed of light completely diminishes our slow
caskets.

According to Mars, the starship won't pass within ten million
miles of us. Nevertheless, we're out in the front line, so to speak.

That's because the starship's extrapolated speed and course are
such that it could use the Sun's gravity for breaking and to slingshot
itself back out toward Jupiter. If it uses Jupiter for further braking, so
as to head in-system again at a more modest velocity, on account of
where Jupiter is right now this manoeuvre will bring the starship
quite close by us the second time. Mars is going to upload all data
regularly into our comp.

"Maybe it's only going to fly by," says Carl. "Whoosh and away."

Marco points out that it's too big to be an automatic probe.
QED, it has a crew.

"That still doesn't mean the monsters won't fly by."

I must protest. "This isn't the right attitude!" This is the Big Discovery. Okay, they discovered us; not us, them. "Anyway, they can't

be the Coffin Makers. Direction isn't quite right, hmm? And the Coffin Makers must have run out of steam millennia ago. Hey, unless of course . . ."

Marco and Carl look at me expectantly.

"Unless their civilization rose and fell, and rose and fell. Like wobbly cycles. That could be how the barbarians got hold of high tech to launch coffins. Suppose they reach another star system. They colonise it. They relapse into barbarism. Or vice versa. Much later, an expedition tries to reestablish contact—one way or the other. Religious barbarians grab the goodies. That way we don't need to invent a second race of aliens they stole from."

"*That way*," says Carl ominously, "means there *are* monsters on board the starship."

Liz has been calculating.

"I *think* . . . on the way inward, this first time . . . I think their starship's going to pass quite close to the Moon. We shan't be at home to see them!"

Oh, be real, Liz. If we were on the Moon, we might only glimpse the starship for an instant or two. If it does the Sun-and-Jupiter trick, we'll get a far longer look.

Horrors.

As the starship streaked close by the Moon it launched a small missile. The warhead must have been of anti-matter—the Sea of Serenity acquired a new crater the size of Posidonius.

Serenity Colony has become silent. Breathless.

"Monsters, monsters!" raves Carl. Our families, our friends, our home, all gone. Our everything, gone. The emptiness is sickening. Only something heroic or splendid could fill it.

SpaceAdmin Mars in the person of none other than Hiroshi Nomura talks to us an hour later. Because of the radio-delay he makes a formal speech, an appeal, which we replay.

Slowed by the Sun, the starship is definitely heading back toward Jupiter. Jupiter will slow the starship more, and put it on an Earthward heading. It'll pass within fifty thousand klicks of our present position. Time enough for us to cram on gees and reach the passing point.

Another thing I recall about those Japanese, aside from *tatami* mats and rice and pickles, is that during the Second Global War they used suicide volunteers to pilot flying bombs and torpedoes. . . .

Nomura-san's plea is that we should accelerate to max, and ram the starship.

No *Prospector* craft is positioned as favourably as we are.

If Serenity is a sample of things to come, the Earth's biosphere may be devastated by titanic anti-matter explosions, equivalent to several comet impacts such as caused mass extinctions in the past. There might be nothing left alive on land but bugs and microbes, and nothing much in the seas but worms and algae.

On behalf of billions of living beings, not forgetting dolphins and elephants and eagles and polar bears, and I suppose flamingos too, Nomura-san beseeches us.

We have about twenty-four hours till the estimated time of collision. A couple of us will be able to abandon ship. We can use our coffin-collecting drones as life rafts, taking extra air-tanks with us. Beacons on the drones. *Ferryman 2* will speed up to max. The two bailouts will become very hungry and thirsty and messy before *F2* reaches them, but they ought to survive, unless they go crazy drifting in the cold empty darkness.

And two must stay on the ship. Because of time lag in uploading data, two need to stay on board for last moment corrections.

Two to stay, two to go. Two to die, two to live, perhaps.

Marco and Carl are already pondering in an old-fashioned way. Accepting Nomura-san's logic.

"It's emotional blackmail," says Marco. "Even so! If I'd been born a couple of hundred years ago, I'd already be dead." That's certainly one way of looking at losing one's life.

"Me too," Carl seconds him. "Those monsters just have to be zapped. We're the only chance." Ah, now he can annihilate his anxieties.

And of course it's Liz and me who must take to the life rafts.

What I say is: "I want to know *why* they're behaving like monsters."

Marco thinks he knows. "They must be utterly xenophobic. They're unable to tolerate the knowledge that aliens exist—namely us."

Kamikaze: that was the name for the suicide pilots whom Nomura-san is asking two of us to emulate. . . .

"Those kamikazes piloted aircraft packed with explosives?" Marco asks me.

We don't need any explosives. Our mass and velocity will be quite sufficient.

It's now that I have my Idea.

"It ought to work," agrees Carl. "We can't tell Nomura. We can't broadcast this. We might seem like cowards."

"What about this business of Sondra and Liz abandoning ship?" Marco wants to know. "Do we pretend they're with the drones? Do we fake it?"

"Ahem." Liz clears her throat. "How about saying that we are all staying together by choice?"

"Mightn't that seem a bit hypocritical? Us pretending to be heroic but not really risking our lives at all."

"Okay, then: *personally* I refuse to spend a week or so stuck in a spacesuit! I'll stink, and I'm not drinking recycled piss."

Oh yes, vanity is a much better excuse. When everyone learns the truth, they can chuckle rather than fume indignantly.

The beauty is this: none of us need die. We have almost two hundred steel coffins in the mag-racks below the ship.

Two hundred torpedoes.

Seemingly a bow-wave precedes the starship, twisting debris and dust aside, some byproduct of the star-drive. However, the starship's flanks remain exposed. So we'll ramp up to max. We'll head for the position the starship will pass through. Then bingo, we demagnetise the racks. We reverse the thrust of the propulsion unit up above *Ferryman*.

I suppose we'll all black out, and our harnesses might bruise us badly, although they oughtn't to snap.

As soon as we reverse the thrust, *Ferryman* starts slowing pretty dramatically. Two hundred loose torpedoes rush on ahead at our former max speed.

Splat, bang, into the starship.

If the coffins diverge a bit, well and good. More chances of hits. Any hits are going to cause havoc.

Trust Carl to point out that the starship mightn't entirely disintegrate.

"It *would* if *Ferryman* hit it. The monsters'll probably all die, whichever, but the wreckage, the wreckage might give us a clue — a clue to the star-drive!"

Oh this is definitely worth a gamble.

Off-watch in our tetherbeds, we're under acceleration and feel heavy. So there's no shooting any rabbits, even if this might be our last opportunity.

Pop some pep pills and stay awake all the time until zero hour? Nomura-san might like us to spend the long interval meditating, but not likely. We want to be super-alert.

I doze. Then I wake because of some irrelevant creak in the ship's fabric. I was dreaming of Graveyard, Graveyard seen on some screen. Not one of *Ferryman*'s screens. A telecast of Graveyard.

Now I remember! A living alien was sitting staring at the screen. The bony ridge on its head sported a crest of bristles like some ancient helmet. The rest of its head was shaven. Its eyes were red. Its lips were drawn back in such a toothy snarl—of outrage.

Creak-creak. Nothing serious. This time I'll dive deep down into the well of sleep.

I'm the great charismatic prophet-leader of the People. I've united all the warring tribes, so skilled in metalwork and pyrotechnics.

A swirling vision has shown me that we must rise up above our world and ourselves and our squabbles. Up, up, into the realm of our sun and the stars which are other suns.

If heroes accept death voluntarily and sacrificially, and if their preserved bodies can be sent to a far star, they will be resurrected as beings of plasma—as gaseous intelligences living in the fires of that star. They will swell its fires so that the star will become a beacon, testifying to their transfiguration.

Meanwhile the People will spread out to other worlds of our sun and then to the worlds of other stars—instead of annihilating one another here, which otherwise seems all too likely sooner or later.

We must rise into space, propelled by this vision. The time scale must be huge. We must not send those sacrificial corpses into our own sun. If no resurrected beings of plasma were to result, my vision would be a failure.

I shall choose a star which we can see with the naked eye but which isn't exactly our next-door neighbour. When we do reach the other stars, let that one star remain taboo. . . .

And now on fifty worlds, on the eve of His Day, vast crowds of the People gaze into the night sky at a certain star in expectation of some transcendental climax, such as that star going nova. Drums beat and pipes skirl and priests chant and hawkers sell little telescopes.

His Name has accumulated vast size and momentum, like a snowball rolling from the top of an Alp or a Himalaya, rolling for a hundred thousand years, despite some ups and downs.

*   *   *

Once upon a time some German chemist discovered the structure of the benzene ring in a dream. He dreamed of a snake curled in a circle, biting its own tail. . . .

"Hell, I was right about the lack of babies, wasn't I?"

"Were you, Sondra?"

"Yes! And I'm right about this. It's more than a hunch about which coffin to collect first. It's a *vision!*"

Eventually, the aliens did colonise all the nearby solar systems —except ours. Maybe their civilization rose and fell several times. But always, from the dawn of their space age, they kept alive the tradition of our sun being specially sacred. Not to be visited. An out-of-bounds shrine to the great founder.

"Okay, since last century they've been able to detect our radio and TV transmissions. Fifteen years ago, the first coffins begin arriving. And we stack the coffins in a junkyard!

"Pretty blasphemous, huh? Maybe they don't exactly believe any longer in our sun flaring up—or at least the wised-up ones don't—but we're committing sacrilege against the spirit which inspired their society!"

Why haven't *we* detected any electromagnetic noise from them? Maybe their civilization doesn't leak much noise. Maybe they only use tight-beam signals.

"If we wreck that starship of theirs," is my view, "then we had better be ready to build a space navy to patrol our fringes. All the nearby star systems might be full of aliens incensed at us."

I guess a psychologist could say that there's a certain mutual *folie* about a small crew who are isolated together for long periods of time. Either you all get on together or you go nuts. And a charismatic personality can swing things.

The idea of more vessels full of angry monsters arriving does not appeal to Carl in the least. Liz likes the idea of a slightly expanded fleet of *Ferryman* ships collecting incoming coffins and ferrying them closer to the Sun for disposal in its incinerator. Or maybe just redirecting them more accurately and tidily, in clusters, with warning beacons attached.

We're all still gutted about the destruction of Serenity, which breeds a gut desire for revenge. Ram the starship! Kill the monsters! It's this response which Marco distrusts, now that he's had time to think about it. When did warfare ever solve anything? How could we possible afford to build and run a huge navy which would be doing sweet nothing most of the time (or even all of the time)?

We shan't involve Mars in our deliberations. Nomura-san wouldn't see things the way we see them, out here in the front line.

We've gyroed *Ferryman*. We've rotated it on its axis. We've maxed the magnetism which holds the coffins. We've programmed the superfusion for pulse after pulse to change course. We're blacking out briefly again and again, ignoring the manufacturer's stress tolerances and nature's own constraints as regards our bodies. We're aching with bruises. We're really suffering. We'll be black and blue. No cracked ribs yet, thanks be. When we boasted to those miners about manoeuverability, little did we think. Even so, it'll be touch and go.

Not *touch* in the sense of us being very near the starship when it passes. Not now we shan't be. *Touch* in the sense of 'Will we have achieved a perfect sun-course soon enough?' The aliens are bound to detect us. (Aren't they?) Surely they'll have instruments to capture and magnify and replay images of our hearse-ship aiming toward the Sun. Out here we're very far from the Sun—but let our good intentions be obvious!

"Starship's on radar," groans Carl. "Five thousand klicks, four-eight, four-six—"

Marco pulses us again and we black out briefly. Groggily I recover vision like a battered boxer.

"Sun-target, spot on—"

At last. At last.

"Three-two, three thousand, two-eight—"

Our closest mutual distance will be about one-four.

"Ready for reverse thrust—"

That's when our strained ship might tear apart.

We'll launch the coffins at two thousand, so the aliens will have time to see what we're doing.

"Two-two—"

The crushing squeeze. Sparkling stars cavorting. Blackness.

Liz moans at broken ribs. Marco's left eye has a haemorrhage. Blood trickles from my nose. Such a headache. I feel as if an iridium miner has beaten me up.

But our two hundred torpedo-coffins have flown true—toward the far-off Sun. Far truer than ever they flew before.

As we limp back toward Phobos there's bitter resentment in the squirts from SpaceAdmin. Odium and opprobrium. We coast along at nowhere near max—not wishing to strain the ship, but nor do we care to arrive anywhere too soon.

Inward bound, the twice-slowed starship is still a week away from Earth.

We're purple with bruises. Liz's ribs have been bound up satisfactorily. The blood is slowly clearing from Marco's eye.

When Marco squirted Mars about my inspiration, he backed me up a hundred per cent. We're never so united as now.

And it happens! It isn't any prank of Carl's when he calls us deliriously to the control room. To play a joke at such a time would be sick.

It's true news.

The starship has lit its antimatter torch or something. It's accelerating. It's veering from an Earthward course. It's going to head out of our system—toward some other star where the descendants of the Coffin Makers must also live.

No communications come from the starship. I suppose we're taboo.

Yet they have analysed what I did. They understood my nonverbal message. They know that now we will carry out our task appropriately.

Such joy, throughout Sunspace. Such applause.

Although I ache all over—and in my heart for lost family and friends—my name reverberates. Norma Notridge, I excel you, I exceed you.

Carl's voice comes over com a few days later.

"Oops, Sondra's coffins have reached the Sun—"

It's months too soon for that.

"My God, the Moon's reporting huge solar flares a million klicks high. . . ."

Timeless moments pass.

"Just joking," he adds.

I rather think that our *Ferryman* fleet should be renamed the Sondra Squadron.

My Vampire Cake

*A*HA, DO YOU SUPPOSE THAT I INTEND TO TELL YOU a recipe?

What could the special ingredient of *Vampire Cake* possibly be? The blood of fresh hot healthy young virgins, of either sex, mixed with cherries or strawberries? Scarcely! Would the cake be in the shape of an alluring alabastrine neck of ivory icing decorated with two toothsome dimples of cochineal, from which thin ribbons of scarlet icing meander downward on to a snow-white shoulder of a base?

Oh no, not at all. The cake I made and decorated so serenely and classically—my masterpiece of the art of sugar, if I may say so—alluded to vampirism neither in its appearance nor in its contents.

I'm truly sorry that I cannot show you this cake. My client forbade any photographs. He was superstitious about visual images, in mirrors or lenses. And he did devour that cake entirely—with the consuming hunger of someone who had not tasted regular food for the past two hundred years. (Not that my cake was in any way routine!) He gorged himself on it with a spiritual as much as a physical appetite.

My cake was a *vampire cake* because it was made especially for

275

a vampire's two hundredth anniversary. I was about to say that this was Philippe Carnavalet's birthday cake. But that's misleading. The anniversary in question was that of his transformation from mortal man to undead person. So I might refer to the occasion as being his *deathday*, and the cake as his deathday cake.

We scarcely ever make death cakes, do we? Birthday cakes, wedding cakes, Christmas cakes, retirement cakes, oh yes. Yet seldom a celebration cake for the wake! At a funeral, bright wreaths and sprays of blooms sound the uplifting note. The sensuality and brio of a splendidly decorated cake would seem unsuitable. Ought the icing to be mournfully black—or angelicly white? If the dear departed succumbed to a heart attack on his favourite golf links, should the icing be correspondingly green (coloured, of course, with spinach juice)? Should there be a model of the golfer swinging his last club? If she was a businesswoman, should she be modeled sitting at a marzipan desk, with her in-tray empty at last?

Do I digress?

Not without a purpose! Philippe's deathday was intimately associated with sweet nourishment—indeed, the sweetest of all.

By his own account Philippe Carnavalet was born in 1770 some seventy miles east of Paris at the little town of Carnaval in the Plain of Champagne. Champagne, and carnival! That may sound like a jolly area, but as Philippe grew into adolescence taxes were steadily increasing to fund the national deficit. Tariffs were being piled upon taxes. The peasantry were suffering direly. Nor were the petit bourgeoisie any too happy. Response to protests all too often took the form of bayonets and gunfire. Revolution and Terror and the mass guillotining of the nobility were just around the corner.

What a mass of nobility and sub-nobility there were in France, all with their various privileges! Philippe's father had prospered by commercial speculation well enough to buy the modest but seigneural Château de Carnaval and change his name accordingly, becoming pseudo-nobility.

Then the shit, as it were, hit the fan. The mob stormed the Bastille. The rioters hoped to loot powder for the up-to-date guns they had seized elsewhere. In the process they freed all seven inmates of that gaol. What a heroic day. (I'm viewing the event with Philippe's jaundiced eye.) Four of these prisoners were forgers. Two were lunatics, one of whom was an Englishman who believed he was Julius Caesar reborn. The seventh was a debauched aristo whose family had locked up to restrain his rampant lechery. A few days earlier, and the mob could have liberated the Marquis de Sade

—but Sade had just recently been transferred to an asylum. The governor of the Bastille surrendered so as to avoid massacring more of the crowd. He was repaid by being hacked to pieces.

Soon the Assembly abolished feudal rights, ruining twenty thousand nobles. Many decamped to Switzerland. Although reduced in circumstances, others remained. Presently châteaux were being looted and burned (though not at Carnaval, where Philippe's father hung on). The King tried to escape. Overcome by a craving to eat pig's trotters, His Majesty broke his journey. He was arrested. As a result of this, the movements of would-be émigrés were strictly regulated—and the Terror began. Committees of Public Safety of the United Indivisible Republic conducted purges. Philippe's father couldn't get away. But by bribery he finessed a safe-conduct for his son.

Philippe de Carnaval guillotined the pretentious pronoun from his name, passing himself off as Citizen Carnavalet. It sounded as if his father and grandfather before him may have served meat at table for some noble family. In fact I think *carne* is slang for bad meat. Revolutionary guards at the frontier could only guffaw at this irony.

Here we introduce yet another gastronomic note—and a culinary delight was to be Philippe's downfall.

Philippe happened to be related to that genius of the dining table, Grimod, who produced regular volumes of an *Almanach des Gourmandes* during the first decade-and-a-bit of the following century. The transformed Philippe was to observe such foody enthusiasms with a bitter disdain since his own diet was by then restricted to human or animal blood. A couple of centuries later this connection (by blood, in the banal sense!) still preyed on Philippe's mind.

"Was I aware," he enquired of me, "that Grimod was born deformed? His right hand was a pincer attached to his arm by a membrane just like a duck's foot. His left hand was a claw worthy of a bird of prey. He had false hands made for himself, constructed of springs and iron. Over these he would wear gloves of white pigskin."

"With these, he cooked?" I was rash enough to ask.

"Bah! How could he? This was the eighteenth century, not today. He never donned an apron in his life. His taste buds and his stomach were his tools. He was solely a connoisseur. A gourmet. Or a glutton."

Did Grimod eat to compensate for a ruined sex life? Because he was unable to bestow seductive caresses by means of springs and iron? Because ladies would be inhibited? Because he could not pleasure himself satisfactorily?

Not at all! Grimod acquired a fine mistress by promising to delight her with foreplay in the style of Tiberius in his grotto in Capri, where trained children swam underwater to nibble the Emperor for arousal. The lips, ah the lips! The gourmet lips. In those days classical references were appreciated.

We don't want to hear this, do we?

However, there's a point.

It's a point concerned with concupiscence—and with gourmet chocolate.

Presently the impoverished though elegant Philippe was employed as French tutor to a Bavarian count's children. In that lonely *Schloss* on the edge of the Alps, Graf von Helmberg jealously guarded the virtue of his family's name. This caused frustration to his bored eldest daughter, Johanna, a considerable beauty.

Philippe fell in love, or in lust, with Johanna. Earlier, in France, Philippe had acquired a recipe for truly ravishing drinking chocolate, a silky melting sweet delight of a drink. He proceeded to obtain the ingredients. He courted Johanna surreptitiously with cups of chocolate. This appealed to her sweet tooth. She developed a craving.

We all know that monks used to be forbidden chocolate in case it aroused libido. We all know that Montezuma always swigged an extra cup of chocolate spiced with chilli before visiting a concubine. For the sake of decorum, Aztec women were forbidden the piquant beverage.

Johanna's craving led to copulation. Alas, Philippe was caught. Enraged, the Graf threw Philippe into the dungeon of the *Schloss*, pending appropriate punishment. Sparing no expense, von Helmberg obtained a large amount of chocolate from Vienna.

On his deathday, Philippe's wrists and ankles were tied. He was laid on his back in a coffin.

"If you can drink enough of the damned stuff, you'll live!" von Helmberg bellowed at him. Into the coffin, the cooks began to pour pot after pot of thick hot chocolate, made to Philippe's own recipe which had been extorted from him on threat of pain. He never confided the recipe to me. Yet I am sure, from his bitterness toward Grimod, that it originally came from that relative of his.

Soon enough the chocolate oozed up over Philippe's face. He craned his neck, to continue breathing. This was a mistake, since the Graf had ordered ample ingredients. From now on, the chocolate was decanted *much* more slowly.

Perforce, Philippe began to lap.

The Graf had no intention of allowing Philippe any real chance. The victim of this bizarre vengeance may have lapped for an hour or more until he was bloated. Remorselessly, sweet liquid engulfed the hapless prisoner. He was submerged. He choked, he drowned.

Yes, *death by chocolate!* We all know the name of the cake. Philippe was the filling.

In slowly congealing chocolate he was buried in the woods well away from the *Schloss*, and his coffin covered over with a shallow depth of loam.

I do not know whether being embalmed within and without by chocolate made to his recipe was responsible for his metamorphosis into an undead person dependent on a diet of blood for nourishment—or whether another vampire on the prowl noted the disturbance of the soil and dug him up. Maybe this conjectural vampire simply sniffed him out from a distance as a pig sniffs a buried truffle! To a vampire's enhanced senses the sweet odour must have been conspicuous, and if not mouthwatering, at least piquing of his curiosity. Or of her curiosity. The whole episode left Philippe with a loathing for the smell of chocolate equal to the vampire's supposed dread of garlic.

Philippe assured me that other vampires walk the Earth, and what's more, that their transformation was often due to circumstances more peculiar than legends would have us believe. But vampires are few and far between, and unsociable. The likelihood of encountering one is low.

So how did I meet Philippe, you are wondering!

Due to my constant involvement with icing, maybe my flesh smells sweeter than most people's flesh. It was also *sweetness* which saved my life.

I had just returned from our Cake Decorators Convention of last year, held in that splendid Hotel de France in St Helier on the island of Jersey. For those of you who missed our stay in that excellent establishment, be it known that the basement houses a small chocolate factory. A shop in the lobby vends the products. Most noteworthy are the champagne truffles—but another popular souvenir last year proved to be the five kilogram chocolate bars, hefty enough to brain a mugger with.

The blessed isle of Jersey boasts many attractions along its lanes so narrow and winding that the Lamborghinis only ever drive in second gear. To my mind the most remarkable is the Neolithic burial mound at Grouville known as La Hougue Bie. *La Oooo-g Beee.* Within the span of a couple of minutes you can step from

Prehistory by way of the Middle Ages to the Nazi period when the island was occupied. Along a low stone tunnel you stoop your way to reach the Great Chamber roofed with twenty-five-ton slabs. Here you are at one with the men of five thousand years ago. Atop the mound is a chapel where a fraudulent cleric set up as a fortuneteller during the gullible Middle Ages. At the side of the mound is the entrance to an underground German bunker of the Second World War. What a juxtaposition of epochs side by side! What an epitome of the layers of history!

I had holidayed on Jersey previously. Consequently, for last year's convention, as you may well recall, I made a cake in the shape of La Hougue Bie, crowned by its chapel, and cut away to reveal not only the monumental passage grave but also the Nazi bunker.

In marzipan and in pastillage I made models of a few German soldiers and of some Neolithic men, and of the medieval cleric up above, and of a Viking scaling the side of the mound—for Vikings were there as well.

The exploration of fantasy is one of the delights of cake decoration, as our Caribbean colleagues demonstrate nowadays so flamboyantly and exuberantly. I fully expect to see a decorator from the West Indies occupy this place of honour next year or the year after.

The passage of a year has mellowed my chagrin at some of the adverse reactions to the décor of my cake. What I saw as virtuosity, apparently other people viewed as a jarring of styles. Perspectives must have shifted within the past twelve months. A reevaluation has taken place! Here I stand today, before you being honoured.

It was on my return from Jersey, as I say, that I met Philippe de Carnaval. The house where I live, alone amidst my cakes-in-progress, is at the far end of a quiet close within a stone's throw—or rather, three or four stones' throws—of the local cathedral. When I pipe icing of an evening how the sound of bell practice thrills me, though my hands never vibrate.

It was late evening and dark when I arrived home from the airport. Floodlights illuminated the cathedral, a veritable Gothic wedding cake. I was so enchanted by the sight that I left my car (the luggage still locked safely inside) and strolled along the pathway linking my close with the cathedral green. I took my in-flight travel bag with me, since it contained documents. The bag also held one of those five-kilogram chocolate bars. I had packed half a dozen of these in a suitcase—then on last minute impulse just before catching the mini-bus to the airfield I bought yet another.

As I stood admiring the cathedral rising immaculately and luminously from the lawns, I became aware of soft footfalls along the pathway behind me.

I turned—to witness this slim figure of a sudden rushing toward me. He was dressed in a black velvet cloak. For a moment he seemed ecclesiastical.

Then I saw his twin fangs gleam, unsheathed.

Plunging my hand into my bag, I hauled out the heaviest object I had with me—that brick of chocolate.

My would-be assailant skidded to a halt. His nostrils flared. He quailed. The chocolate was wrapped in cellophane. With his acute night vision Philippe could recognize it for what it was. With his sensitive nose he could *smell* it. What to me was hardly a whiffer to him was a reek.

He recoiled just as if I'd brandished a silver cross smeared with garlic. He sank to his knees, and wept.

"What are you?" he demanded in a tormented tone.

And so our acquaintance commenced.

I shan't burden you with too many fussy details. Sufficient to say that Philippe was weary of his two hundred undead years. He dearly sought some form of purification which would release him appropriately and, if I may say so, *transcendentally*. He had lived by the tooth. What circumstance could liberate him from that Bastille of his undying body but something which evoked—in inverted form —the source of his present condition?

Is not the arctic whiteness of royal icing the very antithesis of the darkness of the chocolate which once embalmed him?

A well-iced cake takes many long hours to produce. Yet in essence it is ephemeral. It will be consumed—destroyed! It will vanish utterly in a quasi-spiritual affirmation. After two hundred long years, Philippe must likewise attain a climactic nullity.

My cake would be serene. It would possess a classical severity, restrained and dignified, sublime in its nobility. Its architectural sublimity would translate this anguished vampire from undead body into spirit—in the way that a solid sublimates into vapour. By the act of eating such a cake—so paradoxical a novelty after two hundred years—he would gain release. Don't mistake my meaning! My cake would not act upon him as some sort of toxic poison, but as a catalyst of deliverance.

At this point, I must pause to pay homage to Mr Ronnie Rock, icer extraordinaire.

Mr Rock's name is startlingly felicitous. A prosaic-seeming

fellow in an old apron, what an archangel he was with the piping tube! Well may we applaud this departed hero of the common man. Not an aristo by birth, but a *sans-culotte*, although he wore trousers beneath his apron. Ours is a proletarian art in origin.

Once upon a time, as you should know, sugar was only the food of kings and of sultans. Hence the name *royal icing* for the mixture of egg whites and icing sugar—by contrast with the gum tragacanth paste such as I used to model my Nazi soldiers. Yet sugar was to become the very food of the proletariat, the main source of calories. And amongst the working class, who worked harder than bakers? By heaving those overweight sacks of flours and by bending over troughs to heave and tear and pummel the dough, shoulders grew huge and rounded. Feet were permanently splayed. Men's chests became barrels, asthmatic due to all the flour dust.

Within this harsh milieu of slavish labour, cakes were decorated gloriously, during the bakers' spare moments, as a statement of dignity and individuality.

Ronnie Rock: his Grecian columns typically soared tier above tier separated by entablatures, to a drum cupola. So would mine.

Much has been said of the tears and terrors—the sheer panic—of the novice attempting to pipe royal icing as perfectly as Ronnie piped it. In spite of my wealth of experience I confess that I experienced a similar initial qualm, to be piping for a vampire client.

Yet I prevailed. Or else, how should I be here this afternoon, addressing our very own *National Assembly* of cake decorators?

Sugar, of course, is a preservative. How should sugar serve to extinguish a person who had already been preserved far beyond his natural term?

Oh, by its gleaming whiteness, by its angelic purity! This quality, incorporated into Philippe's undead body, would transubstantiate him. It would transfigure him into a body of light, which would all be astral halo! I repeat that I am not alluding to any toxic effect such as a drug addict might experience from a surfeit of purest heroine or cocaine white as snow!

Finally, the night came when my Ronnie Rock cake was ready. With the night, Philippe also came to me, barefoot and silent. During the daytime Philippe was sleeping high up in the cathedral in some concealed coign to which nobody else would dream of climbing without benefit of scaffolding. A week earlier, a courting couple found a lad's body deep in the acre of rhododendrons in the public park. That lad had expired due to loss of blood, although no blood stained his resting place. His injuries were compatible with a car crash, from which he had managed to stagger away. Not far from the park was a burned-out Toyota. Plainly the car had been stolen for joy-riding. Philippe had supped, yet he had not *eaten* for two hundred years.

By candlelight I uncovered the cake to his wondering gaze. After studying it he said to me, "You have done well, Decorator." And I nodded, for I knew this was true; and here was the rightful homage of an aristo to an artisan. Actually, those were the last words he uttered—since the unveiling of the cake led soon enough to devouring and demolition.

Not so much a consuming, as a *consummation!*

A prodigious act of consuming, in itself, given the grandeur of the cake. In his own native era Philippe must have witnessed similar acts of gluttony. Many are the tales of gourmands who died at table from surfeits of oysters, salmon, kidneys, pheasants, lamb, dish after dish demolished with gusto. Yet I had eschewed any rich fruity filling, using only the lightest soufflé, of a sponge mixture as substructure for the soaring columns and walls and entablatures of icing which were the true body of the cake.

A consummation, yes . . .

As Philippe violated his enforced fast and gorged upon the whitest of icing, such sensual and astonished tremors shook him. How exquisitely he trembled, with a terrified ecstasy.

He shed his cloak, beneath which on this night of nights he wore no other clothing. His limbs were radiant in the candlelight, phosphorescent. After a while I could no longer bear to look upon him. Almost in a trance I closed my eyes.

How long was I in this state of stupor, while his rapture intensified? A quarter of an hour? A half an hour? When I looked again, the icing had all disappeared; and so had he. Only crumbs of sponge remained, and his discarded cloak.

Ladies and Gentlemen, I shall say no more except to thank you all warmly for honouring me today. The cake which you admire upon this table—the Colosseum of Rome as it was in antiquity, recreated in royal icing—is undoubtedly a lesser achievement than my vampire cake. Alas, my vampire cake vanished utterly from the world—just as Philippe de Carnaval himself vanished, consumed in brilliant light.

Three thousand copies of this book have been printed by the Maple-Vail Manufacturing Group, Binghamton, NY, for Golden Gryphon Press, Urbana, IL. The typeset is Elante, printed on 55# Sebago. The binding cloth is Arrestox. Typesetting by The Composing Room Inc., Kimberly, WI.